PRAISE FOR

Darling Rose Gold

"Ingenious. . . . A maelstrom of a suspense story."
—Maureen Corrigan, *The Washington Post*

"[A] gripping mystery." —*Good Housekeeping*

"[An] excellent debut. . . . Briskly moves with surprising twists as Wrobel delivers assured character studies." —Associated Press

"Sure to be one of the most unique books of the new year."
—*Newsweek*

"A thorough and delectable novel about class, interfamilial relationships, and the limits of forgiveness." —Shondaland

"Sensationally good—two complex characters power the story like a nuclear reaction, and won't let you forget them. Wrobel is one to watch."
—#1 *New York Times* bestselling author Lee Child

"An absolutely brilliant book; funny, dark, authentic, and a total pageturner. I loved it."
—Lisa Jewell, *New York Times* bestselling author of *The Family Upstairs*

"It's rare for something genuinely fresh to come along in this genre, but this book has it all—a killer premise, twisty plotting, crisp writing, and compelling characters. Dazzling, dark, and utterly delicious."
—JP Delaney, *New York Times* bestselling author of *The Girl Before*

"Two extraordinary narrators drive the nail-biting action in this sensational, compulsively readable debut. A tour de force of captivating psychological suspense."
—Gilly Macmillan, *New York Times* bestselling author of
The Perfect Nanny

"One of the most captivating and disturbing thrillers I've read this year. An astonishing debut."
　　　—Samantha Downing, *USA Today* bestselling author of *My Lovely Wife*

"I absolutely devoured *Darling Rose Gold*! . . . I couldn't get enough of Patty and Rose Gold, alternating my opinion of them at the same speed that I was turning the pages! A fabulous read!"
　　　—Sandie Jones, author of *The Other Woman* (Reese's Book Club Pick)

"An original, stunning debut! Masterful crafting . . . and utterly compelling characters will hook readers from the very first page. . . . An intelligent, beguiling read that should be at the top of every reader's list."
　　　—Wendy Walker, *USA Today* bestselling author of *The Night Before*

"Takes twisted mum and daughter relationships to a whole new level. Think *Misery* meets *Sharp Objects*."
　　　—C. J. Tudor, *Sunday Times* bestselling author of *The Chalk Man*

"Wrobel writes a fascinating and thrilling debut that looks deeply into the complicated reasons a mother and daughter choose to hurt each other. A psychological twister that had me completely captivated."
　　　—Diane Les Bescquets, national bestselling author of *Breaking Wild*

"More than a page-turner. . . . *Darling Rose Gold* [asks] probing questions about why we all hurt the ones we love. An explosive debut from a thrilling new voice."
　　　—Kirstin Chen, author of *Bury What We Cannot Take*

"I inhaled this book. . . . Compelling, intriguing, beautifully written, and paced like a roller-coaster ride, cancel all your plans when you pick up this terrific book."
　　　—Liz Nugent, bestselling author of *Unraveling Oliver* and *Lying in Wait*

"I love it. Fascinating, immersive, whip-smart, with a supremely clever ending that left me gasping."
　　　—Melanie Golding, author of *Little Darlings*

Darling Rose Gold

STEPHANIE WROBEL

BERKLEY
New York

BERKLEY
An imprint of Penguin Random House LLC
penguinrandomhouse.com

Copyright © 2020 by Stephanie Wrobel
"Readers Guide" copyright © 2020 by Stephanie Wrobel
Penguin Random House supports copyright. Copyright fuels creativity, encourages diverse voices,
promotes free speech, and creates a vibrant culture. Thank you for buying an authorized edition of
this book and for complying with copyright laws by not reproducing, scanning, or distributing
any part of it in any form without permission. You are supporting writers and allowing
Penguin Random House to continue to publish books for every reader.

BERKLEY and the BERKLEY & B colophon are registered trademarks
of Penguin Random House LLC.

Berkley trade paperback ISBN: 9780593100073

The Library of Congress has catalogued the Berkley hardcover edition as follows:

Names: Wrobel, Stephanie, author.
Title: Darling rose gold / Stephanie Wrobel.
Description: First edition. | New York: Berkley, 2020.
Identifiers: LCCN 2019033241 (print) | LCCN 2019033242 (ebook) |
ISBN 9780593100066 (hardcover) | ISBN 9780593100097 (ebook)
Subjects: LCSH: Munchausen syndrome by proxy—Fiction. | GSAFD: Suspense fiction.
Classification: LCC PS3623.R628 D37 2020 (print) |
LCC PS3623.R628 (ebook) | DDC 813/.6—dc23
LC record available at https://lccn.loc.gov/2019033241
LC ebook record available at https://lccn.loc.gov/2019033242

Berkley hardcover edition / March 2020
Berkley trade paperback edition / January 2021

Printed in the United States of America
1 3 5 7 9 10 8 6 4 2

Cover art: *Fabric letters* by Ritesh Chaudhary / Shutterstock; *Butterfly* by Ashraful Arefin / Arcangel;
Floral pattern by Spiderplay / E+ / Getty Images; *Spoon* by bogdandreava / Getty;
and *Fly* by Henning K. v. Vogelsang, Liechtenstein
Cover design by Emily Osborne
Book design by Laura K. Corless

For my parents, Ron and Kathy Wrobel

1

Patty

DAY OF RELEASE

My daughter didn't have to testify against me. She chose to.

It's Rose Gold's fault I went to prison, but she's not the only one to blame. If we're pointing fingers, mine are aimed at the prosecutor and his overactive imagination, the gullible jury, and the bloodthirsty reporters. They all clamored for justice.

What they wanted was a story.

(Get out your popcorn and Buncha Crunch, because boy, did they write one.)

Once upon a time, they said, a wicked mother gave birth to a daughter. The daughter appeared to be very sick and had all sorts of things wrong with her. She had a feeding tube, her hair fell out in clumps, and she was so weak, she needed a wheelchair to get around. For eighteen years, no doctor could figure out what was wrong with her.

Then along came two police officers to save the daughter. Lo and behold, the girl was perfectly healthy—the evil mother was the sick one. The prosecutor told everyone the mother had been poisoning her daughter for years. It was the mother's fault the girl couldn't stop vomiting, that she suffered from malnutrition. Aggravated child abuse, he called it. The mother had to be punished.

After she was arrested, the press swooped in like vultures, eager to capitalize on a family being ripped apart. Their headlines screamed for the blood of "Poisonous Patty," a fiftysomething master of manipulation. All the mother's friends fell for the lies. High horses were marched all over the land; every lawyer, cop, and neighbor was sure they were the girl's savior. They put the mother in prison and threw away the key. Justice was served, and most of them lived happily ever after. The end.

But where were the lawyers while the mother was scrubbing the girl's vomit out of the carpet for the thousandth time? Where were the cops while the mother pored over medical textbooks every night? Where were the neighbors when the little girl cried out for her mother before sunrise?

Riddle me this: if I spent almost two decades abusing my daughter, why did she offer to pick me up today?

———

Connolly approaches my cell at noon sharp, as promised. "You ready, Watts?"

I scramble off my Pop-Tart of a bed and pull my scratchy khaki uniform taut. "Yes, sir."

I have become a woman who chirps.

The potbellied warden pulls out a large ring of keys and whistles as he slides open my door. I am Connolly's favorite inmate.

I pause at my cellie's bed, not wanting to make a scene. But Alicia is already sitting against the wall, hugging her knees. She raises her eyes to mine and bursts into tears, looking much younger than twenty.

"Shh, shh." I bend down and wrap the girl in my arms. I try to sneak a peek at her bandaged wrists, but she catches me. "Keep applying the ointment and changing those dressings. No infections," I say, wiggling my eyebrows at her.

Alicia smiles, tears staining her face. She hiccups. "Yes, Nurse Watts."

I try not to preen. I was a certified nursing assistant for twelve years.

"Good girl. Díaz is going to walk the track with you today. Thirty minutes. Doctor's orders." I smile back, petting Alicia's hair. Her hiccups have stopped.

"You'll write me?"

I nod. "And you can call me whenever." Squeezing her hand, I stand again and head toward Connolly, who has been waiting patiently. I pause at the threshold and look back at Alicia, making a mental note to send her a letter when I get home. "One hour at a time."

Alicia waves shyly. "Good luck out there."

Connolly and I walk toward I&R. My fellow inmates call out their farewells.

"Keep in touch, you hear?"

"We'll miss you, Mama."

"Stay outta trouble, Skeeto." (Short for "Mosquito," a nickname given as an insult but taken as a compliment. Mosquitoes never give up.)

I give them my best Queen Elizabeth wave but refrain from blowing kisses. Best to take this seriously. Connolly and I keep walking.

In the hallway Stevens nearly plows me over. She bears an uncanny resemblance to a bulldog—squat and stout, flapping jowls, known to drool on occasion. She grunts at me. "Good riddance."

Stevens was in charge until I got here. Never a proponent of the flies-and-honey approach, she is vinegar through and through. But brute force and scare tactics only get you so far, and they get you nowhere with a woman of my size. Usurping her was easy. I don't blame her for hating me.

I wave my fingers at her coquettishly. "Have a glorious life, Stevens."

"Don't poison any more little girls," she growls.

Strangling her isn't an option, so I kill her with kindness instead. I smile, the epitome of serenity, and follow Connolly.

The intake & release center is unremarkable: a long hallway with concrete floors, too-white walls, and holding rooms with thick glass windows. At the end of the hallway is a small office area with desks, computers, and scanners. It could be an accounting firm, if all the accountants wore badges and guns.

At the reception desk, the clerk's chair is turned toward the radio. A news program plays. *After a short break,* the reporter says, *we have the story of a baby boy gone missing in Indiana. That's next on WXAM.* I haven't watched, listened to, or read the news since my trial. The press destroyed my good name. Because of them, my daughter didn't speak to me for four years.

I glare at the radio. The chair swivels toward me, and I realize I know the clerk sitting in it. I privately refer to the bald and brawny man as Mr. Clean. I met him five years ago. He flirted with me all day, asking what perfume I was wearing while I batted him away. I'd feigned breeziness, but internally I was seesawing between fury at the injustice of my verdict and fear of the next five years. I hadn't seen him again until now.

"Patty Watts?" he says, turning off the radio.

I nod.

"I remember you." He smiles.

Mr. Clean pulls a form from his desk drawer, then disappears into the storage room. After a few minutes, he comes back with a small cardboard box. He hands me a piece of paper. "I need you to look through the inventory list and sign at the bottom to confirm you're leaving with everything you brought here."

I open the box and glance through it before scribbling my signature.

"You can change back into your street clothes now," Mr. Clean says, gesturing to the bathroom and winking at me when Connolly isn't looking. I tip my head and shuffle away, clutching the cardboard box.

In a stall, I rip off the jacket with *DEPT. OF CORRECTIONS* emblazoned across its back and dig into the box. After five years of prison food, my favorite pair of jeans, with the forgiving elastic in the waistband, is a little loose. I put on my Garfield T-shirt and a red sweatshirt embroidered with the initials of my community college, GCC. My old socks are stiff with sweat, but they're still better than the rough wool pair I've been wearing. I pull on my white gym shoes and notice a final item at the bottom of the box. I pick up the heart-shaped locket and think about putting it in my pocket, but instead clasp it around my neck. Better for her to see me wearing her childhood gift.

I leave the bathroom and hand the empty box back to Mr. Clean.

"You take care of yourself." He winks again.

Connolly and I walk down the fluorescent-lit hallway of the admissions building toward the parking lot. "Someone coming to pick you up, Watts?"

"Yes, sir. My ride should be here soon." I'm careful not to say who my ride is; though Rose Gold is twenty-three now, some people still imagine her as a sickly little girl. Some people would not be overjoyed to see us reunited. They don't care that I stayed up all night monitoring her vitals during every hospital stay. They don't know the depths of this mother's love.

We stop at the door. My fingertips tingle as they reach for the push bar.

Connolly scratches his Ditka-esque mustache. "That pierogi recipe was a real hit with my in-laws."

I clap my hands. "I told you it would be."

Connolly hesitates. "Martha was impressed. She didn't sleep on the couch last night."

"Baby steps, sir. She's coming around. Keep reading that book." I've been coaching the warden on *The Five Love Languages* for the past few months.

Connolly smiles and looks lost for a second.

"Now, don't get all emotional," I joke, slapping his shoulder.

He nods. "Good luck out there, Patty. Let's not meet again, okay?"

"That's the plan," I say. I watch him stride away, his clown-sized shoes smacking against the linoleum. He hefts his bulk into an office and closes the door behind him, and then there's nothing left to face but a spooky silence. Just like that, the Illinois Department of Corrections is finished with me.

I try to ignore the wild thumping in my chest. Pushing the door open, I walk outside into blinding sunlight, half expecting an alarm to sound or a red light to flash. But it really is that easy: enter a building, leave a building, no one minds. I can go to a movie or church or the circus. I could get stuck in a thunderstorm without an umbrella or mugged at gunpoint. I am free, and anything can happen to me. I stretch out my fingers and marvel at the breeze on this crisp November day. Shielding my eyes, I scan the parking lot for the old Chevy van. But it's a sea of sedans. No people.

She should be here any minute now.

I sit on the flimsy bench, scowling as the plastic protests under my weight. After several minutes of struggling to get comfortable, I stand. Back to pacing.

In the distance, my maroon van turns onto the long single-lane road that leads to the admissions building. As it creeps closer, I do my best to flatten any frizzies and straighten my sweatshirt. I clear my throat like I'm about to speak, but all I do is stare. By the time the van reaches the parking lot, I can make out my little girl's narrow shoulders and blond-brown hair.

I watch Rose Gold back into a parking spot. She turns off the engine and leans against the headrest. I picture her closing her eyes for a minute. The ends of her chest-length hair rise and fall with every unsuspecting breath. Rose Gold has wanted long hair since she was a little girl, and now she has it.

I read somewhere the average person has a hundred thousand hairs on their head—more for blonds, fewer for redheads. I wonder how many strands it takes to fill a fist. I imagine pulling my daughter in for a warm embrace, twirling her locks through my fingers. I always told her she was better off with her head shaved. You're much less vulnerable that way—nothing to grab hold of.

Daughters never listen to their mothers.

When she lifts her head, her eyes meet mine. She raises her arm and waves like the homecoming queen on a parade float. My own arm glides into the air and mirrors her excitement. I spot the outlines of a car seat in the van's second row. My grandson must be buckled in back there.

I take a step off the curb toward my family. It's been almost twenty-five years since my last baby. In seconds his tiny fingers will be wrapped around mine.

2

Rose Gold

Sometimes I still couldn't believe I was allowed to read whatever I wanted. I rubbed the glossy magazine photos. A flawless couple held hands on a beach. A teenage boy with shaggy hair ducked into a waiting car. A radiant mother cradled her daughter as she walked the streets of New York. All of these people were famous. I knew the mother was a musician named Beyoncé, but I didn't recognize the others. I was sure most eighteen-year-olds would.

"Rose Gold?"

I started. My manager, Scott, stood in front of me. "We're about to open," he said. "Can you put the magazine away?"

I nodded. Scott kept walking. Should I have apologized? Was he mad at me or just doing his job? Could I get written up for this? I was supposed to respect authority. I was also supposed to outsmart them. Mom always had.

I gazed at the copy of *Chit Chat* in my hands. I had been searching the tabloid for mentions of her. During her trial, they had written three stories about us. Now, on her first day in prison, they had nothing to say. Neither did the national newspapers. Mom's imprisonment was nothing but a splashy feature in our local paper, the *Deadwick Daily*.

I put the magazine back on the endcap. Scott began clapping while he walked the store floor, yelling, "A smile is part of your uniform, people." I glanced at Arnie on register two. He rolled his eyes. Had I annoyed him? What if he never talked to me again? What if he told all our coworkers I was a weirdo? I looked away.

The security guard unlocked Gadget World's doors. No one was waiting outside. Sunday mornings were quiet. I flipped on my register's light. The big yellow "5" didn't illuminate. Mom always said a lightbulb out meant something bad was coming.

The tremblies in my stomach tightened. For the past year, I had dreaded any big day of her trial: opening arguments, my testimony, the verdict, sentencing. But the reporters didn't care that "Poisonous Patty" was behind bars. No one but me had remembered it was her first day in prison. She'd still be free if I hadn't gotten on that witness stand. I hadn't talked to her since the arrest.

I tried to picture my mother—five feet five inches and stocky—in an orange jumpsuit. What if the guards hurt her? What if she made the wrong inmate mad? What if she got sick from the food? I knew I was supposed to be happy about these possibilities. I knew I was supposed to hate Mom, because people were always asking me if I did.

I didn't want to imagine her in the present, covered with plum-colored bruises and growing pale from the lack of sun. I wanted to remember the mother I'd grown up with, the woman with broad shoulders and thick arms that could knead bread dough in minutes. Her hair was short and almost black, thanks to a cheap box dye. She had pudgy cheeks, a snub nose, and a big smile that lit up her face. I loved Mom's smile because I liked looking at her teeth: white and straight and neat, a mouth as organized as her file cabinets. But it was her pale blue-green eyes that won you over. They listened, they sympathized. They were kind and trustworthy without her saying a word. When her fleshy hand enveloped yours and she trained those aquamarine eyes on you, you were sure you'd never feel alone.

"Rose Gold, right?"

I started again. A Disney prince look-alike stood in front of me. I recognized him. He came in all the time to buy video games.

The teenage boy pointed at my name tag. "Okay, I cheated. I'm Brandon," he said.

I stared at Brandon, afraid anything I said would make him go away. He held eye contact—did I have something on my face? I grabbed his items off the conveyor belt: a video game with a soldier holding a gun on its cover and four bags of peanut M&M's.

Brandon kept talking. "I go to Deadwick High."

He was younger than me. I was already eighteen and had my GED.

"Okay," I said. I was supposed to say something else. Why was someone as cute as Brandon talking to me in the first place?

"Did you go to DHS?"

I scratched my nose so my hand would cover my teeth. "I was homeschooled."

"Cool." Brandon smiled at his feet. "I was wondering if you'd go out with me."

"Where?" I asked, bewildered.

He laughed. "Like, on a date."

I scanned the empty store. Brandon stood there, hands in his pockets, waiting for an answer. I thought of Phil, my online boyfriend.

"I don't know."

"Come on," Brandon said. "I promise I don't bite."

He leaned over the counter when he said this. Our faces were a foot apart. Tiny freckles dotted his nose. He smelled like boy soap. My heart started doing puppy jumps. I could finally get my first kiss. Did it count as cheating if you'd never met your online boyfriend in person?

Brandon winked, then closed his eyes. How was this so easy for him? I should close my eyes too. But what if I missed his mouth and kissed his nose? Eyes open, then. Should I use my tongue? The magazines said to sometimes use tongue. But not teeth. Never teeth.

My teeth.

I couldn't let him that close to my teeth. Plus, Scott might see us. Our faces were now inches apart. I had been leaning over the counter without realizing it. I was going to mess up. I wasn't ready. I jerked my head back.

"Not a great time," I mumbled.

He opened his eyes and cocked his head. "What'd you say?"

"I said it's not a great time." I held my breath.

He waved me off. "I didn't even suggest a time. Are you busy forever?"

I was never busy, but that wasn't the right answer. I cracked my knuckles and tried to swallow. My throat was dry.

Brandon raised his eyebrows. "Are you gonna make me beg?"

I imagined spending the next forty-eight hours reliving every word of this conversation. I just had to get out before I screwed up. I tucked a strand of hair—short and stringy—behind my ear. "I'm sorry," I said to his T-shirt.

Brandon took a step back from the counter. His cheeks turned pink. I watched his smile morph into a sneer. I must have said the wrong thing. I flinched, waiting.

"Are you busy pretending to need a wheelchair?"

My mouth fell open. My hand covered it.

"And you think you can hide those teeth? They're fucking disgusting. You're fucking disgusting," Brandon hissed.

Don't cry, don't cry, don't cry, don't cry.

"I only asked you out because my friend dared me," he said. On cue, an overjoyed boy popped out from behind register two. Tears began to well in my eyes.

"Like *you* could reject me?" Brandon scoffed, and strolled off with his plastic Gadget World bag. His friend high-fived him. The first fat tear escaped and rolled down my cheek.

As soon as they left, I speed-walked away from my register, ignoring Arnie's stare. I thought about Maleficent and Jafar and Cruella de Vil and Scar and Captain Hook: the bad guys always lost in the end.

The break room was empty. I closed the door and locked it.

I hadn't sobbed that hard since I'd heard my mother's verdict three months ago.

After work I carefully drove Mom's beat-up van nine miles to my apartment. I'd gotten my driver's license two months ago with the help of Mom's former best friend, Mary Stone, who had signed me up for a driver-education course, then taken me to the DMV for my written exam and behind-the-wheel test. The DMV clerk said I was the first person to get a perfect score that month. Sometimes I got in the van and drove in circles around the block, just because I could.

I parked outside my apartment complex. Once I got the cashier job at Gadget World, Mrs. Stone had also helped me search for cheap rentals in Deadwick. Sheridan Apartments was a run-down four-story building—Mrs. Stone said it had been built when she was a kid. Sometimes I had little mouse visitors, but rent was less than four hundred dollars a month. Mrs. Stone said this was a good starter home for me. I wasn't sure what I was starting.

I locked the car doors and headed toward the building. My phone vibrated in my pocket as I walked up the concrete path. I made sure to think of Brandon while I stepped on every crack.

> **Phil:** Chat tonight?
> **Me:** Yes please, rough day
> **Phil:** What happened?

Inside, I kicked off my boots and headed straight for the bathroom scale. Since moving out of Mom's house nine months ago, I'd gained thirty pounds. Recently my weight had plateaued. I looked down. Still one hundred and two.

I avoided the mirror as I left the room. I didn't have the energy to go through the whole routine. (Step one: check whether the whitening strips were working. I rated every tooth on a scale of one to ten, then recorded each tooth's score in a small notebook so I could track improvements. Step two: use a cloth measuring tape to check how much my hair had grown. I'd tried fish oil pills, biotin, and vitamins, but nothing worked; my hair still wouldn't grow any faster. Step three: scan myself from head to toe, body part by body part, and catalogue the things I didn't like. I kept a running inventory in my head so I knew what needed to be worked on.) I tried not to do the routine more than once a day and avoided it altogether on bad days like this one. I turned off the bathroom light. I was hungry.

In the kitchen, I threw a frozen Tex-Mex mac-and-cheese dinner in the microwave and leaned against the counter. I read the meal description on the box and wondered what "chorizo sausage" tasted like. Since moving into my own place, I had mostly lived off of cereal and frozen dinners. I'd been trying to teach myself how to cook, but I kept getting the timing wrong—burning vegetables or undercooking rice.

I missed having someone around to prepare my meals, even when they were PediaSure. Sometimes I lit little votive candles to make dinnertime fancy like Mom used to do.

The microwave beeped, and I took out the mac and cheese. Still standing at the counter, I ripped the plastic wrap off the macaroni and dropped the pasta gently into my mouth, pressing the cool tines of the fork against my tongue. Curly noodles coated with Pepper Jack cheese slid smoothly down my throat, confident of their one-way travel. Bread crumbs crunched between my molars. Then the spice hit me—chorizo had a kick to it! My eyes watered. Goose bumps popped up on my arms. I would never tire of all these new flavors.

I opened the fridge and pulled out a Lunchables meal and a gallon of chocolate milk. I thought about chugging from the jug, until I pictured her lava stare. I poured the milk into a glass instead.

> **Me:** Some high school kid came into the store and acted
> like an a-hole

I thrilled over my casual use of "a-hole." Swearing hadn't been allowed before.

> **Me:** I'm over it
> **Me:** How was your day?

I'd always hoped I was being hard on myself. Everyone else couldn't think I was as ugly as I feared. But Brandon did. My scrawny body looked more like a six-year-old boy's than a woman's. I had no boobs. My teeth were jagged and rotten. Even after putting on thirty pounds, I was still too thin, still couldn't fill a bus seat. No one considered me beautiful, not even Mom, who was always careful to call me a *beautiful soul*, but never beautiful. She chose the worst times to be honest.

Phil: Sorry about the jerk

Phil: My day was snowy ;-)

Phil had moved to Colorado a couple years ago so he could snow-board more often. He had convinced his parents to let him live at his aunt and uncle's cabin in the foothills of the Front Range, forty-five miles southwest of Denver. This rebel streak plus his romantic interest in me had been enough to pull me in. He also helped me figure out what Mom was doing to me, so he pretty much saved my life. We met in a singles chat room when I was sixteen, soon after I convinced Mom to get the Internet to help with my schoolwork. She only let me online for thirty minutes a day, but I snuck on after she was asleep to talk to Phil. Now, two and a half years later, we were texting daily. No calls or video chats, though. I wasn't good at conversations on the fly. With texts I had time to prepare my responses. I couldn't risk losing him.

After tossing the empty macaroni tub in the garbage, I carried my Lunchables to the living room. I sat on one of the BarcaLoungers Mom had bought years ago at a garage sale and popped up the footrest. I stacked a square of cheddar and a piece of turkey atop a cracker, then paused. Was my stomach noodley, or was I imagining things?

Out loud I said, "Nothing is wrong with the macaroni."

I picked up the DVDs on the side table: *Alice in Wonderland* and *Pinocchio*. As a kid I'd only been allowed to watch three movies—*Sleeping Beauty*, *Cinderella*, and *Beauty and the Beast*—so I'd been making up for lost time. So far I had worked my way through half of the library's collection of Disney movies. None of them could beat my all-time favorite, *The Little Mermaid*—I'd watched it thirty times. I was trying to get to thirty-three, for good luck.

But a movie wasn't what I wanted. I studied my khakis and blue uniform shirt. Tomorrow I'd be wearing the exact same outfit, straightening the same stack of magazines, refilling the same kiosk for the next a-hole who came into Gadget World to tell me how gross I was.

What if Brandon came back to the store? What if I ran into him at the gas station or while buying groceries?

Maybe I was overreacting. I had a boyfriend and a full-time job and my own apartment. I'd been to a dentist, who said with some extractions and an implant-supported bridge, I could have beautiful white teeth. Since then, I'd started saving fifty dollars from every paycheck to put toward my new smile. I was making progress, so what was one hot guy's opinion? Brandon was nobody to me.

"You are not disgusting," I said, sick and fidgety. I didn't believe me.

I wasn't ready for a move to a new city. I'd spent most of my life in the same town house, only leaving for doctors' appointments, visits with our neighbors, and school until Mom had pulled me out. Even though a lot of the people in Deadwick annoyed me, at least they were familiar faces. I could hold it together as long as I had our brown recliners, the corner grocery, and Mrs. Stone—known for her oatmeal cookies and eternal optimism—a five-minute drive away. A move was too big. But a short change of scenery could work.

Make a list, Mom whispered. Here were all the people I knew who didn't live in Deadwick: Mom; Alex, who lived in Chicago; and Phil, who was all the way in Colorado. Phil and I had never suggested meeting. Face-to-face meant no more fantasies. If Phil met me, he might call me disgusting too. He might even break up with me. Still, the ants in my pants wouldn't shut up.

I drafted the text for forty-five minutes before settling on the most straightforward approach.

Me: How would you feel about me coming to visit? :-)

Me: I need to leave home for a little while

The three dots hovered, floating on my screen. He was typing and typing and typing. I tugged at a hangnail. *Don't get balloon hopes.*

> **Phil:** Now's not a great time. Sorry babe
>
> **Phil:** Maybe in a few months?

I let out the breath I'd been holding. I didn't dare ask why now wasn't a great time, but instead made another list: Possible Reasons My Boyfriend Does Not Want to Meet Me. Maybe he had another girlfriend. Maybe I was the mistress. Maybe he wasn't allowed to date. Maybe he didn't know how to snowboard. Maybe he was uglier in real life than in his photo. Maybe he knew deep down I wasn't the cute girl he hoped I was—although I'd given him a fake name to stop him from finding me.

The run-in with Brandon was the closest I had come to my first kiss. Eighteen was too old to still be waiting—I had learned that much from the pages of *Seventeen*. I decided to keep working on Phil. He was my best shot. Besides, if we were meant to be together, didn't we have to meet at some point?

I drummed my fingers on the recliner's arm, racking my brain for another way out. I could visit Chicago. For months my best friend and Mrs. Stone's daughter, Alex, had offered to show me around. Gas for a three-hour drive wouldn't cost that much.

On my phone I opened the conversation with Alex. "I think I might come visit!" I typed. I tapped the little blue arrow and chewed my lip.

I scrolled through our chat. Alex hadn't responded to the last three texts I'd sent her. I would have been worried if she wasn't posting on social media sites every day, detailing how much fun she was having with her city friends. Over the past few months, I had been studying some of these sites to figure out how they worked. I even mustered the nerve to create my own account on one, but I still hadn't posted anything. I couldn't decide on a profile picture.

I glanced at the movie rentals again, but instead inserted my copy of *The Little Mermaid*—the one movie I owned—into the DVD player.

Thirty minutes in, Alex still hadn't responded. For once, Scuttle and Sebastian couldn't distract me. I kept imagining the word "DISGUSTING" as a neon sign floating over my head, with two blinking arrows pointing at me. The word tattooed itself across my forehead and cheeks, inside my mouth. I pulled my zebra-striped fleece tie blanket—the one Mom had made for me—up to my chin. The word followed me there, pounding in my ears. I imagined it drifting along the blood in my veins and shook my head to fling the thoughts away. I should have ignored Brandon or kept flipping through that magazine.

The magazine. I grabbed my phone again and scrolled through old e-mails. I found the one from Vinny King, the writer for *Chit Chat* who had sent me multiple interview requests in exchange for a couple hundred bucks. I scanned it again.

> *All the media has done is paint you as a weak, victimized little girl—isn't it time you set the record straight?*

Back then I believed in fate. I thought everything happened for a reason.

When Vinny King had first contacted me, I'd still had the feeding tube. I'd just moved out of our town house to Mrs. Stone's place. Social services had assigned me a therapist. Reporters were camped outside of every building where they thought I might be hiding. By the time I testified against Mom, I was barely holding it together. I wanted to publicly separate the facts from the lies, but an interview with the old Rose Gold would have been a disaster. I could see the headlines laughing that the daughter was as crazy as her mother. They were bad enough as it was: *MOTHER SHOWS NO REMORSE FOR STARVING DAUGHTER.*

But that was then.

Now I was stable. Nothing was perfect, of course. Like, I was maybe a little too fixated on my weight. I still couldn't eat certain foods without feeling nauseated, although I was pretty sure the sickness was in my head. I was bad at talking to kids my own age. Jerks like Brandon still brought me to my knees.

Maybe I wasn't ready to talk about the memories I'd done such a good job bottling up over the last year. But I could either keep taking abuse from people who knew nothing about me, or I could tell my side of the story. The media were no longer interested in Mom and me; I hadn't heard from Vinny in months. But maybe I could convince him to hear me out. Then I could use the money from the interview for my teeth. Or to visit Phil in Colorado.

Alex still hadn't responded to my text. On the TV, Ariel agreed to give up her voice.

I dialed Vinny King's number before I could change my mind. The phone rang. I gazed at my shoes. The laces had come untied.

She was thinking of me.

3

Patty

I stride across the parking lot toward my daughter. Rose Gold jumps down from the driver's seat, her five-foot frame dwarfed by the big van. A woman of twenty-three has replaced the gangly teenager I raised. Her hair is straight and limp, a dull shade somewhere between blond and brown. Her small upturned nose gives her the appearance of a mouse. She wears baggy jeans and a huge crewneck sweatshirt. She darts toward me with that same tiptoe gait she's always had, as if the concrete is covered with hot coals. She looks healthy, normal.

Except for those teeth.

Her teeth protrude from her gums every which way, like old tombstones in a cemetery. They are a range of yellows, from eggnog to Dijon mustard. At the roots some are the color of mud; at the tops they are uneven, jagged. She is smiling—nay, grinning—at me, and I'm reminded of a jack-o'-lantern. To others, her teeth may be hideous. To me, they tell a story. They remind me of the decades of stomach acid corroding the enamel. Her teeth are a testament to her courage.

We meet in the middle of the parking lot. She reaches for me first. "You're free," she says.

"You're a mother," I say.

We hold each other for a few moments. I count to five, not wanting to seem overeager or arouse suspicion. "Can I meet the little guy?"

Rose Gold pulls back from the embrace. She eyes me brightly but wariness slips through. "Of course," she says. I follow her to the van. She yanks open the back door.

There he is, waiting in his car seat. Eyes darting, legs kicking: our little Adam. Just two months old.

On impulse, I reach for his stockinged foot and coo at him. He gurgles at me, then sticks his tongue out. I laugh, delighted.

I reach for the buckle to his car seat, then remember my place. I turn to Rose Gold. "May I?"

She nods. Her eyes match her son's, dashing back and forth between his body and my face. I unbuckle the seat belt and lift him out of his chair.

I cradle him in my arms, drop my nose to his head, and inhale. Nothing beats that new-baby smell. For a second, it's Rose Gold in my arms again. We're back in the town house, and for a few minutes, she's not crying or wheezing or coughing.

"He looks like you," I say, glancing at my daughter.

She nods a second time, staring at the baby with such intensity, I know she's not listening to me. I'd recognize that lovesick gaze anywhere: she is head over heels for her son.

I focus on Adam, who watches me with curious hazel eyes. He sticks his tongue out again, then puts a few fingers in his mouth. All infants resemble tiny, wrinkled grandpas, but on Adam, the arrangement works. He's a cute baby. Lord knows the Wattses aren't lookers, so it won't be long before the ugly stick comes after him. For now, he is precious and adorable and everything I've hoped for in a grandson. I sigh.

"It feels like just yesterday you were visiting me here with that growing belly," I say, handing him to Rose Gold. "Oh, darling, he's perfect."

She nods and nestles him back into his car seat. "I think so too. He almost slept through the night once." She tucks a blanket around his body and under his chin—our miniature mummy. He smiles up at us, dimples forming in his chubby cheeks. We both beam back, awed.

Rose Gold turns to me. "Should we go?"

I nod. We both reach for the driver's door. I realize my mistake and shuffle to the passenger's side. I bought this van when Rose Gold was a toddler. I have never sat in the passenger seat.

Inside, Rose Gold removes her sweatshirt, revealing a ratty white T-shirt underneath. She appears already to have lost some weight. I debate saying as much, knowing most mothers would be overjoyed to hear such a thing—I've been trying to lose my baby weight for twenty-three years—but stop myself. Comments on weight loss have never been a compliment in Rose Gold's book.

She is small behind the wheel. A vehicle of this size is meant for a meaty driver, someone like me. Still, she handles the van with ease, pulling out of the parking spot and pointing it back down the long road. She grips the wheel, hands at ten and two, knuckles turning white. I wonder when she got her driver's license. I never gave her permission. I imagine wrenching the steering wheel away from my daughter, sending the van careening off the road.

We all have little musings like this: what if I screamed in the middle of the meeting? What if I grabbed his face and kissed him? What if I put the knife into his back instead of the utensil drawer? Of course we don't act on them. That's what separates the sane from the not: knowing madness is an option but declining to choose it.

I notice the silence has carried on a beat too long. "Thank you for coming to get me."

Rose Gold nods. "How does it feel to be out?"

I dwell on the question. "Scary. Unsettling. For the most part, fantastic."

"I bet." She chews her lip. "So now what? Do you have to do community service or go to therapy or anything?"

Yeah, like I'm going to serve the community that threw me in prison. Throughout Rose Gold's childhood, I was an exemplary neighbor, cleaning trash off our highways and playing bingo with our elderly. If I want therapy, it has to be on my own dime. I don't have that kind of money in the first place, and if I did, I certainly wouldn't use it to have some quack list all my deficiencies. One of my fellow inmates—a former shrink—gave me some free advice.

She suggested I make a list of goals for my return to society, said keeping busy would leave me less time for getting into trouble. I didn't bother telling her how busy I was during the months leading up to my arrest.

I came up with the following list:

1. Find somewhere to live. My town house went into foreclosure after I went to prison.

2. Find a job. I can't work in a hospital anymore, but I have a promising lead with an old friend from prison. When Wanda got out, she started a nonprofit that helps female former convicts get back on their feet. Ex-prisoners run the company, Free 2.0. (*What about the women who've been in and out of prison a dozen times?* I asked. *Would she call it Free 13.0 for them?* "Patty," Wanda had drawled, "your mind is both your biggest asset and your biggest drawback." People tend to describe my personality via backhanded compliments.) Last time she wrote, she mentioned something about manning a hotline remotely.

3. Fix things with Rose Gold. When my daughter began visiting me a year ago, she was angry and wanted answers. Step by step, I've been winning her back. Soon things will return to how they used to be.

4. Convince my friends and neighbors I'm innocent.

Denial is as good a strategy as any. The word suggests obliviousness, a refusal to see the truth. But there's a mighty big difference between someone who won't see the truth and someone who won't tell it. People are much more inclined to forgive you if you act like you didn't know any better. Let them call me oblivious. Let them think I don't know right from wrong. Beats the alternative.

I glance at Rose Gold. I have one shot to get this right.

"First, I need a place to stay," I say, feigning nonchalance.

She doesn't react, keeps checking on Adam in the rearview mirror.

I was hoping she'd offer so I didn't have to ask. Maybe I've overestimated her renewed loyalty to me. I look out the window. We're on the highway now, nothing but cornfields for miles in any direction. They built this prison where Jesus left his sandals. I keep my voice casual.

"I thought maybe I could stay with you for a little bit? Just until I'm back on my feet," I add. "I know you said your apartment is tiny."

Rose Gold stares at me so long, I get nervous we're going to drift off the road. After a minute, she says, "I don't live in that apartment anymore."

I turn to her, questioning.

"I bought a house," she says with pride. "It's no mansion, but I have three small bedrooms, a bathroom, and a yard."

Bingo. "Well, if you have a spare bedroom, I'd love to spend more time with you. I could take care of the mortgage payments once I have a job." I almost offer to watch Adam while she's at work, but decide to take this slowly. The thrashing in my chest annoys me. I put a roof over my daughter's head for eighteen years. Why shouldn't she put one over mine for a while?

"We've come a long way since I started visiting you in prison," Rose Gold says slowly. "I shouldn't have fallen for the media's story. I wish I had stood up to the prosecutor."

The tide is turning in my favor, so I stay quiet, let her think she's making the decision. Maybe I'm finally going to get my apology.

She turns to me. "But you shouldn't have sheltered me from the world my entire life. I'm not a little girl anymore."

I ignore the slight and nod. I have to pick my battles. She will learn soon enough that the urge to keep your child safe never goes away, no matter how old she is.

"I don't want things between us getting screwed up now that we're finally on good terms. If we try this, if you live with me, it's my house, my rules," she says with a shaky voice. A gentle breeze could decimate her conviction. "I want us to be completely honest with each other."

I nod some more, working to contain my excitement.

She chews her thumbnail for a few seconds.

"Okay, let's give it a try. You can have one of the spare bedrooms." Rose Gold smiles at me. I know it's a real smile because she forgets to cover her teeth.

I can't help myself—I clap with glee and squeeze her shoulder. How have we progressed from arguing across a table in a prison complex to becoming roommates again? But then how could I have doubted my daughter? Of course my flesh and blood will take me in. Think of all the sacrifices I've made on her behalf. Think of all she owes me.

"Are you sure? I don't want to overstep."

She takes a deep breath, eyes never leaving the rearview mirror. "If it doesn't work out, you can always find a place of your own. But I don't want you spending your first night at a motel or something. That's almost as bad as jail."

"Oh, honey, I'd love to stay with you. And I'm happy to take care of Adam if you ever need help." The offer slips out before I can stop it.

"Let's see how it goes." She doesn't sound overjoyed, but gives me a quick smile before her eyes flick back to the rearview mirror. What is she looking for? She has become hard to read, my daughter.

We don't talk for a while, just sit next to each other in either companionable or self-conscious silence—I spend most of the ride trying to decide which it is. When I can't take the quiet anymore, I turn on the radio. Survivor's "Eye of the Tiger" is playing, which cheers me up immediately. I love eighties music. I tap along to the beat on my armrest.

Rose Gold pulls the van off the highway at the exit for Deadwick, and my shoulders sag. Deadwick is, in a word, brown. Everything is always dying here, whether it's from too much snow or not enough rain. And I don't expect the pea-brained residents will throw a parade when they find out I'm back.

I hope her place is in the newer part, with the town houses and apartment complex. You couldn't call the homes there nice or big, but they're farther away from old memories, at least.

We stop at a red light next to Casey's, the town gas station. I note with surprise that gas is less than three dollars a gallon. When the light turns green, we take a right, heading north; the older section, then. Just my luck.

Rose Gold slows the van to a crawl as we travel down Main Street. I focus straight ahead so I don't have the chance to recognize any of the long gray faces or beady black eyes on the sidewalk. My neighbors— people I thought were my closest friends—slandered my good name to the press throughout my trial: *NEIGHBORS DESCRIBE POISONOUS PATTY WATTS AS "PREDATOR," "MONSTER."*

I haven't seen or heard from any of them since.

We've been in the car for over an hour, and I can't keep my mouth shut any longer. As casually as possible, I ask, "Any word from Phil?"

Rose Gold glares. "I told you we broke up."

"I wasn't sure whether that was final. I thought he might have the decency to see his child into the world."

Rose Gold cracks her knuckles at the wheel, tension growing. "You're not going to start up about deadbeat dads again, are you?"

"Of course not." I file away the speech I have been preparing, bulleted in six key points, since Rose Gold's last visit.

My daughter should never have been left to fend for herself. A few years without me, and she winds up pregnant and abandoned. Our neighbors can grouse all they want about my controlling ways, my dubious mothering. But they don't understand how much she needs me, how lucky she is to have me here to run her life for her. I'll right this sinking ship in no time.

"Maybe all Wattses are doomed to awful fathers." Rose Gold sneers. "You always said I was better off without Grant anyway."

She is. I told her that her father overdosed before she was born, a misfortune both timely and fortunate in my book. True, she'd never met him, but at least she could imagine her father was a good guy. He wasn't.

"Well, you're not alone anymore. You have me now." I beam. Fifty-eight years of cheeriness—I deserve a medal.

Rose Gold keeps watching the rearview mirror. She cradles the steering wheel with her knees and wipes her palms on her pants, leaving sweat marks behind. Is she nervous because of me?

She flicks on her turn signal, and I realize how familiar the route is. The right off the highway, the long straight stretch, another right, two lefts. Unease grabs hold of my stomach. I am ten years old again, sitting in the backseat after swim practice, dreading going home.

"Mom?" Rose Gold prods. "Did you hear me? What do you want for dinner tonight?"

I push the memory away. "Why don't I make us something, darling?" My daughter flinches ever so slightly. "It's the least I can do with you taking me in and all."

Rose Gold makes another right turn, and now we're one street away. Maybe she's made a mistake. She slows the van as we approach the stop sign at the intersection of Evergreen and Apple. I clutch the armrests. Beads of sweat form along my hairline. I haven't made a left turn onto Apple Street in decades. There are two houses in that direction, and one of them is abandoned.

The van stalls at the stop sign; it doesn't want to go any farther either. Is Rose Gold making me wait or am I imagining things? The van and everyone inside it—even Adam—are still.

Rose Gold reaches for the blinker and turns the steering wheel left. We can't be turning left; Mr. and Mrs. Peabody live in the house now.

The van creeps down Apple Street, tree-lined but leafless at this time of year. A pothole lurks in the middle of the road; it wasn't there when I was a kid. Neither was the guardrail at the street's dead end— I wonder offhand when it was installed. I try to make sense of the situation. Maybe somebody renovated the Thompsons' old house. But their place is already coming into view, and it's still as run-down as it was when I was a kid.

By now we've reached the end of the subdivision and stopped in front of 201 Apple Street, a half-acre lot with a small one-story ranch house. The brown brick building is still unexceptional, dull but well cared for over the decades. A tall wooden fence surrounds the back half of the property. "To keep the riffraff out," Dad explained while hammering the fence posts into the ground.

I gape at Rose Gold, unable to verbalize the question. She pulls into the driveway and presses the garage-door opener clipped to the sun visor. The door to the detached two-car garage starts to open.

"Surprise," she says in a singsong voice. "I bought the house you grew up in."

I'm too dumbstruck to formulate sentences. "The Peabodys?"

"Gerald died last year, and then Mabel moved into a nursing home. But we made an agreement they'd sell it to me once they were ready to move on. I got such a good deal. Way better than anything else I could have bought around here." Rose Gold is proud of herself, like the day she learned to tie her shoes. She pulls the van into the garage, empty without my dad's yard tools and all the cases of Budweiser.

I feel sick.

"I was going to wait a few weeks to show it to you, so I could decorate more. But maybe now you can help with that"—she lowers her voice and squeezes my shoulder the way I had squeezed hers—"since we're reconciling and everything."

My mind is fuzzy, like a room with carpeted walls. I keep reaching for clues, but instead am consumed by one thought: I can't go in there.

Rose Gold pulls the key out of the ignition and opens her door. "I knew you'd be surprised." She simpers, then gets out of the car.

"You know what happened here," I say, still in shock. "Why on earth would you buy this house?"

Rose Gold's eyes widen. "I thought we'd keep it in the family," she says earnestly. "Four generations of Wattses—think of the history!"

She opens the backseat door and makes baby noises at Adam. He kicks his feet. She takes him out of his car seat.

"I missed you," she coos, hugging Adam tight to her body. He nestles into her, yawning.

I am still belted in, hand frozen on the buckle.

Rose Gold carries the baby toward the garage's side door, then turns back when she realizes I'm not following her. "Come on, *Mom*." Why does she say it that way, sarcastically, as though I'm not her actual mother? "Come see what I've done so far."

I should have stayed at a motel. I could have stayed in prison. The hair on my arms stands straight up. My mouth is dusty. I press the buckle, and the seat belt strap retracts. My fingers reach for the door handle. The soles of my feet find the running board.

"You coming?" Rose Gold watches me, cradling Adam in her arms.

I nod and muster a grin, the ever-agreeable Patty. Slamming the van door behind me, I drift out of the garage and toward the house.

4

Rose Gold

January 2013

The reporter tapped away on his phone while waiting in line for our coffees. Vinny King had slicked-back hair, wore a small silver cross on a chain around his neck, and looked like he'd slept in his baggy clothes. I wondered if he'd woken up late.

It had taken us two months to find a date to meet in Chicago. On the drive up, I was sure Vinny would cancel on me last minute. When I got to the café, I was still convinced the interview wouldn't happen. Yet here we were, on a freezing but sunny January afternoon.

Vinny had suggested a coffee shop in Bucktown. I had to google where Bucktown was, but I found my way. I watched stressed customers order their drinks to go. Others sat at old wooden tables and pecked away at their keyboards. I'd drunk coffee once and hated it, but Vinny didn't need to know that. Coffee was a rite of adulthood—only a kid wouldn't drink it. So when Vinny offered, I asked for a Nutella latte. Maybe the chocolate would disguise the coffee flavor.

I had decided this interview would go well because of two good omens on my way into the shop: a baby with its hand in its mouth, then three blue cars parked in a row.

I had started paying attention to good and bad signs when I was seven—first because Mom did, and later because I wanted a way to predict what was going to happen to me. While waiting in a doctor's office lobby, I'd get that familiar nervous thumping in my chest. But instead of sitting there thinking how scared I was, I'd record everything I observed in a small pink notebook.

Man with eye patch, I wrote, watching an old guy make his way across the lobby. Thirty minutes later, my doctor announced I didn't need the MRI after all. An eye patch became a good omen.

Two gray hats, I noted in a hospital parking lot. That afternoon, the doctor took my vitals and said I'd lost six pounds. A gray hat meant something bad was coming.

Seeing the world this way gave me certainty at a time when I had zero control over my body and health. I knew now that these signs didn't actually predict anything, but they were like a childhood blankie—I just felt better holding on to them.

Vinny walked two big mugs over and set them on the table. Coffee spilled over the side of one cup and onto Vinny's hand.

"Shit," he grunted.

I stared at him.

"Can you grab me some napkins?" Vinny said, jabbing a finger at the dispenser. I rushed to pull two from the metal box. Vinny rubbed his wet hand on his jeans, where a dark coffee stain was forming. He took the napkins from me and rubbed at it.

Dab. Don't rub, she chided. *See what happens when you don't carry a Tide to Go pen?*

Vinny glanced up and saw me watching him. I looked down and studied my drink. Someone had drawn a heart in the steamed milk. I wanted to take a photo, but when I scanned the café, no one else was photographing their coffee. Maybe I wasn't supposed to care. "Thanks for the drink," I said.

Vinny stopped rubbing his jeans and tossed the crumpled napkins on the table. He let out a disgusted sigh and sat across from me, defeated. "I got you some muffins too," he said. He looked me up and down. "First time in Chicago?"

I nodded.

"You in town long?"

"Just the weekend," I said, making sure I blocked my mouth with my hand. "I'm visiting a friend."

Alex had been at the gym when I'd arrived this morning, so I went straight to the café. I'd texted her a couple times but hadn't heard back.

"She was my neighbor in Deadwick," I explained.

The barista set a basket of muffins in the middle of our table. I counted five. Vinny blew on the coffee he had left. He didn't take a muffin, so I didn't either. I wondered how old he was—early forties, maybe?

"She was the first person I told about my mom," I mumbled. I'd tried making muffins last weekend, but they weren't very good. I wondered if these would be better. Under the table, my leg pogo-sticked.

Vinny shook his hair out of his bloodshot eyes and sat up a little straighter. "Why don't we start with your illnesses?" he said. "What have you been diagnosed with? And can you speak up a little?"

My eyes widened at the thought of listing them all. "I was a preemie, born ten weeks early. That's how it started," I said, rubbing my hands on the thighs of my jeans, not making eye contact. "At the hospital, I had jaundice and then pneumonia. I think those were real—the nurses wrote it down in my medical records."

Vinny still hadn't touched the muffins. Starving, I grabbed a blueberry one and popped a piece in my mouth. I nearly moaned in appreciation. The base was moist and fluffy, the top buttery, the blueberries fresh—these were a million times better than the batch I'd made at home. I took bite after delighted bite before remembering I was in the middle of a story.

Once Mom was allowed to bring me home, I told Vinny, I had issues with sleep apnea. Mom got me a CPAP machine and medicine. She said I also had constant fevers and sore throats, and these awful ear infections. A pediatrician put tubes in my ears.

Mom was most worried about my digestive issues. I couldn't keep anything down—formula, real food, none of it. I was shrinking when I should have been growing. When I got down to the tenth percentile in weight, the doctor agreed with Mom that I should get a feeding tube. All of this before I turned two.

I don't remember when Mom came up with her "chromosomal defect" theory, but she clung to it for the rest of my childhood. How else to explain all the bizarre symptoms—the headaches and stomachaches, the dizziness, the near-constant fatigue—that weren't connected to any single disease? A chromosomal defect sounded serious enough to be devastating, but vague enough that any illness might stem from it.

Mom had a solution for everything. As I grew up, my hair started falling out in clumps—she shaved it so I wouldn't be embarrassed by the uneven growth. When my vision problems didn't go away, Mom bought me glasses. I started fainting more often, so Mom got me a wheelchair. All her solutions created the appearance of a chronically sick child. What healthy ten-year-old had a buzzed head and was more or less confined to a wheelchair? Nobody doubted my illnesses. Including me.

Vinny thought for a minute. "How much of this do you remember?"

I picked up the second half of the muffin and took a bite. When most people looked back at their childhoods, I assumed they thought of oven-baked chocolate chip cookies at Grandma's house or the salty-sweet mixture of coconut sunscreen and sunburned skin after a long summer day.

When I thought of my childhood, I smelled disinfectant.

"I was too young to remember the appointments when they started," I said. "But Mom explained them to me once I was old enough. She said no matter how many doctors we visited, no one could ever figure out what was wrong with me."

Vinny watched a pretty young woman gather up her belongings and leave the café. Was he losing interest in my story? What if he cut the interview short and I didn't get the money for my teeth? I grabbed a second muffin: chocolate chip. I might as well get a free lunch out of this.

"The pattern was always the same. Mom would find a new doctor, and before the appointment, she'd give me a fresh buzz cut. She said I could wear my wig in the lobby, but had to take it off in the doctor's office. That he needed to see how sick I was."

When I was a kid, I hated showing my shaved head. I could pass for a little boy. But I never seriously considered letting my hair grow out. I couldn't remember what my real hair looked like, but based on my mom's descriptions, I didn't want to find out.

"Mom told me what to say before the doctor came in," I continued. "'I need you to be brave. You have to tell the doctor how you've been feeling. About the headaches and dizziness and vomiting. Don't hold back. If you don't tell him, he can't help you.'"

I worked my way through the chocolate chip muffin and told Vinny that when the doctor came in, I'd just repeat the words Mom had used. I wasn't lying about being sick—I was in pain every single day. But a four-year-old doesn't know what fatigue is. Everything I knew about my body came from Mom. I trusted her.

Mom would get annoyed with my two-word responses and pump up the pain. "These are debilitating headaches, Doctor, and she's getting them all the time." She'd run through my entire medical history, starting with apnea when I was a preemie. I'd sit in silence, bracing myself for when she reached eighteen-month-old Rose Gold. That was the age I got my feeding tube, and Mom always lifted my shirt to show it to the doctor. That horrified me every time.

"Thirty minutes later, the doctor was ready to do anything to get Mom to stop talking. He'd listen to my heartbeat, take my blood pressure and temperature. My stats were normal, with the exception of my weight, which was always way too low. He'd offer to run a few tests, and if he didn't, Mom had a few ideas on a legal pad in her purse to get him started.

"'Have you thought about a chemistry panel? What about a CBC?' She'd lean in with this little wink and whisper, 'I was a nurse's aide for twelve years,' letting the doctor know she wasn't your ordinary over-protective mother. She knew what she was talking about.

"Anyway, the doctor would agree—'Sure, I could run a CBC'— and Mom would clap her hands, all excited. She loved nothing more than being on the doctor's team. She just wanted everyone to work together to get the best possible treatment for her little girl."

I reached for a third muffin and glanced up at Vinny. To my surprise, he was leaning forward, watching me with SpaghettiOs eyes. I put a few crumbs in my mouth, self-conscious. He stared at my hand covering my mouth while I chewed.

Vinny scrunched his brows, eyes never leaving my mouth. "What about your dad? He wasn't in the picture, right? The trial reports said he died when you were young."

For the first time in I didn't know how long, I took my hand away from my mouth when I talked. I let Vinny see my teeth. He scooted closer and winced, but he was also intrigued. I had his attention.

"He died before I was born," I said.

"Of what?"

"Cancer," I lied, guilty for a minute but too embarrassed to tell him the truth. I couldn't believe how the fib slipped from my tongue, how quickly Vinny bought it. I'd been wondering how Mom kept her own stories straight all those years. Turned out, lying was much easier than telling the truth.

Vinny bowed his head for a moment, as if praying for my dead father. *Don't let the silver cross around his neck fool you,* Mom whispered. *He's never prayed a day in his weasel-faced life.* Vinny picked his head back up and opened a voice-recorder app on his phone. "Okay if I tape?"

I nodded, and he pressed the record button. I smiled at him, a big openmouthed grin. Vinny shuddered a little, but didn't even bother hiding his stare. I ignored the heat of humiliation in my face. I was going to get the money for my teeth after all.

"What about family on his side?" Vinny asked. "You ever meet any of your relatives?"

I shook my head.

"Okay, so your ma is telling everyone you're sick, and both you and the doctors believe her. You're going to the doctor's office all the time. What about life at home? What was that like?"

I dug into the third muffin, teeth first. "She pulled me out of school in first grade after one kid was mean to me, said homeschooling would be easier on my health. I spent most of my time alone with her until I was sixteen."

"How'd she justify that?" Vinny asked.

"She said I was too sick to be around other kids. My weak immune system wouldn't be able to resist their germs. She was always holding the chromosomal defect over my head. I was too scared of my sicknesses to argue. So I sat in my chair and let her shave my head and played the good patient."

"But you had to get out once in a while," Vinny said.

"We left the house for doctors' appointments, running errands, and visiting neighbors," I said. "Before Mom's arrest, our neighbors thought she was a saint. She took part in every food drive, roadway cleanup, and raffle. And all this with a sick daughter at home. 'That Patty is something, isn't she?' they'd say. Their praise was just what she wanted."

Vinny thought for a minute. "You said you didn't hang around a lot of other people until you were sixteen. What changed?"

I smiled. "We got the Internet."

When I explained to Vinny how I stopped Mom, I'm not sure why I left Phil out of the story. I mentioned once in our chat room that broccoli and turkey and potatoes reminded me of maple syrup mixed with cotton candy. Phil was the first person to tell me none of those foods was sickly sweet. I described the weird bitterness on my tongue and throat as I swallowed Mom's meals, how the tingling lingered no matter how hard I scratched. Nothing could get rid of the taste—not mouthwash, gum, water, more food.

It's odd that hospital food never makes you sick. Only your mom's food, Phil said.

I remembered that moment in perfect detail, like it was preserved in a snow globe. I was sixteen, sitting at the desk in Mom's bedroom, where she insisted we keep our computer. It was the middle of the night—the only time I dared talk to Phil. Mom was snoring loudly in her bed a few feet away.

I stared at the computer screen, fingers frozen on the keyboard. *My illness. My mother. Illness because of my mother.* The connection had never crossed my mind.

I have to get to bed, I told Phil. *Thanks for listening. XO.*

I signed off but stayed up all night, following link after link like a scavenger hunt. The sun was starting to rise when I found it: an image of a small brown bottle with a white cap and blue lettering. I had seen the bottle once before while putting away laundry.

Holding my breath, I tiptoed to Mom's dresser and, an inch at a time, opened her sock drawer. Buried in the back was the same brown bottle. Lettered in blue were the words "Ipecac Syrup."

I hurried back to the computer and scanned the page for more information. Ipecac syrup was used to make kids or pets vomit when they accidentally swallowed poison.

My mother had been poisoning me.

I became aware of a throbbing in my chest. My hand couldn't feel the mouse it was holding. The chair fabric under my thighs disappeared. I was terrified of reading further.

Suddenly I felt hot, angry breath on the back of my neck.

I whipped around in my chair, expecting Mom to be looming over me. What would I say? But I was imagining things. She was still in bed, the quilted comforter rising and falling with her steady breath. How confident she was, even in sleep. Nothing kept her up at night. I read for as long as I dared, then erased my search history.

I climbed into my bed that morning with no idea what to do next. I understood Mom was putting ipecac in my food, but it still didn't occur to me then that I didn't have any food allergies or digestive issues. It took me another six months to figure out I probably didn't need the feeding tube. Piece by piece, I realized everything she'd told me was a lie: the vision problems, the chromosomal defect, all of it.

Back in the café, Vinny said, "So lemme get this straight: the only thing wrong with you was your ma put ipecac in your food?" He sounded disappointed.

"When I was given food at all," I pointed out. "The ipecac explains the vomiting. The rest of my symptoms were malnutrition."

"But you had the feeding tube."

"After Mom was arrested, I found out she'd been feeding me half of the daily calories I needed."

Vinny let out a low whistle. "At the risk of offending, I've gotta ask"—he paused—"how did you not know? I get not understanding when you were a kid, but even at fifteen, you had no idea?"

Vinny King was an a-hole. I wished I could dump my gross coffee in his lap. I'd heard comments like these before: *Why didn't you get up out of the wheelchair? Why didn't you cook your own meals? You really didn't know you were playing sick?* They were judgments more than questions.

I narrowed my eyes at Vinny. "What Mom said was true—I was sick all the time. I did throw up every food she put in front of me. I did get really bad headaches and dizzy spells. I never had the chance to make my own food, because I was too weak, and she was always a step ahead of me. If your mom and your doctors and your neighbors all say you're sick, why would you question them? The pain was there. The proof was in my medical file."

By the time I was ten, I'd had ear and feeding tubes, tooth decay, and a shaved head. I needed a wheelchair. I was allergic to almost every food on the planet. I'd had cancer scares, brain damage scares, tuberculosis scares. I told Vinny I'd been weeks away from a heart catheterization, which wasn't totally true. My doctor had rejected that idea as soon as it came out of Mom's mouth. But by now Vinny was hanging on my every word.

I took a breath and continued. "How could I have known malnutrition was causing my hair to fall out and making it hard to breathe? How was I supposed to know the ear tubes and the allergies were all one hundred percent made up, all lies my mother told before I could even talk?" I thought of her betrayal for the thousandth time and let my eyes fill with tears, heard the pitch of my voice rise. "When you're a kid, there are things you don't question. This is your mom. This is your dad. Your name is Vinny. This is your birthday. When you turned fifteen, did you ever ask your parents if your birthday was really your birthday?"

A couple tears rolled down my cheeks. This was not at all the cool person I'd been hoping to be, but this version of me was even better, because this version of me was the one Vinny paid attention to.

He made a sympathetic face, like a nurse right after she stuck a needle in you. "You're right. I'm sorry. That was a dick thing to say. It's like Stockholm syndrome or a cult or something—impossible for people on the outside to understand the inside."

I didn't say anything, let an awkward silence fall between us. I wanted to eat another muffin, to show my teeth some more, but I thought I might throw up if I had another bite.

Vinny cleared his throat. "What about the doctors? You blame them? How could they not have known?"

I had this part memorized from the trial. "Doctors rely on the parents to understand a kid's health. They assume the parent has the kid's best interest at heart and is telling the truth. If any of my doctors got suspicious after a few months, we'd move to a new doctor's office. I went to dozens of doctors all over the state." I combed my fingers through my hair. "Mom told me we were moving on because the doctors weren't smart enough to fix me."

Vinny shifted in his seat. "So how'd you stop her?"

I started the chain of events that got Mom arrested by accident. I told Alex about Mom's abuse not because I thought she'd call the cops, but because I wanted to impress her. Alex had boyfriends—*plural*—went to school in a big city, and majored in graphic design. She had fascinated me my entire life. All I'd wanted was to fascinate her once.

"I had to take action," I said instead. "But I was too scared to do it by myself, so I went to the friend I mentioned earlier, and she helped me do the right thing."

"Any chance you'd tell me your friend's name?"

I shook my head. Alex would love the spotlight, but this was my story, not hers.

"Fair enough."

Vinny and I talked about the trial. I told him what he would have already known from following the news: nobody from Deadwick would testify in defense of Mom. One of my old doctors came forward to say he suspected "something foul might be afoot." But it was my testimony that sent her to prison.

The *Deadwick Daily*'s headline the next morning shouted *JUDGE SAYS POISONOUS PATTY WATTS MUST PAY.* Reporters said the jury's deliberation was the quickest in the history of our county. Mom was found guilty of aggravated child abuse and sentenced to five years. She couldn't contact me unless I said so. By now, she'd been in prison a few months. This was the longest we'd ever gone without talking.

I wanted to leave the café and get away from Vinny King. He was only interested in Rose Gold the Freak Show. Still, I answered the rest of his questions. Vinny was just the messenger. I needed him to get out my version of the truth. Without him, I had no money to fix my teeth. I could already see my blinding white smile. Strangers would return my grin instead of cringing.

My little trooper, she said.

"How do you think your ma got so—pardon my French—fucked up? Anything happen when she was a kid?" Vinny was enjoying himself now.

"Your guess is as good as mine," I said.

I gazed out the coffee shop window. An icicle fell off the roof and shattered on the sidewalk.

Vinny watched me, his tongue making sucking noises against his teeth. I silently dared him to ask what I knew was coming next.

"Your ma sounds a little crazy. Do you ever feel kinda sorry for her?"

Every single day, I wanted to scream.

But people didn't get excited by stories of forgiveness. They wanted bridges to burn. They wanted dramas that made their own lives feel normal. I was starting to get it.

I turned my head from the window to stare at Vinny. I imagined a falling icicle stabbing one of those baby blues. An ocular kebab.

"Not even a little bit," I lied.

5

Patty

Rose Gold and I stand at the front door of my childhood home, my throat clutching a cry. I take Adam from her so she can search her purse for the house keys. Holding the baby—watching his little fingers and toes wiggle—calms me. I remember why I'm here.

Rose Gold sighs in frustration. She digs deeper into her purse. I sneak a peek around while I wait. To the right of the garage are the woods. When I was young, they went on for miles, but by the time I moved out, a strip mall had replaced half the trees.

Across the street is the Thompsons' wretched house. When I was a kid, the two boys were always playing with scrap metal in the yard, their faces covered with dirt, even first thing in the morning. "Like barbarians," my mother would cluck, watching them from our window.

The Thompsons intrigued me because they had a horse. I never saw the horse leave its pen. Until, one day, it was gone. The Thompsons too. No one knew where they went, but they didn't take any of their junk with them. Now the yard is littered with knee-high weeds, spare tires, and fast-food wrappers. I guess this is still the hangout for Deadwick's derelicts.

I can't believe the Peabodys never hassled someone into cleaning up the place. What an eyesore out their front window.

Behind the garage is the pool deck David, my dad, and I built. I take a few steps toward the deck. The wood has splintered, the paint is chipped, and the giant hole in the middle of the deck is still empty. Dad had grand plans for an aboveground pool, but never got around to finishing the job.

Rose Gold finally pulls her keys from her bag, unlocks the front door and steps over the threshold, but not before taking Adam back from me.

"Hello, handsome." She smiles, rocking the baby, touching his cheeks, and kissing his forehead. She has forgotten about her mother. He is all she cares about.

We'll have to fix that.

I follow close behind and find myself face-to-face with my old living room. Dark wood paneling still covers the walls. The steel blue carpet is worn and needs to be replaced. The furniture is sparse: two brown BarcaLoungers, a coffee table, and an ancient television. The walls are bare—no family photos, no art, nothing. The place is somehow less welcoming now than it was when I was a child.

"How long have you lived here?" I ask. Rose Gold motions for me to follow her down the hallway to the bedrooms.

"A few months. I haven't had time to decorate with the baby and all."

We walk toward my parents' bedroom. The door is closed. Rose Gold pushes it open.

The first thing I notice is the color, or lack thereof. Everything is white, from the walls to her bedspread to the dresser. Even the crib in the corner is made of white wood. I would've bet my left boob I'd find some combination of pink, purple, and sea green on her walls. Those used to be her favorite colors.

Her bed is tidy, although the pillow is deflated on one side, as if the stuffing has been torn out of it. There are no photos of Adam or me or anyone else. Every surface is clean, organized, characterless. The room reminds me of a psych ward crossed with a convent.

I realize Rose Gold is waiting for my reaction, so I bob my head. "It suits you."

She keeps moving, entering my childhood bedroom. "I thought you could stay in this one."

The walls are sponge-painted lilac. The one piece of furniture inside the room is a flimsy twin bed with a plain white sheet. I suppose it would be unreasonable to expect my daughter to give me the master bedroom. I'm in her home now, a guest—long-term if I play this right.

I follow her gaze upward. Painted on the ceiling are two giant lifelike eyes. I yelp and jump back. The eyes are blue and watery, like they're upset with me.

Rose Gold chuckles. "Those Peabodys sure had a strange sense of humor."

I have a hard time believing the Peabodys were responsible for commissioning this "art." Even when they were young, their idea of a wild night was staying up until ten to play chess. They were the types to decorate their house with the kids' school crafts. Someone with talent painted these eyes.

Scooting closer to the door doesn't help. The eyes watch me wherever I am in the room. They'll have to be painted over. Immediately.

"And this is, as you know, the third bedroom," Rose Gold says from my older brother's room, across the hallway. I close the door to mine, eager to put the eyes behind me. I glance inside David's room, empty except for a handful of unopened boxes. I can still picture the desk covered with doodles, the leather journal shoved under the mattress, the Swiss Army knife on the nightstand, spear-point blade out. I rush past the room and stop in the bathroom all four of us shared.

Rose Gold follows me, clutching Adam. "Everything okay?"

I loosen my grip on the countertop and smile weakly at her in the mirror. "A lot of memories in this house."

Rose Gold returns my smile. "I thought we could relive some of them. I'd like to learn more about my extended family." Rose Gold never met her grandparents; my father's been dead almost forty years, my mother for thirty.

My daughter leaves the bathroom, rocking Adam and walking down the hallway toward the kitchen. I stare at my pale complexion in the mirror, racking my brain. Why would Rose Gold buy my parents' house? Maybe she's still upset with me. Maybe she hates me enough to buy a house solely to taunt me. But if so, why agree to let me live with her in the first place? Why not move away—new state, clean start?

Of course, if she left, I would find her.

I rush out of the small bathroom, feeling claustrophobic. I make a quick pass through the kitchen—still the same dark wood cabinets and olive countertops—and head back to the living room, ready for my recliner.

"Wait," Rose Gold says, opening the door to the basement. "You haven't been downstairs yet."

My upper body stiffens and my legs turn to jelly. When I was a kid, the basement was unfinished, walls and floor made of concrete. The idea was to create a second family room, but the space became Dad's hideaway. He had a workstation with all his tools, plus a coffin-sized freezer, where he stored all the deer meat he hunted. I haven't been down there since I was seven. I won't even touch the doorknob. Every October 3 since 1961, try as I might to forget, I always remember.

"No need," I say. "Has it been remodeled?"

"No, but I put a treadmill down there. Mr. Opal gave it to me. He bought a new one and had left this at the end of his driveway. I happened to drive by one day and saw it and knocked on Mr. Opal's door and asked how much and he said, 'For you, dear? You've been through so much. Take it for free.'"

Rose Gold grins, and I get a very unmotherly urge to knock the smirk off her face. (See? I'm honest about my shortcomings.) I don't care if a full Thanksgiving feast is down there—I'm not going into the basement.

I lower myself into the recliner and settle in. "I'll look at it later. I've had a long day."

Rose Gold nods. "Of course. I didn't mean to overwhelm you."

My attention turns to the TV, and my heart rate spikes again. "You aren't watching the news on this thing, are you? Those good-for-nothing reporters ruined our lives. You realize that, right?" My voice is shriller than I want it to be, but I can't help myself. "If you believe any of their lies, I don't know what I'd do."

"Mom, calm down," Rose Gold says patiently. "I don't have cable or even an antenna for basic channels. I use the TV to watch movies and Netflix."

I nod, unsure how all of this works or what I've missed while in prison. When Rose Gold was little, she was only allowed to watch a few Disney movies and *Blue's Clues*. I didn't want the boob tube to rot her brain. "I'm sorry. This is a lot to take in. I think I might take a nap."

"Then I'll go pump." Rose Gold has not put Adam down since we entered the house. She heads down the hallway with the baby in her arms, singing "Pat-a-Cake, Pat-a-Cake, Baker's Man" as she goes.

"I don't mind if you want to do it out here," I call after her.

"That's okay," she calls back. The door to my parents' bedroom shuts, and then, ever so quietly, the lock clicks.

I find it hard not to be irritated by the locked door, but try to understand. Maybe pumping breast milk embarrasses her. Maybe she's still getting used to motherhood. Maybe she wants privacy. Maybe, maybe, maybe.

I must have dozed off, because when I next open my eyes, Rose Gold is sitting in the other recliner, rocking Adam and watching me. I startle, reminded of the eyes on my bedroom ceiling. Rose Gold keeps staring, so I heave myself out of my chair. "Why don't I start dinner?"

Rose Gold shrugs. "Sure. I have the ingredients for tortellini soup."

I used to make tortellini soup when she was a child—for myself, of course. She would have gotten sick eating it.

In the kitchen, I pull the prepackaged tortellini, Italian sausage, and herb cream cheese from the refrigerator. I rummage around the pantry for tomato soup, diced tomatoes, and chicken broth. After a few minutes, the sausage is sizzling in the pan, and all the liquids have been added to my old stockpot. Of all the things I missed while imprisoned, cooking was not one of them. But it has its advantages: brainless grunt work requires just enough concentration so your mind can't stray.

After an hour, I've melted the cream cheese in the broth and cooked the pasta and sausage. I ladle the soup into bowls, marveling at my first productive deed as a free citizen. I know I'm being silly, but I'm proud of myself. "Dinner's ready!"

Rose Gold joins me at the dining table, and we sit across from each other. I push her bowl toward her, then pick up my spoon. I have been dreaming of my first meal for months. In my dreams, I savored each bite, relished each sip. In reality, I slurp the soup as fast as my hand can bring it to my mouth.

"Guess I'm hungry," I say sheepishly, looking up from my soup. Rose Gold's bowl is still filled to the brim. "What's wrong? Do you not like the soup? Did I make it wrong?"

Rose Gold shakes her head. "I'm not hungry. I had a late lunch before I picked you up. Are you mad?" She sounds truly sorry, so I decide to forgive her.

"Of course not. We'll have plenty of leftovers. You can have some tomorrow."

I sit down with my second bowl. Rose Gold scoops and drops a spoonful of soup six times in as many minutes. A less patient mother would tell her not to play with her food. But I have always been a patient mother.

After we (I) finish dinner, Adam begins to cry in the bedroom. "You go get him," I say. "I'll clean up here."

I load the dishwasher and clean the stockpot to the sounds of my daughter soothing my grandson. She coos and shushes, and the baby quiets down. I'm surprised by my daughter's maternal instinct, but then I haven't known her since she was a teenager. I have to keep reminding myself she's a grown woman now. Still, there will be something she's ill-equipped to do, and that's when I'll swoop in.

Rose Gold brings Adam to the kitchen, nuzzling her face against his. He smiles back at her, wrapping his tiny fingers around one of hers. I make goofy faces at him and wipe the table. He is still so tiny.

Once the kitchen is clean, we move to the living room, each taking a recliner. Rose Gold situates Adam in her lap, then grabs the remote and scrolls through a list of films. I notice she doesn't seem to own any DVDs—all the movies are on her TV. When did that happen?

She stops scrolling, pausing on a film I've never heard of.

"What's *The Hunger Games*?" I ask.

Rose Gold stares at me like I'm from another planet. "It's a dystopian universe where a boy and a girl from each of twelve nations are recruited once a year to fight to the death in a televised competition."

My hand flies to my mouth. "That sounds horrifying."

She shrugs and keeps scrolling. I'm surprised when she chooses *Titanic*. The themes of the movie are awfully adult, but I keep quiet. I steal a glance at the other recliner.

"Why don't I take Adam for a little while?" I offer. "You're exhausted."

Rose Gold gives the baby a once-over, hugs him close, then hands him to me.

I tuck him into my baby-cradling-sized arms. I hold a bright green rattle in front of him, and he bats at it with his hand, excited. He babbles at me when I tickle his feet. I stick my tongue out and wink at him. I do not say aloud I was born to be a mother.

I want to ask my daughter so many questions: how difficult labor was, how she's handling the new baby, whether she's happy at her job. I want to know everything Rose Gold is willing to tell me, but right now, she looks like Wile E. Coyote post–boulder crush. I keep quiet and focus on the bundle in my arms.

After a minute or two, I realize I'm counting his breaths. No, I'm counting the seconds between his breaths. Old habits die hard.

When I brought Rose Gold home that first night, I was captivated. Give me another kid to watch sleep, and I'll tell you I'd rather watch a couple of geezers golf eighteen holes. But when it's your own kid? Ask any mother. They know.

She was breathing until she wasn't. Time loitered. Every second lasted four. My eyes bored a hole in her little skull. I gulped air, willing her to do the same. My hand shot out and grabbed the phone. I'd dialed "9" when the breath came. A quiet purr amplified to an ocean wave. It could have been thirty minutes, maybe an hour, when all I did was stare at her, frozen, listening to the bundled body produce roar after roar of inhalations.

I didn't sleep that night. Instead I thought about our time at the hospital, when there was always someone who knew what to do, people who watched over my baby like she was their own.

I moved the rocking chair next to her crib and counted the seconds between breaths. *One-Mississippi.*

I forced myself to say the state slowly in my mind, to let all four syllables have their due. The brain is a tricky organ: it can condense words into a single sound, squish them like an accordion or a car crash. *Two-Mississippi.*

How many "Mississippis" before I'd call someone? Most of us didn't have the Internet in those days. I dared not leave the room for my copy of *What to Expect When You're Expecting*, a book with more pages dog-eared than not by then. Mom and Dad were dead. So were David and Grant. *You're alone,* I reminded myself. *You are ready. Three-Mississippi.*

You're never ready for your baby to stop breathing. I decided five was an appropriate number. Reasoning my Mississippis were coming out slower than a second each, I figured I could tell the doctor eight to ten seconds had passed between each breath. *Four-Mississippi.*

You don't want to be that mom. The overreactor. The nonstop caller. The one who makes the nurses roll their eyes. Then again, Rose Gold's immune system was barely functioning. She had a speck of a liver. Didn't that require some dispensation? *Five-Mississippi.*

I picked up the phone.

The pediatrician told me Rose Gold had to cease breathing for twenty seconds for apnea to be considered. Anything shorter was "something to keep an eye on." As if my eyes could go anywhere else while I counted the moments my daughter was not breathing. As if there were a way I could unload the dishwasher or do a load of laundry when I was obsessing over five seconds becoming twenty becoming a minute becoming death.

Over the next few days, I did nothing but count the "Mississippis" between Rose Gold's breaths. The longest was fifteen. I put my hand on the phone after nine. I punched one digit to the doctor's office per second from *ten-Mississippi* on. The phone would ring by the time I reached twenty.

A week after I'd brought her home, I got to eighteen and dialed anyway. "It's been twenty seconds," I said. "I want to bring her in for a checkup." The next day I left the pediatrician armed with a CPAP, medication, and a plan. That was how it started.

"Mom?" Rose Gold says, interrupting my reverie. "What are you thinking about? You have this look on your face."

I glance at Adam. He's fallen asleep again. I keep rocking my chair. "Just remembering," I say.

Rose Gold considers me, but doesn't say anything. We turn back to the TV, where Jack and Rose are dancing a jig belowdecks in third class.

"How did you and Grant meet again?" Rose Gold asks.

I whirl around in my chair, almost forgetting the infant in my arms. "Where did that come from?"

She gestures at her sleeping son. "I have a baby of my own now. Someday I want to be able to tell him where he comes from."

He comes from a mother whose head was up her derriere and a father who was worse, I want to say.

Rose Gold has asked this question before, but I've always managed to put her off. I decide to be honest this time.

"I was visiting GCC, where I got my CNA certificate way back when. I was looking at CNA-to-RN bridge programs to become a nurse. I met him in the cafeteria."

"How old were you?"

"Thirty-four."

I had finished an appointment with the admissions office and headed to the cafeteria for lunch. The food at Gallatin Community College wasn't fresh or healthy, but I'm a sucker for nostalgia, so I went anyway. I ordered and paid for a plate of mozzarella sticks. (Forget His only Son—mozzarella sticks are God's greatest gift to mankind.)

I was making my way through the second mozzarella stick when a kid who looked to be in his early twenties sat at my bench. Not too close to me. In fact, I thought he'd chosen the perfect distance: not so close he'd be intruding, but not so far we couldn't talk. He wasn't sexy, but his shirt was pressed, body lanky.

"Hi," I said, more to my mozzarella stick than to the boy with the blond crew cut.

He swiveled around. "Hi?"

He said it like it was a question. I should've known from the first syllable he wouldn't be the kind to step up.

Rose Gold interrupts my reminiscing. "How long were you together?"

"A few months," I say.

"Did you ever think about marrying him?"

I choke on my laughter. "Lord, no."

"Why not?" she asks so seriously that I know I need to be careful.

"Because I was ready to grow up. He wasn't."

I tell my daughter that Grant Smith became my boyfriend too fast. I say I ignored the signs, as every smitten girl does: the dilated pupils, the heavy sweating, the shoving of objects under the couch cushion when I came over unannounced. It had been a long time since I'd had a boyfriend, an embarrassing number of months (fine, years) since I'd had sex. I never heard wedding bells with her father—a man twelve years my junior—but I thought he was a good way to pass the time until someone more appropriate came along. He could string several sentences together without sounding like a moron. I never said we were soul mates.

I was thinking about babies at that point. A lot. Not babies with him, but a baby for me. I spent countless nights dreaming of tiny toes and names for little girls. Sometimes I think I jinxed myself, dreaming about babies so often while I slept next to him. How else can you explain getting pregnant while on the Pill?

I thought about the predicament for a while before I told him. Was this a predicament at all? I'd wanted a baby for so long, and now I'd somehow found one in my belly. Maybe we could become a happy family. Maybe he would step up to the plate, hit the home run. (I've now exhausted my knowledge of sports metaphors.) Maybe he needed a baby to straighten out his life.

Right.

Her father was horrified in the way most young men would be. He didn't want a baby; he had his whole life ahead of him. He couldn't believe I'd "done this." He was paranoid and irritable, and I told Rose Gold it became hard to discern whether Grant or the meth was talking. I couldn't bring a baby into his world. I'd have to go it alone.

We wouldn't be the *Brady Bunch* family I'd hoped for, but let's face it: Mike Brady was a drag. I could raise a kid on my own. I'd raised myself, hadn't I? And I turned out okay. I ended the relationship and started checking out town houses.

Rose Gold pipes up again. "And he died of a drug overdose?"

"That's what I heard."

"So you don't know for sure?"

"I know." I scowl at my daughter. "All I meant was we weren't in touch by then. Someone from the neighborhood told me."

"Who?"

"I don't remember," I say, irritated.

"Where is he buried?"

"How on God's green earth should I know?"

"I thought you might have heard," Rose Gold says. She's being smart with me.

"I'm sorry if this comes off harsh," I say, "but Grant didn't want to be your father."

"Tell me about it," Rose Gold says, dripping with bitterness.

The movie's end credits roll, and we watch the names scroll by. I turn the TV off, shrouding the room in silence. Rose Gold yawns and stretches in her baggy sweatshirt.

She takes Adam from me and curls him against her chest. She opens her mouth to speak, but her cell phone vibrates loudly on the coffee table in front of us, stopping her. I lean forward to see who's calling, but she snatches the phone away before I catch a glimpse.

Rose Gold glances at the screen. The blood drains from her face. Her hands begin to shake. I worry for a second she's going to drop Adam.

"Can you take him?" she mumbles as she thrusts the baby into my arms. She hurries down the hallway, clutching her ringing phone. A few seconds later, her bedroom door slams shut. The lock clicks into place.

I sit back in my chair and begin rocking Adam again, thinking about what I've just seen.

Someone wants to talk to my daughter.

The real question is, why doesn't she want to talk to them?

6

Rose Gold

When the interview was over, I picked up the paper grocery bag holding all my sleepover stuff and left the café. I got back in the van and typed Alex's Lakeview address into the map on my phone.

I drove north on Western Avenue and took a right on Fullerton, thinking about the lies I'd told Vinny. Of course I felt bad for Mom. On more than one night in my apartment, I'd gazed at the recliner to my right and wished she were sitting in it. She used to draw the alphabet on my back and braid my wigs. She made up wild vacations, without us ever leaving the house. She gave hugs that squeezed the air from my lungs. She fought for me. In spite of all her sins, I knew how much she loved me.

But no one wanted to hear about the redeeming qualities of a child abuser. I was beginning to understand people needed to put one another in buckets: good or bad. No room for the in-between, even if that was where most of us belonged. Anyone who knew our story imagined Mom was evil. The jury must have slept well the night of the verdict, picturing themselves as my white knights. But they took my mother away from me. Some days I was thrilled. Others I felt like a vital organ was missing.

I mulled over all of this while searching for parking on Belmont. A Patty pity party was not how I wanted to spend my weekend. I had looked up Stockholm syndrome at a stoplight. Vinny was wrong—I wasn't a captive, and I didn't trust Mom anymore. Nothing she did to me was justifiable. I locked the van and walked toward Alex's apartment.

My pocket vibrated.

> **Phil:** Do you have anything fun planned today?
>
> **Me:** Nope, just working
>
> **Phil:** I've been stuck at my desk all day too

I paused. I thought Phil worked as an instructor at a ski resort? That was what he'd told me anyway.

> **Me:** New job?
>
> **Phil:** Oh, yeah, the lodge has me doing back office work
> once or twice a week

The key safe was bolted to the fence. I took the spare key out of it and let myself into the building, like Alex had instructed. By the time I'd climbed three flights of creaky stairs, I was huffing and puffing at the apartment door. Shortness of breath—I knew this pattern from childhood. Soon I would get dizzy. Fuzzy spiders would creep into my vision. If I couldn't stop them, I'd faint. I would lie unconscious on this dirty carpet until someone found me. What if Alex or her best friend Whitney didn't come home for hours? I could slip into a coma. I'd have to go to the hospital. They'd stick thick needles in me. They might perform surgeries I didn't need. I knocked on the wooden doorframe, trying to unjinx all the thoughts I'd had. I heard panting and realized the gasps were coming from me.

I braced myself against the door, waiting. The fuzzy spiders never came. I didn't get dizzy.

"Quit being a freak," I said, unlocking the apartment door. No one was home.

Alex and Whitney's decorations almost disguised the cheap furniture and old appliances. Colorful swirly paintings hung over the couch. A big white canvas leaned against one wall. The words "NO SHIT" had been sprayed onto the canvas with red paint, but the words were upside down. I didn't get it, which made it even cooler. I sat on the blue couch and pulled out my phone to text Alex.

Me: I'm back from my *Chit Chat* interview. I can hang out
whenever

I hadn't told Alex about the interview until now. Half of me had been worried she'd want to come with me. The other half had been saving the news for a moment I wanted to get her attention.

Thirty seconds later, my phone rang. Alex was calling. I tried to remember the last time she'd called.

"What interview?" she said in place of a greeting.

"Hi, Alex," I said.

"You had an interview with *Chit Chat?*" she shouted, loud enough so anyone near her would have heard. I wondered who she was with.

"The reporter even bought me these incredible muffins and a Nutella latte." I tried to steady my voice.

"I want to hear everything. I'll be back at the apartment in ten minutes."

We hung up.

Eight minutes later, a key turned in the lock. Alex—long, lean, and wearing her trademark high blond ponytail—marched through the door with a backpack slung over one shoulder. She wore designer workout clothes, purchased at a 40 percent discount from the athletics store where she worked part-time. She tossed the bag onto the floor and sat across from me on the couch. Sometimes I couldn't believe how little she resembled Mrs. Stone. Alex used to sneak me candy when my mother wasn't looking.

She grabbed me by the knees, something she hadn't done since I'd told her about Mom. I resisted the urge to reach out and stroke her ponytail.

"Tell me everything," she commanded.

I spent the next hour describing each painstaking detail of the interview. Alex hung on my every word. I decided to forgive her for ignoring me the past few months. I could tell she cared—she had even silenced her phone.

"That must have been so hard for you," she said when I was finished, twirling her ponytail, deep in thought. "I'm so proud of you for putting yourself out there." She squeezed my knee. I wished I was wearing shorts—I had shaved my legs that morning, and they were silky smooth. I thought back to Mrs. Stone's bathroom ten months ago, when I'd applied shaving cream for the first time.

I gave her a closemouthed smile, though I was grinning inside. "I was tired of being the victim," I said, borrowing Vinny's words.

"So when does the issue come out?" Alex hopped off the couch and walked to the kitchen. "Smoothie?"

I'd never tried a smoothie before. "Sure. And in a month or two, I think."

Alex looked disappointed.

"But I get to do a photo shoot soon," I lied. Vinny had made clear they'd use one of the photos they already had of us. "Nothing with my face," I added. "Maybe my profile or something."

Alex nodded. "You don't need people hounding you more than they already do."

"Or for the entire country to see how ugly I am."

Alex didn't say anything. I took notes on my phone as she added half a bag of frozen strawberries, one banana, ten ice cubes, and a splash of milk to the blender. Now I could try the recipe at home. I watched the long blond ponytail bob while she worked, imagined cutting it off and gluing it to my own head.

She brought two pink smoothies back to the couch and handed me one. "Your face is not ugly," she said. "It's unique and it's yours."

I stared at Alex, wondering if anyone had ever told her that she had a "unique" face. Probably not, or she wouldn't have thought it a compliment. I sighed and took a sip of the smoothie, surprised by how refreshing and creamy it was.

"When is the photo shoot?" she asked.

"In a week or so. Vinny said the photographer would call me." For the second time that day, I marveled at how effortlessly the untruths flowed from my mouth. If I wasn't careful, this could become a habit.

"Can I come?"

Alex was so excited, so eager. She had never beamed at me this way before, as if *I* had something to offer her. My stomach clenched at the thought of disappointing her.

"I don't know, Alex." I hesitated. "The more people there, the more awkward I think I'll feel."

"Oh, come on," she said. "I can help advise on hair and makeup stuff. That way you won't end up looking like a total stranger. I mean, you want to look like yourself."

Sometimes I wondered whether Alex and I had anything besides a hometown in common anymore. We had been so compatible when we were little: making roller-coaster rides out of odd stuff around the house, pretending the living room carpet was lava, hosting dog pageants with Alex's Puppy in My Pocket toys. Friendships were easier when you were a kid.

She was waiting for an answer, and it wouldn't be no. I could make up some reason they'd canceled on me later. "If you really want to," I said.

"Yes." Alex clapped her hands together. "Oh my God, this is so exciting. *Chit Chat!*"

I smiled, hiding my teeth behind the smoothie glass. I owed Alex this, after everything she had done for me.

She picked at an imaginary split end in her ponytail. "How's my mom?"

I realized I hadn't been to Mrs. Stone's in at least a month. I vowed to visit once I got back to Deadwick. She had helped me through so much.

"She misses you," I said. "You should come home more often."

"Why?" she said to the strand of hair she was examining. "Now that she has you, there's no time for me."

I was stunned for a moment—Alex had never said anything like that before.

"That's not true," I protested.

"She used to call me every day until your mom went away." Alex glanced at me and shrugged. "I mean, no big deal. I get it."

I didn't know what to say. "You should go home and see her."

"I will," Alex said.

No eye contact, bowed head: I was starting to learn how to read body language. I wasn't the only liar in the room.

Later that night, Alex and I met her friends at a bar. Alex had told me on the ride over that she knew the bouncer, so I wouldn't have any trouble getting in, even though I was only eighteen. Sure enough, he was too busy flirting with her to check either of our IDs. We walked inside. The floors were sticky, the crowd was loud, and the bartenders were unimpressed.

I was nervous because we'd seen four white cars on the ride over—a bad omen. Plus I had stepped on a crack when I got out of the cab.

We stood in a tight circle by the door, taking turns getting jostled. Alex introduced me to the group: three guys and two girls, one of them Whitney. "This is my friend from childhood, Rose Gold. She's going to be on the cover of *Chit Chat*." That wasn't even close to true—I'd be a two-page interview at the back of the magazine—but I didn't correct her. My heart pounded when they all turned to look at me. I gave a small wave and remembered not to smile.

The five of them stared in my direction, so I assumed Alex had told them about me. They all sipped their drinks—beer, except for Whitney's vodka cranberry. Were none of them going to tell me their names?

Whitney caught me staring at her drink. "You want some?" She handed it to me.

I took a sip and tried not to make a face. The cranberry juice was fine, but the liquor was gross, like Windex or something. Still, I'd done it: my first sip of alcohol. My nineteenth birthday was a month away. I handed the drink back to her.

Alex tapped one of the guys on the shoulder. He was wearing a track jacket with a moose stitched onto the left side of the chest. "Can you grab Rose Gold a drink? Vodka cranberry."

Moose Shirt wandered off. Alex, satisfied, turned back to the group. "I get to go on the photo shoot with her," she said, tossing her ponytail over her shoulder.

The girls both got Christmas eyes.

"So cool," said Whitney.

"Amazing," agreed the other. She had freckles all over her face.

Alex nodded. "Rose Gold used to let me do her makeup when we were younger." She turned to me and smiled. "Remember that huge Caboodle case I had? You always wanted the sparkly purple eye shadow."

I gave her a small smile back and nodded. I would still let Alex do my makeup if she offered. At least now I wouldn't have to worry about Mom scrubbing my face clean when she saw Alex's handiwork.

Moose Shirt pushed through the crowd and handed me the red drink in a plastic cup. I turned away from the group and opened my purse. "How much?" I asked.

"What?" he yelled.

"How much?" I repeated, louder this time.

"Five," he said.

I found my wallet and handed him a five-dollar bill. He accepted it without a word.

Moose Shirt walked around the circle and back to his spot between Alex and one of the other guys. They stepped aside to make room for him. I admired the ease of this group, how in sync they all were with one another's bodies and movements. They took their friendships for granted. This was their average Friday night.

I guzzled the vodka cranberry. It made my head spin. I didn't have anything else to drink that night—I'd been through enough dizziness for one lifetime.

Instead, as the night went on, I watched Alex and her friends get tipsy, then drunk. The drunker they got, the more they rambled.

"Do you think I could get the photographer to take my photo?" Alex asked the group.

"For sure," said Freckles, swaying. "You're so pretty."

"And so photogenic," Whitney agreed.

"In case I need headshots one day," Alex explained to the boys.

"You're a graphic design major," Moose Shirt said.

"Maybe I'll be an actress on the side." Alex threw her arms up with dramatic flair. Everyone laughed. The way Alex said it, it didn't sound far-fetched. I pressed my lips together and smiled at her. She winked, ponytail bouncing and flirting.

I'd wanted to pee for forty-five minutes, but I'd been holding it in fear of missing anything: a funny joke, a compliment from one of the guys or Alex. But I couldn't hold it any longer. "Be right back," I said to Freckles. She didn't respond, too busy ruffling one of the guys' hair.

I pushed my way through the crowd to the women's bathroom and found a long line of girls already waiting. I joined the end of it and wondered why the men's bathroom was empty. Three girls in front of me giggled and tiptoed toward the men's room, pretending they were sneaky. They were breaking the rules so obviously. Weren't they afraid of getting in trouble?

They went into the single stall together. I wondered if they peed in front of one another. By the time they came out, I'd reached the front of the women's line. I locked the bathroom door and checked my face in the mirror while I peed. So far, the night had gone unbelievably well. No one was paying attention to me, but no one had asked any intrusive questions either. Maybe Alex would let me come back and go out with them again. I just had to follow their cues.

I wound my way back toward the group. Moose Shirt had slung his arm around Alex. He whispered in her ear. Alex chuckled and intertwined her fingers through his, but kept chattering to the group.

Freckles kept stealing glances at Moose Shirt. I bet she had a crush on him, but he liked Alex. I was prouder of having figured out this puzzle than of any social studies quiz Mom ever gave me.

I imagined Phil and me at a bar, maybe a lodge in Breckenridge. We'd sink into a big brown leather couch by a cozy fireplace, exhausted after a day of snowboarding. He'd sling his arm around me without asking, my shoulders an extension of his body. I'd intertwine my fingers with his, and he'd kiss me on the forehead. Someone to take care of me again.

Alex didn't know about Phil because I kept him a secret. She would think an online boyfriend was weird. *How can you be sure this guy is who he says he is?* she would ask. Or *Why don't you get a real boyfriend?* As if we all had guys lining up to woo us.

I had reached the group, but they were all too absorbed with Alex to note my return.

"She's so tragic," Alex shouted over the roar of the crowd. "Really struggling."

"Isn't her mom, like, in jail now?" Freckles yelled, laughing.

"I was the one who called the cops," Alex bragged.

My face grew hot and my hands shook. I balled them into fists. I was about to spin around so they wouldn't see me, but then Whitney called out, "Rose Gold, there you are!" A few months ago, I would have thought she was excited to see me. Now I knew she was clueing in the rest of the group to stop talking about me.

They were all either too drunk to notice or didn't care that my eyes were wet. I wiped them with the back of my hand and watched Alex, waiting for her to mouth a subtle *Sorry* or wink at me again. But she was too busy laughing at Moose Shirt to acknowledge me.

Alex didn't want to be my best friend. She wanted a few minutes of fame, to see her name or face in a magazine, to say she used to live next door to a total freak. I was nothing but the butt of a joke to her friends when they'd run out of things to talk about. Alex Stone had betrayed me, just like the other person I'd most trusted.

I told you that little hussy never had your best interest at heart, Mom whispered.

Shut up, I hissed.

Alex tipped her head back to laugh at Moose Shirt's latest witty remark. I watched that perky blond ponytail cascade down her back and imagined ripping it off her head, this time with my bare hands instead of scissors. Now she was just a baldhead running around the bar, crying for help. But no one would help the charming Alex Stone, because they were too busy laughing at her—doubled over, tears running down their cheeks, clutching-their-stomachs-in-pain kind of laughter. How humiliated she would be, how alone she would feel. She'd find me in a corner of the room and fall to her knees, eyes pleading, hands clutched. *Sorry,* I'd yawn. *You're just a little* tragic.

I stood in the wicked circle, watching the ponytail swing back and forth like a pendulum. I counted the seconds until I could wrap my hands around it.

But what good would it do me to confront Alex here? She had a group of friends to back her up, to defend and protect her. What point was there in me yelling at her when they'd all burst out laughing as soon as I stomped away? And where would I sleep tonight if not at Alex's apartment?

Tonight was not the night for teaching a lesson. Alex and I had been friends for a long time, and the least I could do was give her a chance to apologize when she was sober again. I owed her that much—no, I didn't owe her anything—but I would grant her another chance.

She and her ponytail would remain attached. For now.

But I needed to be more careful about people. I was too quick to trust. My mom had fooled me and Alex had too. I had to quit letting people walk all over me. Quit letting people like Phil call the shots.

Why couldn't I go see him the same way I had come to see Alex? Soon I would get the interview money. I didn't have to wait for him to invite me. Phil was shy and would never take charge. I could catch a bus so I didn't have to drive across the country on my own. I sent him a text.

> **Me:** I wish we were together tonight

I made a resolution among the group of friends. Sometime in the next year, I would visit my boyfriend and get my first kiss. I was long past overdue in finding out who was on the other side of the screen.

When Moose Shirt went to the bar to buy more drinks, Alex finally made eye contact with me across the circle. She blew me a kiss, oblivious or cruel or maybe both. I smiled at her, teeth exposed. About time I let her see the ugly side of Rose Gold.

7

Patty

I spend my first night out of prison tossing and turning in the twin bed. The eyes on the ceiling watch me. I listen to Adam's piercing screams in the next room. Whenever he stops crying, I'm convinced I hear the snap of a belt outside my bedroom door. I plug my ears and chide myself for being such a wimp. During my five years in prison, I snored soundly every night, give or take the first month of adjusting. Even after some of the women found out what I'd been convicted of, I had never lain awake all night, never seriously worried for my safety.

I like to think my time in prison was made easier not because of my size, but my charisma. The key—inside prison and out—is befriending the people in power. Once I had the guards and the warden in my pocket, the inmates fell in line too. They began to see me as more than an obnoxiously jolly doppelgänger of the Kool-Aid Man. I became useful.

A new round of wailing interrupts my six a.m. musings. I forgot how shrill babies can be.

My parents' bedroom door opens. I cannot hear Rose Gold's footsteps over the shrieks of the baby. The cries move farther away—the kitchen or the living room. I swing my legs off the mattress and sit up. I need to get away from these watery blue eyes.

I make my way to the living room, where Rose Gold is giving Adam a bottle.

"Good morning," I say.

I notice the door to the basement is open. I rush to close it.

She glances at me, hair sticking up in several directions. The dark rings under her eyes are pronounced. "Morning. Did he keep you up all night? I'm sorry."

Those two little words ring in my ears. So she can apologize for her crying son, but not for sending me to prison.

"Slept like the dead," I chirp. "Have you eaten? I'll make us eggs."

In the kitchen I turn on the radio. When I realize "Every Breath You Take" by the Police is playing, I turn up the volume and smile. I pull a carton of eggs out of the refrigerator.

Rose Gold sets the empty baby bottle on the kitchen table. She begins to burp Adam. "That's okay. I'll have a granola bar or toast."

"Toast? That's not enough to fill you up."

Rose Gold shrugs. "I'm not a big breakfast person." She keeps patting the baby.

"Have at least one egg," I protest. I suppose I shouldn't be surprised she's not a huge fan of my cooking.

"Not everybody eats as much as you," she snaps.

Wounded, I shut my mouth. I put two pieces of bread in the toaster and pull three eggs from the carton. A blue flame crackles when I turn on the burner.

Even as a girl, I was on the cusp of too big. My body was square before it turned round, and I winced at the words people used to describe it. Stocky. Big-boned. Thick. They were all unsubtle ways of reminding me I looked more like a boy than a girl. I took up too much space. I finished every brown-bagged lunch. Jimmy Barnett used to joke, "You eat the napkin too?" But no one bullied me over my weight. Their matter-of-factness was almost worse. Everyone knew Patty was the burly one, like they knew the Earth circled the sun and never to order the chili dog from Dirty Doug's unless you were ready to butt-trumpet your way through the following twenty-four hours.

Imagine showing up to the Dress Barn at ten years old and being told dresses weren't "for you." "None of them?" I managed to squeak. I glanced at the hundreds of styles in every color and shape. The saleswoman's grimace was answer enough. It's hard to be a little girl when you're not little.

I used to have dreams of getting in shape, of going on some bonkers pepper juice diet and hiring a trainer to shriek at me on the treadmill like they do in those reality shows. But Oreos and Diet Coke were easier to scarf down between Rose Gold's feedings and schooling and doctors' visits. Not until prison did I realize how powerful I am, how useful my body can be. The more space I take up, the less people push me around.

I scramble the eggs, butter Rose Gold's toast, and tuck my hurt feelings aside. I glance at my daughter, now glued to her phone. "Whatcha looking at?"

"Instagram," she says.

My silence gives me away.

"It's a social media platform," she adds.

"Like Facebook?" I ask, hoping the question isn't absurd.

"Yeah, but better."

I don't care to learn the finer points of Facebook versus Instagram, so I move on to what I really want to know. "So who called last night?"

Rose Gold's zombielike expression sharpens. "No one."

"Didn't look like no one," I say casually. "Looked like you saw a ghost."

Rose Gold doesn't say anything. We stare at each other across the kitchen. I wait for her to budge and am surprised when she doesn't.

"Was it Adam's father?" I guess.

Rose Gold hesitates, then nods slowly. "All of a sudden he wants to get back together. After nine months of wanting nothing to do with me. I told him to leave me alone."

"Why didn't things work out between you two?" I ask, keeping my tone soft.

"When he found out I was pregnant, he bailed." Rose Gold's voice shakes, but she lifts her chin in defiance. "I'd rather do this alone than with a flake."

I can't fault that logic.

Rose Gold looks ready to cry, so I change the subject. "What's on the docket today?"

"Work," she says.

"Do you need me to watch Adam?" I erase any trace of hope from my voice.

Rose Gold gives me a once-over. "Mrs. Stone has been watching him since I went back to work last week."

This is news to me. Rose Gold said during one of our visits that she doesn't talk to Mary Stone much anymore. I haven't seen my former neighbor and best friend since the trial.

I set the plate of toast in front of Rose Gold. "Do you drop him off or does Mary pick him up?"

"She picks him up. You might want to make yourself scarce when she comes by."

"Why?"

"You're no longer one of her favorite people." Rose Gold smirks.

"Oh, that." I wave my daughter's comment away. "Mary and I have a lot of catching up to do. Set some things straight."

Rose Gold looks skeptical. She pushes away her plate of toast, one slice uneaten.

"Why don't I watch Adam while you shower?" I offer.

"That would be awesome." This is the nicest thing my daughter has said to me since we got up this morning. Her relief is palpable. We both know how hard it is to raise a child alone. I watch her watch him, eyes drowning in love for her son. With the slightest of hesitations, she hands Adam to me. My plan is starting to work.

Rose Gold closes the bathroom door behind her. The shower turns on. I consider the pile of dirty dishes in the sink, but decide to take care of them later. Who knows how long I'll be allowed to play with my grandson?

I set Adam on the living room carpet, belly down. His head wobbles as he tries to lift it. I clap for him and his blossoming neck strength. He sticks his tongue out at me. Cheeky imp.

From our spot on the floor, I can see a worn plastic high chair in a corner of the kitchen. Adam is too young to need it anytime soon. I wonder if this is another of Rose Gold's neighborhood finds. My mother used to keep my wooden high chair in the same corner.

Adam watches me with big hazel eyes. I babble at him. His bottom lip quivers, and he opens his mouth to wail. I scoop him up, grab his hat and a thick blanket, and rush him through the side door into my parents' backyard. I can at least give Rose Gold twenty minutes of peace.

The baby starts to cry, and I pull out all my old tricks. I rock him from side to side in big swooping motions. I stick his pacifier in his mouth. I try to burp him some more. Nothing works—Adam keeps screaming.

"Who pooped in your Cheerios?" I ask the baby. He's not amused.

After a while, I get him to quiet down. He's still not silent, but his wails have calmed to a whimper. He was so relaxed yesterday—I'd pegged him as an easy baby. I keep rocking back and forth.

The yard is in sore need of attention. My father used to keep the grass trimmed like his buzz cut, nary a stray blade in sight. Now it's both overgrown and dying in places, like something you'd find near a haunted house. The oak tree with thick arms still holds our home-made swing, but the red seat has faded to pink. Dad fashioned the swing when I was a kid. He tested it a dozen times before David and I were allowed to give it a whirl.

The side door flies open. Rose Gold bolts through it, wrapped in a towel with dripping wet hair. "What did you do to him?" she screams, her eyes darting around the yard until they land on Adam in my arms.

"We've been out here the whole time," I say calmly. "Adam started fussing, and I didn't want you to worry while you were in the shower. He's just quieted down."

Rose Gold keeps yelling. "I thought you left!" Her eyes are open as wide as they go, like a terrified horse. I half expect her to start foaming at the mouth.

I shush her, hoping to rein in the hysterics. At Rose Gold's screeching, Adam starts to cry again. To my surprise, Rose Gold begins to cry too. She rips the baby from me and holds him so tight, I worry she might break him.

"I was just trying to help," I say, shocked. She must know if I wanted to steal her baby, I'd do a cleaner job of it than this. Wattses are nothing if not meticulous.

Rose Gold turns on her bare heel, baby in arms, and marches back toward the house. Her sharp shoulder blades protrude above the towel as she flees. They remind me of a younger Rose Gold—a sick Rose Gold. She slams the door behind her. The yard is quiet again.

I feel a little guilty for upsetting her, but realize what I've learned. Since she picked me up yesterday, Rose Gold has had a certain swagger, a confidence she didn't possess before I went to prison. She brought me back to this house, knowing full well I hate it here. She wants to go for my jugular? That's fine. None of us is without weak spots.

Now I know hers.

Walking to the side door, I head back inside and tiptoe down the hallway. Rose Gold's bedroom door is closed. I put my ear against it, straining to listen.

Rose Gold's footsteps creak on the wooden floor as she paces the room. She soothes Adam with little shushing sounds. He quiets down. I can't make out the first part, which she whispers.

"—soon. I promise." Her voice breaks. "I'm sorry."

Soon what—what's going to happen? She must have something planned. Is she going to terrorize me in this house? Kick me out and leave me homeless? Physically hurt me? She isn't strong enough to overpower me, and I can't imagine her resorting to violence, but I suppose anything is possible.

I listen at the door for another minute, but Rose Gold doesn't speak again. The bedroom floor stops creaking, so I tiptoe back down the hall and into the living room. I settle into my recliner, thinking. When I got out of prison, I extended an olive branch to Rose Gold, ready to start fresh. This is her response? Not only does she refuse to take responsibility for her actions, but she thinks she's going to teach *me* a lesson. A weaker woman might run off, tail tucked between her legs. But I'm not going to desert my daughter when she needs me most. Underneath all that anger and scheming is a woman in need of her mother. Let her think she has the upper hand for now. She's not the only Watts capable of forming a plan.

Like I said, now I know her weak spot: Adam.

I wait for my daughter to reemerge.

Half an hour later the master bedroom door unlocks. Rose Gold walks to the kitchen, places a bottle of milk in the freezer, and pulls two others out of the fridge. She washes her pumping supplies in the sink, then puts them in a backpack.

"I'm sorry," she whispers, joining me in the living room. She wears khakis and a royal blue shirt with a small Gadget World logo embroidered on the chest, plus her pump bag. She sets down a baby carrier with Adam bundled inside. "I overreacted."

"Being a new mom is hard," I say, forcing sincerity into my voice. Rose Gold doesn't say anything.

"I'm here for you, darling."

I scan her up and down, searching for clues. Even in long sleeves and pants, I can tell she's lost weight. When we were in the yard, she looked gaunt in that bath towel. I think back to her weekly visits during my last year in prison. She'd seemed a normal size until her bump started to show, and she only got bigger from there. Of course some mothers lose pregnancy weight fast while nursing, but I didn't expect Rose Gold's new body to resemble the old one. She hasn't been this thin since she was sixteen.

The teenager I raised was all elbows and knees, a hunched skeleton. She stopped growing at five feet and was excruciatingly self-conscious about her body. Back then I tried to reassure her that thinness was in vogue. I told her that millions of girls would die for her shape, but her body always embarrassed her. It didn't help her chest was roadkill flat. She was stuck in a kid's frame.

That was before her food allergies went away. Before her feeding tube was removed. She had a reason to be skeletal back then: she was sick. Now she is healthy. At least that's what she's told me.

The doorbell chimes. I stand at once, but Rose Gold rushes past me. She opens the door a tiny bit. Mary Stone's warm voice floods the house.

"How are you doing, sweetie? Are you getting any sleep?" I miss this concern, the genuine care I know is etched on Mary's face. She used to reserve that kindness for me. When she knew I was having a tough day with Rose Gold, she'd bring over a plate of brownies or a pitcher of iced tea. We'd sit and talk for hours.

"I'm okay," Rose Gold murmurs.

I pick up the baby carrier and walk to the door. "Little Adam is a spirited one," I say, forcing the door open wider.

Mary Stone hasn't changed a bit in five years: sensible-mom hair-cut, dull but trustworthy face, wearing too much pink. God bless her.

Mary's eyes bug out, and her jaw drops at the sight of me. She's such a cliché sometimes.

"Hello, Mary," I say warmly. "It's been far too long."

I lean forward to give her a hug, but she shrinks away from me.

She stares at Rose Gold, fingering the rhinestone butterfly brooch pinned to her blouse. "Whose idea was this?"

Rose Gold doesn't meet Mary's eyes. "Mine. Mom had nowhere else to go."

Mary's eyes narrow. "I know somewhere she can go."

This is, without question, the most aggressive statement the lamb-hearted Mary Stone has ever made. Apparently distance does not al-ways make the heart grow fonder.

"I've missed you so much, Mary," I gush. "I thought about you all the time while I was away."

Mary grips the doorframe, face purple and knuckles white. How hard would you have to slam a door to cleave a finger from a hand? She snatches the carrier from me and peers inside, as though I might have gobbled Adam whole for breakfast. I need a pointy black hat.

Mary turns to Rose Gold. "Why don't you come by my house after work? We can catch up."

Rose Gold shrugs her shoulders to her ears, eyes cast toward the

floor. This submissive version of my daughter almost makes me miss the maniac screaming at me in the backyard half an hour ago.

"I'd love to join you," I butt in. "You and I have a lot of catching up to do as well."

"You are not welcome in my home," Mary says. "Ever again."

She grips the baby carrier and rushes down the driveway to her car. I guess it's safe to assume I'm no longer the Mister Rogers of the neighborhood.

I step outside the house into a morning cloudy and full of fog. Mary buckles Adam into the backseat of her car. A movement across the street catches my eye. Standing at the darkened window of the abandoned house, watching me, are three shadowy figures. They don't move when they realize I see them. One of them crosses their arms. I cross mine back, though the hair on my forearms is on end. I glance at the driveway. Mary is gone. When I squint at the abandoned house, the shadows are too. I shake my head and go inside, locking the door behind me.

My daughter studies me, waiting.

"Reporters did a number on this town." I shrug.

"People might forgive you if you were a little less chipper," Rose Gold points out.

"Honey, when you spend five years in prison for a crime you didn't commit, you've got to make up for lost time when you get out," I say. "I'm not going to pretend to be something I'm not."

Rose Gold's jaw stiffens for a second. Then she conjures up a smile. Maybe she fools Mary Stone with this act, but she can't hide her anger from her own mother.

"I have to get to work," she says. "I'll be home around six."

Rose Gold slams the door behind her and walks toward the detached garage. From the living room window, I watch the garage door open. She begins to back the van down the driveway, but then sits there for a moment, staring at me as I stare at her. Her lip curls in contempt, an expression I'd seen on her once before.

August 22, 2012: the day she took the witness stand.

The courtroom sweltered on that Wednesday. The gallery was crowded. Most of Deadwick's residents had shown up to stick their noses in our business. Plenty of reporters had come as well; they couldn't resist weaving a few more scandalous lies into their stories. My lawyer—an incompetent public defender who would have been more at home behind the counter of a medical marijuana dispensary—fanned himself and fidgeted in his baggy suit. The day I met him, I knew I was doomed.

The prosecutor had just finished questioning one of Rose Gold's former pediatricians. This imbecile of a doctor claimed I'd acted "fishy" during office visits. Funny, he'd never said a word about my behavior ten years ago. He never reported this supposed fishiness to any superiors or state CPS agencies. If you asked me, all the prosecutor had established was that this key witness was a key moron, another seeker of the limelight armed with tall tales. The doctor returned to his seat.

The prosecutor, chin raised and shoulders back, looked the part of the justice-seeking hero. He glanced at the notes on his table before turning to face the judge. "Your Honor, at this time I'd like to call Rose Gold Watts to the stand."

My stomach churned. My lawyer had said Rose Gold would testify against me, but I'd hoped she would back out before this day came. I turned to peek at my daughter, in her usual spot in the gallery, sandwiched between Alex and Mary Stone. Rose Gold had been living at the Stones' town house for six months, since the day I was arrested. I wasn't allowed to contact her.

Alex squeezed her arm around Rose Gold's shoulders. The little con artist—Alex might have fooled the reporters with her concerned-best-friend shtick, but I knew all she wanted was fifteen minutes of fame. She hadn't given two hoots about Rose Gold until my trial.

Rose Gold stood, bony shoulders propping up the sleeves of her cardigan. Eyes wide, she swayed a little, as though she might faint. Her skin was even paler than usual. She looked much younger than eighteen.

My daughter was terrified.

Sit back down, I wanted to tell her. *Let's call this whole thing off. I'll drive you home and tuck you into bed, and we'll make up stories about princesses and magic spells in faraway lands.*

Rose Gold took a shaky step forward, one after another, until she was close enough for me to reach out and touch. I had to stop her. I couldn't let her put herself through any more of this agony.

"You don't have to do this," I whispered.

Rose Gold turned to me. Her eyes were sad, begging me to take her home.

"Ms. Watts," Judge Sullivan—who resembled a walrus—barked, "if you try to communicate with the witness again, I'll hold you in contempt of court."

At the sound of the judge's voice, Rose Gold turned away and continued shuffling toward the stand. Was everyone in the courtroom blind? Could none of them see how much my little girl hated being there? They must have realized she was being forced to testify against her will.

Rose Gold sat in the witness box. She raised her right hand and swore to tell the truth. The prosecutor asked her to state her name for the jury.

"Rose Gold Watts," she mumbled. The jurors leaned forward, straining their necks to hear.

"A little louder, please," the prosecutor said.

She cleared her throat. "Rose Gold Watts," she repeated.

"What is your relationship to the defendant?" the prosecutor asked.

"She's my mom," Rose Gold said, eyes cast down, hands gripping the arms of her chair.

"And it was just you and your mom living at 1522 Claremont, correct?"

Rose Gold nodded.

"Can you give us a verbal affirmation, please?"

"Yes," Rose Gold said.

"No dad? No brothers, no sisters?"

I gripped the arms of my own chair. This simpleton was going to make my daughter relive every rotten moment of her childhood— every absent family member, every infection, every missed school field trip. I had tried to shield her from her disadvantages. In our house, we focused on positives. These buffoons were trying to drown her in her own sorrows.

"Can you describe your schooling from preschool up through now?" the prosecutor asked.

Rose Gold launched into a nervous explanation of her transition from elementary school to homeschooling. She lifted a trembling hand to smooth a flyaway on her head. I wondered if she was on her period. The time of month was right. I still hadn't taught her how to use a tampon. There were so many things I had yet to teach her. She wasn't ready to face the world alone.

The prosecutor moved on. "I want to ask you a few questions about your diet."

Rose Gold had never fixed a sandwich or folded laundry. I cleaned her room and made her bed and drove her everywhere she needed to go. I had tried to encourage her independence once in a while, offering to leave her at the library for a few hours or sit in the waiting rooms during her doctors' appointments, but she always wanted me there. "Stay," she'd beg, and grab my hand. So I did. Maybe I should have pushed her harder. She was eighteen years old with no driver's license or friends. She was not equipped to handle the meanness of this world. She was up there, shaking like a leaf, because of me. I should have been firmer, should have said no, should have spoiled her less. But all those years, I had needed her as much as she needed me.

"Were you allowed to have friends?" the prosecutor asked.

I had been deserted time and again throughout my life. I wasn't good enough for my family, wasn't good enough for Rose Gold's father. Then suddenly I had this little angel who was dependent on me, who loved me more the longer we were together. I had someone to zip the back of my dress all the way to the top, to laugh no matter how cheesy my jokes were. She never got sick of my stories, never asked me to leave her alone. Some evenings, after we'd finished school for the day, I'd head to my bedroom or the kitchen to give her some privacy. She always came looking for me.

Rose Gold seemed far away, dreamy.

The prosecutor repeated his question. "Miss Watts, were you allowed to have friends?"

"No," she answered, not making eye contact with anyone, but especially not me. "My neighbor Alex Stone was the only person my age I was allowed to talk to—almost always under my mother's supervision."

"What was her reason for keeping you away from the other kids?" the prosecutor asked.

Rose Gold tucked her hands under her legs, arms stiff. She shivered, obviously freezing. Mary hadn't bothered to pack her an extra sweater. Some stand-in mother she was.

"She said she was worried my immune system wouldn't be able to fight off their germs. Because of my chromosomal defect."

"Which we now know you do not have," the prosecutor pointed out. The two of them must have rehearsed this little scene.

"Right," Rose Gold said reluctantly. "That was an excuse. She wanted us to be together all the time."

"Why do you think that is?"

Rose Gold mumbled, just loud enough for everyone to hear, "She said she wanted to give me the childhood she never got."

My face burned to the tips of my ears. My stomach flipped.

"What kind of childhood did she have?"

Rose Gold watched the prosecutor with wide eyes, searching for the same approval she'd always sought from me. "She wouldn't say much, but I know neither of her parents was very nice to her. Actually, her dad was abusive. I guess that's where she gets it from."

I wiped my clammy hands on my pants. The jurors watched me with curiosity; one even wore an expression of pity. I stared down at the table, pretending to examine the wood grain.

In Dad's defense, he had PTSD during an era when there was no such thing as PTSD, let alone a treatment plan. If I had to guess, I'd say the Battle of the Bulge was tolerable next to his battle with the bottle. He never laid a finger on my mother, but he applied all ten of them and then some to David and me. The country was ready to boil over in the sixties, and my house was no exception.

Dad ran his house with military precision, all "Yes, sirs" and never at ease. My mother, with her gelatinous spine, was his second in command. She never hit us herself, but I came to dread the threat "Wait till your father gets home" almost as much as the inevitable pounding that would follow. To this day, I can't look at a belt, let alone wear one. They make the scars on my back itch.

Rose Gold studied the prosecutor, brows furrowed, debating something. In my head, I pleaded with her not to say whatever was supposed to come next in their script.

She sat back in her chair, decision made. Quietly she said to her lap, "One time I found her in the kitchen, crying that her parents never loved her."

A lump formed in my throat. I have tried to be a cheerful person all my life, but the morning Rose Gold was referring to, I didn't have it in me. When my ten-year-old daughter found me crying over the sink, I confided in her. I slid to the tile floor, slumped against the cabinets, and sobbed that my parents hadn't loved me. Graduations, parent-teacher conferences, school talent shows: my dad never came to any of them. *Not like you're going to win,* he'd say, while my mother sat next to him, acquiescing with her silence.

On the kitchen floor, Rose Gold had nuzzled her face into my shoulder. *I love you more than all the people in the whole wide world combined,* she'd said. Her love helped me pick myself up, allowed me to get breakfast on the table and finish the dishes.

I know I've made some awful mistakes, but I would never expose the thing she hated most about herself to everyone she knew.

In the courtroom, the prosecutor drove his point home. "Is it fair to say Patty Watts created a toxic environment for a child to grow up in?"

Rose Gold nodded. "She wouldn't leave me alone."

For the second time in as many minutes, I felt like I'd been slapped. *Wouldn't leave her alone?* I couldn't go to the bathroom without Rose Gold following me. She needed my opinion on everything: her outfits, her hairdos, her Barbie dolls' names. Less than a year ago, she had asked to sleep in my bed, and now she had the nerve to act like I was the one suffocating her? If there was an unhealthy codependence between us, it went both ways. Sure, outsiders would find our relationship odd—since when had we cared about outsiders? I'd trusted her. She was my person.

Rose Gold went on. "My mom talked over me to my doctors." *You asked me to do the talking—you were shy and nervous around strangers.*

"My mom picked out my outfits every day until I was seventeen." *You didn't trust yourself to match your clothes.*

"My mom chewed up the foods she thought I could tolerate before I was allowed to eat them." *You said you might not get sick if the food was ground up first.*

Through my mind flicked memory after memory. Weren't we laughing in most of them? Wasn't she begging me for more hugs, more stories, more approval? More, more, more. Did I ever say no? Did I ever once bad-mouth her to a neighbor or a teacher or a doctor? Did I ever leave her on a Friday night to go on a date or see a friend? Did I ever ask for space from her, ever say I wanted the bed to myself, that I wanted to sleep in, that I wanted to take a bubble bath without waiting for her call for more apple juice?

Rose Gold's chin quivered. "I knew she was controlling, but I didn't know the medicine she gave me was making me throw up over and over and over again, until my teeth started to rot. She starved and poisoned me"—her voice shook—"and she ruined my entire childhood." She played with the cuff of her sweater, sliding the fabric between her index and middle fingers, a method of self-soothing she'd used since childhood. She used to stroke the edges of her blankie that way as a toddler. When I remembered how small and naive she still was, my anger began to subside.

I could protest all I wanted, but the truth was, I had no one to blame but myself. If I'd kept a closer eye on my daughter, she wouldn't have been on this witness stand testifying against her own mother. I wished I could take the past six months back, start over. Maybe we could go to family counseling.

"Thank you, Miss Watts," the prosecutor said. He turned to the judge. "No further questions, Your Honor."

"All right," the judge said. "Let's take an hour recess for lunch."

The bailiff approached the witness stand. Rose Gold's fingers twisted in knots. She peered around the room. Her eyes found mine.

I love you, I mouthed to her, smiling.

Her expression darkened. She glanced at the jury, who were gathering their things, and leaned into the microphone. When she spoke, her voice rang out loud and confident. "My mother belongs in prison."

The bailiff hurried Rose Gold off the witness stand. The gallery buzzed behind me.

My jaw clenched. I fought the urge to rip the tie off my dumbfounded attorney and shove it in my daughter's mouth. All those months I thought some shadowy *they* had gotten to her: Alex Stone, the police, the prosecutor, reporters. I thought she was someone else's mouthpiece, parroting back what she was supposed to say like a good girl. But she was up there—blabbing about the intimate details of our lives—of her own volition. She wanted to see me rot in a cell, even though I'd devoted my entire life to taking care of her. The shock of her betrayal zipped through me like two thousand volts. I was sure my heart would stop at any minute.

How could you? I thought, watching her. *You were more than a daughter to me—you were my best friend. You were my everything.*

Rose Gold turned toward me, as if I'd spoken aloud. Our eyes met again, and in hers, I saw regret, a plea for forgiveness. That was when I knew: she would come back to me someday. She would pay a price for her betrayal, of course, but we would get through this.

On that day of my trial, and for many years after, my daughter was lost. But in the end, I was right: all the vicious people in the world couldn't keep us apart. She found her way back to me.

This time, dear girl, I promise not to let you go.

8

Rose Gold

August 2014

In Gadget World's break room, I ate my lunch at the rickety plastic table. Today I'd made a Cobb salad. My cooking wasn't going to win any awards, but at least my meals were edible now. It'd been a year and a half since my interview ran in *Chit Chat*. Vinny had claimed he wanted to tell my version of events, but I still came off as a victim in his final article. I was a two-page sob story toward the back of the tabloid. I had six copies of the issue at home.

My life hadn't changed like I'd hoped it would. No Disney princes were knocking down my door. My neighbors were still nosy. Work was boring.

Across the table sat my coworker Brenda. She'd given birth a couple months ago, so was constantly in the break room pumping breast milk. A blanket covered her boobs, but the machine was so loud, I could barely think. Every time I saw Brenda, she asked if I'd talked to Phil about visiting him yet. I'd made the mistake of telling her I had an online boyfriend a couple months ago.

"So," Brenda said, "have you asked Phil yet?"

"No," I said, hoping to cut the conversation short.

"Rose Gold, these are your twenties! Someday you'll be thirty-five with two kids like me, and trust me, girl, you will want some adventures to look back on to get you through the day. What's it gonna take for you to ask him?"

I shrugged, uncomfortable. Brenda and I weren't friends.

She watched me for a minute, head cocked. "Tell you what," she finally said. "I'll give you five bucks if you text him right now."

I pictured my new teeth. Every little bit would help. I took out my phone.

> **Me:** What's your cabin like in the summer?
>
> **Phil:** There's so much wildlife around right now! I saw a black bear and her cub the other day, and a couple of foxes too
>
> **Me:** Your house is in the mountains, right?
>
> **Phil:** Yes, not too far from Platte Canyon. My cabin is small, but I like it
>
> **Me:** You mean your uncle and aunt's cabin?
>
> **Phil:** Right. They've been traveling so much, I guess the house feels like my own
>
> **Me:** That's so cool. Your own mountain cabin!
>
> **Phil:** It's really something. . . .

This was my chance. I sucked in a breath. Brenda watched me equivocate. She fished her wallet out of her purse. I rattled off the text before I could chicken out.

> **Me:** Why don't I come see it for myself? :-)

I showed the text to Brenda. She hooted and handed me a five-dollar bill.

His reply was almost instant.

> **Phil:** I don't know, Katie. . . .

I had lied to Phil about my name. I didn't know much about the Internet back when I met Phil, but I knew you weren't supposed to give your real name to strangers you met online. By the time I was ready to be honest with him, Mom and I were in the newspapers, with headlines like *POISONOUS PATTY WATTS FINALLY GETS WHAT SHE DESERVES; JUSTICE FOR ROSE GOLD.* I didn't want Phil to find me. I prayed the newspapers in Colorado wouldn't cover a story so far away. One of these days I'd tell him the truth.

> **Me:** But you said we'd meet soon. You promised
>
> **Phil:** I know, honey. I just don't want to ruin what we have

What did we have? I was twenty years old and no closer to my first kiss. I threw away my empty Capri Sun and put my lunch bag back in my locker. I plopped onto the black fake leather couch and closed my eyes.

"That bad, huh?" Brenda asked guiltily.

I nodded, eyes still closed. What would Alex do? She might not have been the greatest friend, but she had a lot of luck with guys. I thought for a minute. Alex was all about ultimatums. Either he does this or I'm done with him. I'd heard her say that more than once. But Alex was beautiful and cool. Plus she had that *hair.* She could get away with saying things like that. I was no Alex. Still, maybe she was onto something.

I checked the wall clock. My lunch break was almost over. I pulled myself off the couch, waved to Brenda, and left the break room, walking back to register one. The store was quiet today. Plenty of time to figure out the Phil situation.

I stopped by the kiosk at the end of my register, waiting for a customer. This was Scott's new rule—he said we needed to appear more accommodating. I watched people browse the video game aisle. They were teenagers, with the exception of one neatly dressed man in his forties. I took a few steps over to check out the DVD aisle: empty, like always.

I peered back down the video game aisle. The man in his forties was staring at me, but looked away when he realized I'd caught him. He was probably from one of the next towns over, here for a glimpse of the freak show. I told myself not to jump to conclusions. I had a bad attitude lately—I hadn't even told my last customer to have a nice day.

I focused on organizing my kiosk, straightening the magazines and packages of gum. After a minute, I peeked over my shoulder. The man was watching me again. He jumped when I turned. This time, he walked farther down the aisle, away from me. He picked up a video game, then set it back in its place.

The man was average height with blond-brown hair and had one hand in his pants pocket. He was studying his surroundings as though he'd never been in an electronics store before. He looked like someone who gave back dropped wallets, pulled pranks on his wife, enjoyed a water gun fight more than his kids. A TV dad. Not the typical guy to nose himself into my business.

I walked back to my register. At least I could make it harder for him to stare at me. I scanned the registers to make sure Scott wasn't lurking. I checked my phone. No texts.

I put my phone back in the register cubby, then started when I realized the man was now examining the items I'd just arranged in my kiosk. Was this guy an alien? He was handling a pack of gum as if it were a precious valuable. I didn't acknowledge him, but he kept stealing glances at me. Enough was enough.

"Can I help you with something?" I asked, decidedly unaccommodating. I hoped he could tell I was annoyed.

He dropped the pack of gum he was holding, then put it back on the kiosk. He walked over and placed a bottle of Diet Pepsi on the conveyor belt.

"This is it?"

He nodded and cleared his throat, staring at my name tag. He fidgeted.

"Rose Gold," he said.

I nodded, losing patience, heart starting to pound. I steeled myself for more humiliation—I wouldn't let him off the hook like I had Alex, Brandon, and all the others.

He paused, considering something. The color had drained from his face. "I'm Billy Gillespie," he said, emphasizing his name and offering me his hand.

I watched him, confused.

He squinched his eyes and pulled his hand back. *"Billy Gillespie,"* he said. He pronounced his name like a secret password to a hidden grotto. Billy Gillespie seemed to expect me to know him. I frowned and scanned the Diet Pepsi to break the awkwardness.

"Cash or credit?" I asked.

Billy Gillespie held up his credit card and swiped it in the reader. He sighed. "You don't know who I am."

I shook my head and turned to the receipt printer, glad for something to do. I handed him the piece of paper. "Do you need a bag?"

"No, thanks," Billy Gillespie said, getting tomato cheeks when some customers walked by us. "Listen, can I talk to you outside for a minute?"

By now my curiosity had evolved into alarm.

"Sorry," I said. "I'm on the clock." I crossed my arms. The man didn't seem like a threat, but why was he being so weird?

Billy Gillespie looked like he wanted to say more, but instead let his shoulders sag in defeat. "Okay, I understand." I watched him trudge toward the door. He peeked back at me once, then was gone.

I rang up another customer and racked my brain for any Billy Gillespies I should have remembered. I was positive I'd never heard of him.

After the customer left, the sliding-glass doors opened again. Billy Gillespie was marching back through them, now heading toward me.

"If I could have five minutes of your time—," he pleaded before I could cut him off.

"Do I need to get my manager involved?" I said, trying to sound brave.

Billy Gillespie put his arms up in surrender and started rambling. "I didn't want to do it like this, but okay. The thing is, I'm pretty sure I'm your father."

My jaw fell open. Of all the nutjobs that had stopped me, none had gone this far.

I raised my voice. "Is this your idea of a joke?"

Billy Gillespie was mortified. "Your mother is Patty Watts, right?"

Anyone who lived within thirty miles of Deadwick and read the newspaper knew that.

"My dad died before I was born," I said through gritted teeth.

"You're twenty, right? Born around February nineteen ninety-four?"

I stared at Billy in alarm and tried to remember whether any of the articles had stated my birthday. I'd memorized most of them—I was pretty sure they hadn't. Still, he could've found that information online.

"You should get out of here, or I'll have to call security." My voice sounded squeaky and pathetic.

"How do you know your dad died?" he asked.

"Please, go," I said, not looking at him anymore.

Billy Gillespie slipped his hand into the back pocket of his khakis and pulled out a photo, folded in half. He opened it and smoothed it out. He held it up for me to see, jabbed at the people in it. "See?" he said, handing it to me.

I was about to summon Robert, the bulky security guard, who was already watching us with interest, trying to figure out whether he needed to intervene. Then I saw Mom's face in the photo.

She was twenty years younger and smiling at a young Billy Gillespie.

"Everything okay, Rose Gold?" Robert said behind me.

"Where did you get this?" I whispered.

"I'm telling the truth," Billy Gillespie said sadly. "Now will you talk to me?"

I scanned the store floor. Would anyone notice I was gone? I checked my watch. "I'm good, Robert," I said to the security guard. "Five minutes," I told Billy Gillespie. I followed him out of the store.

We stood on the curb. I hugged my arms across my chest. "What do you want?" I said.

He looked surprised. "I don't want anything. I just thought this was the right thing to do." He gave me a sidelong glance. "Maybe I was wrong."

"My mom had lots of friends before she went to prison," I said. "All this photo proves is you knew her when the two of you were young." I realized I was still clutching the photo and tried to hand it back.

"Look closer," Billy said.

I examined the photo. The two of them were lying in a bed, pillows under their heads. Both of them were topless. Mercifully, the photo cut off above the chest. Mom's short hair was messy. Billy had taken the photo, arm extended.

"But my dad's name was Grant Smith," I protested.

"What'd he die of?" Billy asked.

"A drug overdose." I felt sick. I longed for the feeling of my forehead against cool bathroom tile, even though that normally meant neon green drool was hanging from my mouth. My stomach lurched again.

Billy sighed. "Your mom lied to you."

Which was more likely: that a strange man was pretending to be my father, or that my mother had lied to me—again?

Shit.

If you're going to do something, do it well, she said.

Billy continued. "I'm not proud I left you behind, but I thought you'd be okay. I had no idea what Patty was. And then I was at the dentist's office a few months ago and saw this old issue of *Chit Chat* with your interview inside," he said, embarrassed. "I realized you thought I was dead. I tried to look you up in the phone book or find your e-mail, but I kept hitting dead ends."

"What do you want?" I asked again, dizzy. Was I going to cry or scream? My body felt turned inside out. I pinched the skin between my thumb and forefinger hard.

"I don't know." Billy fidgeted. "I just feel guilty."

I stared at him. I should have known today would be a bad day— I'd found a calculator in the middle of the street this morning.

"I wanted to make sure you're okay," he said. He scanned me top to bottom, as if he'd find evidence of all I'd been through on my uniform shirt. His eyes stopped at my teeth. I realized my mouth was hanging open.

"Am I okay?" I said. My brain had become a merry-go-round, which I had never been allowed on—Mom thought it'd make me sick. Same with slides and swings and basically every childhood pastime that was in any way fun.

I blinked back tears, hands throbbing. "You ditch me for *twenty years* and now you come slinking back here, wanting to know if *I'm okay*?"

Billy winced, but I was just getting started. How did this keep happening? First my mother betrayed me, then Alex, and now this man—my apparent father. Plus, Phil kept dodging me. Would I never learn? Would I never stop letting people walk all over me?

"You deserted us," I shouted. "My whole life, all I wanted was to have a dad like every other kid. You left us to fend for ourselves. Mom was always worried about money. Of course I'm not okay. None of my screwed-up life would have happened if you'd stuck around."

I had that ache in my throat, the one you get when you're trying hard not to cry. But I'd said too much—I couldn't stop the tears now. I sat on the curb and buried my face in my arms. My shirt smelled like Mom's perfume: the Bath Shop's Vanilla Bean. I'd sprayed it around my apartment this morning to pretend she was still here.

Billy squatted next to me, not saying a word. After a couple minutes, my shoulders stopped trembling. I imagined the mascara streaks on my face. What a mess I must have looked like. I didn't want to face him.

"I'm so sorry for everything you've been through," he said, voice shaky. "This is all my fault." He sounded like he meant it.

I picked up my head and studied Billy. He had the same hazel eyes and small nose as me. Both of us had dishwater blond hair. His leg pogo-sticked on the curb the way mine did when I was nervous.

"You're really my dad?" I said.

Billy nodded. He hesitated, then wrapped an arm around my shoulders. He smelled like woodsy aftershave and McDonald's. "After I read the article, I didn't know what to do. I thought maybe I should leave you alone, not drop this bomb on you when you've already been through so much. But then I thought maybe you might want to meet your father, or at least to know I was alive. I kept having these awful nightmares. So I drove down from Indiana, where I live. I'm sorry if I made the wrong choice." Billy removed his arm from my shoulders and chewed his lip. I did the same thing when I was worried. There were too many similarities to ignore.

"I have so many questions," I said. Would we spend Thanksgiving together? Would he try to have "the talk" with me? Would he expect me to root for his favorite sports teams?

A knock sounded on Gadget World's windows. Scott stood in the vestibule and glared at me, hands on hips. Billy helped me up.

"When do you get off work?"

"I'm done at five," I said. I was already thinking about Billy's half hug, already wishing for another one.

"Can we have dinner? How about Tina's Café at five? I'll answer anything you want," he said. "I want to start to make this up to you."

I thought about the number of Christmas mornings I'd wished for a third stocking above the fireplace. "I could do Tina's," I heard myself say.

Billy beamed. "Okay, Rose, see you then."

I put my hand up to wave and watched him cross the parking lot. He climbed into a red Camry. Nobody called me Rose, not within earshot of Mom. She'd correct anyone who tried to abbreviate my name.

Actually, "Rose" was the first idea Mom came up with while thinking of baby names. She said she'd always liked the phrase "rose-colored glasses." She wanted her little girl to be full of optimism for her future, in spite of her missing father and extended family. But Mom thought "Rose" was a little too ordinary for Patty Watts's daughter. "Rose Gold," on the other hand—wasn't that just the perfect hue? "It reminded me of blushing cheeks. Or a pale pink sunset. It's the name of a little girl you can't help but love," she'd said to me one night, beaming.

I plodded back into Gadget World and stood behind register one while Scott lectured me about attending to personal matters on my own time. If Billy was my dad, then he'd been alive my entire life. The only reason I'd grown up without a father was because Mom had lied to me about him. How many times had I asked her about my dad? How many times had she brushed me off, called him vile?

A customer approached, stopping Scott's lecture, thank God. I smiled weakly at her and rang up her new camera. *Mom kept him from me.*

She wanted me all to herself. If Billy had been around, she couldn't have gotten away with the poison. She never could have starved me. Billy would have been there to intervene, to protect me.

Of all the crimes my mother had committed against me, this was by far the worst.

The next four hours of work crawled by. The store was dead that day, and I barely had any customers aside from old Mr. McIntyre, who worked at Walsh's Grocery and who I'd known all my life. I assured him that his grandson would like the LEGO City Undercover video game in his hand. Before he shuffled away, he told me for the millionth time that he hoped to see me at church on Sunday—Jesus's teachings were exactly what someone like me needed. For the millionth time, I ignored him and waved goodbye.

All afternoon I kept replaying my blowup at Billy, already embarrassed by it. True, he'd made some bad decisions, but I could at least hear him out. At four fifty-five, I grabbed my coat and purse from the break room and tucked them into my register. While I waited for five o'clock, I pulled out my phone and texted Alex. I had to tell someone.

Me: You will never believe what happened today. . . .

Me: I found out my dad is alive!

Alex: wow. crazy!

Alex and I hadn't talked much since that night at the bar. She had been disappointed when I told her the photo shoot was canceled, but she got over it when my interview was published. The next day, she video-chatted with me and a bunch of her friends.

She never apologized for what she'd said behind my back, so she either didn't know I'd overheard or was too drunk to remember saying it in the first place. I was still a little mad at her, but was giving her a chance to redeem herself. I didn't want to be someone who tossed friends aside after one mistake. Besides, I didn't have any other friends to replace her.

Me: We're going to Tina's to talk. I'm so nervous

Alex: good luck

So far her redemption had been underwhelming.

The clock on my phone changed to five p.m. I put on my coat and waved at Robert, then scurried out.

How many hours had I spent searching for Grant Smith online? Every minute I wasn't piecing together my medical history or talking to Phil, I had tried to find proof of my sleazy dad. But there were too many Grant Smiths. I couldn't find anyone by that name who had died in central Illinois the same year I was born. After a couple weeks of late nights and dead ends, I'd given up.

I parked the van at Tina's, then put on some lip gloss. I spotted the red Camry a few spaces away and walked into the café. Billy was sitting in the back corner. He smiled and waved. I waved back, then wiped my palms on my khakis. I wanted this dinner to go well.

"Thank you for coming," he said. I sat across from him. "I was a little worried you wouldn't show."

"I'm sorry for yelling earlier," I said. "I've had some people in my life treat me not so well."

Billy squirmed.

"But that's not your fault," I added.

He exhaled. "How about we start over?" he suggested. He drummed his fingers on the table. He was tenser than he was letting on. I noticed the gold ring on his left hand.

"You're married?" I said, pointing to the ring.

Billy nodded. "My wife's name is Kim."

I tried to picture Kim. I decided she would be thin and have pretty red hair. She would be nothing like my mother.

"What do you and Kim do for fun?" I asked. I imagined the two of them taking grand adventures together—going on safaris, hiking Mount Everest, things like that.

"I have a little garden in my backyard—tomatoes, cucumbers, on-ions. I even make my own pickles." Billy paused. "To be honest, I spend most weekends carting my kids around to basketball or swim practice."

I blinked. "You have kids?"

Billy nodded. "Three. Sophie's thirteen, Billy Jr. is eleven, and Anna is six."

They were my half siblings, I realized. I had always wanted a sister or brother. This could be my chance. We could go ice-skating at Christmastime, or to the local pool during summer, or to matinee movies on Saturday afternoons.

"What do you do in Indiana?" I asked.

"Work way too many hours." Billy forced a laugh. "I sell life in-surance."

We were silent for a minute. His life was so charming, already full. Would he have room for another kid? Should I ask?

"Patty told you I was dead?" he said.

I nodded. "She said you overdosed, that you were an addict."

Billy stared at his lap.

"Were you?" I asked.

He glanced up, startled. "I've never overdosed on anything—except maybe birthday cake." He forced another chuckle, embarrassed. We both winced at the lame joke, but it made me like him more. I wondered if this was considered a "dad joke."

"So you never did drugs?" I asked, hating how hopeful my voice sounded.

He shook his head, serious now. "Aside from smoking pot once in a while in college."

I believed him. Billy Gillespie's face was so squeaky clean, he was practically a rubber duck. He was the kind of parent you could look up to—someone who didn't lie to people he supposedly cared about.

The server stopped by to take our orders. I chose lemonade and a club sandwich, and he did too—a good omen, for sure. The server walked away, and there was an awkward silence. Billy cleared his throat but didn't say anything.

"How did you meet my mom?" I asked.

"I was taking a few classes at Gallatin, this small community college thirty minutes from my house. I thought I'd get a head start—transfer a few credits toward my bachelor's degree when I started at Purdue the next year. I met Patty in the school cafeteria. She was flirty and charming, not afraid to make the first move. She kept inviting me to see a movie with her. The third time I said yes."

He paused, as if trying to answer the unasked question: why?

"She was funny as hell," he said. "I liked being around her."

The server dropped off the lemonades at our table. Billy and I reached for the packets of sugar at the same time. Another sign. I smiled, stirring the sugar into my cup with a straw. This man seemed kind and normal. Maybe I didn't need my mother. Maybe I'd just needed my father all along. I signaled for him to continue.

Billy took a long drink of lemonade. "Patty was a lot of fun, but I didn't want a girlfriend at the time. I was twenty-two, about to go to college after doing odd jobs around my hometown for a few years. Nothing was going to get in the way of me getting my degree." He stared at me. "My dad got my mom pregnant when they were eighteen, so they did what they were supposed to: married and settled down. Never left our small town. Born and died in the same hospital. Never saw the world, never had any big passions. Happiness was a frivolous goal in their eyes. Maybe frivolous is the wrong word. Unattainable."

Billy folded his straw wrapper. He looked like a little kid, the way he kept fidgeting. "I respect my parents' choices. I do. But I didn't want that life for myself. So when Patty told me she was pregnant . . ."

He wavered. He drank from his glass for a few seconds, then sat back in his chair as if he'd finished his story. I had to hear the rest.

"When she told you she was pregnant . . . ," I repeated.

He groaned. "Do we have to dredge all of this up? I've told you how sorry I am."

I needed to tread carefully; I didn't want him to change his mind about getting to know me. "I'm trying to understand this from your point of view, that's all."

Billy chewed his lip. "I had no idea how she'd gotten pregnant in the first place. She told me she was on the Pill. It has like, a ninety-nine-percent success rate—I remember looking it up." He rubbed his eyes. "She said it was a sign the baby was meant to be. When she offered me an out, I realized she'd planned the whole thing. I'd been bamboozled." Billy said this last word in a goofy tone to try to lighten the mood, but his jaw clenched for a second, and his smile didn't reach his eyes. Mom always called those "fakies." I batted the thought of her away.

"Two club sandwiches," the server said. She set down the plates. "Can I get you anything else?"

I shook my head and grabbed a French fry. "Then what happened?" I asked him.

Billy took a bite of his sandwich, then sighed. "Patty said as long as I paid child support, I didn't have to be involved with her or her baby. I said yes without a second thought. I'd been so close to having it all ripped away from me—Purdue, falling in love, waiting to have kids until I was ready. I sent her a check every month until you turned eighteen."

Mom told me the checks in the plain white envelopes came from my grandpa. She said they were part of the inheritance he'd left us. I wondered if anything that had come out of her mouth was true. Billy had made some mistakes, but at least he was honest.

"She was so excited to have a baby. I thought she'd be an excellent mother. More than capable of providing the love of two parents." His shoulders slumped. He gazed at me. "Rose, I hope you know how sorry I am."

My father hadn't wanted me, so he'd left, simple as that. Now that I was sitting across from him, though, his abandonment was less important. He'd been a dumb kid, but he was here now. He had apologized over and over, when no one else in my life would.

I reached across the table, touched his hand, and smiled. "It's okay."

He smiled back, relieved. "I'd love to have you over for dinner sometime. You can meet Kim and the kids. What do you think? It's a five-hour drive, but I can give you gas money. We'll make something fun. Is there anything you've been dying to try?"

I couldn't believe he'd driven five hours to see me. I gripped the table, unable to contain my excitement. I was going to have a normal family. Today was the first day of the next phase of my life—a better phase. I rolled the word "Dad" around in my head.

"I would love that," I said. "I've never had a cheeseburger. Well, I mean, I've had the fast-food version, but not, like, a homemade one."

Billy feigned a look of horror. "An absolute crime."

Then he grinned and put his arm up to hail the server. "Let's exchange numbers, and then we'll figure out a date when everyone's free." He handed me his phone. I typed my name and number in it. He reached for my phone to do the same, but I held on to it and added his information myself. I didn't want him to see how few numbers I had.

The server dropped off the check. Billy pulled out his credit card. I reached for my wallet, but he waved me off. "This is on me," he said.

"Are you sure?" I asked. He nodded. I couldn't help but beam, almost forgot to cover my mouth. This was just like on TV, where dads paid for their families' meals and all the kids said, "Thanks for dinner, Dad!"

"Thanks for dinner," I said.

Billy walked me to my car, and I smiled again. He was like King Triton at the end of the movie, after he stopped being so hard on Ariel. I had to make sure he knew I'd forgiven him. He was one of the good guys.

"This was the best day I've had in a long time, so thank you," I said, peeking at him sideways. "And I hope you know I'm not mad at you or anything. Thanks for being so honest," I finished.

Billy watched me for a while. "I'm glad we're getting a second chance," he murmured.

I couldn't resist. I pulled him into a hug, this time a tighter one. Softly I sniffed him. One more whiff of that dad smell.

He pulled away and held me by the shoulders, his palms damp but strong. Up close, I could see all the wrinkles on his forehead, the stress in his eyes. "We'll talk soon, okay?"

I nodded, climbed into my car, and waved one more time. "See you soon—Dad!" I waited to see how he'd react.

He stumbled a little when I called his name, but turned and waved
back to me with a quick smile before getting into his Camry. I watched
his car pull out of the parking lot and drive away. My hands shook
against the steering wheel. I couldn't stop grinning like a dope. *Cheesing,* she called it. I frowned.

I reached for my phone. One more text.

> **Me:** I did it, I met him! He's the greatest guy ever. I couldn't
> ask for a better dad. I'm going to visit him in Indiana
> soon!!!
> **Alex:** yay

I opened a new note on my phone, listing all the questions I'd
forgotten to ask at Tina's. I wanted to know everything about my dad.
I'd have to space them out, maybe one text per day.

I couldn't risk scaring him away.

9

Patty

One morning I wake up and decide today will mark my return to society. The good people of Deadwick have been Patty-less for too long, and they need someone to spice up their otherwise tedious lives. Mary might not be ready to forgive me, but the rest of them will be. Besides, it's been two weeks since I got out of prison, and I haven't left the house since then. Thanksgiving is next Thursday—a trip to the grocery store is the perfect stage for my resurrection.

My social calendar may be empty, but I've made progress on other fronts. I started the Free 2.0 job, I've begun decorating the house, and I wrote my old cellmate Alicia the letter I'd promised. Rose Gold even left me home alone with Adam once, although only for twenty minutes. I'm no closer to figuring out what she's up to.

Sometimes I have to remind myself how patient I am.

In the shower, I realize my legs have turned into Chia Pets and groan. Some people find shaving relaxing, but I am not one of them. Keeping up with body grooming is exhausting. There're leg shaving, armpit shaving, bikini waxing, eyebrow threading, nail clipping, nail painting, hair dyeing, hair cutting, daily bathing, and an unfortunate patch of peach fuzz around my throat that means neck tweezing. By the time I get through a round of all these chores, it's time to start over and do them again. Sometimes I want to embrace my inner hippie— be the type of woman not bothered by hair all over her body. Mostly, I wish I were hairless.

After showering, I stand in front of my closet, weighing a few options. I choose my favorite T-shirt. Printed on it in purple lettering is *Not a morning person doesn't begin to cover it.* Actually, I am a morning person. I've woken up at five thirty every day for the last decade. But a lot of folks find morning people insufferable. Better if I bring myself down to their level.

The house is quiet, humming. Rose Gold left for work hours ago, dropping Adam off at Mary's on her way. I've started trying the doorknob to her bedroom each morning after she leaves. But the door is always locked. Today I try using a bobby pin to pick the lock, but end up breaking the pin. My curiosity swells from an itch to a rash. I want to get inside that room.

I set the task aside for now and bundle up in my heavy winter coat. I decide to walk the twenty minutes to Walsh's Grocery. Not like I have much choice without a car. I head outside, surprised by the ferocity of the cold.

Most people in Deadwick view the months from November to April as a feat of endurance. I inhale. All the hairs inside my nose feel glued together. Even the houses look cold, driveways empty and living room curtains closed. I stand at the end of our driveway and squint at the Thompsons' old house, looking for signs of life. Maybe I'll take a quick peek inside, reassure myself no one's watching me.

I take small steps across the street until I've reached the edge of the abandoned lot. I hesitate, then tell myself not to be ridiculous. Striding across the lawn, I pick my way around the piles of trash. The wind moans, and I pull my jacket tighter around me. I pause before the two stairs leading to the porch, debating whether this is a good idea. The air around me stills, suddenly silent, save for a distant creaking noise. Is it coming from inside the house?

I climb the first rickety step. The wood immediately cracks and gives way, taking me with it. I shriek and thrash my arms, trying to keep my balance. Turning on my heel, I flee the yard and cross the street back to my own sidewalk. I stand there for a minute, hands on knees, huffing more from shock than exertion. I glare at the house. It glares back.

Point taken.

I march down the sidewalk, trying to look braver than I feel. Curtains are pulled aside as I walk. The faces staring out at me are haggard, and their eyes burn into the back of my head after I pass. None of them has come to our house or otherwise acknowledged me. A crone pushing a cart crosses the street when she sees me coming.

When I pass each house, I bend to pick up the newspapers, then toss them in the oversized trash bins. I don't mind doing my part to save the neighbors from reading this filth. The news is all lies and sensationalism. We won't encourage them with our money or eyeballs. I made sure Rose Gold didn't have a newspaper subscription the day I moved in with her.

Deadwick is old now—just a handful of kids here to replace the diseased and dying. No hope, no verve, no ambition in this town. Just row after row of deteriorating houses with owners to match. One by one, we'll all fall down.

A window opens. A bag of trash flies out of it, exploding on the lawn ten feet in front of me. I cast a scathing look toward the window, though I can't see who threw the bag. I keep walking.

I'm determined to stay positive today, so I try to focus on what I once loved about this town. Deadwick's population has hovered steady at four thousand since the nineteen seventies. Newcomers were noticed and typically welcomed twenty years ago. While the rest of the country worried about unmarked white vans, Deadwick's parents didn't have to fret over the safety of their children. Most adults knew the name of every kid who sailed by on his or her bike, and who that kid belonged to in case tattling became necessary.

I made a splash when I moved into the town house—I'd grown up on the old side of Deadwick, so I was a newish face on the newer side. My neighbors were just happy I'd replaced the Gantzers, who had kept to themselves in a community that emphasized togetherness. The Gantzers had never participated in the town Easter egg hunt or made dinners for grief-stricken families. Plus, their cat, Dante, had antagonized the neighborhood dogs. I made mental notes of what was expected of me as I rubbed my pregnant belly. I have always been a good neighbor.

My community participation paid off when my own time of need came. I'm not sure how I would've gotten through Rose Gold's childhood without my neighbors stopping by to drop off casseroles and cheer me up. There was always someone to rub my back, to sigh sympathetically, to bounce an idea off of when the doctors wouldn't listen.

By now I'm standing at the entrance to Walsh's. I lift my head, straighten my shoulders, and plod through the doors, ignoring the growing knot in my stomach. I guide a shopping cart down the first aisle, gathering the items on my list. No one pays me any attention. I don't recognize most of their faces, thank God. The coil in my stomach loosens a little.

I approach the deli counter. Ancient Bob McIntyre is working the slicer. Bob is harmless. I will start with him.

"Hiya, Bob," I say to his back. Hiya? A bit much, even by my standards.

Bob turns, a grin on his face, until he sees me. A crease forms between his skimpy eyebrows. "I heard you were out of prison," he says.

"You heard right," I say. "I'm planning a Thanksgiving dinner for my family."

"You're living with Rose Gold now?" he asks, arms crossed.

"Sure am. How's your family been? How's Grace?"

"She's fine," Bob says. "What can I get for you?"

"A pound of honey ham. For sandwiches," I add. "I've already got my turkey." I pat the twenty-one-pound Butterball strapped into the child's seat in front of me. I'll plump my daughter up one way or another.

"I see a turkey, all right," Bob says under his breath. He pulls the ham from the display window and turns back to the slicer.

I almost laugh. If this is the worst insult Deadwick's residents can lob at me, I'll be fine.

"What puzzle are you working on these days?" I say to Bob's back. Bob is a puzzle fanatic.

Reluctantly he answers, "A thousand-piece of the solar system."

I resist a pun about his abilities being out of this world. Bob is not in the mood to pal around. He hands me the bag of sliced ham.

"Well, it's good to be home," I say.

Bob snorts. "Have a nice day."

I wave goodbye and keep walking. Not a horrible start. Baby steps.

I force myself to take my time in the store. I catch a few dirty looks and hear a lot of whispering out of earshot, but I keep packing produce into bags, pretending I don't notice any of it. I have as much of a right to be here as they do.

I'm searching for the stuffing when I find a store employee crouched down, restocking shelves. I tap him on the shoulder. "Excuse me," I say, then stop short when I realize who it is. "Josh Burrows." I cross my arms.

He glances up, rodent eyes searching my face, trying to place me.

Josh Burrows: the little boy, now young man, for whom I wished a low SAT score, early male-pattern baldness, and a lifetime spent with exclusively feline company. I have resisted the urge all these years to look him up, to find out what sort of psychopath he's grown into.

"Can I help you?" he asks, feigning politeness, pretending he doesn't remember me.

"Do you remember my daughter?" I say.

He scratches his pockmarked face. "I'm sorry. I don't. Did we go to school together?"

"She left school because of you." I keep my voice low so he has to lean in to hear me.

Josh Burrows squints, confused. I should have known he'd grow up to be a dunce.

I sigh in frustration. "Just tell me where the stuffing is."

"Aisle nine," he says with a smile, glad to have an answer. "You have a nice day."

I roll my eyes and push the cart toward aisle nine.

That March afternoon when Rose Gold was in first grade, I'd allowed myself a rare couple of hours to relax. I think I had almost finished a crossword when I received a call from the school administrative office asking me to please come by, because Rose Gold was "okay but unwell." They'd adopted this phrase over the course of two years, having phoned me dozens of times. *Unwell is not okay,* I wanted to snarl.

I raced over to the school, where I found Rose Gold gasping for breath with tears streaming down her face. Her wig was in her hands, covered with dirt. She strangled the dirty golden locks with her fists, shaved scalp exposed. "It hurts, Mommy," she cried, clutching the wig to her chest. I noticed someone had put Band-Aids over scratches on her knees. The scratches hadn't been there that morning.

"What hurts, baby?" I said, tugging her toward me. The question was redundant, a stall tactic. The reality was everything hurt: her chest, her lungs, her stomach, her head. If the pain lessened in one area, a different region gobbled it up, intensified the flame. The pain never disappeared, just shifted in levels of manageability. The tide was always high with my daughter. She exhausted me.

Rose Gold shook her head, refusing to answer. The school staff asked me to sit down for a meeting, but I ignored them. I carried Rose Gold to our beat-up old van, cradling her like I had when she was an infant. I buckled her into the backseat and put the key in the ignition. On the drive home, I watched the rearview mirror, my eyes focused backward more often than not. My little girl stared out the window, silent.

I pulled into the garage and turned off the ignition, letting my head rest against the seat for a minute. Closing my eyes, I imagined finishing the crossword, taking my daughter to the park, cheering her on as she descended a slide headfirst.

"Darling, why is your wig dirty?" I asked with a sinking feeling, already knowing the answer.

Behind me, Rose Gold began to whisper. "At recess Josh Burrows said my hair is fake, and he pulled off my wig to prove it. And then he and the other boys kept throwing it but I couldn't catch it and it fell in the dirt and I tried to get it but Josh pushed me and I fell in the dirt too. Then they all shoved dirt in my mouth. To match my teeth, they said." A solitary tear slid down her cheek. "Mommy, what are cooties?"

Josh Burrows and his cronies had been bullying Rose Gold for months, spilling ketchup on her clothes, leaving dead bugs in her backpack, and calling her cruel nicknames the rest of the students picked up on. This was the first time they had physically hurt her. I wished those boys a thousand fiery deaths that day and have every day since. It mattered not one whit to me that Josh was seven years old.

I had tried to teach my daughter how to defend herself, but she was an easy target with all her ailments. I was a bit clueless in this department—I had been popular in school, getting straight A's and learning the art of self-deprecation at a young age. Rose Gold was too sensitive to laugh anything off.

I relaxed my fists into hands. "Your hair is beautiful, sweetheart. And you don't have cooties. Josh Burrows is the one with cooties." (Undoubtedly the wrong lesson to teach in that moment, but I am, after all, human.)

Growing up, my father had preached resourcefulness above all else. No use listening to someone's problems if you couldn't fix them. I could fix my daughter. I ached to help. "Do you want to stay home with Mommy from now on? What if Mommy was your new teacher?"

Rose Gold hesitated. She had mentioned last week that she loved her teacher, and there was a girl in class she talked about a lot. Maybe the two of them were friends for the time being, but how long until that girl turned on her too?

This transition would make both our lives easier. I could squeeze in classroom lessons during those interminable waiting room visits. I could make the doctor's office an opportunity for fun, rather than something she dreaded. As long as those checks kept coming every month, we would make this work.

Rose Gold took off her glasses with the clear frames and cleaned them on her Tweety Bird T-shirt. This gesture always made me smile—such a wise old action for a child. I'd grown to love those glasses. Her eyes looked beady without them, as if they might scamper off her face without the frames to hold them in place.

"What do you think?" I asked again.

She put the glasses back on and watched me. "Can we still have recess?"

My heart swelled, imagining her participation in recess these past two years. I pictured her standing off to the side of red rover and tag, more out of breath than her classmates, who were running around.

I jutted out my chin, toughened the shell. "Of course we can, sweetheart. We'll have two recesses a day. How about that?"

Rose Gold nodded and took off her seat belt. I hoped Josh Burrows and his goons were already fading from her memory. Supermom had saved the day again.

Back in the grocery store, I grab the last couple items on my list and head for the checkout. One lane is open. Four people wait in line while the teenage cashier slowly scans canned goods. I join the back of the line.

A very tall man, thin as a flagpole, stands in front of me. Only one person I know of in Deadwick is almost six feet five inches. The man turns as if he can hear my thoughts. I come face to face with Tom Behan.

He's almost as startled to see me as I am to see him mustache-less.

"You shaved your mustache," I blurt.

Tom hovers over me, adjusting his glasses. "I heard they let you out," he says.

"I seem to be the talk of the town," I say, chilled by his tone. "It's strange not to see you in scrubs."

Tom and I went through the CNA program together at Gallatin. He had been my closest friend. We'd stay up late at his apartment, goofing off when we were supposed to be quizzing each other on infection control. He'd gone on to get his nursing license, and we sometimes worked overlapping shifts at the local hospital. I think Tom had a crush on me back then, although I always thought of him as a brother. Now he has a wife and two kids.

"Let's cut the horseshit." He jabs a finger at me. "You may have tricked your daughter into forgiving you, but the rest of us have long memories."

"That was all a big misunderstanding," I say. "I made a few missteps, but I served my time. Rose Gold and I are closer than ever." Not strictly true, but Tom Behan doesn't need to know that.

Through gritted teeth, Tom says, "I vouched for you. I helped you research her symptoms and suggested treatments and let you cry on my shoulder." Tom gets this haunted expression and lowers his voice. "Do you know the damage we wreaked on her poor body? On a perfectly healthy body? We took an oath—"

"She could barely walk. I wouldn't call that perfectly healthy." I look Tom Behan straight in the eye, suddenly desperate to win my old friend over, and try a softer tone. "I thought we could put the past behind us."

Tom stares at me. The cashier has gotten through one customer in all this time. Another cart joins the line behind me.

"Well, well, well."

I turn to see Sean Walsh, a lumberjack of a man I barely know, but who had an awful lot to say about me to the press five years ago. Tom nods at Sean.

"Patty here thinks we should all put the past behind us," Tom says, loud enough for everyone in earshot to hear. I cringe.

"The past behind us, huh?" Sean says, scratching his beard. He leaves his cart and takes a few steps forward.

"Yes," I say, because he's waiting for my response. Sean takes another step closer. I wish he'd back off. Everyone in line in front of us is pretending to examine the register kiosks while they rubberneck.

"We've known each other since we were seventeen," Tom says to me. "Maybe that's the past we should put behind us."

Sean takes a sip from a travel coffee mug. "I think the whole town would like to forget you were ever a part of it."

His drink could use more than a few drops from the small brown bottle with the white cap in my purse.

"Tom, be reasonable," I say under my breath.

Tom takes a step toward me. "Reasonable?" he chokes. "This coming from the woman who starved her little girl?" He raises his eyebrows at Sean. Tom is putting on a show, but I recognize the pain in his voice. I know how upset he is. If it were just the two of us, I'd give him a bear hug, like I did the day he failed his first certification exam. I was the one who convinced him to try again. If I hugged him right now, in front of Sean Walsh and the rest of the customers, he might slap me.

"Don't talk to us about *reasonable*," Sean says, taking another step forward. He's close enough to reach out and touch. "The *reasonable* thing for you to do right now is walk out of this store before I remove you myself."

Someone, a few feet away, starts to clap. Heat rushes to my cheeks. "But—" I gesture to my cart full of food.

"My brother doesn't need your business," Sean says, pointing to the door. Bill Walsh owns the grocery store. "Buy your food elsewhere."

Tom and Sean form a semicircle around me. The only way out is toward the store exit. Outside, the bare branches lean forward with the wind, reaching for me.

I imagine a tree for every citizen of Deadwick. The long arms of timber lift the people up higher, higher, higher still. Then, when every Tom and Sean and even the little Timmys are fifty feet in the air, the trees release their catches, all at once, in harmony. I am their conductor. The bodies crash to the ground, the opposite of rose petals. They land on the tops of their heads and the backs of their necks and the flats on their spines. Their bodies are my carpet, painted red. I wipe my shoes on their faces.

I stand my ground for a second, chin out, fists clenched. I try to meet Tom's eyes, to plead for mercy, but he won't look at me anymore. His facial expression suggests he just stepped in a pile of dog doo.

They've left me no choice. I shuffle toward the door, head down, leaving my full shopping cart where it is. I think of the empty fridge at home, of Tom Behan's misty eyes.

I walk out the door.

Behind me, the crowd erupts in applause.

10

Rose Gold

November 2014

I had been on the road for four hours, driving east along I-74 and then north on I-69. Today was the big day: I was going to meet Dad's family and stay the night in Indiana. Over the past four months, he and I had texted a lot and talked on the phone several times. All I had to do was listen during these conversations; Dad was chatty enough for both of us. I pointed this out once, and he conceded that with age, he'd started to talk to strangers everywhere, whether he was in a checkout line or stopped at a tollbooth.

I'd friended him, Kim, and the two older kids on social media. I had hoped the family would grow to love me before they'd even met me in person. Dad and Kim weren't as active online, but the kids were, especially thirteen-year-old Sophie. I liked every single status update she posted; there were a lot, and they were random.

My second toes are longer than my firsts. As a kid, someone told me that means I'm a genius. Even then, I knew it just meant I have hideous feet.

*I'm calling it now: I suspect cancer will be my eventual
demise. All four of my grandparents died from breast, throat,
skin, and/or prostate cancers. The only mystery is which of
these I will succumb to, the last being unlikely.*

I suspected people would call Sophie a "character."

Last summer was a long one, but now, in November, the weather
was cooling down. My mother had been in prison for two years. The
closer I got to Dad, the angrier I got at her. He was such a loving, kind
man, and she'd kept him from me. All this time I'd thought she cared
most about me. Even when I testified against her, I wasn't sure I
was doing the right thing—I only went through with it because
Mrs. Stone and the police said I should. I'd doubted myself the whole
way through. But the reporters were right: she was a monster; she was
poisonous. My mother was a selfish woman. She loved herself more
than anyone else.

Since Dad had walked into Gadget World last August, I'd been
erasing all traces of Mom from my life. I'd looked into changing my
last name, although "Rose Gold Gillespie" felt like a mouthful. I'd
distanced myself from Mrs. Stone, because she reminded me of memories tied to Mom. I'd stopped using Mom's stupid sayings—no more
"Christmas eyes" or "puppy jumps." No more wondering what she
would do every time I needed to make a decision. I was done being her
doormat, done with her altogether. I had a new family now. I hoped
they would leave me in one piece.

I'd gotten so caught up in the reunion with my dad that I had to
put the visit to Phil on hold. The five-hour drive to Fairfield was more
important than the trip to Colorado. I could—and would—do both,
but for now, Phil would have to wait. When I told him about my dad,
he'd been supportive and sweet. Phil understood I loved him but

wouldn't be as available as usual. I had to make up for lost time with my dad.

The last hour of the drive flew by, and I found myself in a tidy suburb faster than expected. This town was a polished version of Deadwick—the houses were bigger, the grass was greener, and even the dogs looked happier. I pulled into the driveway of 305 Sherman Street. How fitting my TV dad had a TV house: a two-story brick structure that was sturdy and well-kept but not flashy. Outward appearances suggested the Gillespie family was comfortable, not rich. I couldn't wait to get inside.

I pulled my brown paper bag of sleepover stuff out of the backseat of the van and walked up the driveway. Dad opened the front door.

"Welcome!" he said.

I hugged Dad and held onto him tight, relieved he still smelled like woodsy aftershave and McDonald's.

"Come in, come in," Dad said, ushering me inside. Waiting in the hallway was a woman I'd guess was in her late thirties, but the fake tan made her look older. I opened my arms to give Kim a hug, but she extended a hand full of acrylic nails instead. She had a French manicure, chipped on one nail. She was different than I'd expected.

"Kim," she said, watching me. "Nice to meet you."

I took her hand and smiled, mouth closed. "Nice to meet you too." I'd try again for a hug before I left tomorrow.

"Let me give you the grand tour," Dad said with a wink. He set my paper bag to the side of the foyer.

We walked through the living room first. Two shabby beige couches and a TV took up most of the space. A bin of thick blankets sat next to one of the couches. The walls were covered from floor to ceiling with framed black-and-white family photos—trips to Six Flags, first communions, birthday parties, the kids running through sprinklers, the kids waiting in line for the ice cream truck, the kids holding up their first lost teeth. *Look at us,* they shouted. *See all the places we've been, the things we've done, how adorable we are.* My chest tightened as I saw all I'd missed.

We moved on to the kitchen. Evidence of a busy family covered the refrigerator. Alphabet magnets held up report cards, baby shower invitations, and to-do lists. A few Christmas cards had already been taped to the side. I thought back to before my mother's arrest, when all our neighbors in Deadwick sent us Christmas cards. Mom let me tape them around the doorframe between the living room and the kitchen. I shook the thought away.

Dad showed me the dining room, where a six-person table stood. Along one wall was a china cabinet, full of Precious Moments figurines and other fragile pieces. A LEGO set was scattered next to the cabinet. Kim drifted behind us from room to room. I felt her eyes on the back of my head, scrutinizing me while I couldn't see her. I tried to focus on Dad's tour.

We walked down a hallway, and Dad pointed out the downstairs bathroom. We headed back toward the staircase, and I noticed a little door built in underneath it.

"What's this?" I asked, reaching for the handle.

"Our seasonal closet," Dad said, gesturing for me to open the door. "Holiday decorations and wrapping paper and stuff. No one ever goes in there."

I ducked my head and stepped inside the small, unfinished room. Wreaths, Christmas stockings, Easter baskets, a big sewing kit, Halloween costumes, and more filled the room. The closet was stuffy, nothing special, but I liked the intimacy of it, as though it were hiding secrets in its exposed insulation.

Dad gestured for me to follow him. He opened a sliding-glass door in the living room that led to the backyard. I stepped out onto the patio and into a chilly evening. The sky was just starting to darken.

The Gillespies' yard had a swing set in one corner, a trampoline in another. On the patio were a couple chairs and a grill. Dad paused at the grill. When I stopped looking around and focused on him, he pointed to the grill shelf with a flourish.

"Ta-da!" he said. On the shelf was a tray with a dozen uncooked beef patties.

He'd remembered. I blinked back tears.

"Now," he said, "for a lesson." He grabbed an apron—*I cook for kisses* embroidered on it in bubbly lettering—from the patio chair and tied it around his waist. He fired up the grill.

"First, we sprinkle garlic and onion salt on the patties," he explained as he worked. "Then a few splashes of Worcestershire sauce." He threw each burger on the grill. The meat was still raw, yet already my mouth watered.

"Never press down on the burger while cooking," Dad said. "You'll squeeze all the juices out. Only flip your patties once—about three minutes on each side. And finally, we'll toast and butter the buns."

I stayed quiet, but thrilled at the normalcy of grilling in the backyard with my dad. When the burgers and buns were ready, Dad and I brought the platters of food back inside and set them on the kitchen counter. "I'll introduce you to the kids while we let the burgers rest for a few minutes." Before I could ask, he added, "So the juices can redistribute into the meat."

I followed him to the hallway stairs.

"Kids," Dad called up, "come down and meet Rose."

I braced myself, eager to meet them. Someone thumped down the stairs. Two others plodded behind.

I met Anna, the six-year-old, first. She grinned at me, two front teeth missing, a good omen. Dad put his hand on her shoulder.

"Anna, this is Rose Gold," he said a little nervously.

I crouched down at the same time Anna stepped forward, and we landed in a tight hug. "Your hair smells nice," Anna whispered, twirling a strand around her fingers. I imagined the two of us building sand castles at the beach, me pushing her on the swings at the park, her inviting me to a tea party.

"Rose, this is Billy Jr.," Dad said. A skinny boy of eleven stood with his hands in his pockets, not meeting my eyes. He looked uncomfortable, but then, I guessed all boys that age did. He gave me a small wave before returning his hand to his pocket.

"And this is Sophie," Dad went on. The thirteen-year-old girl stood on the middle of the staircase, arms crossed. She had mild acne and braces. What I wouldn't have given to have had braces at her age.

I smiled at her, mouth closed. She smiled back, then peered out the front window at the street. "You drive a van?" She sounded unimpressed—and a little rude.

I had expected my new siblings and stepmom to welcome me with open arms. I thought they'd be as excited about me as I was about them. So far everyone but Anna seemed apathetic.

"Sophie," Kim called from the kitchen, "help me put dinner on the table."

Sophie trotted past me without a word. I tried to forget the bad feeling; we had the entire night to turn this first impression around.

"Why don't we sit down, kids?" Dad said. His kids included me. I was one of his kids. I beamed, pretending to examine my nails so he wouldn't notice how pathetically happy I was to be one of their group.

"Can I help with anything?" I asked.

He shook his head.

We reentered the dining room. The table had been filled to the brim with toppings and condiments.

Anna, Billy Jr., and I took seats at the table.

"That's Mommy's seat," Anna said, pointing at the chair I'd chosen. I jumped up, wincing.

Billy Jr. rolled his eyes. "It doesn't matter, Anna."

"Don't roll your eyes at your sister," Dad said.

Billy Jr. sighed and took a bag of Goldfish crackers out of his pocket. He ate them ten at a time, like a toddler without self-control.

"Put those away. You'll ruin your appetite," Dad grumbled.

Billy Jr. slid the crackers back into his pocket.

"Where should I sit?" I asked them.

Anna patted the seat next to her. I sat in it. She started playing with my hair again. I had forgotten how good it felt to be doted on.

Kim came in with the plate of burgers, and Sophie followed close behind with the buns. Dad filled everyone's glasses with milk. Once we were all seated at the table, Dad started to say grace. Kim bowed her head and closed her eyes, but the kids just stared at the burgers. I decided to bow my head but keep my eyes open, to make sure I didn't miss anything. Nothing happened, though; the kids sat there, waiting.

When Dad was finished, he rubbed his hands together. "Okay, Rose, we have five cheese options for tonight's meal: American, Cheddar, Jack, Swiss, and provolone. You've got yellow or Dijon mustard, as well as ketchup, mayonnaise, and barbecue sauce. And here we have tomatoes, lettuce, and red onion. The world is your oyster. Go nuts."

I didn't know where to start or which options to choose. I watched Kim make a burger for Anna before serving herself. Billy Jr. was halfway through his first sandwich by the time I picked out a patty and bun. I marveled at how quickly the kid could put away food. I hoped he'd take seconds so I could too. I carefully sliced a tomato and pulled a piece of lettuce from the head.

"Have you been to Indiana before, Rose?" Dad asked.

"No, first time," I said. Everyone kept stealing glances at me when they thought I wasn't looking. I pretended not to notice, piling red onion atop the tomato.

"Well, welcome, then," Dad said. "We're all so glad you could make it."

They ate in awkward silence for a few minutes. I wondered if they were always this quiet, or if I made them uncomfortable.

Kim spoke up. "How was the drive? Not much to see along the way, was there?"

"It wasn't bad," I said. "A lot of cornfields, but this was my first road trip, so it was kind of fun. I bought Doritos and played the alphabet game."

"How nice," Kim said at the same time Billy Jr. muttered, "By yourself?"

I squirted ketchup and mustard onto my bun, spreading them evenly with a knife. I arranged each ingredient just so, as though my burger might be on the cover of a food magazine.

Billy Jr. stared at me, incredulous. "Just eat it already," he said under his breath.

"Leave Rose alone," Dad said. He watched me expectantly.

I cleared my throat and picked up the sandwich, inhaling the scent of chargrilled meat. I opened my mouth wide and put the burger inside, making sure I got a little piece of every ingredient. I suspected the first bite was the most important. After that, the burger would become less art, more fuel.

I closed my teeth around the sandwich and bit hard. I let the mixture roll around inside my mouth: the tanginess of the mustard, the crunch of the lettuce, and the salty, juicy patty. The burger was absolutely delicious. They'd gone to all this trouble, just for me.

I made satisfied noises, even dancing my head around a little to show my pleasure. Dad smiled at Kim. After a minute of watching me, they went back to the food on their own plates. We all ate quietly.

"So your mom is in prison?" Sophie said flatly.

"Sophie," Dad scolded, turning to Kim for support. But she was looking at me, waiting for my response.

I cleared my throat. "About two years now."

"You must hate her, huh?" Billy Jr. said, eyes trained on his mom. When Kim didn't discourage him, he added, "If everything you say is true."

"This isn't appropriate for the dinner table," Dad snapped, an edge to his voice that hadn't been there when he chided Sophie.

Sophie flashed Billy Jr. a look. Neither of them acknowledged our father. I felt sorry for Dad and even sorrier for myself. I bit my lip.

In a low tone, Kim spoke up. "They're just trying to learn more about Rose Gold."

"What I don't get," Sophie said, "is why you didn't just eat or brush your teeth. Anna knew how to brush her own teeth a year ago."

I managed to stop my jaw from dropping, but stared at Sophie, unsure how the conversation had taken such a fast turn. Mom always said you had to give bullies a taste of their own medicine. And sure, I would have liked to smash Sophie's burger in her face, but hadn't I decided I wanted to be nothing like my mother? Besides, Dad and Kim would never let me join their ranks if I wasn't nice to their kids. Maybe having a sister meant wanting to shove food in her face 60 percent of the time.

Anna grinned to show me her teeth. "I floss too. Right, Mommy?"

"That's right, honey." The tension on Kim's face morphed into pity. "Rose, we were so sorry to hear about all that happened to you growing up."

I smiled tightly. "Thanks, Kim." I hoped they would take a hint and realize I didn't want to discuss the past. I had been recovering steadily for almost three years, but people still liked me more as a weakling than as the healthy woman I'd become. I needed a subject change, fast.

I gave Billy Jr. my warmest smile. "I've always wanted a brother."

"Half brother," Sophie mumbled to her plate.

My cheeks flamed. Dad turned to Kim again, expecting her to say something, but she took a long drink of milk.

"A sister too," I added, thinking maybe Sophie felt left out.

"Half sister," Billy Jr. corrected me.

I couldn't win with these two. They were like Cinderella's evil stepsisters.

"Enough," Dad barked at Billy Jr. "Is this the kind of man you want to grow up to be? One who bullies people weaker than you?"

Billy Jr. lowered his eyes.

Dad gave me an apologetic glance, then turned to Sophie. "How was practice today?"

Sophie launched into a ten-minute explanation of the new drills their basketball coach had the team do. I had no idea what any of it meant, but I was relieved not to have all five Gillespies staring at me, at least for a little while. I tried to appear interested while I finished my burger. This was not how I'd expected dinner to go.

I had to try again—maybe sports were the way in. I wished I were more of an athlete.

"Did you guys watch the London Olympics?" I asked when Sophie stopped talking. "I loved Gabby Douglas, especially her routine on the uneven bars."

Billy Jr. rolled his eyes. "That was two years ago."

Dad gave his son a withering glare. "Rose was a little busy in the summer of 2012, what with serving as a star witness in a criminal trial and all. She didn't have the luxury of sitting around in her pajamas all day, like you."

Billy Jr. stared at his plate but didn't say anything. Kim gave Dad a pleading look. He ignored her. I felt a little bad about the way he was beating Billy Jr. up, but I was also bursting with joy that he was defending me instead of his son. Besides, Billy Jr. deserved to get in trouble. He was a brat.

Kim turned to me. "We all love watching the gymnastics team. Gabby Douglas was our favorite too." I guessed she was ready to play peacemaker, anything to break the tension between her husband and son. We continued eating in silence.

When Billy Jr. had finished his second burger, I figured I could take another one too. Kim was asking Sophie about her teammate's injured ankle and whether she'd be starting at this weekend's game. I leaned forward.

"Could you please pass the buns . . . Dad?" I murmured.

Kim's head jerked toward me. Sophie stopped speaking. Their eyes met across the table. Dad pretended not to notice and passed me the plate.

I broke the silence with a compliment—this always worked for my mother. "Your house is beautiful, Kim," I said. "I love how cozy it is, with all the family photos in every room."

Kim smiled stiffly at me. Dad rested his hand on hers.

"We've been very blessed with these three," Kim said, nodding at her kids. "They're not angels, but we think we got pretty lucky."

Anna beamed. Billy Jr. rolled his eyes. Sophie winced.

Dad put his arm around Kim, lightening up. "We'd have liked to have one more, but—"

"Dad," Sophie groaned, mortified. "Gross."

Anna tugged on my arm. "We're going to sleep in a tent," she said, excited.

I looked around, confused.

"We're going to Yellowstone next summer," Dad explained. "On a camping trip."

The whole family perked up at the mention of the trip. They spoke over one another in their eagerness.

"We're going to rent canoes," Sophie said.

"And roast marshmallows," Anna announced.

"I get to build the bonfire," Billy Jr. added. "And we're going to go fishing. Right, Dad?" He peered at our father so earnest and full of hope that I realized he might not be a brat after all. Maybe he was just a kid who wanted his father's approval, who didn't know how to act around his long-lost sister.

Dad nodded and grinned, his bad mood gone.

"When is the big trip?" I asked.

"Over the July Fourth holiday," Kim said, relaxing a little. She smiled at the kids' excitement. She was pretty when she smiled. "We haven't gone camping in years, not since before Anna was born."

"When I was in your tummy?" Anna asked.

"Even before then," Kim said.

Anna looked confused, but didn't comment.

Sophie piped up again. "Anna thinks she saw me and Billy in Mom's tummy." Everyone started to laugh. "She said there was a Toys 'R' Us in there too."

"No, I didn't," Anna protested.

"Yes, you did," they all chimed back. They sounded happier now, laughing and playful. This was the kind of family I'd wanted.

"I'm going to show these guys how to make waffles over a fire," Dad said. He was as thrilled as the kids. I imagined myself wedged between Sophie and Billy Jr. on a log in the dark, telling the scariest ghost stories I could come up with. We'd stay up all night, eating and laughing. Dad would put me in charge of grilling the burgers.

"I'd love to join you," I blurted.

Kim did a double take. Even Dad was at a loss for words. Sophie and Billy Jr. watched their parents.

Anna clapped her hands and yelled, "Can Rose come? I want to sit next to her in the car!"

Dad smiled weakly at Anna. "We'll see, honey." He turned to me. "Let's talk about it later, okay?"

I nodded. That meant no. Crap—had I screwed everything up? My heart pounded. I shouldn't have invited myself like that, but they'd made the trip sound so fun. I could picture myself next summer, not alone on my couch in Deadwick with a sad stack of movies, but nestled in a sleeping bag with my siblings snoring quietly beside me in our tent. I hadn't wanted something this bad since Disney on Ice when I was ten.

Kim began clearing the table. "Anna, why don't you take Rose to the living room and show her the DVDs? How about we let her choose the movie for tonight?"

Anna pulled me by the hand to the living room and showed me her collection of Disney movies. My fingers brushed the spines of the films I'd watched tirelessly for the past two years: *Peter Pan*, *Mulan*, *Dumbo*. I pulled the last title from the shelf.

"I hate that movie," Anna said bitterly.

"Why?" I asked with surprise.

She looked at her feet. "The girls at school say I have Dumbo ears." My heart hitched.

I squatted to her height. "You know, Dumbo gets to fly at the end. He's the coolest of all the elephants."

Anna glanced up at me, doubtful.

I tucked her hair behind her ears, which were big, but not as big as she probably feared. She watched me, waiting. What was I supposed to do, tell her to love her flaws while I saved every spare dollar to get rid of mine?

"What's your favorite Disney movie?" I asked.

"*Frozen*," she said immediately.

I gasped. "Mine too! Let's watch that, and I'll braid your hair."

Anna shook her head, letting her hair cover her ears again. "I don't like braids."

No, you don't like that they show your ears. I knew every trick in the book.

"Oh, come on, you'll look just like Anna and Elsa!" I said. "Tell you what. If you hate the braids, we can take them right out. But let's see if you like them?"

Anna thought about it, then nodded. "Deal."

While the rest of the family cleaned up dinner, I braided Anna's hair like my life depended on it, even weaving a purple ribbon through. I'd practiced on my wigs countless times, but had never braided a person's hair before. Now I knew all my practicing had been for this moment. When I finished, the braid was perfect. Anna ran to the bathroom to check herself out in the mirror. I held my breath. Seconds later, she darted back into the living room and hugged me tight. I grinned, resting my cheek on the top of her head and basking in the simple joy of making another human being happy.

Once the dining room was cleaned, all the Gillespies settled on the couch to watch *Frozen* together. Anna informed me I was sitting in Daddy's spot, but Dad said that was okay and he wanted to try a new spot tonight. I beamed, thankful he was including me in his family.

Billy Jr. and Sophie didn't enjoy the movie as much as Anna and I. They were on their phones the whole time. Sophie sighed when Anna sang along to "Let It Go" at the top of her lungs. I thought she was cute. She played with her braid the entire time.

After the movie, Kim told the kids to get ready for bed and led me upstairs. She gave me a brief tour of the second floor: the master bedroom and bathroom; Sophie and Anna's room; Billy Jr.'s room; and the guest room, where I would sleep.

The guest room had a queen-sized bed and pastel yellow walls. The bottoms of the walls had ducklings stenciled onto them. Kim noticed my gaze.

"This used to be the nursery," she said, pulling an extra quilt out of a trunk for me. "We haven't gotten around to repainting yet. God, is Anna six already? Now I'm embarrassed." She forced a laugh. I waved her off, said I loved it.

She draped the quilt along the foot of the bed. "In case you get cold."

A whole-body ache washed over me. I missed being mothered.

Kim pointed to a bathroom between my room and Billy Jr.'s. "If you want to wash up, there's face cleanser and toothpaste and stuff in the medicine cabinet."

Anna rushed into the room and jumped on the guest bed. "I want to sleep with Rose!"

"You're supposed to be in bed," Kim scolded her. "You'll see Rose tomorrow. Right now we have to let her sleep. She's had a long day of driving."

Anna pouted. "But—"

"No buts, no cuts, no coconuts," Kim said, pointing to the door. "Quit stalling."

Anna sighed the same way Sophie had earlier. She marched to her room.

Kim followed Anna, starting to close my door behind her. "Let me know if you need anything."

I grabbed Kim's hand and squeezed it. "Thank you for everything," I said, meeting her eye so she'd know I meant it.

"Sleep tight," she said, squeezing back.

Kim headed into the master bedroom and pulled the door behind her, leaving it a bit ajar. I washed my face in the bathroom and thought about our old town house. We had one bathroom. The Gillespies had three. Each one was nicer than ours. I'd always thought it was my fault Mom and I didn't have any money; if she didn't spend all her time taking care of me and carting me to doctors' appointments, maybe she could have hung on to a job. But I'd had it all wrong. Mom had used me to mooch off of Dad and our neighbors. She only worked odd jobs—cleaner, in-home caregiver, bookkeeper—if we were in danger of coming up short on that month's mortgage payment. She chose for us to scrape by.

After I finished brushing my teeth and turned off the faucet, I heard murmurs coming from Kim and Dad's room. I stepped to their door and peeked inside. They were both in the bathroom, door closed. I tiptoed into the room and stood as close to the bathroom door as I dared, straining to listen.

"You can't expect them to act like she's their best friend," Kim was saying. "She's a virtual stranger! And inviting herself on our family vacation? Where did that come from?"

"I know, honey," Dad said. "I know it's a big change, but I don't know what to do. She doesn't have anyone else."

"Doesn't she have any friends?" Kim asked. "Tell her to take a trip with them."

Silence for a few beats.

"I'll talk to her," Dad said. "But I can't hang her out to dry."

The bathroom door started to open. Alarmed, I backpedaled as fast as I could out of the bedroom and darted back into the guest room. My heart felt like it would pound straight out of my chest. Their conversation continued at the same volume, but I couldn't hear the rest of it.

I quietly closed my door and climbed into the big, cushy bed. I lay like a starfish under the sheets, stretching my arms and legs wide. I'd never slept in anything but a twin bed. Maybe once I had enough money to fix my teeth, I would save up for a queen for my own place.

Surprisingly, I wasn't that upset. True, Kim wasn't taking to me at lightning speed, but Dad was. He'd invited me here and let me hang out in his house, and now he had defended me to his wife. We were already creating an unbreakable bond. I'd have to work to win Kim,

Sophie, and Billy Jr. over the way I had Dad and Anna. I needed a story, an ironclad reason, why I had to go on that camping trip next summer. After a whole week of bonding, they'd see I wasn't an outsider at all. I was the same as them. I listened to the Gillespies get ready for bed and stared at the ceiling, thinking.

———

The next morning, Dad and I went for a walk around the neighborhood before I had to hit the road. I had work the following day and needed to get home.

We walked in comfortable silence for a while. I was still thinking about what I'd overheard the night before. I had to bring up the camping trip at some point, to give him another chance to invite me. My new family was about to make all these memories we'd reflect back on in thirty years. Our first family vacation—I had to be there.

We rounded the corner. Dad's house came back into sight.

"When can we hang out again?" I asked.

"We'll figure out something soon," Dad said. "You know where to find me now." He winked. I gave him a small smile. One day I'd be able to grin with confidence, put all my perfectly straight teeth on display.

"Rose," he continued, "you haven't told me about your friends. Do they all live in Deadwick?"

All? "Well, my best friend is Alex. She goes to school in Chicago," I said. "But things haven't been great between us."

"Why not?"

"I don't know," I said, trying to memorize every inch of the neighborhood—the old man shuffling to pick up his newspaper, the kids skateboarding in the street, the pet walker trying to control seven dogs. "We're not seeing eye to eye on some stuff."

"How long have you known her?" Dad asked.

"Since we were kids," I said. "She was my neighbor in Deadwick before she left for Chicago."

"That sounds like a pretty strong relationship, to make it that long," Dad said. I shrugged. "Maybe you should sit down and level with her," he said. "Friends like that are less common than you'd think."

I nodded. "Okay, I'll give it a try."

Dad seemed satisfied.

I turned to him. "Do you think Kim likes me?"

He feigned surprise. "Of course she does. Why would you ask that?"

This was my chance. "I, um, overheard you guys talking last night. She doesn't want me to come on the camping trip." I stared at him, but he avoided meeting my eyes.

"Rose," he said, touching my shoulder, "don't read too much into that. You and I have had months to get to know each other, but the rest of my family met you yesterday. This is a lot to take in, but they all loved you. I'm sure of it."

A small smile formed on my lips. "I love them too."

He still hadn't invited me. He wasn't going to, I realized.

This *was* just like the Disney on Ice show.

When I was ten, I saw a poster at Walsh's for Disney on Ice. For weeks I begged Mom to take me to the show in Chicago. *I'll stay in my wheelchair,* I promised. *I won't bring my wig. I'll do whatever you say.* I imagined meeting Ariel in real life and getting one of those spinning light-up wands like Alex had. Maybe I'd even get to talk to the other kids.

Finally, Mom relented. We picked a date—May 10, 2004—and she bought the tickets, or told me she did anyway. I'd already planned to buy her a "thank you" gift for taking me; I would get her a Mrs.

Potts key chain for her car keys. Every day for six months I counted down the number of days until our show.

The morning of May 10, an hour before we needed to leave for Chicago, I began vomiting and couldn't stop. I tried to hide it from Mom, but she caught me with my head in the toilet. *I'm so sorry, darling,* she said. *We'll go another time.*

We never did.

Dad and I kept walking, almost to my van in his driveway now. I had to go on this vacation. I could not leave Indiana without a promise. I racked my brain, frantic. I remembered Kim's look of pity at dinner the night before—the single moment that she'd truly been on my side. Maybe, like everyone else, the Gillespies liked the old me better.

Nothing ventured, nothing gained, Mom said.

I stopped walking, so he stopped too. "The thing is," I said, "I'm sick."

Dad tilted his head, trying to understand.

I took a deep breath. The story came tumbling out so rapidly, it felt like the truth. "I've been having night sweats and fevers and stuff the past few months. I didn't think anything of it at first, but then I thought I should go to the doctor just in case. So I did, and he wanted to do a biopsy. They removed a lymph node from under my arm and sent it out for testing. The doctor called me with the results two days ago. I have Hodgkin's lymphoma."

Tears sprang in my eyes. For a moment, I imagined I really was sick. I could almost feel the night sweats and fevers, could conjure up the thin line of the doctor's mouth as he delivered the news.

Dad stuttered a little, the color draining from his face. I hated to lie to him. "That's . . . It's . . . God, just, how—horrible. Rose, I am so sorry." He gathered me into his arms. I shuddered with relief. How comforting to be held, to feel like you were home.

"What stage?" he asked.

"Three," I said, gripping him tighter.

My mother's encyclopedic knowledge of illnesses had finally become useful. She'd once had a doctor perform a biopsy on me, insisting I had all the symptoms of someone with Hodgkin's lymphoma. The results came back negative, of course.

"I start chemo in two weeks," I said, "but who knows if that'll work? That's why I want to go on this camping trip so much. I'm sorry. I know I shouldn't have invited myself, but I've never been on a family vacation before. Visiting you this weekend was my first trip out of state. There's so much I still want to do. So many things I never got to because, well, you know the story."

Dad hugged me even tighter, petting my hair. I could have stood there, on that sidewalk with him, forever.

"I just want to go on one trip," I whispered, tears streaking my face. "What if I don't . . . ?"

Dad shushed me. "Hey, you're going to be fine, okay? Look at me." He tilted my chin up so our eyes met. "We'll figure it out. Together."

I closed my eyes and let him rock me. *Together, together, always together, together always.* I grinned and sniffed. I'd have to start researching hiking boots.

We stood there until I felt someone else's gaze on me. I opened my eyes and peeked at the Gillespies' house. Standing on the front stoop, watching us, was Kim.

"Everything okay?" she called to us.

Better than okay, Kim. Everything was fantastic.

11

Patty

At four o'clock sharp, Thanksgiving dinner is served. After I set the final dish on the kitchen table, I step back and examine my handiwork. I may have sweet potato in my hair, but "triumph" is still the word that comes to mind.

In the center of the table is a roasted turkey. Surrounding it are half a dozen dishes filled with stuffing, mashed potatoes, candied yams, broccoli casserole, cranberry sauce, and roasted butternut squash. Apple pie and chess pie stand at the ready in the fridge. I have made all of it on my own, without burning a single dish. The kitchen is a mess, but I'll worry about that later. I have prepared a feast. My love for my daughter is laid out on the table.

I straighten the linen napkins I bought at TJ Maxx and light the votive candles. I've been so busy preparing this meal that, for a few hours, I haven't thought about the pained expression on Tom's face, the irate round of applause at my back when I left Walsh's. Afterward, I had to take a bus to a grocery store two towns over to buy our food. The whole humiliating experience has been playing on a loop in my mind for the past week. I would have to find a new Tom, befriend a new nurse at the hospital. My legs tremble when I think about never talking to him again.

"Dinner's ready," I call to the living room, where Rose Gold is singing "Row, Row, Row Your Boat" to Adam.

She joins me at the table, Adam tucked into her arms. She kisses both his cheeks before putting him in his bassinet. Her eyes bug out when she takes in the spread. "You outdid yourself," she says, smiling.

I wave her off, though we both know this is a big deal. Not known for my cooking prowess before prison, I served whatever Stouffer's family-sized dishes were on sale. Rose Gold could never eat them anyway.

She reaches for the mashed potatoes, but I stop her. "Before we eat," I say, "I think we should each say something we're grateful for. You go first."

Fine, so I'm hoping for more adoration.

Rose Gold thinks for a moment. "I'm thankful for Adam." She beams. "He's going to change my life."

Adam?

Did Adam prepare the immaculate feast in front of her eyes? Was Adam offering to pay her mortgage? All he does is poop and refuse to sleep through the night.

The miracle of life is a lot less interesting when it's someone else's miracle.

I glance over at the baby in his bassinet. He kicks his legs and smirks at me, as if to remind me what an adorable leprechaun he is.

I squeeze Rose Gold's hand tight. "He already has."

"What about yours?" Rose Gold asks.

"I'm thankful for you." I meet her eye. "You and second chances." She holds my gaze, then turns away, uncomfortable.

"Let's eat," I say, breaking the silence.

We both fill our plates with the steaming food on the table. I break into the turkey first; this is the dish I'm most nervous about. But the bird is perfect: full of flavor, not at all dried out. I pile the food into my mouth, barely remembering to breathe between bites. After working on my feet all day, I'm famished.

"You have tomorrow off, right?" I ask. I scoop more stuffing onto my fork.

Rose Gold shakes her head, twirling her spoon through mashed potatoes. "Black Friday—I'm working overtime. I have to be in at six."

"Six in the morning?" I cry. "Who in their right mind wants to buy a TV that early? These people aren't getting enough tryptophan if they're up and at 'em the morning after Thanksgiving."

Rose Gold shrugs.

"Why don't you leave Adam here with me, then?" I suggest. "That way Mary doesn't have to come over at the crack of dawn to pick him up."

Rose Gold considers the proposition. "Okay," she says after a few seconds. "If you're sure you don't mind."

I clap in excitement. This is the first time she's agreed to leave us alone for an extended period. A whole day with little Adam—the possibilities are endless.

By the time I finish my second helping, I can no longer ignore that Rose Gold's plate is still full. "Darling, you haven't eaten much. Everything taste okay?" She wouldn't dare insult my magnum opus.

Rose Gold nods and takes a bite of the potatoes. "It's all delicious."

"You can't keep working these hours and feeding a baby on so little food. You have to keep your strength up," I say. "If not for yourself, then at least for Adam." I scowl at my daughter. "Promise?"

"Okay, okay." Rose Gold puts her hands up in surrender, glancing at the baby with concern. "I promise."

Satisfied, I nod and get up. I open the freezer door to search for the vanilla ice cream. I want it to soften to get to the perfect consistency to pair with my pies. I search every shelf, but can't find the tub anywhere.

"Did you eat the ice cream?" I ask, turning to Rose Gold.

She examines a piece of turkey on her fork. "I put it in the basement freezer," she says, "to make room for my milk."

I put my hands on my hips. She knows I hate the basement. The upstairs freezer has plenty of space.

"Would you mind going to get it?" I haven't been down there since I moved home.

Rose Gold grimaces. "I would, but I made a promise to someone that I'd eat all this food." She gestures to her overflowing plate and sticks the piece of turkey in her mouth. "I've got a lot of work to do." She chews and smiles sweetly. Someone still hasn't learned who's in charge here.

I grit my teeth and walk out of the room. She watches me go.

I open the door to the basement. I can see the gleaming white freezer to the right of the staircase. I'll run down, find the ice cream, and come right back up.

I take a tentative first step down the stairs. Think of Adam. Second step. Think of Rose Gold. Third step. Adam. Fourth step. Rose Gold. Seventh step. Dad. Ninth step. Mom. Tenth step. Him. My mouth dries. My knees buckle. I slide to a sitting position on the stair, breathing hard. I peer at the rafters. My brother, David, swings from one end.

Dad and the paramedics took David away before I got home from school. Sometimes I forget I wasn't there, but I might as well have watched his suicide for the number of times I've pictured my seventeen-year-old brother alone here. In reality, the last time I saw David was that morning at the breakfast table. I don't think either of us said goodbye before I flew out the door to catch the bus. I was seven.

He used Dad's belt, the one that had beaten us bloody hundreds of times. Dad never used that belt, or any other, on me again.

"You find it?" Rose Gold calls from the table.

I push myself off the step and return to standing. My legs shake. I get the ice cream out of the freezer and climb the stairs. I head for the bathroom instead of the kitchen and lock the door behind me. I set the ice cream on the counter and sit on the toilet with my head between my knees. When my pulse returns to normal, I splash water on my face in the sink. I watch beads drip down my nose and cheeks.

After a few minutes, I'm in control again, ready to face her. I head back down the hallway. Out of habit, I try Rose Gold's bedroom door, forgetting for a second she's in the house and might hear me. As always, the door is locked. I'm no closer to figuring out why. It's time to start unraveling this mystery.

A couple days ago, I tried to force my way into the room through her window, but the window is also locked and heavy and old. It didn't budge. I panted outside in the cold with my hands on my knees and remembered the abandoned house with eyes. I peeked over my shoulder. A curtain moved in the window of the Thompsons' house. A chill dove down my spine.

I am never alone here, even when I'm the only one home.

When I come back to the table, I'm pleased to find barely any food on Rose Gold's plate. She takes a final bite of turkey. I pull the pies out of the refrigerator. I set them and the ice cream on the table.

Rose Gold groans and laughs. "Not dessert too." She shows no signs of remorse for the hell she has put me through—back when I was on trial or now.

I will myself to relax. "What kind of Thanksgiving dinner doesn't have pie?" I scoff. "You're getting the real deal today, kiddo." I dish a piece of chess and apple pie each onto my plate. I top them with a scoop of ice cream.

"I'll just have a bite of yours," she says, lifting a little chess pie off my plate and into her mouth. I scoot my plate closer to her in case she wants more, and watch my daughter. Maybe she's ready to talk.

I muster as much nonchalance as I can manage. "So," I begin, "why did you really buy my parents' old house?"

Rose Gold glances up, taken aback—or pretends to be anyway. "I told you: as a surprise for you. To help you move on."

"And I told *you* about my dad's abuse," I say, trying not to grit my teeth. "Not to mention my brother's suicide in the basement. You thought it was a good idea to force me to relive those memories?"

Rose Gold cocks her head, studying me. "Don't you think it's time to stop letting your dead dad control your life?"

"He does not control my life," I start to protest before I realize what she's doing. She's forcing me on the defensive, putting me back on trial at my own kitchen table. This is an interrogation of *her*, not me.

"Then why are you still afraid of this house?" Rose Gold continues. "Your dad's been dead for decades. He's not going to pop out of the wall and hit you."

Time to change tack. I twirl my fork in my hand and gaze at Adam, who is awake in his bassinet and watching me. "You know," I say casually, "by two months old, most babies recognize their mother's voice and face. Have you ever noticed Adam doesn't turn his head when you talk?"

Rose Gold winces, as if she's been stabbed through the heart. "That's not true."

I shrug. "He doesn't seem very bonded to you." I let Adam wrap his fingers around mine.

Panic fills Rose Gold's face. She scoops Adam out of his bassinet and holds him close, searching his face for clues. "He's a good baby," she says, more to herself than to me.

"He is," I agree. "He doesn't cry at all when you're gone."

She jerks her head up and stares at me. I smile warmly at her. She bites her lip—doubt piles on top of fear. I can almost see the wheels turning in her head. She's wondering if I'm telling the truth, if I'm right about Adam. Maybe this conversation will make her realize she needs to focus on taking care of her family instead of pushing us away. Maybe she'll start worrying more about the future and less about the past.

We finish our dessert in silence. I offer Rose Gold another bite, but she shakes her head no. Her eyes are glued to Adam's face as she rocks him.

As soon as my plate is empty, Rose Gold stands up and hands Adam to me. "You go relax in your chair," she says, patting me on the back. "If you don't mind keeping an eye on Adam while I clean?"

"Of course not," I say, shuffling to my BarcaLounger with the baby in my arms.

This is more like it. I hate to make my daughter doubt her mothering capabilities, but I'm not going to be terrorized or condescended to in my own house. I'll restore Rose Gold's confidence as soon as she falls in line. I need to know for sure that she's moved past this childish desire to get back at me.

An hour later, Rose Gold joins me, plopping down in the other chair. "All clean," she announces. She turns to me. "This was the best Thanksgiving I've had in a long time."

"Me too." I smile, remembering the last five Thanksgivings of freeze-dried turkey and watery mashed potatoes served on cafeteria trays with plastic utensils. Every time I think of the grocery store debacle, I'll replay this compliment. I decide to forgive my daughter for her earlier mistreatment.

Rose Gold turns on the TV. I wait to make sure she isn't watching the news, then doze off.

I wake up to Rose Gold patting my arm. "We're going to bed," she whispers. "Night, Mom."

She carries Adam down the hall. "Are you ready for sleep?" she asks him. "Will you dream of puppies? Or maybe kitties?" She closes the door behind her and begins to sing to him.

I stretch, long and lazy, then pull myself out of the chair. Yawning, I amble through the kitchen on my way to bed. I open the fridge. A dozen plastic containers of food are stacked neatly. The countertops and kitchen table are spotless. Rose Gold's done a thorough job of cleaning up my mess. Then I spot a forgotten Ziploc bag, filled with bacon grease, on top of the refrigerator. I pick it up and carry it out the side door, remembering how delicious the stuffing was.

The floodlights turn on. I step outside into the freezing night. I open the garbage can and toss the bag of grease into it. I'm about to replace the lid when I notice a bit of loose food underneath a black garbage bag. I make tsk-tsk noises with my mouth—if there's a hole in the bag, Rose Gold should know better than to leave the garbage spilling out. Forget the plundering raccoons; the garbage men have strict rules. Everything has to be bagged.

I pull the bag of trash out of the can, expecting its contents to spill everywhere. Instead, the bag holds its shape. I lift it to eye level, examining for tears. There aren't any. I peer into the can. Inside are turkey, mashed potatoes, candied yams, broccoli casserole, cranberry sauce, and butternut squash—about one plate's worth. I think back to Rose Gold's empty plate when I came back from the bathroom.

Well, what do you know? My daughter is hiding something from me. That something appears to be an eating disorder. I've turned a blind eye to it this long, but the facts are slapping me in the face. Her shrinking frame, granola bars for meals, hiding the food she's throwing away: I can't deny it anymore.

All these years, I've been telling people she was sick.

Look who was right after all.

12

Rose Gold

January 2015

I eyed the cartons of Chinese food. Alex and Whitney were already digging in, chopsticks between their fingers. I had never tried using chopsticks. My first attempt would not be in front of them.

"Can I have a fork?" I said to the space between them.

Alex didn't stop eating. Whitney mumbled, "Drawer to the right of the fridge," while continuing to scroll through her phone.

When I came back, they'd started discussing plans for the night, calling out options that materialized from their screens.

"Jenna wants to go to the Hangge Uppe," Alex said.

"Dollar bottles at Kelsey's," Whitney volunteered. "Some of the basketball team is going."

"Tyler and the guys are going to Kirkwood." Alex took a sip of pink wine from her stemless glass. I examined the bottle label—Sutter Home White Zinfandel—and made a mental note to buy that wine on my twenty-first birthday. Less than a month now.

My pocket vibrated. I pulled out my phone and took a bite of

Mongolian beef. The meat was lukewarm, but still tasty—both savory and sweet, which I'd come to realize was my favorite flavor combination.

> **Dad:** Anna can't stop talking about her ear piercings. She
> said all the girls at school love her earrings

Two months had passed since I'd stayed the night at Dad's house in Indiana. I'd seen the Gillespies a handful of times since then. On my last trip, I'd convinced Dad and Kim to let Anna get her ears pierced, thinking cute earrings might help with her self-consciousness. After some hemming and hawing on Dad's part, he'd finally agreed. Kim, Anna, and I had piled into their car and driven to the mall, where we'd found the Claire's boutique and requested one set of pierced ears, please. Anna and I had painstakingly weighed the pros and cons of pink versus purple studs. In the end, she chose pink. When the technician brought out the gun, Anna squeezed Kim's hand with her left and mine with her right. But she didn't cry, barely even flinched. Afterward, she was ecstatic.

> **Dad:** She let Kim put her hair in a ponytail for the first time in
> a year
> **Dad:** Thank you so much, Rose

I smiled, proud to have had the answer for once, to finally belong somewhere. I had never fit in at school, but because of me, Anna would.

> **Me:** I'm just glad I could help
> **Me:** Also, I made it to Alex's okay. She says hi

I took a photo of Alex while she wasn't paying attention and sent it to him.

Dad: Tell her hi back. And make sure you take it easy this
weekend, okay? Be safe

He'd become even more attentive since I'd told him about my cancer diagnosis, offering to come to chemo appointments with me. I said
no, of course, explaining Mrs. Stone would be crushed if she couldn't
take me. The few times Dad and I had gotten together since then, at
his house or at Tina's Café near me, he'd been surprised by how
healthy I looked. I pointed out not everyone loses their hair during
chemo. I was nauseated and fatigued, I told him, and had no appetite.
To prove it, I had two measly bites of a breadstick when I met all the
Gillespies for dinner at an Olive Garden one Sunday. They'd watched
me with pity, but still no one mentioned the camping trip. When I
brought it up over dessert, Dad patted my back. He said being that far
from medical care wasn't a good idea.

Didn't see that coming.

Still, I insisted I'd be done with chemo well before the trip. I told
them my doctor said I'd be fine to travel this summer. Now, as a show
of good health, I'd come to stay with Alex. If I could already handle a
weekend with friends, Dad and Kim would have to let me go with
them six months from now. Road trip games, stargazing, Dad putting
his arm around me by the campfire—this vacation would be the best
weeks of my life.

"I'm sick of Kirkwood," Whitney was saying.

"I want to see Tyler," Alex pouted.

"Who's Tyler?" I asked.

Alex jerked her head in surprise, as though she'd forgotten I was
there. She probably had.

"The guy I'm seeing," Alex said, swinging that long blond ponytail off her shoulder. She turned to Whitney. "We're going to Kirkwood. You owe me one."

Whitney didn't argue. Based on my observations of her and Alex's friendship, she was constantly repaying Alex for invisible good deeds.

Whitney sighed and started clearing away the Chinese food. "Fine. Then I'm borrowing your new leather jacket."

I followed Alex to her bedroom. She began applying makeup in the dresser mirror. I sat cross-legged on her bed. "What kind of bar is Kirkwood?" I asked.

"Sports bar."

"So I shouldn't get dressed up?"

"We always get dressed up. But you don't have to." She paused, lipstick tube in hand, to study me. Then she went back to her makeup.

"How do you choose a lipstick shade?"

"Depends on your skin tone," Alex said. "Cool tones make your teeth look whiter."

I made a note to research "cool tones" later. The right lipstick would make my future teeth look even better.

"You have a fake ID?" Alex asked.

She could be so thick. *Yes, Alex, I had my first drink a year ago with you, haven't had one since, and spend all my time selling video games to teenage boys. I totally have a fake ID.*

"No," I said.

"Ohhh," Alex said. She sounded like the *Wheel of Fortune* audience when a contestant missed a no-brainer puzzle. "Kirkwood is twenty-one and up."

I stared at her. "Do you have a fake ID?"

She bit her lip. "When I turned twenty-one, I sold it to a girl at work who looks like me."

"What are we going to do?" I asked.

"What do you mean 'we'? You've been here before. You know Chicago bars are twenty-one plus."

"Can't Tyler meet us somewhere else?"

Alex gawked at me as if I'd suggested Tyler waltz in front of a snowplow. "I didn't ask you to come this weekend. You invited yourself."

My mouth hung open.

Whitney sashayed into the room. "Carmen is going to Kirkwood too," she announced. She stopped when she saw my expression. "What's with Sally Sadface over here?"

Without a trace of remorse, Alex said, "Rose Gold isn't twenty-one. She's not coming."

She finished her lipstick and then turned back to me. "But my DVR is full, so you can watch anything you want. There's a makeover show that might be of interest."

Whitney tittered. I flushed.

Alex continued. "We'll have a girls' day tomorrow. How about that?" I hated her patronizing tone, hated every rotten thing about her.

"We have those face masks," Whitney said.

"I've been wanting to tint and wax my eyebrows for weeks," Alex added. She glanced at my forehead. "We can wax yours too."

The two girls eyed each other, making tiny adjustments to their hair, tops, and lips before scurrying out the door. They laughed and yelled until I couldn't hear them anymore. They had ditched me in minutes.

I wanted to stab something sharp and poisonous through Alex's face, but she wasn't here. Instead I found a pair of scissors and got ready to cut the head off Bobo, her childhood teddy bear. I'd pull Bobo's eyes from his face, leave the two buttons on her dresser, and throw the bear in a dumpster down the street. I watched the scene play out before my eyes, but in the end, I had to leave him be. I'd known Bobo as long as I'd known Alex, and it wasn't his fault she was a terrible person.

Afterward, I was tired from all the screaming, so I lay on the couch, turned on the TV, and flipped through the channels until I found *10 Things I Hate About You.* I'd moved on lately to all the nineties teen movies I'd missed, and while I usually loved this one, I couldn't stop fuming over Alex. Three hours I'd driven to see her. She deserved to lose more than a beloved toy.

I walked back to Alex's room and dug through the bag of makeup she'd been ransacking an hour ago. The shade of lipstick she'd used was called Raspberry Kisses. I puckered my lips and applied the color the way I'd watched Alex do. In the mirror, a healthier, prettier version of me gazed back. I put the lipstick in my pocket.

I jammed the bottles and pencils back in her makeup bag. When was someone going to teach Alex she couldn't treat people like crap and get away with it? All her life, she'd done whatever she wanted, and because she was pretty and charming, nobody ever told her off.

I opened and closed the bathroom medicine cabinet. Nothing of interest. Under the sink, I found hair accessories, cold medicine, shaving cream, a box of tampons, and a bottle of depilatory cream. Unfamiliar with the word, I turned the bottle around and read the back label.

A quick and pain-free way to say goodbye to unwanted hair.

Skeptically, I applied the lotion to a small patch of hair on my thigh. I waited eight minutes instead of the instructed five, because five was bad luck, then wiped the patch with a washcloth. My hair came off.

Why had no one told me about this stuff?

I applied the cream to both my thighs and bikini area and kept rummaging while I waited for my phone timer to ring. Alex and Whitney's organization system made no sense. In the bottom drawer, I found a bunch of Band-Aids and a box of blond hair dye.

The timer sounded. I wiped my bikini line and legs clean. Alex would use that blond dye to tint her eyebrows the next day. Picking up the dye box again, I peered inside. The bottle's seal had been broken. I removed the cap and sniffed the colorant, wincing at the chemical scent. I placed the brow dye on the counter next to the depilatory cream and gazed at the two products side by side. My lips curled at the ends before I even knew I'd made a decision.

Being adored was easy when you were pretty. But if you took away Alex's beauty, what was she?

Another Rose Gold.

———————

B y the time my rage had worn off, it was too late.

I didn't sleep at all that night, tossing and turning while I thought about the bottle under the bathroom sink. Twice before Alex and Whitney came home, I got off the couch to throw it away.

Then I'd remember Alex skipping out her front door, leaving me behind without so much as a glance. I forced myself back to the couch, back under the thin blanket. When Alex and Whitney came stumbling home at two in the morning, I pretended to be asleep. They were too drunk to notice or care.

Now it was noon. They were each lying on a couch, hungover and moaning. I was sitting on the floor, intimate with the concept of having your heart in your throat. I worried I might throw up, that the guilt was plain on my face.

"When are we starting this girls' day?" I asked, voice squeaking.

Both girls groaned.

"Alex, you promised," I forced myself to say. "Come on, I'll get everything ready."

"Fine," Alex said, a sleeping mask covering her eyes. "The face masks and hair dye are in the bathroom. Get a face towel from the hall closet too."

I sprang up from the floor. I had to calm down. As slowly as possible, I walked to the bathroom. I brought the stuff back to the living room, where Whitney and Alex were drinking red Gatorades. I placed each item before Alex, like an altar offering. She scanned all of it. I wondered if she could hear my heartbeat.

Alex motioned for me to sit in front of her. I leaned in. She applied the exfoliating mask to my clean face. The pads of her fingertips were gentle.

"Your skin is so soft," she said with real admiration.

I watched her focused face while she worked, regretting what I'd done.

"How long do I leave this on?" I asked.

"Five minutes," she said.

I nodded. I would do eight.

"Whit, you want to do my brows?" Alex asked, lying back on the couch.

Whitney grabbed the face towel and covered Alex's eyes and the rest of her face below them. All I could see were her eyebrows and forehead. Whitney yawned and pulled the brush and bottle of dye from the box. She shook the bottle, then loosened its lid, not bothering to put on the gloves. She'd performed this ritual for Alex many times.

After a few minutes of Whitney's dabbing, Alex's eyebrows were coated in purplish cream. Whitney put all the supplies back in the box, then turned on the TV and flipped to a channel with cartoons. She slumped against the couch and closed her eyes.

I counted every second—one-Mississippi, two-Mississippi—in my head. After four minutes, I wondered if Alex had fallen asleep under the towel. Whitney hadn't stirred. I resisted the urge to say anything.

"You going to take this off or what?" Alex said. I fled from the room.

My hands shook. I splashed water on my face again and again, long after my skin had been cleared of the grainy cream. I dried my face with a towel. I stared at myself in the mirror. I was even paler than normal.

A shriek came from the living room. Whitney's.

I wanted to stay in the bathroom, lock the door until this was all over. But the old Rose Gold would come running as soon as she heard her friend's alarm.

I dashed back to the living room.

"Your eyebrow is coming off," Whitney cried, staring at the damp paper towel in her hand.

Alex ripped the towel off her face. "What do you mean, coming off?" She recoiled in horror when she saw the hair on Whitney's paper towel. "What did you do?" She ran past me to the bathroom. Her right eyebrow was missing. Not just sparse—the hair was gone.

Alex let out a bloodcurdling scream. Whitney and I exchanged a look, then rushed after Alex to the bathroom.

"Where the fuck is my eyebrow?" she yelled when we reached her.

"I don't know what happened," Whitney said in panicked confusion. "It . . . came off."

"I can see that, you dipshit," Alex snapped.

Whitney bristled. "I told you you're not supposed to use old hair dye."

"You think my hair fell out because the dye is expired?" Alex thundered. "How fucking stupid are you?"

I watched Whitney try to redirect Alex's wrath away from herself. "What are we going to do about your other eyebrow?"

Alex gaped at the mirror and moaned. "Try to get this shit off without any hair coming out." Whitney moved to grab toilet paper, but Alex snarled, "I'll do it myself."

Whitney and I watched with held breath. Alex dampened a wad of toilet paper with water from the faucet. Even with the lightest touch possible, the cream still stole her hair when she blotted it away. She managed to salvage some of her left eyebrow, but the effect was almost worse. I could tell Whitney was thinking the same thing, but neither of us dared suggest that Alex finish the job and go for a hairless forehead.

If Tyler could see her now, I thought in spite of my terror.

By then, Alex was bawling, hangover long forgotten. "Look"— sob—"what"—sob—"you"—sob—"did," she cried. I had never seen Alex lose her marbles before. I kept reminding myself that she'd had this coming. No one should be able to be so awful for so long and get away with it. I'd taught my mother that lesson the hard way.

Whitney apologized over and over. "What can I do?" she pleaded.

"You've done enough," Alex screeched. She ran to her bedroom and slammed the door behind her. Then Whitney and I were alone in the bathroom.

I turned to face Whitney. Tears brimmed in her eyes. "I think I should go," I whispered, patting her shoulder. "She'll be all right."

Whitney followed me to the living room, like a lost puppy in her own apartment. For the first time, I felt a swell of power. I had the ability to make those girls behave the way I wanted. Maybe I couldn't force them to like me, but I could punish them if they didn't.

I picked up my paper bag of sleepover items, ensuring I had everything with me. I was never coming back. Whitney walked me to the door, crestfallen.

"Thanks for letting me stay over," I said. "Sorry it ended on such a crummy note."

Whitney nodded, in a trance.

I couldn't help myself. Before I left, I lowered my voice. "She's just so *tragic.*"

13

Patty

I raise my knuckles to the familiar door and knock with more confidence than I feel. For weeks I've been trying to work up an excuse
to pay Mary Stone a visit. The discovery of my daughter's eating disorder is as good a reason as any. Mary might be able to abandon me,
but she won't leave poor Rose Gold to the Big Bad Wolf.

I found the discarded Thanksgiving food a week ago. Since then
I can't decide what to do with my daughter. Reasoning hasn't worked.
Leaving her to her own devices is not an option. I've never been above
seeking outside help, particularly if it involves a good and petty "told
you so."

Someone pads down the hallway. The door will swing open in a
few seconds. Mary doesn't peek through the peephole before she opens
her door. How many times have I told her she's too trusting? She's going to wind up in the trunk of someone's car.

The door opens, and the expression on Mary's face is warm. Then she recognizes who's standing on her doorstep. By now I'm used to people's smiles turning into frowns when they see me.

"I told you you're not welcome here," Mary says. She starts to close the door.

"Wait," I say, pushing back against it. "It's Rose Gold. I think she's in trouble."

Mary hesitates, watching me. Then she sighs and opens the door wide. "Come in," she says.

Bingo.

The house is just as I remember it, painted and carpeted in Easter pastels. Mary's collection of angel statues in the living room has somehow grown—there must be more than fifty now, fashioned from ceramic, concrete, glass, wood, and marble. I wonder if she's ever driven past a yard sale without stopping.

I sit on the couch. Two glass bowls are on the coffee table: one full of potpourri, the other of M&M's. I'm already concocting a slapstick routine that involves pretending to eat a handful of the dried petals, but remind myself this is supposed to be a somber visit. I am here to play the role of Concerned Mother. I grab a handful of M&M's. Concerned Mothers still need to eat.

"What do you want, Patty?" Mary says.

I toss the M&M's into my mouth. "I think Rose Gold is sick."

Mary's face softens. "Sick how? Is this an emergency?" She reaches for her phone.

"No, no," I reassure her. I stare at my folded hands in my lap, like this is hard for me to say. Timing is key before a big reveal. You want your audience on the edge of their seats, hanging on your every word.

Mary leans forward, as if she can read my mind. "Are you going to tell me what's wrong with her?"

I take a deep breath. "I think Rose Gold has an eating disorder."

I've played Mary's reaction a hundred times in my head, but never did I imagine it would be a laugh of disbelief. She crosses her arms. "Funny, she never had any trouble with food while you were in prison."

"How do you know?" I ask.

"She used to come over here for dinner all the time," Mary says, gazing at the cherubs dancing on her fireplace mantel. "She usually had multiple helpings."

"How do you know she didn't make herself throw up afterward?"

Mary's expression darkens. "I know."

"How?" I prod.

She sighs. "I would have known if she went to the bathroom every time we finished dinner. She didn't. She helped me clear the table, and then we'd come in here. I never heard her get sick—not while she was pregnant, and certainly not before."

"She could have waited until she got home," I insist, trying to fit the puzzle pieces together.

"Patty, she was over here for hours after dinner sometimes. We'd watch a movie or just talk."

I try not to picture Mary Stone serving as Rose Gold's surrogate mother. The image makes me feel like tiny spiders are crawling all over my body.

Mary crosses her arms. "You're doing it again."

I study her, questioning.

"Creating an illness where there isn't one," she says, lips forming a tight line.

If Rose Gold doesn't have an eating disorder, why have I never seen her eat? I turn the question over and over in my mind. She doesn't eat my meals, but she doesn't make her own either. I haven't seen her eat more than a few pieces of toast and granola bars since I moved in with her. My silence continues for a beat too long.

"You don't know what you're talking about," I say, keeping my voice steady.

"Here's what I know," she says. "The only time Rose Gold has looked healthy in her entire life was during the five years you were locked up."

I picture my friend Mary up on the mantel among her angels, stripped naked, hot tar poured down her back, wearing seraph's wings of filthy pigeon feathers. She holds her hands together in prayer.

"We've all seen her jogging around town," Mary says, gritting her teeth. "That girl is being starved or poisoned again. She may not be able to see through you, but the rest of us are watching. We know you brainwashed her. And if baby Adam so much as catches a cold on your watch, I'll call the police so fast, you won't see the handcuffs coming."

I suppose I shouldn't be surprised by the accusation, given all I've been through. The truth is, I haven't put anything in her food. Rose Gold and I have been sharing meals, which means if I'd tainted the casseroles or soups, I'd also have been poisoning myself. Even if she were ridiculous enough to be afraid of my cooking, that doesn't explain why she's not making her own food.

"I know she started visiting you during your last year in prison," Mary says. "Before that, she hated your guts, wanted nothing to do with you. I don't know how you changed her mind, but since then, she's been acting different."

"Different how?" I ask.

"That's enough questions. It's high time you left my house." She ushers me—rather forcefully, I might add—off her couch and down the hallway.

As I near the door, something clicks into place. Mary thinks I'm to blame for Rose Gold's size. They all think I'm to blame. What if that's what Rose Gold wants? What if she's trying to turn them all against me by pretending to be sick?

"If you love Rose Gold, if you're even capable of love, you will move out of her house and leave her alone." Mary opens the door and shoves me outside.

"Mary—"

She silences me with a stony expression. "Take care, Patty."

The door closes in my face. I am left standing on her stoop, speechless. The dead bolt clicks.

I pound on the door. "Mary, what if she's making it up?"

No response.

I pound again. "Mary!"

Still no response.

I pound a third time. "Mary, maybe she's lying."

On the other side of the door, Mary sighs. "I was there for you," she says, sounding more tired than angry now. "I held your hand and listened to you cry. I made you dinners and gave you money. You were like a sister"—here her voice wobbles, and I can tell she's trying not to cry—"to me."

I hang my head. She clears her throat. I imagine her dabbing her eyes, regaining her composure. I hear her pad down the hallway. She's done with me.

I move away from the front door and sit on the stoop, my head in my hands. I don't think I can muster another ounce of peppy Patty positivity today.

One afternoon Mary and I decided to make French macarons. I got powdered sugar and almond flour everywhere when I forgot to put the lid on the food processor. By the time we'd piped the batter onto baking sheets and cleaned up the kitchen, we were exhausted. We settled onto Mary's couch to catch up on *All My Children* and were horrified when our favorite hunk, Leo du Pres, plummeted to his death over Miller's Falls. While our macarons burned in the oven, we made plans to send an angry letter to the showrunners, demanding Leo's return. We never did write that letter.

One spring Mary and I signed up for a 5K. For months we trained side by side, progressing from walking to slow jogging to running the three miles. Together we raised five hundred dollars from our neighbors and donated the money to the Leukemia & Lymphoma Society. On the morning of the race, we both had nervous jitters. Our goal was to finish in thirty-five minutes. We'd just crossed the starting line when Mary tripped over a stick and twisted her ankle. She insisted she still wanted to complete the race and could walk if I supported some of her weight. We crossed the finish line an hour and twelve minutes after we started.

One September Mary and I took the girls to the nearby cul-de-sac for wheelbarrow races. Rose Gold had been bedridden for days. She was too weak to run around outside, but she was bored out of her skull. So Mary and I wheeled her and Alex around in circles, huffing and puffing and laughing at how out of shape we were. Mr. Grover, a crotchety old man, stopped us for a lecture about the appropriate uses of wheelbarrows. Every time he turned to face Mary, I made hand puppets behind his back and imitated his stern expression, while Mary tried not to laugh. She even rolled her eyes once—the Mary equivalent of giving someone the finger—while he was chastising me.

I realize I have lost my closest friend, maybe for good. Even if I can get her to come to the door, she won't believe me.

I turn and begin the long walk home, concentrating on the sidewalk in front of me. Glassy eyes peer from dark garages and second-floor windows. Every time I leave the house, everywhere I go—they watch me. I feel their eyes on me in the shower, while I'm napping in my recliner. They crawl across my skin, but when I look, they aren't there.

I speed up, distract myself by replaying the conversation with Mary. I keep coming back to the same question: *is Rose Gold sick or not?* If not, what does she hope to gain by faking an eating disorder?

Attention? Sympathy? Making my neighbors hate me even more? Regardless of her motive, if she's starving herself, that still means she's sick, right? Maybe she has depression or an adrenal insufficiency or cancer. Shouldn't I find her some help?

When I get back, I pace the house, nervous energy burning me up. Rose Gold won't be home for a while. She took Adam to the pediatrician for his vaccines.

I sit in my recliner, but my legs won't stop trembling. I stand and pace the house some more. I need to shake off that visit to Mary—I can't strategize until I calm down. Maybe Rose Gold has the right idea with exercise.

In my bedroom, I change into sweatpants and a ratty old T-shirt under the gaze of the watery blue eyes on the ceiling. I tie the laces of a pair of gym shoes. My legs are leaden, but I walk to the kitchen and fill a water bottle under the faucet. I screw on the bottle top. I search the living room and kitchen to see if Rose Gold has one of those iPods for listening to music, but I don't see one anywhere. Finally, I head toward the basement. Jogging outside, with all those evil eyes watching me, is out of the question. That leaves me with one option.

I breathe in, breathe out, then twist the basement door handle. I descend the stairs, keeping my eyes on the floor. The rafters are all I can think about, but that doesn't mean I have to look at them. I scurry to the treadmill. *Stay focused on the task at hand.*

Rose Gold has tucked it into a corner so the right and back sides of the machine are nearly flush with the walls. I climb on and press the start button.

The machine's screen illuminates, but the digits in the speed section are gibberish. I sigh, pressing the button to increase speed. This is what Rose Gold gets for picking up someone else's trash. There's a reason our neighbor was about to throw this old thing away.

The treadmill belt still isn't moving. I press the buttons harder. The list of people who have humiliated me in this town is getting long. Someday they'll regret the way they've treated me. I jab the ^ button, pretending it's Mary Stone's face. The nerve of that—

The treadmill belt rips to life under my feet. The garbled numbers on the screen straighten themselves. I recognize a speed of 16.5. The force of the machine flings me backward. I flail my arms, try to lean forward, but the belt throws me off.

My back hits the wall with a thud, knocking the breath out of me. A burning pain screams from my lower shins. I glance down and see my feet are wedged between the wall and the treadmill belt. It peels layer after layer of bloody skin from my shins.

I am screaming. Watching my own legs get shaved like gyros on a spit. The treadmill belt has blood stuck to it. I might pass out. I flail. I fall to my left. My palms smash into the concrete. I pull my legs toward me. They're still burning. I glance at my shins—free now, but a bloody wreck.

The treadmill is plugged into the wall outlet beside me. From my position on the floor, I rip the cord from the wall. The belt stops. The machine is silent. I'm still screaming. My throat is dry. I close my mouth.

I can't tell if the ringing in my ears is from shock or pain or all the yelling. I lie on the floor for another minute, eyes closed. The concrete is cool against my cheek. My shins throb. I examine them. They'll be a mess to clean, but nothing Neosporin and bandages can't fix. I will be okay. Someday this will be a funny story, maybe.

Overhead: footsteps. Someone is whistling a song from *The Little Mermaid*. The one Ursula sings in her lair.

Rose Gold.

Has she been home the whole time? Was she up there, listening to me scream in pain? Or am I being paranoid? Maybe I'm still a little woozy from the accident.

"Rose Gold?" I call out.

The whistling stops. The basement door opens.

My daughter chirps, "Coming, Mom!"

14

Rose Gold

July 2015

It was not the greeting I'd been hoping for.

"Rose, what are you doing here?"

Dad jogged across the street, away from the blue SUV he was packing in his driveway. I opened my van door and jumped down from the driver's seat.

"Hi, Dad," I said.

The door to the Gillespies' house opened. Sophie came out first, carrying thick sleeping bags under each arm. Billy Jr. carried two paper bags of groceries. Kim followed them, but spotted me before either of the kids did. She frowned. I hadn't seen that frown since my first dinner at the Gillespies' house. She'd been much nicer to me since she found out about my cancer.

I'd seen the Gillespies at least once a month since our first dinner eight months ago. Since Anna's ear piercing outing, even Sophie and Billy Jr. were being nice to me. Dad and Kim had been especially hospitable. Sometimes I felt like an actual member of their family.

Dad stopped next to the van, letting the duffel bag on his shoulder slide to the ground. Out of breath, he said, "We talked about this on the phone. You can't come with us to Yellowstone."

Actually, he had said *it wasn't a good idea, given my condition.* But he'd never said no. I'd come prepared.

I pulled the folded note from my pocket and pushed it into Dad's hand. "My doctor says I'm fine to travel."

Dad glanced down at the note, squinting while he read.

I'd made up some mysterious postexercise chest pains to get a doctor's appointment. After the nurse took my vitals and left, I locked the door and dug through the cabinets until I found Dr. Stanton's prescription pad. I took two pages from the pad—one for practice—and tucked them into my purse. I unlocked the door and was back on the exam table before Dr. Stanton knocked. He and I agreed we'd *keep an eye on* the chest pain.

I was beginning to understand how my mother had gotten away with all those lies for so many years. Doctors were walking Band-Aids; they were eager to fix every leak, squeak, and pain. All you had to do was provide your medical background, list your symptoms, and ask for help. Dr. Stanton assumed I was telling him the truth. The two of us were a team with the same goal in mind. Model patient was a role I'd mastered decades ago.

And yes, I realize the hypocrisy of lying about being sick while condemning my mother for the same act. The difference is her lies hurt someone. My lie was supposed to heal, to strengthen the bond between father and daughter.

Dad handed the note back to me. "I'm glad Dr. Stanton thinks you're doing so well," he said. He didn't meet my eyes, though. I'd learned the meaning behind that cue years ago. When I was a kid, every adult about to give me bad news—doctors, teachers, my mother—avoided looking at me.

"You still can't come," he continued.

"But why?" I asked, failing to keep the disappointment from my tone. "I'm done with chemo. Dr. Stanton says everything looks good."

I was beginning to regret this whole cancer story.

"All I do these days is worry about you," Dad said, frowning. "I'm tired. This is my vacation too. I need a break from"—he gesticulated at me—"this. It's too much."

He gazed back at his family. They kept packing the car. He straightened. "This is *my* family trip."

My fists clenched. "But I am your family."

"You know what I mean." Dad looked away.

I thought about the fishing pole, jumbo marshmallows, and bag of charcoal in the backseat of my van. I had seen Sophie's Facebook post the night before, saying the Gillespies were leaving at nine sharp this morning for their big trip. I'd left my apartment at three a.m. to make sure I didn't miss them."

"I can't believe you're not going to let me come," I said, crossing my arms.

Dad chewed his lip. "Why don't you spend the weekend with Alex?"

I tried not to laugh. I hadn't seen or heard from Alex in six months. A week after the eyebrow fiasco, she'd sent me a text.

Alex: i know what you did. don't ever contact me again

I didn't respond. I had to hand it to Whitney—she was smarter than I'd thought. Apparently she'd passed the "tragic" comment along to Alex, and one or both of them had put two and two together. I couldn't blame either of them for not wanting to be friends with me anymore. What friend left another friend eyebrow-less?

I wasn't sure how to react to the loss of Alex. She'd been my friend since we were kids. But was it a loss if that friend treated you like crap? Without her to text the daily minutiae about my life, I'd been texting Phil, and especially Dad, twice as much.

I shrugged. "She's out of town. I guess I'll go back to Deadwick and obsess over whether the chemo worked."

Dad glowered at me. "Don't do that," he snapped.

"Do what?"

"Try to guilt-trip me. I offered to come to all your appointments. You didn't want me there."

"Well, I need you now." I knew how pathetic I sounded, but the camping trip was slipping through my fingers. I peered at my brand-new hiking boots—I could already feel a blister forming on my right pinkie toe.

Dad hoisted the duffel back over his shoulder. "For Christ's sake," he said, exasperated. He gestured to the driveway. "You want to see us off or not?" I followed him across the street to his SUV.

Kim yelled inside the house, "Anna, we're leaving."

A few seconds later, Anna skipped out the door and down the driveway, holding a Frisbee and wearing a rainbow backpack. When she spotted me, she dropped the Frisbee and ran to my side.

"Rose, Rose," she yelled, hugging my legs. "Is Rose coming?" she asked Dad.

Dad shook his head.

I leaned down and hugged Anna. "I want to," I said. "But Dad won't let me."

"Why not, Daddy? Why?" Anna burst into tears. "I want Rose to come."

Dad's jaw tightened. "Get in the car, kids," he said, never taking his narrowed eyes off me.

Sophie and Billy Jr. stood limply while I hugged them goodbye. The kids climbed into the SUV and began arguing about whether they were going to play a game first or watch a movie. Anna was the only one bothered by my absence. Here I thought they had all accepted me.

"I really, really want to join you," I said to Kim, making one last-ditch effort. I hated the pleading tone in my voice.

Kim didn't say anything. She tilted her head and watched me. Her eyes rested on the ends of my hair, which by now grazed my shoulders. The kids had grown quiet in the car—eavesdropping, no doubt.

Dad broke the silence. "What did you say the name of your doctor was?"

"Dr. Stanton," I said. "Why?"

"What street is his office on?"

"Kinney," I answered. A bead of sweat formed at my hairline.

Dad pulled out his phone. "Why don't we give him a call," he said, impassive, "to make sure he's okay with this?"

I gnawed on my bottom lip, heart beating faster. "He's on vacation this week," I said. "Out of touch." I didn't like where this was going.

Dad touched a few buttons on his phone. "There must be an assistant or nurse we can talk to."

I snuck a peek at Kim. She wouldn't meet my gaze. I had to get out.

"Maybe you guys are right," I said. "Maybe this is too big a trip for me. I'll get out of your hair."

Dad and Kim watched me, both tense.

From the car, Billy Jr. gave me a small wave and sad half smile. Now that I too had been on the receiving end of Dad's meanness, he was willing to acknowledge me. I bet it wasn't often someone else served as Dad's punching bag.

I glared at Dad for a minute. He was supposed to be kind, a decent man. "I thought you cared," I spat, and marched down the driveway toward my van.

Before stepping into the street, I heard footsteps behind me. Dad grabbed my arm. I turned around, hoping my cheeks weren't as red as they felt.

"Rose, listen, I'm sorry," Dad said, and he did sound contrite. "I've been under a lot of stress, but I shouldn't have taken it out on you. I care about you. I do."

I waited for him to continue.

"I know I'm the parent here, so maybe I'm supposed to know what to do. But there's no rule book for getting to know your long-lost daughter. I feel like I'm botching things every step of the way." He rubbed his face, and for the first time, I saw how exhausted he was by all of this, by me. "Why don't you and I get together once I'm back from this trip?"

I nodded, not trusting myself to speak. He gave me an awkward hug before retreating to Kim's side. I waved to both of them, plastering a fake smile on my face. They waved back, studying me.

In my car, I pretended to get something from the glove box so they couldn't keep watching me. What parents wouldn't let their cancer-riddled daughter go on the family trip? Who the hell did they think they were, deciding my capabilities for me? Dad had already abandoned me once—now he was trying to do it again. But they weren't getting off that easy. When their car doors slammed, I sat upright.

Dad started his car, so I did the same. He was waiting for me to drive off, but I waved him on to let him go first.

I couldn't let the Disney on Ice disaster happen again.

They were not taking this trip without me.

The garage door closed. Dad eased the Explorer down the driveway. He honked when he passed me. Kim stared straight ahead. I watched them drive down the street and halt at the stop sign. I put the van in drive and followed them.

Ten minutes later, we reached a two-lane road with a bunch of strip malls on either side, and I realized Dad and Kim were watching me in their rearview mirror. I pretended not to see them. The first highway they needed—US-30 W—was coming up on the right. I'd memorized the twenty-four-hour-long route so I could help Dad navigate if their satellite signal didn't work.

But the SUV didn't get on the highway. Instead, Dad changed lanes. I did the same. Then, without much warning, he turned on his left blinker and pulled into a Subway parking lot. I pulled into the auto repair shop lot across the street and watched the Gillespies traipse inside Subway. Sophie glanced over her shoulder at my car. They all knew I was following them.

I gripped the steering wheel until my hands hurt. Mom once told me about her own childhood camping trip in Pokagon State Park. On the second day, a white skunk had wandered through their campsite. Her dad jumped onto the picnic table and froze, trying not to alarm the skunk. Mom said that was the one time she saw him scared. After the skunk moved on, the rest of the family burst out laughing at him. He looked, my mother said, like a robot turned off mid–dance move. They laughed until their stomachs hurt, until tears dripped off their faces and onto their melting sticks of ice cream. Weeks later, someone dubbed the close call "Pepé Le *Phew*."

I wanted my own close call, my own inside joke, a story retold at every family gathering. I wanted the bonfire smell to get stuck in my jacket—I'd been planning not to wash it for at least a couple months so I could sniff it every day back in Deadwick. I could almost taste the crunchy exterior of my roasted marshmallow, then the gooey inside as my teeth dug further. I was already sitting on a log, listening to Billy Jr. tell ghost stories, with Anna on my lap.

I thought I'd done everything right. I'd been polite and funny and laughed at all their jokes and gone out of my way to help them every chance I got. When Kim mentioned blisters from gardening, I'd bought her a pair of gloves. I told Dad over and over how lucky I was to call him my father. I'd helped Anna learn to love something she thought was ugly about herself; she wasn't scared to go to school anymore. How did they decide when I was good enough to be one of them and when I wasn't? Why wasn't I ever enough for anyone?

Don't get mad. Get even, she hissed.

Her instructions cleared my head. First I had to get rid of this van. It was too big, too recognizable. I googled the nearest bus station.

Twenty minutes later, I was examining the bus schedule and map. At the counter, I bought one ticket. We departed in an hour.

I spotted another Subway across the street and realized I was hungry. Sitting on one of the hard yellow benches with a ham-and-cheese sandwich in hand, I imagined I was with Dad's family, eating lunch alongside them.

"Ew, ham?" Billy Jr. said, wrinkling his nose. "Salami is the best."

"No, turkey is the best," Sophie corrected him.

"Rose Gold is right," Kim said, winking at me. "Ham is my favorite." She took a big bite of her sandwich and chewed, smiling.

A minute later, Kim began to cough. The cough turned into choking. She clutched her throat, motioning to Dad for his bottle of water, but he'd started choking too. Dad and Kim, red-faced and eyes bulging, stared at their four children.

We kids glared back.

"Let's get going," I said to the others, "if we want to get there in time to catch lightning bugs."

The kids nodded, rubbing their hands together with glee. Kim and Dad fell to the floor, writhing. Their faces turned purple. Sophie and I helped Anna hop over them on our way out the door.

I checked my watch: my bus would leave in twenty minutes.

Standing, I threw away my sandwich wrapper and went back to the van. I left most of the stuff I'd packed in the car, except for the small suitcase and the jumbo marshmallows.

Walking down the long row of parked buses, I stopped at bus 942 and scanned the list of stops for my destination: Bozeman, Montana. There it was. I clutched my bag of marshmallows tighter, handed the driver my ticket, and climbed onboard.

I'd catch up to them in no time.

15

Patty

I flick on my turn signal and switch lanes. It feels good to be behind the wheel again. Just Adam and me on the open road.

I glance at the baby in my rearview mirror. "Where to?" I ask him.

"Gadget World, Jeeves," I respond in a squeaky baby voice.

Adam stares, but grins when I turn on the radio. He shares my love of eighties music. I begin a rousing rendition of "Didn't We Almost Have It All." Adam munches on his fist.

After over a month of being on my absolute best behavior, I've finally earned Rose Gold's trust and convinced her to let me watch the baby while she's at work. No more Mary Stone whispering nasty lies about me in my grandson's ear. I'm sure Mary threw a fit when Rose Gold told her, but Adam isn't Mary's child, now is he? About time she stopped trying to take what's rightfully mine.

"You'll spoil your appetite," I warn the baby. He keeps sucking on his fingers.

I've also convinced Rose Gold to let me drive her to work so I can have the van. She balked at first, but there's no sense in leaving the car in a parking lot all day when I can use it to take Adam to the doctor or to buy groceries. I suggested she jog home after work since she loves exercise so much all of a sudden. I'm not going to cart the little liar to *and* from work every day. I have better things to do with my time. Besides, the run takes only forty-five minutes.

Since Thanksgiving, Rose Gold has been even more attentive toward Adam, so my pep talk must have worked. With the increase in time spent with the baby, she has ceded bits and pieces of her life back to me. To be honest, I think she's relieved not to have to make every decision for herself. Adulthood can be exhausting. Being cared for is much easier. I'm all too glad to provide my services.

Proof of Rose Gold's need for help: she forgot her lunch today. She's lucky to have a mother willing to drive it to her workplace for her. She didn't even ask—I saw the brown paper bag on the kitchen counter, bundled Adam up, and got into the van. Though I'm not sure why I bother: inside are a handful of carrot sticks and an apple. She still isn't eating.

I lift my foot from the brake to the gas pedal. The skin on my shins pulls taut. I wince. The wounds on both legs have scabbed over. The more I think about it, it's ludicrous to believe Rose Gold had something to do with my treadmill accident. You can't rig an old piece of machinery to work only when you want it to. I'm pretty sure you can't anyway.

I expect to find Rose Gold at one of the registers, but don't see her. She told me she's a cashier here, but, come to think of it, I've never visited her during a shift. I wonder, for a second, if she's lying about this job.

I stop at register two, where a kid—six feet tall, college-aged, and a dead ringer for a young Bill Nye—is playing imaginary drums on the counter with his eyes closed. He doesn't see me approach.

"Arnie?" I say, glancing at his name tag.

Arnie's eyes fly open. His set ends. I hope he got a standing ovation.

"Is Rose Gold working today?" I ask.

"Yes," Arnie stammers. He blushes. "She's in the break room. Ever since she got back from maternity leave, our manager lets her take a couple extra breaks during her shift."

I sigh with relief. One household can only take so many lies.

"She forgot her lunch," I say, holding up the brown bag. "I brought it for her."

An all-too-familiar curiosity crosses Arnie's face. "Are you her mom?" he asks.

Warily, I say yes. I thought I loved any spotlight, but being the town scapegoat has gotten old. It'd be nice to run an errand without getting the stink eye.

"Is that her baby?" he asks.

I nod. "His name is Adam." Adam gurgles, as if to confirm.

Arnie smiles at Adam, but the baby doesn't interest him as much as the woman holding him does.

"How long have you been out of prison?" he blurts.

The bar for manners is low these days. "Five weeks."

"Is the food as bad as they say?" he asks, sounding hopeful.

"Worse," I lie, wanting a little sympathy.

"What's the worst thing they fed you?" He's enjoying this a little too much, methinks.

I lean in and whisper, "Rat brain."

Arnie scoots a couple feet away from me, half horrified and half unbelieving. He shakes his head no, questioning.

I raise my eyebrows and nod.

He makes a disgusted face.

I could torture this poor kid all day, but I'd rather get back to my comfy chair at home. How long of a break does Rose Gold need?

Arnie stares first at Adam on my chest, then at the brown bag in my hand. "Rose Gold has told us some things," he says. He wants to shock me back.

"Oh, yeah? What kind of things?" I ask, indifferent. I'm sure this twerp is the last person my daughter would confide in.

"Well, that you're controlling." He watches for my reaction.

I yawn. Not exactly a secret Patty Watts craves control.

Arnie keeps at me. "And she can't eat any of your food."

Now he has my attention. Has Rose Gold told him about her supposed eating disorder? I have to tread lightly here. If I act too interested, he'll clam up.

"And why is that?" I say, examining my nail beds.

Arnie is silent for so long, I'm forced to look away from my cuticles and study his face. Some internal struggle is taking place. He mumbles something I can't make out.

"Speak up, Tiny Tim," I snap.

A little louder, he mutters, "She said you're trying to poison her."

So I was right—she *is* trying to make everyone think I'm guilty. But why? Is this a ploy for sympathy from our neighbors, or is she after something more serious? Does she really believe I want to hurt her?

I stare at this punk, unsure what my response should be. He could be lying. Maybe the whole town is baiting me, trying once again to get me to confess to a crime I didn't commit. For all I know, he could be recording this conversation. When you're not sure if you're on firm ground, it's best to move softly.

I smile. "I see why she likes you—same weird sense of humor. I don't find jokes about poison funny, but to each their own, I guess."

Arnie says nothing, just watches me. I give him a casual wave and make my best attempt at a mosey toward the DVD aisle.

I pretend to browse the selection. Clumps of staff members congregate nearby. Arnie has sounded the alarm, and now a dozen or so hoodlums want their turn to ogle me. Two older employees, disheveled and breathtakingly hideous, whisper to each other and jerk their heads in my direction. A teenage girl takes out her phone and starts filming me. A goateed man grimaces as he twists an extension power cord in his hands. The employees inch closer, none of them smiling. I hate their bold stares, their entitlement.

"Mom?"

I swivel on my heel and spot Rose Gold at the end of the aisle. I have never been so relieved to see her ugly mug. The surprise is plain on her face. She looks so young, so innocent, standing there. Maybe she really is sick, and I'm the only one who can see it.

I stride toward her and hold up her lunch bag. "You forgot this," I say, conscious of her coworkers watching us. I hand it to her.

"You didn't have to bring that," she says, taking Adam from me, brushing his wispy hair with her fingertips. "I would've bought my lunch."

Then she too becomes aware of the number of people hanging on our conversation. I watch my daughter transform. Her eyes move from my face to the floor. She hunches over, shoulders inching toward neck, like a turtle retreating into its shell. When she speaks again, her voice is a whisper.

"Thank you," she says.

I lift a hand to tuck a messy strand of hair behind her ear, determined to demonstrate my maternal instinct to these people. Rose Gold flinches when my hand gets near her face. If I were a stranger watching this interaction, I would think she's afraid of me.

Arnie's claim runs through my mind again. Maybe he's telling the truth.

I smile at my daughter, let my hand fall to her shoulder, and give it a soft squeeze. "I'll see you at home," I murmur.

Rose Gold nods, still staring at the floor. I take Adam from her and stride out of the store. Adam clutches one of my fingers the whole way. I speak silly gibberish to him. He grins when I talk; he recognizes my voice now.

In the car, I run through the possible scenarios in my head. Arnie could be lying, though it's unlikely. Or he could be telling the truth: Rose Gold is sullying my name to him, Mary, and anyone else who will listen. But why? Does Rose Gold have an eating disorder, or is she trying to fool everyone into thinking she does? If the latter, why lie about it? Maybe she got used to being the center of attention while I was gone. Maybe she likes playing the victim. Maybe she found the small brown bottle with the white cap in my purse and is paranoid. I reach into my bag, through a small tear in the lining, and root around until my fingers find it. I stroke the cool glass. My chest tightens. I start the car.

Maybe this is nothing more than a power play. It could be her way of getting back at me after I made that jab about her bond with Adam. I knocked her down a peg, so perhaps she's knocking me down one to even the score. Silly girl. A rookie doesn't challenge a master. This is not a game she can win.

I'm reminded of the summer when she was ten years old. We were bored out of our gourds on one of those boiling, muggy days when you had to sit so one fold of skin didn't overlap any others, or they'd suction-cup together, then rip apart when you shifted. Without air-conditioning in the town house, we were miserable. We took turns sticking our faces in front of the floor fan, making E.T. sounds into the blades.

Weekend activities required imagination. Options were limited with little money or mobility because of Rose Gold's chronic fatigue. She was the one who suggested the lemonade stand.

She'd seen other kids' stands over the years. The concept delighted her: kids running a legitimate business, handling money, talking to customers. It all sounded very grown-up to her.

We had a few pieces of scrap cardboard lying around, so I figured, what the heck? And I let her go to town. She lettered the cardboard first with pencil, then colored in the business name with scented markers: Rose Gold's Lemonade Stand. (She must have inherited her father's creativity.) When she finished the sign, we made lemonade: a packet of Kool-Aid mixed with water. We didn't have the means for fresh squeezed lemonade or whatever exotic berries kids are putting in their juice these days. Our neighbors wouldn't know the difference anyway.

After stacking the supplies in the backseat of the van, my daughter and I got in the car, excited for an adventure to break up the monotony of her illness. We set up the table and chairs in an empty strip mall parking lot, affixed the cardboard sign to the front of the table, and unloaded the lemonade and cups. A quarter was Rose Gold's asking price.

She was ecstatic at first, calling out singsong but questionable rhymes, like: "It's a hot day, so get your lemonade" and "Twenty-five cents makes a lot of sense." I didn't have the heart to tell her the latter made no sense. Without a customer in sight, it didn't take long for her enthusiasm to waver. After an hour with zero takers, she was using the cardboard sign to fan herself, head lolling on the back of her chair.

"Where is everyone?" she whined. "Four people have walked by. We've been here for hours."

Rather than deliver dual-pointed lectures on whining and patience— my natural instinct—I went around to the other side of the table.

"Excuse me, miss," I said. "I'd like to buy a lemonade, please."

Rose Gold rolled her eyes. She peered around to ensure no one was witnessing this embarrassing scene with her mother.

"Is the lemonade still for sale?" I prompted again.

Rose Gold narrowed her eyes at me. "You have twenty-five cents?"

"Sure," I said, grabbing my purse from under the table and opening the pouch of coins.

Rose Gold reached for the filled-to-the-brim pitcher, using both hands to fill the red Solo cup, trying to pretend this task wasn't important to her. I did my best to keep a straight face to maintain the decorum required of the occasion. She handed me the cup. "Here you go."

I handed her the quarter. "And here you go."

Lifting the cup to my lips, I took a long drink. "What did you put in here? Pixie dust? Sparkles? What's your secret ingredient?"

In spite of herself, she laughed. "Mom, you're blocking the cardboard sign." She swatted me out of the way.

From whom? I wanted to say, but bit my lip. I sat back in my chair, letting the lemonade's tartness tickle my taste buds. I offered my cup to Rose Gold. She guzzled the drink. Lemonade was one of the beverages her stomach tolerated. Sometimes.

After another half hour, a total of ten cars had driven past us. Seven sped by, two slowed to read the sign before speeding away, and one dotty senior—that fossil must have been old when the Dead Sea was still sick—pulled up and tried to haggle over the price. He argued the lemonade wasn't worth more than ten cents. (And it probably wasn't, back in 1720 when he was born.) My daughter refused to grant him the discount. He left beverage-less. Served him right, cheapo.

Two hours of effort, with one sale to a blood relative, did not a happy girl make.

"Let's go home," Rose Gold said. "No one wants my dumb lemonade."

I suggested we move the stand to Main Street, an area with more foot traffic. Nothing but stale air and leftover fish sticks awaited us at home, and it was not yet noon. I'd run out of ideas to entertain her and was set on milking this one for at least another hour. She shrugged and agreed to the location change, indifferent by now.

I packed the table and chairs into the van. Rose Gold's eyes lit up. "Why don't we get my wheelchair?" she said.

"Why?" I asked. My daughter never volunteered to get in the wheelchair.

She shrugged. "My butt hurts from the metal chair."

I agreed to her request and headed home, lugging the cumbersome wheelchair into the trunk, then drove to our new stand location, starting the entire setup process again while Rose Gold sat in her chair.

True, the new area had more foot traffic than our previous spot. And it's much harder for people on foot to ignore a child's lemonade stand. But I've always wondered how many people stopped that afternoon because they saw a little girl in a wheelchair trying her hardest to sell some lemonade. More important, I keep returning to the question of whether Rose Gold was shrewd enough, at ten years old, to understand how to win sympathy. To use her disadvantages to her advantage, shall we say?

She sold two pitchers of lemonade in twenty minutes, for a total of six dollars and forty cents. She bought a Beanie Baby with the money—Nuts the Squirrel, if I remember correctly.

I am not the only manipulator in my family.

———

Later that night, I wake to the sound of glass breaking outside. I swat at the clock face: three thirty-five a.m. Yawning, I sit up in bed and shuffle to the window. I rub my eyes and let my vision come into focus. When it does, I yelp.

Something on our lawn is on fire.

The blaze is closer to the sidewalk than to our front door, but big enough to be a legitimate concern. I run to Rose Gold's bedroom and try to open the door. Like always, the door is locked.

I knock. "Rose Gold."

Stepping back, I expect the click of the lock, the door to swing open any second. But nothing happens.

"Rose Gold!" I pound my open palm against the door.

I put my ear to the door and hear Adam start to whimper. No sign or sound of my daughter.

I run back to my bedroom and gawk out the window. The fire has gotten bigger. Panicked, I pound on her door one more time before running down the hallway and outside. A freezing gust bites my bare feet and arms. I reach for the side door to the detached garage. I throw it open and flip on the light, eyes scanning until they find a fire extinguisher in the back corner. Tossing junk out of my way, I scoop up the extinguisher and run back out the door toward the driveway.

The sensor floodlights come on and illuminate the front yard. Now I can see it's our trash can that's on fire. On my way to the flames, I notice a big chalk drawing on the driveway's blacktop. The pink lines cover the entire surface. I step around it, trying to interpret the meaning. Then I see it: a skull and crossbones.

The universal symbol for poison.

The heat on my back reminds me of the flames. I turn and pull the pin from the extinguisher's handle. Aiming the nozzle at the base of the fire, I squeeze the lever. Liquid shoots out and douses some of the flames. I keep at it, sweeping from side to side for what feels like hours, but couldn't be more than thirty seconds. When the last flame is gone, I sink to my knees in the grass, staring at the charred can and listening to my shaky breath.

The smell of gasoline lifts me from my stupor. *Someone started this fire,* I think stupidly. I squint into the darkness toward my neighbors' houses, searching for the culprits. There's no sign of life out here except my own. I shiver, my brain registering how cold my body is.

I find a flashlight in the garage and sweep it along the sidewalk and up the trees. I'm too scared to leave our property. Maybe in the morning I'll do a more thorough search for evidence. For now I want to get back inside, safe behind a locked door.

I hurry into the house, closing the door behind me. I stand there for a few seconds, soaking in the strength of the door at my back, then take another unsteady breath.

At the end of the hallway, I pound on Rose Gold's bedroom door again. This time, the door opens right away.

Rose Gold stands there, blinking with bed head. "What time is it?" she asks, groggy.

"How did you not wake up?" I cry.

"I took a sleeping pill." She yawns. "What's wrong?"

"Someone set our trash can on fire," I say. My voice sounds hysterical, unfamiliar to me.

Rose Gold raises her eyebrows, starting to wake up. "What are you talking about?"

"I just put out a fire in the front yard!" How can she be so dense?

Her jaw drops. "Are you serious?" Finally, the reaction I'm looking for. The two of us stare at each other for a moment with matching agape expressions.

Then Adam lets out a shrill cry. Rose Gold fixes me with a glare and goes to the crib to get him. How dare I wake the baby in the process of stopping her lawn from going up in flames?

I forget the fire for a second and peer into the dark room, searching for the reason my daughter needs to keep this door locked all the time. But the bedroom looks the same as the day I moved in here. Nothing is out of the ordinary.

Rose Gold comes back to the door, yawning. "Would you mind getting him to sleep?"

Is she going back to bed right now? I won't be able to sleep for weeks.

I take Adam from her. She smiles before closing the door gently in my face. I carry the baby to the living room, rocking him in my arms until he stops crying. He sticks his tongue out. I laugh in spite of the situation. My heart pulses against his small body.

Someone has taken their anger too far this time. I figured the people of Deadwick might be petty when I got out of prison, but I never thought the town would become unsafe. Yet unsafe is exactly how I feel. I rack my brain for who's behind this: Mary Stone, Tom Behan, Bob McIntyre, Arnie, the other Gadget World employees? Any of them might be playing white knight, might be hell-bent on teaching me a lesson.

I gaze at the innocent bundle in my arms. He would be much better off growing up somewhere else, far away from the maniacs of Deadwick.

With a sigh, I try to enjoy these last few minutes of rest. I will stay up all night if that's what it takes to scrub every remnant of chalk from the driveway. None of Rose Gold's crusaders will get the satisfaction of seeing their threats in the light of day.

Nor will Rose Gold.

16

Rose Gold

After twenty-four hours on the bus, we'd made six stops across Indiana, one long transfer in Chicago, and two stops in Wisconsin. We had crossed the border into Minnesota when my phone vibrated. A text from Dad. In spite of his earlier rudeness, I was still happy to see his name on my screen.

> **Dad:** I wanted to let you know we're almost there
>
> **Dad:** Kim's doing the last leg of driving
>
> **Dad:** I'm sorry for not letting you come on this trip
>
> **Dad:** And for being short earlier
>
> **Dad:** I'm so happy you're beating this illness, but I still think it's too soon for you to take a big, active trip like this

The stream of messages paused.

> Dad: I know I said we should get together after my vacation, but now that you're getting better, I think I need some space for a while

What? How long was "a while"?

> Dad: I hope you know how great it's been getting to know you
> Dad: And I mean that

Why did it feel like he was breaking up with me?

> Dad: I've gotten as much out of this as you have
> Dad: But with all the driving back and forth to Deadwick, and constant texts and e-mails and worrying about you, I've been neglecting my family

I started to type, *I AM your family*, but deleted the sentence.

> Dad: With the promotion, work has been busier than ever
> Dad: I want to be there for my wife and kids with the little free time I have

I blinked back tears. What if he never wanted to see me again?

> Dad: I know you're my kid too, but you're already a grown-up, and look at you—you beat cancer, for Pete's sake!
> Dad: You have Mrs. Stone and your neighbors, but my kids don't have anyone else
> Dad: Anna's only 7

> Dad: I could never forgive myself if they grew up without a
>   father

A bone-shaking scream threatened to escape from my chest. I gripped my jaw closed with my hand, wild with fury. How could he do this to me?

> Dad: I already made that mistake once
> Dad: I'm sorry
> Dad: I'm so sorry, Rose

His use of my nickname—the only nickname I'd ever been given—deflated my anger. For the first time since I'd stepped onto the bus, I saw what I was doing with crystal clarity: my dad wouldn't let me go with his family to Yellowstone, so I was following them there. What was I thinking? That I'd steal their food? Cut the straps to their tents? Drill a hole through their canoe? Now that my fury had quieted, I realized I was going to drive him away for good if I showed up and ruined his summer trip. I had to take smaller, saner steps to win over the Gillespie family. I couldn't go to Bozeman right now.

I stood and stepped into the aisle. "Stop the bus!" I yelled.

The driver's eyes glanced at me in the rearview mirror. "Miss, sit down, please," she said, bored.

I gathered my few belongings and made my way to the front of the bus. "I need to get off," I pleaded.

"You think you're on some kind of movie set? We're on a highway," she chided me, incredulous. "Now, take a seat."

I sank onto the nearest bench. "But I'm going the wrong way," I said, close to tears. "I made a mistake."

"Minneapolis in ten minutes," the driver called to the group. To me, she said in a low tone, "We all make mistakes. You can always start fresh."

I clung to the bench in front of me, thinking of the brand-new fishing pole in my van back in Indiana. I could see the Gillespies on the six-seater boat they'd rented, five poles lined up and waiting to be used. Dad helped each kid bait their hooks. Kim tried to slather sunscreen on Anna while she wiggled away, peering into the water and naming every fish she saw. On my empty seat, Dad plunked a cooler full of drinks, the kids fighting over who got the blue Gatorade. When would I ever ride in a boat or learn to fish? The idea of trying to do these things on my own struck me as absurd. Another family outing had slipped through my fingers.

I wiped my eyes. My predicament wasn't Dad's fault. In a normal family, I wouldn't have to force my way onto summer trips. There'd be no such thing as overstaying my welcome. I wouldn't be making up for lost time if it weren't for my mother. By now, Mom had been in prison for almost three years. I hadn't spoken to her once. I hoped I'd never see her rotten, lying face again. She deserved to be hacked to pieces, not Dad.

When the bus pulled into the parking lot, I darted off of it, apologizing to and thanking the driver.

How had I gotten here? Not to Minneapolis, but to this place in my life. My best friend—even if she was a jerk—was no longer speaking to me. My dad wanted space from me; my mother was in prison. I had no one. I was alone.

I couldn't bear the thought of turning around and going home. Not when I'd begged Scott for a week off. I could stay here, but I didn't know anyone in Minnesota.

For the second time in as many days, I studied the bus schedule and map. I had to go somewhere—I couldn't stay at this bus station. Where do you go when you're all alone?

My eyes stopped roaming the map. I wasn't alone at all. All these years, I'd promised to visit, and when would be more perfect than right now? I already had the time off, had already headed west.

I marched to the ticket counter. I'd gone too far north, but we would correct course. By the weekend, I'd be there.

"Can I help you?" the man at the counter asked. He wore an eye patch—a very good omen.

"One ticket to Denver, please," I said.

I was long overdue to meet Phil in the flesh.

A t ten a.m., when the bus was an hour outside of Denver, I decided to text Phil my real name. I didn't want our first in-person exchange to start with me correcting him when he called me "Katie." I couldn't go on pretending to be someone else forever.

> Me: I haven't been honest with you
>
> Phil: What do you mean?
>
> Me: My real name is Rose Gold
>
> Me: I lied because I didn't want you to find my messed-up
>   family story online or in the papers
>
> Me: I'm sorry

I dropped my phone in my lap, hands shaking, and let out a sigh of relief. I'd taken a risk by admitting I'd lied, but it felt good to come clean with Phil. I hoped he wouldn't google me in the next hour and figure out what I looked like, or he'd never want to meet me. I waited for his response.

> Phil: Huh
>
> Phil: I'm both surprised and not. It's the Internet, after all

Me: I'm so sorry

Phil: Hey, I understand

A pit formed in my stomach. I had to ask.

Me: Do you still want to talk to me?

Phil: Of course

Me: Good, because I'm almost in Denver

Phil: What?

Me: I knew you'd never agree to meet unless I surprised
     you. I'm on a bus, and I'm almost there

Me: Meet me at the Denver bus station in an hour. The one
     on 19th Street. I'm wearing a purple hoodie

My heart was hammering again, but I was also proud of myself. More and more these days, I had taken control of my life. I'd stood up to Alex and taught her a lesson. I'd demanded my manager let me have this week off of work. I'd gotten to know my father and cut off my mother. And now I was giving Phil commands. Timid Rose Gold had been ousted.

Phil: Okay, I'll be there

I blinked a few times at his message, not believing it. I was going to meet my online boyfriend.

Phil: I'll be wearing a gray beret

I was so excited at not being hung out to dry that I tried to ignore the bad omen of a gray hat. I had never seen a beret-wearing snowboarder before, but then, I had never met any snowboarders. I would have to wait and see.

The last hour of the bus ride dragged by. I spent most of the time watching YouTube tutorials on applying makeup. In the end, I put mine on the same way I'd seen Alex do hers. After that, I practiced poses that would allow me to talk to Phil while concealing my teeth— not that I needed the practice. I'd figured out every mouth-covering move years ago.

The bus pulled into the parking lot. I had butterflies. Good or bad, this day was going to be a memorable one. I peered out the window, trying to catch a first peek at Phil. But the parking lot was mostly empty. A few cars waited, but I couldn't see any of their drivers.

The bus stopped. The doors opened. A handful of people shuffled off the bus with me, yawning and stretching their legs. I willed them to move faster. I descended the three steps to the sidewalk, the last one off the bus. I watched some of the passengers head to the waiting cars. They poked their heads in the driver's-side windows, offering hugs and kisses to invisible loved ones. I scanned the parking lot, but didn't see a gray beret.

What if he'd stood me up?

I tapped my foot on the concrete and crossed my arms. *No one here is paying attention to you,* I told myself. *And if they are, they'll assume your ride is late.*

I'd give it fifteen minutes. If he didn't show up by then, I'd have my answer. I was already dreading getting back on the bus.

Someone tapped my left shoulder. "Rose Gold?"

I whirled around to see a man standing behind me, arms stiff at his side. In one hand, he held two crushed daisies. Under his gray beret was a reddish blond ponytail. He had a potbelly and a mustache with white wisps, wore glasses, and had to be at least sixty.

This couldn't have been Phil.   •

The man extended a hand toward me. "I'm Phil," he said.

"Rose Gold," I said numbly, shaking his hand.

The guy was old enough to be my grandfather, and I'd told him I loved him more than once during our late-night chats. I was going to projectile-vomit all over Phil's Birkenstocks.

"You hungry? I thought we'd get a bite at the Crispy Biscuit down the street. Great diner." Phil scratched his elbow. A flaky patch of skin flew off. It dawned on me I had been very stupid and made a giant mistake.

Phil began walking toward a black pickup. I plodded behind him, stalling. I did not want to get into this guy's truck. I'd recently started watching horror movies, and it seemed like all the characters put themselves in harm's way—failing to call the police, hiding in obvious places, getting into strange cars—while I screamed at them for being idiots. I vowed not to be an idiot twice in one day.

"How far is the diner?" I asked.

"Two-minute drive. Not even," Phil said, clearing phlegm from his throat.

"Maybe we could walk over," I said. "I've been sitting for, like, twenty-four hours."

Phil glanced at me sideways. "No problem," he said. He stopped walking, so I stopped too. "You don't think I'm out to hurt you or anything, do you?"   •

I gave him a small smile. "Of course not. Just want a little fresh air."

We walked the rest of the way to the restaurant in silence. Phil offered to carry my suitcase, but I declined, although I didn't have anything valuable inside. If I had to leave it behind in an emergency, so be it.

At the Crispy Biscuit, an apathetic waitress seated us in a sticky booth and handed us menus. Phil took off his beret to reveal a receding hairline that made me wince. He hummed to himself while he examined the menu. Meanwhile, I planned an escape route.

I'd get through this meal, then make up some excuse about having an aunt in town who would pick me up. In fact, maybe I should tell him about the aunt now so he'd know someone would notice if I was missing. But how many times had I told him in past conversations that I had no living relatives but my mother? Maybe this could be a long-lost aunt. Or wait. I'd told him about finding my dad. I could say my dad was on a business trip in Denver, and he was picking me up after his meeting. Maybe I should actually text Dad to let him know I was in danger. He'd said he needed space, but I doubted that included emergencies. Maybe this could be the thing that brought us back together. He'd feel guilty and forget all the stuff he'd said. He could be the proverbial dad sitting on his porch with a shotgun, waiting for his daughter's sixty-year-old boyfriend to bring her home. I tried to imagine Dad holding a gun. I couldn't.

"What's it gonna be?" Phil asked, watching me. I bet Phil owned lots of guns.

I started. "Sorry?"

"I'm going to have the Denver omelet. Anything sound good to you?"

In spite of my nerves, I realized I was starving. I hadn't eaten a real meal in two days. I glanced at the menu and picked the first thing I saw. "Blueberry pancakes."

"Good choice." Phil smirked and leaned in. "You know, you don't have to look so scared. I'm not some crazy ax murderer or something."

I squawked out a laugh. "Isn't that exactly what a crazy ax murderer would say?" I sounded like my mom.

"You invited me to meet you," Phil reminded me.

"You're just . . . ," I faltered.

"Old?" Phil guessed.

"You said you dropped out of high school."

"I did. A long time ago." Phil chuckled.

"You said you live at your aunt and uncle's house."

"I do. They sold it to me a while back."

I scowled. "You're different than I expected."

He gave me the once-over. "So are you."

What was that supposed to mean? Was I uglier than he'd predicted? Flatter chested? Scrawnier? I wondered if he was sizing me up, guessing how much I weighed, how much of a fight I'd put up if he carried me to his truck. Or what if he wasn't forceful but instead tried to woo me? Under no circumstances did I want to have sex with this man.

"I never wanted to become a lifelong bachelor, reading Kafka alone in my cabin in the woods." Phil paused. "I'm kidding—Kafka's full of shit. You ever read him?"

I shook my head.

"Don't bother. I'm more of a Margaret Atwood fan myself. I've read *The Handmaid's Tale* at least thirty times. Gives you something different to chew on with every read, you know? But I'll be the first to admit I like a little *Eat Pray Love* as much as the next guy. Elizabeth Gilbert is a national treasure." The way Phil was babbling, I wondered whether he had spoken to anyone in the last sixty years. I had to admit, he didn't strike me as an ax murderer.

"Do you really live alone in a cabin in the woods?" I asked.

He chuckled again. "That's all you took away? I told you I live in a cabin."

"Yeah, with your uncle and aunt," I glared, becoming less scared of him.

"Let's be honest." His eyes twinkled. "Nobody wants to talk to an old guy online, even if he's a nice old guy. Sometimes we have to get creative with the truth. You understand, don't you, Katie?" He was enjoying himself, as though this were all some master prank.

I guessed it was. I'd spent five years of my life thinking I was in a real relationship, yet I was no closer to my first kiss. I wanted to both laugh and cry.

"I take it you don't snowboard either," I said.

Phil belted out a laugh and slapped his belly. "Not since I threw my back out in oh-eight. I did take a lesson once. Hunter said I was a natural." He beamed.

Hunter—now that was the name of a plausible twentysomething snowboard instructor. I wanted to smack myself.

"Don't you get lonely, living by yourself?" I asked.

"I thought you said you live alone too," Phil said.

I stared at my hot chocolate. "I never said I wasn't lonely."

Phil's expression softened. "Sure, I'd rather have a wife and kids, and even grandkids by now. But I strike out every time I try courting someone in real life. Had my heart broken one too many times, so I've accepted the hand I was dealt." My face must have been filled with pity because he continued. "Look, I make the best of it. I grow vegetables and bake bread. I get my meat from a butcher in Denver. I'm trying to make my house self-sustainable, but I'm not a total recluse or anything. I sing in a church choir once a month. As Thoreau said, 'I never found the companion that was so companionable as solitude.'"

In any other story, Phil would be a serial killer. In this one, he was a philosophical hermit.

The waitress dropped off our food. I drizzled a heap of blueberry syrup on top of the blueberry pancakes, cut off a piece, and ate it. A shiver still ran through me when I took a first bite of an especially delicious meal, and this time was no different. The pancakes were thick and fluffy and melted in my mouth. I ate forkful after forkful, not caring if I looked insane.

"What do you mean, 'self-sustainable'?" I asked between bites.

"I have my own hydroponic garden for water. I use my own

heating and cooling systems. No bank accounts. I pay cash and get paid in cash."

"What do you do for work?"

"Sell my produce, tutor high school kids, snow removal in the winter." He leaned in and gestured for me to do the same. "Create fake identities."

I almost laughed, then realized he was serious. Where was this guy when I needed to pretend I was twenty-one so I could join Alex and Whitney at Kirkwood?

"Is Phil your fake identity?"

Phil raised his eyebrows, suggesting the answer was yes.

"What's your birth name?"

Phil shook his head. "Sorry, kiddo. No can tell. I changed my name thirty years ago to get away from my past." He studied his omelet. "I also have a mother I'd like to forget."

I couldn't believe real Phil and I had something in common. I had forgotten that all this time, I'd been telling him about the horror show that was my own mother.

"I know what you mean," I said, anger creeping into my voice. "My mom ruined my life."

Phil gave me a sad smile. "Don't hold on to that bitterness, darlin'. It'll crush you."

"How do you let it go?" I asked.

"That's the million-dollar question." He took the final bite of his omelet.

I realized I probably needed the real Phil in this moment more than the online version I thought I'd been dating. I smiled at him, a genuine smile to let him know I was happy to be there, grateful to be sitting across from another human being with a lousy childhood.

Phil cringed a tiny bit—at my teeth, what else? My cheeks flushed. This whole time, I thought I'd been the only one repulsed. I imagined meeting Phil at this diner again, a few years from now, once I had my gleaming white teeth. I'd never be embarrassed to smile again.

"Excuse me," Phil said, rising from the booth and folding his napkin. He placed it where he'd been sitting. "Need to use the facilities."

When he'd left, I pulled out my phone and texted my dad.

> **Me:** I decided to meet up with a guy in Colorado I've been talking to online
>
> **Me:** Turns out he's, like, 60 and lives alone in the woods. I thought he was 20
>
> **Me:** He seems okay, but if you don't hear from me for a while, just call the Denver police, okay?

I reread the texts. Everything I'd said was true. So what if I left out some minor details that would have assuaged my father's fears? No way could he ignore me now. I'd have to wait for his phone to find service; he had warned me he would be out of touch while they were camping. I put my phone back in my purse.

Phil returned from the bathroom and sat. He noted my empty plate, impressed I'd finished. "Good?" he asked.

"Delicious," I said.

"The Crispy Biscuit never disappoints."

The waitress brought the check. Phil laid two twenty-dollar bills on the table. I reached for my own wallet, but he waved me off. I didn't object.

He cleared his throat. "Well, I don't think either of us is hoping for something physical."

I shook my head. Part of me was overjoyed Phil wasn't interested; the other part was ashamed I was being rejected by a sixtysomething loner.

"For me, our relationship was never about the physical anyway," he said, fidgeting. "All those years ago, you seemed like you could use a friend."

I opened my mouth, but couldn't think of anything to say. I felt pathetic, listening to Phil describe sixteen-year-old me. Worst of all, five years later, the description still fit.

"I needed a friend too," he tried to reassure me. "Which is why I didn't want to leave you hanging at the bus depot today. I was also once a kid running away from abuse."

Was that what I was doing? The question flickered while Phil kept talking.

"Here's my idea. Why don't I drive you to the airport? I'll give you four hundred bucks for a plane ticket, and you can fly anywhere you want. You can start over."

He watched me with hope. I'd read this man completely wrong. He wasn't out to hurt me—he wanted to help. I was too exhausted and overwhelmed to tear up.

"I don't want to get back on that bus." I laughed weakly.

"You don't have to. Let me help you," Phil said. "When I was your age, someone helped me get back on my feet. And I vowed to do the same someday."

"Are you sure?" I asked.

"Absolutely," Phil said.

We left the diner together. I had the urge to hug this stranger I'd known for so long, but didn't want to chance sending any wrong signals. Just in case.

The thirty-minute ride to Denver Airport was a quiet one. While Phil drove, I thought about where I'd go. I could fly to California and see the ocean for the first time. Or the Statue of Liberty in New York. I wondered if four hundred dollars was enough to buy a ticket to Mexico—it was supposed to be sunny and warm, and no one would know my story there. I could be Rose or pick a new name, like Phil had.

I allowed myself these fantasies, although I already knew where I'd go when I reached the counter. I'd book the next flight to Indianapolis. From there it would be a two-hour drive to the bus station to pick up my van, and then a five-hour drive home.

I couldn't give up on my dad or the life I was rebuilding. I had a job, a car, a savings account with actual money in it. In a few years, I would be able to pay for the dental procedure. I was not yet done with Deadwick. I couldn't up and run away like Phil had, as tempting as it might have been.

Phil pulled his truck over to the departures drop-off area. From his wallet, he drew four crisp hundred-dollar bills.

He grinned and handed me the cash. "Promise me you'll take care of yourself?"

I beamed. "I promise. Thank you so, so much."

Overcome with gratitude, I kissed his cheek. We both flinched, but pretended not to notice. I got out of the pickup, waved once, and watched the truck drive away.

17

Patty

Christmas in Deadwick is a pathetic affair. We have no town square, so the "festivities" are set up in the parking lot of our strip mall. Fabric and hardware stores, a nail salon, a pizza place, and a Hallmark—I thought they'd gone the way of Blockbuster—all stand as sad witnesses to the holiday spectacle.

Thousands of cotton balls have been scattered across the pavement. That still isn't enough to offer a passing likeness to snow, and more blacktop is poking through than white clumps. In one corner of the parking lot is a row of gingerbread houses—I have to assume their decorators were blindfolded. The reindeer are garden deer statues, made of flimsy plastic and antlerless. Someone has drawn a grin on each of their mouths with red paint, so they bear a striking likeness to Heath Ledger's Joker. (Rose Gold and I watched *The Dark Knight* the other evening; my, her movie tastes have gotten sinister.) At the center of it all is a five-foot, Charlie Brown–ish Christmas tree. The ornaments are scratched, the garland is balding, and the angel on top looks embarrassed for all of us. A homemade countdown sign reads: *9 days until Christmas.*

Kitty-corner from the gingerbread houses is the reason we're here: Santa. Though it's ten a.m., a line has already formed, all the kids dressed in red and green. Some are jumping in excitement; others look like they're waiting for sentencing. (I would know.) One little girl is bawling. I wish I could join her.

I wanted to take Adam to the mall Santa two towns over, but Rose Gold begged me to come with her to Deadwick's "Christmaspalooza." She wants everyone to see we're three peas in a pod—and also Adam's adorable reindeer outfit (this one complete with antlers). I glance over at her pointing things out to Adam, like he has a clue what's going on. Her excitement is somewhat endearing. I'm glad I came.

The day after our property was set on fire, I confronted Rose Gold about her odd behavior the night before. She admitted she'd thought I was exaggerating. In her sleeping-pill-induced state, she hadn't realized the gravity of the situation. Of course, *she* had nothing to do with it, she insisted, insulted I would insinuate as much. She suspected Arnie was involved. He had a crush on her and had said something about teaching me a lesson a few weeks back. She promised to do a little digging.

A couple days later, she came home from work with an update: Arnie said he didn't start the fire, but she had a feeling he knew who did. She thought his younger brother, Noah, and his friends were to blame.

"But why would they come after me?" I asked.

Rose Gold shrugged. "A lot of folks in Deadwick have grudges against you—even people you don't know."

My eyebrows reached for my hairline. "We should call the police."

Rose Gold shook her head. "Don't be silly. They're harmless."

"I wouldn't call juvenile delinquents with a penchant for arson harmless." I chewed my lip.

Rose Gold sighed. "I don't know what to tell you, Mom. People in town think it's their job to keep me safe, and they believe the best way to do that is by getting you away from me. Listen, why don't we go to Christmaspalooza next weekend, and we can prove to everyone how close we are?"

Which is why we are now standing in a ramshackle parking lot, her arm hooked through mine, waiting to stick my grandson on a strange man's lap. I'm not completely satisfied with Rose Gold's explanation—I've seen Arnie, Noah, and their gawky friends around town. They seem incapable of operating flyswatters, let alone vandalizing someone's property.

I've decided to leave it be for now. I don't want to spook Rose Gold by making accusations or asking pointed questions. I need to keep her close so I can figure out what she's up to. Once I have more answers, I can regain control of this family.

I pat my daughter's arm. She beams at me.

Five families wait in line ahead of us. Blessedly, I don't recognize any of them, and they don't recognize me. Santa is also an unfamiliar face, a fortysomething guy, if I had to guess. Bob McIntyre always used to play the town Santa. Maybe he couldn't find his dentures in time this year.

Two little boys hop off Santa's lap after their parents take four million pictures. What happened to one and done? They're not going in *National Geographic,* for Pete's sake. Santa "ho-ho-hos" and "Meeeeeeerry Christmases" them away. While the next parents in line straighten their children's Sunday best, Santa's gaze skims the parking lot and lands on me. His eyes squint, then widen in recognition. I may not know him, but he knows me.

He glowers at me. I try to stand my ground, frown back, but feel creepy having a staring contest with Santa. I turn away. His eyes are still trained on me, even as the new group of kids climbs onto his lap.

Maybe I'm being paranoid. Maybe he's not staring at me at all.

I glance over my shoulder to see if he might be watching someone behind me, and whom should I spot across the parking lot but the walking Gumby that is Arnie Dixon and, presumably, the creatures that spawned him. A level of rage builds within me that I have not felt since Rose Gold took the stand at my trial.

I stride across the lot toward them. Arnie sees me coming and looks scared. I stop in front of him and put my hands on my hips.

"You and your fire-loving derelict of a brother better stay away from my family," I yell.

Arnie gawps and peers around, like I might be talking to someone else. His parents, slender, bespectacled folks who smell like cat lovers, are also caught off guard.

"Tell your little crew to feed their pyromania elsewhere. If I catch any of you on my property again, I'm calling the police." My head pounds from shouting.

Arnie's mom steps in, raising a soft-spoken voice. "You stay away from my sons, you crazy witch."

I wheel around on her. "Your sons set my trash can on fire."

A tall man grabs me by the arm and looms over all of us. "How about you leave the spectacles to Santa and let the Dixons alone?"

Tom.

He's not the only spectator, I realize. The flurry of activity in the parking lot has more or less ground to a halt. Moon-faced dimwits wrapped in sleeping bag parkas stare at me, their faces filled with animosity. One couple hurries their little girl to the car, but the rest stay and watch with crossed arms. They want a show? Fine.

I rip my arm from Tom's hold and raise my voice even more, flailing my arms for emphasis. I want everyone to hear me. "You've all been awful to me since I came back. You know nothing about my relationship with Rose Gold, how close we've become. And yet you're all conspiring against me."

The PTA moms make a show of pulling their children close. A group of high school wrestlers cracks their knuckles. I realize I am raving. Those who don't know about the fire might think I'm a lunatic. I have a sinking feeling the town mob is going to force me to leave again when a raspy voice speaks up behind me.

"Why don't we all let Patty enjoy her holiday, and you all can enjoy yours?"

I whirl around to find Hal Brodey, an old friend of my dad's, gazing down at me. I haven't seen Hal since I was a kid. He has to be pushing ninety now, but other than a wrinkled face and slightly stooped posture, he doesn't seem much worse for wear. Hal never went out of his way to be kind to me when I was younger, so I'm not sure why he's defending me now.

Tom stares at Hal, incredulous. "You're going to defend her? After what she put Rose Gold through?"

Hal takes off his Chicago Bears baseball cap, then settles it back on his head. "I know what she did, Tom." As he speaks, his eyes never leave mine. "Most of you didn't know Patty as a kid, what she went through. I do."

The crowd stills. My lungs feel emptied of air.

"Her daddy beat the crud out of her for years." Hal wears a haunted expression, his mind somewhere dark. "I still remember the bruises."

So that's what this is about. Hal Brodey needs to clear his conscience after looking the other way while his best friend beat his kids to a pulp. I didn't know Hal knew. I didn't know any adults knew, besides my mom. Blood rushes to my face—I'm half horrified to relive the memories, half humiliated to have my shame shared with so many people again.

"A lot of us got the belt as kids," someone in the crowd grumbles. "None of us grew up to be monsters. We didn't poison our daughters or starve our sons."

The rest of the group murmurs their agreement. Someone claps.

Hal frowns. "Well, you'll get a goddamn gold star in heaven. Is that what you wanna hear? All I'm saying is this woman's had a hard life, and she needs a second chance now. Maybe we should give it to her."

Nobody says anything. I wish I could freeze this moment right here. Hardly anyone has said a kind word about me in six years. I feel a tear coming and blink it away.

Hal keeps going. "What about forgiveness? From what I remember, that's a big part of the Good Book you all are always preaching from."

The parking lot is quiet for a moment. I could kiss Hal Brodey square on his weathered face. This is the moment I've been waiting for. I glance at Rose Gold. She looks livid.

"You know, Hal," Jenny Wetherspoon—our wet noodle of a town librarian—speaks up, "the last thing I need right now is a lecture on my faith. Forgiveness has limitations."

Jenny's husband, Max, steps forward. "If Patty wants a second chance, she should try a new town. The people of Deadwick have long memories."

Max spits out the side of his sneer. I wonder whether he still keeps a handgun tucked into the waistband of his pants.

"What was she expecting, a 'welcome back' party?" Max continues, watching me.

The PTA moms snicker.

Jenny pretends to consider this. "She always did love a handout. Had no trouble eating our food, 'borrowing' our money. How much did she take from us over the years, Max?"

Max clears his throat and walks toward me. "Somewhere north of seven hundred dollars, I'd reckon." For a second, his tough-guy mask slips, and I see the pain in his eyes.

Jenny nods, avoiding my gaze. "Plus all those hospital bills. The library ran at least half a dozen fund-raisers to cover them."

This isn't about the money, though they're pretending it is. I held Jenny and Max in my arms after every fertility clinic appointment, helped them research and brainstorm other options until there weren't any. Rose Gold and I bought them Campbell's chicken noodle soup and recorded silly home videos, whatever I could think of to cheer them up. Twenty years before they decided I was a monster, they'd called me their guardian angel.

I take a step back. "You leave my daughter and me alone," I shout at all of them. "I'm sick of your lectures."

Max sticks his hands in his pockets, pulling the jacket open wide. On the left side of his belt, metal flashes. "If you're tired of the conversation, I'd be happy to show you how we all feel," he says agreeably.

My blood runs cold. I glance at Hal, hoping he'll speak up again. He chews the inside of his cheek, squinting at Max Wetherspoon, but doesn't say anything.

"You aren't welcome in Deadwick, Patty," Jenny says. "We can't force you to leave town, but don't think we won't try."

Rose Gold rushes over, head ducked, and holds me by the elbow. "Let's get out of here," she murmurs. She's not angry anymore. Back to gentle, subservient Rose Gold. I'd give myself whiplash trying to keep up with her personality changes.

I nod, dazed. She puts her arm around me, steering me toward the van. The blinking black eyes of the human hive stare at us. Hal Brodey shakes his head, the only one sad to see me go.

Back at the house, I pace the living room, still furious. Rose Gold returns from feeding Adam in her bedroom, singing "Twinkle,

Twinkle, Little Star" as she walks down the hallway. When she reaches the living room, she lifts Adam to her face and kisses him four times: on the forehead, both cheeks, and his chin. He giggles.

"They have no right to treat me this way," I say, watching my daughter. "Every single day I try to be nice to them. And every single day, all they do is bully me."

"Why don't you play with Adam for a bit?" Rose Gold suggests cheerfully, hugging the baby before handing him to me. "I'll make us dinner."

"They've gone too far this time," I say, lowering my voice now that Adam is in my arms.

"I know, Mom," Rose Gold says, trying to sound solemn. I catch a hint of a smile right before she turns away. "Tell you what. I'll make your favorite."

She disappears into the kitchen. Her good mood irks me, but I resist the urge to tell her off. I sit in my recliner and try to focus on Adam, rocking him back and forth. At least he would never remember the awful Christmaspalooza scene. Maybe at dinner, I'd broach the topic of raising him somewhere other than Deadwick. Rose Gold might be ready to start fresh if I could get her away from the influence of these spiteful people. They have nothing better to do than gossip and plot ways to hurt people. I have had it with this town.

Half an hour later, Rose Gold calls me to the kitchen table. She's filled two plates with Polish sausage, kapusta, boiled potatoes, and a salad—my favorite meal. She sets one of the plates in front of me. In spite of the day's earlier events, I smile. This is the first dinner she's cooked us since I got out of prison. We settle Adam in his bassinet and sit at the table to eat.

"You'll have to let me know how it is," she says, gesturing to our plates. "I've never made this on my own before. I hope I didn't mess anything up."

"I'm sure it's all perfect," I say, cutting into a piece of sausage. I pop it into my mouth. "Really good." I slice another piece.

Rose Gold beams and picks up her own fork and knife. She slices all of her sausage and potatoes, then begins to eat. I startle when I realize the significance of this simple act.

My daughter is eating. She doesn't scoot the food around her plate or try to condense it into smaller piles. She chews and swallows, chews and swallows same as I am. Why the sudden appetite? Maybe she's grown tired of her ruse. Maybe she's sorry for me now that she's seen the unrelenting wrath of Deadwick's residents. Maybe she feels guilty for her role in their hatred. Maybe she's ready to start acting like we're a normal family.

I pull the serving dishes closer to me for second helpings. My stomach rumbles.

Odd.

I use the tongs to pick up another sausage and cut a slice. The sausage is halfway to my mouth when a wave of nausea hits me so hard, I drop my fork.

Rose Gold jumps in her chair. "What's wrong?"

Another wave of nausea—this one more powerful than the first—washes over me. I'm going to be sick. My chair squeals against the floor when I scoot it back. I bolt toward the bathroom. Rose Gold calls, "Mom?" but all I can think about is the toilet.

No sooner is my head over the porcelain bowl than I begin to retch. I squeeze my eyes closed, not wanting to see the contents of my chewed-up dinner reappear. Gripping the toilet bowl's base, I am dizzy and shaky and sweaty and chilly. The stench of throw-up fills the air. I keep heaving. I flush the toilet, desperate to get the smell away from my nose, but too scared to lift my face from the bowl. I am reminded of an article I read: when you flush a toilet, feces particles shoot fifteen feet into the air, covering the sink, toothbrush, and now my face. But I am too queasy to be disgusted. I will never stop retching.

A knock sounds on the door.

"Mom, are you okay?" Rose Gold calls.

I keep my face in the bowl. Only bile is coming out of me by now. "I think the lettuce was bad."

"I feel fine," she says, borderline chipper.

You want a medal? I want to yell.

"Can you get me a Seven Up?" I ask.

She pads down the hallway and returns a minute later with a glass and a can of 7 Up. She empties the soda into the glass, then taps the glass on the counter to get rid of all the bubbles—the same way I used to when she was sick.

"Put it on the counter," I say, head still in the bowl, waiting for the next round of nausea.

"Oof," Rose Gold groans. "Smells awful in here. I don't know how you stood it all those years."

I say nothing, willing her to shut up and get out.

"Let me know if you need anything else," she says, skipping down the hall.

How is it possible that I, with my hardy stomach, got sick, but Rose Gold's wimpy digestive system is fine?

When I haven't puked in five minutes, I pull my head from the bowl and sink to the tile floor, too exhausted to reach for the glass of 7 Up or brush my teeth or even sit. I pray this nightmare is over. I lie as still as possible, not wanting to provoke any of my organs.

Rose Gold checks on me a few more times and offers little tips that irritate me. They're the same things I told her when she was young: small sips of 7 Up, a cool washcloth on the forehead, deep breaths.

I don't know how much time has passed, but eventually she pops her head in and says, "Adam and I are going to bed. Hope you feel better in the morning."

The baby wriggles in her arms, making my daughter smile.

I say nothing.

She watches me on the floor, her voice flat now. "I don't know how you did it all those years."

Didn't she already say that? I think with impatience. I lift a hand. "Night, honey."

The master bedroom door closes. The lock clicks. The house is silent. I am left alone with my thoughts.

I pull myself to my feet and stagger to the living room. My recliner reaches for my body. I sink into it. My eyes close.

No, earlier she said, *I don't know how you stood it.* Just now she said, *I don't know how you did it.* My body, dehydrated and exhausted, says, *So what?* But something nags at my brain.

By "did it," did she mean take care of her all those times she vomited? Or something more accusatory?

My eyes open.

Rose Gold made dinner. Rose Gold ate dinner. Rose Gold didn't get sick.

But I did.

This line of thinking is preposterous—but is it? Did my own daughter poison my food?

Maybe Arnie or Mary or Tom got to her. Maybe she believes the media, the judge, and the jury. Maybe this is the lesson she wants to teach me, the reason she let me stay with her. She wants my attention. Well, sweet girl, you have it.

No one in this town wants me here, not even my own daughter. Scare tactics and bullying are one thing, but harming me is another. The treadmill accident, the yard fire, the poisoned food: some of the people in this town are deranged, and my daughter is one of them. Am I supposed to wait for them to burn me at the stake?

My mind reels, drawing conclusions and making decisions faster than I'm prepared for. How could I be so naive to think she took me in with honest intentions, out of the goodness of her heart? Forget trying to fix Rose Gold. Forget figuring out her plans. This has become more serious than a power struggle.

I can't stay here. I have to leave. If my daughter is unstable, she could also be dangerous. Has proven she *is* dangerous, in fact. Meaning I can't leave Adam here either.

He's going to have to come with me.

18

Rose Gold

November 2015

I hadn't seen my father in four months. He paced the sidelines of the soccer field, shouting encouragement to his team. Five little girls sat behind him on the bench, watching the match unfold.

On the field, Anna went to kick the ball, but missed. I noticed her hair was in a ponytail and beamed. A girl on the other team ran past Anna, taking the ball with her. She was halfway across the field before Anna realized the ball had gotten away from her.

Dad was trying very hard to look patient with his daughter. Maybe he assumed she would have Sophie's athletic prowess or at least Billy Jr.'s adequate handling skills. Anna had neither—she was more Billy than Kim, more me than Sophie. Her unenthusiastic trudge down the field made me love her more.

Kim sat in the stands with the other parents, cheering for Anna's team and laughing with her friends. She seemed years younger when she was grinning. She had never smiled at me like that.

Four months ago, Dad had asked me for space, and I gave it to him. But I thought "space" meant fewer texts and visits, not cutting off communication altogether. He'd texted me back, alarmed, when he saw my comments about Phil. But after I reassured him I was okay, he went quiet again. Since the Yellowstone trip, he'd responded to half of my messages, and the responses were one word or a sentence at most. He wouldn't pick up when I called. We hadn't seen each other since the morning the Gillespies had left for their trip. I'd tried to be patient. I focused on work and saving the money I needed for my teeth—I was halfway there—but I was still lonely. I was afraid if I stopped initiating contact, I might never hear from my father again.

The day Dad had walked into Gadget World, he acted like he wanted a real relationship with me. But now, after a year and a half, he was already throwing in the towel a second time? Who did he think he was? Apparently no one had told him a parent's love was supposed to be unconditional. I wasn't asking for much—just to be a part of the Gillespie family.

So I did what any good daughter or sister would: I kept tabs on the family via social media. When I discovered Anna had a soccer match this afternoon, I got into my van and drove five hours north to cheer her on. I hadn't worked up the nerve to get out of the car yet, but I had a decent view of the field from the parking lot. The score was zero to zero. Not a riveting game, but I marveled at how easily this group of seven-year-olds ran up and down the field. They were boundless in their energy, legs strong and obedient. They would spend their childhoods running and rolling around in the grass, not hooked up to IVs or confined to hospital beds. They were luckier than they knew, and they took all of it for granted.

A whistle blew, signaling the end of the match. Each team lined up to shake one another's hands. I stretched and opened the van door, hopping down to the concrete, stomach in knots. Watching Anna high-five the girls on the other team, I couldn't help but grin and relax a little. I loved my sister—and I'd missed her all these months. I wanted nothing more than her stubby arms around me. When was the last time I had been hugged? The last time another human being had touched me at all?

I made a beeline for Anna, ignoring the stares of the parents in the bleachers, the refs walking off the field, and the girls on both teams. When Anna saw me, her eyes lit up.

"Rose," she yelled. She sprinted toward me, much faster than she'd chased any soccer ball in the last couple hours.

When we reached each other in the middle of the field, she pounded her little body into me. I scooped her up and swung her in circles. Anna laughed with delight, squealing. I swung her faster and faster. I wanted to be good to her the way Phil had been good to me. I wanted to pay it forward.

"I'm gonna barf," Anna said, but kept laughing, so I kept spinning. This reunion was exactly how I'd pictured it. "Look at my new earrings!"

I stopped twirling and set Anna down. The two of us swayed, waiting for the dizziness to pass. I oohed and ahhed over the tiny Minnie Mouse studs. I had the urge to lie down in the grass, to stop the afternoon right there.

"Rose, what are you doing here?" a voice behind me said. Kim.

"She came to see me play," Anna said.

My gaze shifted from Anna to her mother. Sometimes I couldn't believe they were related. I tried to adopt Anna's carefree tone. "I missed you guys."

Kim put her hand on Anna's shoulder and tugged my sister toward her. "Go join the team huddle, honey," she said, pointing to the circle of girls Dad was giving a postgame speech to. Anna trotted off.

Kim watched Anna go, then turned toward me. "You shouldn't have come," she said. "Billy told you he needed space."

I frowned at Kim for a minute, debating the best way to approach this conversation. She crossed her arms.

"I'd rather talk about this with my dad," I said. I had a better shot of getting through to him.

"Billy is busy," Kim said. "What is there to talk about?"

I had never cussed anyone out before, but Kim would have made the perfect first candidate. I bit my tongue, watching Anna's team stack their hands in the middle of the huddle and then yell, "Team!" on the count of three. Kim followed my gaze and moved over a few steps, trying to block my view of Dad and the girls.

Anna tugged on Dad's sleeve and pointed at me. Dad followed her finger, squinted, and recognized me. He nudged her toward a couple of the other girls and came jogging in Kim's and my direction, clipboard and backpack in hand.

When he reached us, he was out of breath. I opened my arms to hug him.

"Dad!" I said.

He hugged me back stiffly. I tried not to think about the looks or mouthed words he and Kim were exchanging behind my back.

Dad pulled out of the hug. "What are you doing here? We talked about this."

I smiled in spite of the knot in my stomach. "I've been giving you space for four months now. How much space do you need?"

I'd tried to keep my tone light, but the question came off desperate. Worse, no one was answering. Dad scowled at me, cheeks reddening. Kim looked ready to explode—if her arms crossed any tighter, she'd turn into a pretzel.

The seconds felt like hours. I willed someone to say something, anything. Even Kim's voice would have been preferable to silence at this point.

I wished too soon. "Billy," Kim snapped, "if you don't say it, I will."

Dad turned on his wife. "Kim," he said, voice deadly quiet, "go wait in the car."

Kim pouted but slunk away.

He watched me with emotionless eyes. "We know, Rose."

"Know what?" I asked, my heart rate quickening.

"Stop playing dumb," he said flatly. "I know you lied."

I tried to keep my face blank. "Lied about what?"

Parents had collected their daughters. The fathers had their arms around the little ones, congratulating them on a great game. The mothers packed up the coolers. The kids chattered and sipped their juice boxes. They all walked toward us, heading for their cars in the parking lot.

"About the cancer," Dad hissed, struggling to keep quiet, aware of the parents nearby. I had never seen him this mad. "You lied about having cancer! What the hell is wrong with you?"

I flushed. My outrage had to match his to be believable. "Excuse me?"

The parents nearby stared, their interest piqued. I bet they'd never heard Billy Gillespie raise his voice.

"I called Dr. Stanton's office," Dad said.

Shit.

"He's a general practitioner, not an oncologist," he said, hands shaking with fury. "Do you have any idea how humiliated I was?"

I'd worried this might happen. I did what my mother would have done—deny, deny, deny.

"Dr. Stanton is my GP, but I also have an oncologist," I said, indignation building. "Why were you calling my doctor anyway?"

"Your doctor's note was from Dr. Stanton," Dad said, jaw muscles tensing.

"Yeah." I jutted out my chin. "He's capable of deciding whether I'm healthy enough to travel."

"You told us Dr. Stanton was the one treating you." Dad waved his arms like a lunatic. "So who is this mystery oncologist?"

Quietly I said, "I asked my oncologist to write me a note but he said no. So I convinced Dr. Stanton to do it instead."

Dad's forehead wrinkled. "Why did your oncologist say no?"

I shrugged. "He said my body had been through a lot, that I should rest a few more weeks and then we'd see."

Dad was quiet for a minute, watching me.

"Rose," he said, his voice full of pain, "is a family trip really worth risking your health?"

Without hesitating, I said, "It is to me."

That much was true.

Our eyes met. I bit my lip.

For a second, I had him.

Then he blinked a few times and rubbed his forehead, like he was waking up from a spell. "Christ, what am I saying?" he fumed. "Why would one doctor say yes if the other said no? You never seemed sick. You were vague about treatment. You wanted all this support but then wouldn't let me come to your appointments." He paused, fresh anger brewing. "You pretended to have Hodgkin's lymphoma to guilt-trip me. So I would let you come camping. What the hell is wrong with you?" he yelled.

The other parents exchanged shocked looks; they were watching their kids' soccer coach ream out a helpless young woman. I imagined them speaking in hushed tones later: *Is this the kind of man we want around our children?* I wondered if they'd kick him off the team.

I felt about two feet tall. I could see now how colossal a mistake I had made. My mother had never been caught in a lie—until the end. How had this all gone so wrong? I just wanted a family, my family.

I cleared my throat and opened my mouth, having no idea what to say next.

Dad cut me off before I could speak. "Don't you dare keep lying. Don't you dare even think of opening your mouth and saying one more word about cancer or being sick or how much you need me and my family."

Anna scurried over, hair disheveled, but she was smiling. She stopped short when she saw the livid expression on her father's face. "Daddy?" she said, hesitant.

Dad's eyes flicked toward Anna. "Go to the car and find Mommy."

Anna didn't protest. She walked straight to the car, turning back once to glance at me.

I tried not to squirm under the heat of Dad's stare. Peering up, I marveled at the blue-sky day. The sun was shining, not a cloud in sight. How could my world crumble on such a beautiful afternoon? In the movies, it would be pouring right now, and I'd be stuck without an umbrella. I could have used a good-sized tornado right about then to scoop me up and take me somewhere else. Anywhere far, far away.

I'd banished the voice inside my head last year, yet I still found myself waiting for her to tell me what to do. She'd been silent since I'd arrived at the soccer field, though. I realized that, for the first time in my life, her voice was gone. She'd been guiding me through every day for the better part of twenty-one years. She told me how to eat, dress, behave, scheme. I hadn't realized how dependent I was on her directions until she took them away, and I hated that I wanted her help. I'd been sure I'd never need anything from that woman ever again, but I'd been fooling myself. Now, when I needed her most, I had to rely on myself instead.

Dad stepped forward and wagged a finger in my face. "You stay away from my family—you got that?" He was trying to intimidate me, but fell a few feet short. I wasn't scared of Dad—I was scared of *not*

Dad. I was scared of the void I knew was coming. Warts and all, he was still better than having no one.

"Leave *me* the hell alone too," he added. He was beginning to annoy me with this self-righteous act. Like he was a saint. Like he'd never made a mistake. He'd lied by omission for twenty years. *He* was the one who had come looking for *me*, who had dangled the promise of a family in my face and then yanked it away.

We had reached the point of no return. There would be no coming back from this. There would be no big happy family—at least not one that included me.

"I expect my son to act out," he said, face still red with anger, "but girls are supposed to behave."

I guessed my mom never got that memo.

Dad watched the other families pack their trunks, climb into their cars, and drive away. A few stragglers were stalling, trying to watch our little drama reach its conclusion.

"You're just like your mother," he jeered.

I wished he'd shut the fuck up and leave already. I imagined putting hexes on the four oldest Gillespies, wrapping them in tumors and stab wounds until they were mummies bound by their own blood.

But he couldn't know that. He needed to think I was anything but a threat, that I was contrite even. Sugar and spice and everything nice, that was what he expected.

"I'm so sorry," I said, wincing at the pathetic desperation in my voice, though I knew it was necessary. "I didn't mean to hurt you."

Dad put the clipboard in his backpack. Before stomping off, he shook his head. "I'm sorry I ever went searching for you."

I stood very still, squinting. He shouldn't get off that easy. I swallowed my rage.

"Dad, I'm sorry," I called after him, channeling the old Rose Gold, the meek girl, all shoulders and no spine. She was a lifetime ago. She was dead. I danced on her grave. "I said I'm sorry."

Dad spun around, glowering at me. "I know one thing for sure," he said.

We had the same small noses and hazel eyes. He clenched his hands.

"You deserve every rotten thing you got."

19

Patty

I stare at the watery blue eyes on my bedroom ceiling, too exhausted to be scared of them. After my four-hour embrace with the porcelain throne last night, I have nothing left to give. I swing my legs over the side of the bed; I have to drive Rose Gold to work. First, I want to confront her about last night.

I shuffle to the living room just in time to hear the front door close. Rose Gold walks by the window in running clothes: a tank top, mesh shorts, and gym shoes. She looks ridiculous in that getup in the middle of December. I watch her for a minute. She sets off at a plodding pace down Apple Street, all elbows, shoulder blades, and knees. I shake off the urge to run after her with a scarf and mittens. She takes a right on Evergreen and disappears from sight.

Fine, the conversation can wait until I have her cornered in the van.

Forty minutes later, we leave the house together, at our usual time. While I lock up the house, she buckles Adam into his car seat, then climbs in beside me. I take the wheel, start the engine, and head for the highway.

"Are you feeling any better?" Rose Gold asks.

I say yes, though my stomach is still a bit wobbly. I don't want to betray any signs of weakness.

Rose Gold plays peekaboo with Adam while I debate the best way to confront her. Perhaps she had nothing to do with the treadmill or the yard fire, but I know she's been making herself out as a victim to Arnie, Mary, and Lord knows who else. And now she's poisoned my food. This has gone too far.

"I can't believe you didn't get sick at all," I say.

Rose Gold shrugs. "I'm sure the prison food did a number on your digestive system. You must still be adjusting."

"I got out a month and a half ago. I've never gotten sick before." *Composure, Patty, keep your cool.*

"That's true. . . ." Rose Gold trails off, content to leave my sickness a mystery. But I'm determined to pin her down today. I will not let her slippery excuses and noncommittal shrugs slide.

I stare straight ahead. We're going fifty in a forty-five-mile-per-hour zone. *Just right, Patty. Keep it above the legal limits but not fast enough to get caught.*

"Did you put something in my food?" I ask, keeping my voice flat.

Rose Gold turns to me, eyes bulging. "What?"

"We ate the same meal. How could you be fine while I was a wreck?"

The look of shock, the feigned innocence—I want to slap it right off her face.

"Are you suggesting I poisoned you?"

She is outraged. The speedometer climbs to sixty. Adam babbles in the backseat.

"How else can you explain it?" *Stay quiet, Patty. Deadly calm.*

"I don't know, *Mom*." There it is again, that sarcastic emphasis on my name. "Do you know how fucked up it is that *that* is the first place your mind goes? After everything I've done for you?"

My teeth clench so hard, my jaw starts to shake. After everything *she's* done for *me*? She's taken me in for all of six weeks. I gave her every single piece of me for eighteen years. Right up until she thanked me for my sacrifice by sending me to prison.

And she knows she's forbidden from using curse words.

The speedometer hits seventy.

Rose Gold raises her voice. "Why on earth would I want to poison you?"

I am the surface of an undisturbed pond, a cactus in the still heat. The rational mind always wins. "Maybe to get revenge."

Rose Gold narrows her eyes, her tone mocking. "Why would I need revenge if you're innocent?"

Her smirk fills the air between us, taunting me, daring to suggest she knows more than I do, that she has outsmarted me in some way. The insolence.

"Maybe the media got in your head the way it brainwashed everyone else."

I pull off the highway and am forced to slow down. I can see the Gadget World parking lot around the bend.

"Everyone but you, huh?" Rose Gold sneers. "Everyone in the whole town has gone crazy, with the exception of Patty Watts. Always someone else's fault, isn't it? You're never, ever to blame."

I can feel the soft flesh of the neck oozing between my fingers. My thumbs silence the voice box. The spinal cord bends to my will.

How dare she? I think over and over.

I will not stand for this abuse.

A dam and I watch the frozen pond, searching for signs of life in the park. But the animals have all moved south for the winter. The wind picks up. I zip Adam's snowsuit all the way to his chin.

The weather is a bit nippy for a day at the park, but I needed to get out of that house. We drove forty minutes south to find a playground where nobody knows us. No Mary Stones or Tom Behans or Arnie Dixons to try to hurt us. No one at all—the park is empty today.

I pull Adam out of his stroller and bounce him on my knee. Already he is growing his own little personality: smiling when he farts, chewing on his hands, drooling all over every piece of clothing I've laundered. He's used to me now, spending more time in my care than Rose Gold's these past few weeks. At least he won't be leaving with a stranger.

Because we do have to leave. I realize that now. Neither of us is safe with his mother.

My daughter has turned this town against me, flaunting her skin and bones during neighborhood runs. Mary and the rest of them think I'm poisoning her. Her coworkers believe I'm torturing her. All this time, I blamed Tom or Arnie or maybe a few neighbors teaming up to destroy me.

But Rose Gold has always excelled at playing the victim.

Never mind all the attention she got while she was sick. Never mind the free toys and extra lollipops from the nurses and the total adoration of every citizen in Deadwick. She had them eating from the palm of her hand—she chose to throw it all away. And now she wants it back.

I have tried to be the doting mommy I thought my daughter wanted. But I didn't suffer through five years of prison to be turned into a villain again. She wants to drive me away? Fine, I'll go.

I study the baby in my arms. "You look like your mother when she was your age," I say. Same hazel eyes, same petite nose. I hope he's stronger when he grows up.

I toss Adam in the air and catch him, swinging him down through my legs and back up. He giggles with delight, watching me with those wide, curious eyes.

So far he has been a healthy baby.

That won't last long.

After all, Rose Gold's digestion issues began around Adam's age. He's shown no signs of apnea or pneumonia like she did, but there must be something sinister lurking beneath those rosy cheeks. No baby is perfect.

I set Adam down on his stomach in the frosty grass. A little exposure to the elements will make him stronger. He stretches his legs and kicks his feet, facedown in the cold.

"Adam," I whisper. "Adam, look at Grandma."

As if he understands me, the baby raises his head. He balls his hands into fists, kicking his legs harder. His mouth opens. I wonder whether I should let him cry.

At the last second, I swoop down and scoop him up, tossing him in the air again. That's enough for one day. His whine turns into a laugh. I laugh too and palm his forehead. His cheeks are pink—or are they green? Could he have a cold or the flu? I think a trip to the doctor is in our future. Better safe than sorry.

I put Adam back in his stroller and walk him to the van. Starting it, I head toward Deadwick.

Odd how you adjust to life's new circumstances. I've already become used to pulling into the driveway of my childhood home. My stomach tightens at the sight of the house for a different reason now.

In the kitchen, I move two bags of Rose Gold's frozen milk from the freezer to the refrigerator, then take out a bottle of chilled milk.

We have our routines down pat: Rose Gold pumps breast milk and puts it into the freezer; then I thaw it to feed Adam. I may have to switch him to formula, but that's not the end of the world. I grew up on formula and did fine.

Adam sucks at the bottle. He has a big appetite and rarely throws up his food. His weight and height won't convince any doctor he's having digestion issues. He is not his mother's son in that regard. He gazes at me, the essence of goodness, while he drinks. What I love most about babies: their dependence. They need us in order to survive.

All I've ever wanted, as a mother, is to be needed. The first few years of your child's life, no one is more important to her than you, not even her father. That biological imperative demands to be satisfied, over and over and over. And then your child turns ten or twelve or eighteen, and suddenly you're no longer critical. How are we supposed to cope? We mothers give up everything for our children, until they decide they don't want our everything anymore.

Isn't it just like a daughter to blame all her shortcomings on her mother? Whether it's limp hair or a penchant for lying, every character flaw is our fault, not theirs. Naturally, all our daughters' best traits have nothing to do with us. What other traps does she have waiting for me behind closed doors? She has this wretched house rigged for my demise.

I put Adam in his bassinet, leaving him in his snowsuit. It couldn't hurt to get his body temperature up, for his cheeks to look a little redder than normal. The baby begins to whimper. Maybe he needs a diaper change.

I walk down the hallway to the bathroom. Out of habit, I try Rose Gold's bedroom door handle. Locked, as always.

Opening the cabinet under the sink, I pull a diaper from the box of Luvs. Adam cries louder. I rush back and change him. He keeps crying. I try burping him, rocking him, distracting him with toys—all of it on maternal autopilot. I need him to stop so I can make a plan. I need a minute to think.

He quiets down before I resort to putting him in the backyard.

I glance at the baby in my arms. I can't leave Adam behind with Rose Gold, not if she's become this unhinged. There will be time to take him to a doctor later. Besides, a new doctor in a different state won't know my name or recognize me. Why wouldn't she believe the story of a grandmother raising her grandson alone after a family tragedy?

I pick up my phone and search for flights out of Chicago. Where will we go—California? Maine? Montana? I have only ever lived in this godforsaken town. Maybe I should book the next outbound flight, no matter where it's going.

"Hang on a minute, Patty," I say, trying to calm down. "Think it through now. You're the logical one. She's the emotional one."

I check my watch: four fifty-eight p.m. Rose Gold is supposed to be home from work in forty-five minutes. I need more of a lead than that. If I take Adam, Rose Gold will move mountains to find him. He and I will never be at peace.

This would all be so much easier if she just . . . disappeared.

Out the window, snow has begun to fall. Christmas is eight days away. Neither Rose Gold nor I have decorated the house. We're the only ones on the block without red and green lights lining our roof. No doubt she expected I would take responsibility for this year's festivities. She took everything I did for granted—the hand-cut snowflakes, the miniature-scale village, the Kolaczki cookies I bought from the Polish bakery. I worked tirelessly, every year, for her.

I squeeze Adam, relieved I'm not in this alone. We can't go anywhere until Rose Gold comes home from work. I swivel my recliner toward the front door.

For now we wait.

20

Rose Gold

November 2016

The stone-faced security guard at Mordant Correctional Center tapped the dotted line with his pen.

"Need you to sign here," he said, glaring.

I signed the form, then pushed the clipboard back toward him.

"Have a seat. Someone'll take you through." He gestured to the row of plastic chairs behind me. I caught a glimpse of the gun on his belt. I wondered what it would feel like to shoot someone.

The prison was quieter than I'd expected—or at least the reception area was. I was the only person waiting. I stared at the ugly linoleum, feeling the guard's eyes on me. I hoped I'd be taken through soon.

It had been over a year since my dad turned out to be the worst. I hadn't spoken to Alex or Phil in just as long. I'd tried to make new friends at work, but none of my coworkers were interested, so I'd opted to start watching all the Oscar Best Picture winners instead. I'd also begun drawing in my spare time. To my surprise, I was actually good.

Not saying my artwork will end up in a museum or anything, but my renderings of Dad's bones breaking on a medieval torture rack were shockingly realistic. I had a gift for sketching faces.

By then I was close to having enough money to get my teeth fixed, to being someone who *beamed*, hands at her side instead of blocking her mouth. After my teeth, I planned to start saving for a down payment on a house. Every day at Gadget World, I reminded myself what I was working toward.

Still, watching my savings account grow couldn't occupy all my free time. One year after Dad blew up at me at Anna's soccer game, I realized I was miserable. I had learned the hard way that our parents didn't have all the answers. We wanted them to. We believed they did for the first couple decades of our lives, depending on the parents and how good they were at covering their asses. But in the end, discovering our parents were mere mortals was no different than finding out about Santa and the Easter Bunny.

Now every day was the same: wake up, go to work, eat dinner in front of the TV, watch a movie, sketch, go to sleep. After the Gillespie family had ostracized me, I told myself I didn't need them to be happy. I bought a fern, named her Planty, and told myself she would be more than enough company.

Then my coworker Brenda, the one who used to tease me about visiting Phil, didn't come in to work one day. Or the day after that, and so on. No one knew where she had gone, until weeks later, when Scott gathered us in the break room before the store opened. He said Brenda had been diagnosed with stage IV pancreatic cancer. A month later she was dead. Her four-year-old daughter and two-year-old son were motherless.

I had never really been friends with Brenda—she had kids, was in her thirties; we were in different stages of life—but I couldn't stop thinking about all those afternoons in the break room with her hooked up to that breast pump. Now she was gone. I would never talk to her again. This was the first time someone I personally knew had died. It sounds stupid, but Brenda's death made me realize I wasn't going to live forever. If I didn't like the way my life was turning out, no one else was going to fix it for me. I had to do something. I needed to go back to the beginning, back to the first wrong turn—which meant going back to Mom.

When I had gotten the restraining order against her, did I truly believe I would never see or speak to my mother again, for as long as we both should live? Maybe I liked to think so during fits of anger, but the honest answer was: no, of course not. I had permanently cut other people from my life for less, but none of them was my mother. Mom still held the key to so much information I wanted: her childhood, my childhood, and most of all, *why?*

The one-word anthem pounded in my ears when I woke up in the morning and lay in bed at night: why? Why? WHY? I needed her to explain, to tell me the truth, to say she was sorry.

Which was why I'd finally come to Mordant Correctional Center.

I was trying not to pin big hopes on this reunion. Mom was the biggest liar I knew—maybe she wasn't capable of honesty or apologies. If so, I'd have the restraining order reinstated. Our relationship, and her second chance, would be on my terms from now on. After four years on my own, I had no interest in being anyone's puppet anymore.

A uniformed man—enormous with thick biceps—ambled through the door.

"She the only visitor?" he asked. He had a mustache—a bad omen.

The first guard nodded.

"Follow me," the second guard said.

I slid off the chair and wiped my clammy hands on my pants. I'd told myself I didn't care enough to be nervous.

The giant guard led me down a long concrete hallway. A light flickered overhead. Swearwords and initials were scratched into the walls. A stain on the floor was rust colored.

We reached a door at the end of the hallway and stopped. The guard scanned his badge in a reader, and the door clicked as it unlocked. The guard pulled the door open. I followed him through. A sign next to the door read *Visitors Center.*

The room was filled with empty chairs and tables, set up for groups of two, four, and six. In one corner, a few children's drawings were taped to the walls. They were Thanksgiving turkeys, traced over little fingers and palms. The feathers had been colored red and orange and brown. "I love you, Mom" was written on one. I didn't want to think about where those kids were now or what their lives were like.

"Have a seat," the guard said. He left the room. I was alone.

I pulled out a chair—same as the hard plastic ones in the waiting area—and sat. Maybe I shouldn't have come.

A door opened on the opposite side of the room from where I'd entered. The same guard came back in, followed by my mother. She looked smaller than I remembered. Was it possible she'd shrunk in height? Or had I gotten bigger? Maybe it was her posture. She used to walk around Deadwick with her head held high, but this woman's shoulders sloped forward. She was stooped, a turtle wanting to curl back into its shell. The transformation was shocking.

Her gaze flicked from the guard to me, and her whole face lit up. *Christmas eyes,* I thought.

Her shuffle turned into a stride as she came closer. I didn't want to give her the satisfaction of an embrace, didn't want her to think she was forgiven. But my chest ached for one of my mother's infamous bear hugs. Before I had time to decide whether I'd allow her the intimate gesture, she had enveloped me in her fleshy arms. My body relaxed into hers.

"Oh, my baby," she murmured into my ear, stroking my hair. "You have no idea how good it is to see you."

I forced myself to stiffen and pull away. I needed to remember that my mother's hugs and hand-holding were never about love; they were forms of control. A therapist had helped me figure that out. I'd gone to a few sessions before deciding I'd rather spend the money on my teeth.

I reached for the back of my chair, was in the process of returning to my seat, when I saw her fat lip—ugly, purple, and split open.

"Oh, my God. What happened to your lip?" I asked, unable to hold back.

Mom sat across from me and tapped it with one finger. "Oh, this," she said. "I was walking the track the other day and tripped and split it. What a klutz."

I had never known my mother to be clumsy. "You fell and landed on your lip?"

"Well, no, I landed on my hands and knees. But I bit my lip on the way down."

Her hands were on the table in front of me. They weren't cut or bruised or bandaged—they looked fine, except for more dirt under her fingernails than usual.

I had assumed my mom ran the prison. I figured she had the warden in her back pocket, that she'd upended whoever had reigned supreme here. She was the sparkly, effervescent one; she was supposed to be untouchable. She had been the protector of the bullied.

Now she was being bullied herself.

The woman in front of me had bloodshot eyes, messy hair, and a dull complexion. To a stranger, she would have resembled the same person who had raised me. To me, she looked nothing like the woman I'd grown up with. I remembered everything I had said on the witness stand: how I had humiliated her, left no sordid detail untold. Her split lip was, in part, my fault. If I hadn't turned her in, she would never have gone to prison.

"Are you sure you're okay, Mom?" I asked.

I cursed myself. I'd been planning to call her "Patty" to put some space between us—and to hurt her feelings.

This is not your fault. She's in prison because she abused you.

I was finally starting to listen to my own voice instead of hers.

She waved me off and forced a smile. "I'm fine, honey. Don't you worry about me." She rested her chin on her hand, then winced in pain and adjusted her position. "Now, tell me everything that's going on with you. Are you working? Do you have a boyfriend? I want to hear it all."

I told Mom about Gadget World, about the money I'd saved, and that I'd been named employee VIP three times in the last few years. She beamed. Then I told her about Phil, my first real boyfriend, and our visit in Denver. I left out the fact we hadn't spoken in a year and a half—and that he was older than she was. I considered telling her about my dad, but decided to save that story for another time. Something in my gut told me to keep it from her.

"And what about Deadwick?" Mom asked.

"What about it?" I said.

"Do you still talk to anyone? Our old neighbors and friends?"

"I rarely see Mrs. Stone anymore, if that's who you mean," I said without thinking. I knew this news would please Mom, but it was also true. Mary Stone had failed me just like everyone else. She still treated me like a child and kept reminding me she was my shoulder to cry on. But I was tired of crying, tired of people caring more about who I had been than who I am. Mrs. Stone liked me better broken. With every good deed, she needed confirmation that she was my savior.

I'd be my own goddamn savior, thank you very much.

Predictably, Mom was pleased. When Mrs. Stone had lambasted

her to reporters during the trial, my mother was not happy. Until she was arrested, no one had ever turned on Patty Watts.

"How is my old friend?" Mom's voice dripped with fake sweetness. This was the mother I knew: color had returned to her cheeks, her eyes bright and attentive. She hung on my every word, noting every detail.

"Annoying," I said, trying to put an end to the topic. I'd come here for answers, and so far I'd been the one doing all the talking. My mother was manipulating me the way she manipulated everyone, the way she'd controlled my entire childhood.

"Listen, Mom," I said, giving up altogether on calling her "Patty." "If we're going to start over, I need you to be honest with me. No more trying to steer the conversation or deflecting my questions by turning around and asking your own."

Mom watched me, not saying anything.

"If you lie to me, I'm out of here," I said, staring at the table between us. I forced myself to meet her eye. "And I'm not coming back."

A beat of silence passed that felt like three eternities.

"Are we clear?" I said.

Mom nodded. "Of course, darling," she murmured. "I would never do anything to screw up our relationship again. I already lost you once."

I wasn't sure whether she was telling me the truth, but this seemed like the right tack. I had plenty of questions to test her commitment to honesty.

"Good," I said. "Then let me ask you again: how did you split your lip?" I crossed my arms and leaned back—my best no-BS pose.

Mom folded her hands in her lap. I knew if I peeked under the table, she'd be twiddling her thumbs. She told me she had gotten that habit from my grandfather. I'd caught myself twiddling my own thumbs while watching TV one night last month. I sat on my hands for the rest of the episode.

Mom sighed. "Another inmate hit me."

"Why?" I demanded.

"She doesn't like me very much."

"Mom," I warned, "don't be evasive."

Her eyebrows rose in surprise. I wondered if she was questioning where I'd learned the word "evasive." She hadn't taught me the term during any of her hundred vocabulary lessons, so where could I have picked it up? I was supposed to be an extension of her, a product of her creation and fine-tuning.

She rubbed her eyes. "Stevens has had it out for me since I got here. Every few months, she gets her band of cronies together to gang up on me. Two of them pin me against a wall while she takes a few swings." Mom shrugged. "Don't ask why she hates me. I haven't done anything to her."

Based on my mother's track record, I doubted that, but decided to let it go for now. I had bigger fish to fry.

"Why did you lie about how you hurt your lip?"

"Because I didn't want you to worry," Mom said, exasperated. "Because that's what mothers do. We shelter the hardest truths from our children to keep them safe. We take the hit so they don't have to feel the pain."

"I'm not a child anymore," I said calmly. "And I've dealt with some pretty hard truths the past few years."

Mom patted my hand. "It doesn't matter how old you are. The desire to protect your kid never goes away. I'm not going to apologize for that." She winced. Good—she was taking my threat to leave seriously. "You'll see when you have kids of your own," she added.

I snorted. Like I'd ever have kids after the f'ed-up childhood I'd endured.

"I want you to tell me about your family," I said. "Every time I've asked about them, all you've said was you had a tough childhood. I want to know specifics. What was so tough about it? What were my grandmother and grandfather like? And my uncle David?"

Mom groaned. "This is how you want to spend our first afternoon in almost five years together? Talking about our degenerate ancestors?"

"Mom," I warned again, "you promised you'd be honest."

"That doesn't mean I have to like it," she grumbled. She pushed up her sleeves and leaned her chest forward on the table. "My father was drafted when he was nineteen and went to Belgium in nineteen forty-four. This was after he'd met my mother, but before they got married."

For the next thirty-five minutes, Mom painted a picture for me of her childhood. She told me, in sickening detail, about my grandfather's abuse. She told me about her brother's suicide. She told me about her mother's miscarriages: three, to be exact, between David and her. She explained the Wattses had been an every-man-for-himself family. Her mother hadn't stood up for her. Neither had her brother. As soon as Mom had turned eighteen, she'd moved out of the house into an apartment on the other side of town and found a job as a certified nursing assistant. She cut all ties with her parents. Sometimes she'd see one of them at Walsh's or the bank and would turn around and leave without saying a word. Mom never reconciled with either of them.

"I'm sorry I never told you any of this," Mom said. "You deserve to know if you want." She sat back in her chair, exhausted, and I knew she was finished.

I was exhausted too. I'd expected a sad story, but not this sad. I understood now why she had been so cagey all those years when I'd asked for details about my extended family. She wasn't trying to hurt me: she was being protective. I thought back to the morning I'd lied to Dad about having cancer. I wasn't trying to hurt him—I just wanted the Gillespies to accept me. Our methods might have been warped, but Mom and I had good intentions. We needed to be loved.

Nobody had ever looked at me the way my mother did. Not Dad, not Phil, not Alex. When I opened my mouth, the rest of the people in the room ceased to exist for her. When I was hurt, she ignored her own throbbing pain. Mom wanted to destroy my bullies more than I did. I might have forgiven them, but my mother would never forget.

The debt between a child and her mother could never be repaid, like running a foot race against someone fifteen miles ahead of you. What hope did you have of catching up? It didn't matter how many Mother's Day cards you drew, how many clichés and vows of devotion you put inside them. You could tell her she was your favorite parent, wink like you were coconspirators, fill her in on every trivial detail of your life. None of it was enough. It had taken me years to figure this out: you would never love your mother as much as she loved you. She had formed memories of you since you were a poppy seed in her belly. You didn't begin making your own memories until three, four, five years old? She'd had a running start. She had known you before you even existed. How could we compete with that? We couldn't. We accepted that our mothers held their love over us, let them parade it around like a flashy trinket, because their love *was* superior to ours.

"Thank you," I said. "And I'm sorry for everything you've been through."

Mom shrugged, cheeks flushed. I could tell she didn't want to talk about it anymore.

My mother's childhood stories were a warm-up to the questions I really wanted to ask. I felt bad about her past, but worse about my own. I wanted her to admit she'd taken my childhood from me, the same way hers had been taken from her. I wanted Mom to take responsibility for her wrongs. I needed her to look me in the eye and say she was sorry.

I had rehearsed this speech since the day I'd had the restraining order lifted. For months afterward, I hesitated to call the prison. Did I want to reopen this drama? I had no business poking a beehive.

"Another thing," I said.

Mom glanced up. "Anything," she said. This was the most earnest I'd ever seen my mother. She knew how to play earnest like an Oscar-winning actress.

The door on the far side of the room opened. The guard from earlier emerged. "Time's up, Watts," he barked.

"Already?" she said.

She stood, so I did the same. She wrapped me in another bear hug and whispered in my ear, "To be continued?"

This first visit had gone better than I could have hoped. I'd come to see my mother as a last resort, expecting the meeting would end in me storming out and never seeing her again. So far, she'd been willing to meet me halfway. She hadn't lied, as far as I could tell. Maybe we could get past our past, after all.

"How about next week?" I whispered back.

She pulled out of the hug and gripped me by the shoulders, searching my face for signs I was kidding. When she saw I was serious, her face broke into a wide grin, split lip and all. She squeezed my hand tight. "I would love that."

I watched my mother follow the guard through the door, shoulders back, head held high. She whistled, winked, and waved one more time before the door closed behind her.

That was the Patty Watts I knew.

21

Patty

Rose Gold is still not home. She should have been back an hour ago. She hasn't called or texted.

Maybe Gadget World is busy today. Maybe her manager asked her to work late. Maybe she's getting drinks with friends I don't know.

I send her a text.

> **Me:** Hi honey, will you be home soon?

I stare at the screen. No reply comes back.

Adam gurgles from his bassinet, unaware his mother is MIA. I get off my recliner and walk to the kitchen, pull his bottle from the fridge, move more frozen milk from the freezer to the fridge. Thank God Rose Gold has been pumping and storing all this milk.

I warm the bottle, then bring it back to the living room. I cradle Adam in my arms.

"Big strong boys need to eat, eat, eat," I sing. He gulps the milk.

I distract myself with attending to Adam. After he finishes the bottle, I burp him. I give him an extra-long bath, making sure he's spotless. I dress him in his duckling jammies, then rock him back and forth. I imagine every night like this one from now on: Adam and me winding down in a quiet house somewhere. Just the two of us.

I was born to be his mother.

I move the bassinet from the living room to my bedroom. By seven thirty, Adam is sound asleep inside it. For now the bassinet will do. His crib is in Rose Gold's locked room.

I call her phone twice. No answer.

We could leave first thing tomorrow.

I force that line of thinking from my mind. It would look fishy if I took off the morning after Rose Gold didn't come home.

I call Gadget World, but no one answers the phone there. I'll call again in the morning, if she hasn't come home by then. It'll be good to have a record of texts and calls, proof I was worried about and searching for my daughter. In case she doesn't turn up.

> **Me:** I'm worried about you, honey. Please text me back

Of course she doesn't.

I pace from the living room to the kitchen to the hallway to the living room. Around and around in circles I go, my phone clutched in my hand. This is what a Concerned Mother would do, wouldn't she? That is the role I need to play.

In the hallway I pull strings off the grass cloth wallpaper, like I used to when I was young and eavesdropping on my parents' arguments. I ball the string up into a little pile between my thumb and forefinger. These rooms are haunted with the spirits of all of them— Mom, Dad, David, and now Rose Gold.

I call my daughter's cell phone another dozen times, leaving stressed voice mails, even stubbing my toe so I cry in the last one. At eleven, I give up and get ready for bed. I wash my face and brush my teeth.

I'll deal with my missing darling in the morning.

I barely slept at all last night, between Adam's nighttime feedings and my anxiety about Rose Gold. At six, I get out of bed.

She's not coming home.

I check my phone, although I'd turned the ringer volume all the way up, in case she called in the middle of the night. No e-mails. No texts. No missed calls.

I feed Adam a bottle and weigh my options. A Concerned Mother would call the police, but they're going to ask too many questions. Besides, Concerned Mother doesn't know for sure Rose Gold is in any danger. For all I know, my daughter got fed up with Adam and me and decided to leave.

I like that explanation. If anyone tracks us down, I can say I left because Rose Gold left first. No one was keeping Adam and me in Deadwick. We wanted a fresh start.

As I burp Adam, I think about checking the news for information, but decide against it. It's been five years and two months since I tuned in, and I'm not about to start now. Besides, the authorities would reach out to me before the reporters got wind of any "scoop." They never get the story right anyway. I think back to an op-ed that ran in the *Deadwick Daily* right before my trial started: *HOW THE PATTY WATTSES OF THE WORLD ENDANGER ALL OUR CHILDREN.* Ridiculous. I put my grandson in his bassinet and promise I'll be quick.

I call Rose Gold, shower, then call her again. I cross the hallway to my bedroom to get dressed and pause at Rose Gold's door. What has

she been hiding from me these past six weeks? Maybe Concerned
Mother will find clues to her daughter's whereabouts.

After dressing and checking on Adam, who's fallen asleep, I return to the master bedroom. I try the door handle for the millionth
time—still locked, of course. With a bobby pin from the bathroom, I
try again to break the lock. Again the bobby pin snaps in half.

I walk outside and around the house to the exterior of Rose Gold's
bedroom. All the curtains are drawn, covering the windows, per usual.
It doesn't make sense to break a window when I can break down a
door. Besides, my snooping neighbors can't see what I'm doing if I'm
inside. I head back into the house, picking up my pace.

I consider googling "how to break into a room," but decide there's
no time. A Concerned Mother wouldn't be so logical as to research
steps for finding her missing daughter. She'd go ahead and break
down the godforsaken door.

I approach the door again. First I try shoving my shoulder into it.
It doesn't budge, but I'm confident I've bruised my arm. I ram the door
again and again, switching sides when my right shoulder begins to
hurt. After five minutes, the door is starting to give but still hasn't
broken open.

Marching to my bedroom, I pull on a heavy pair of boots, lacing
them tight. I return to the bedroom door, sigh, and start kicking it. On
the fourth kick, the wood begins to splinter. On the sixth, a long crack
forms. On the eighth, the door gives way altogether. It bangs back
against the wall. I've done it.

I peer inside, almost afraid. The bedroom looks the same as the
day I got out of prison, when Rose Gold gave me a tour of the house.
The bed is made. The crib is in order. The windows are closed.

I drag my fingers along the dresser. I open all eight drawers: no
clothes are missing. I search her jewelry box: all the cheap earrings and
bracelets are in place. I move on to the closet, opening the sliding-

mirror door. A cursory glance tells me nothing is missing from there either—the closet is as jam-packed with junk as before.

At her desk in the corner, I dig through the three drawers to the right of the chair. They are crammed with creased papers and old journals. I check the dates of the journals, but there's nothing here from the past few months or even the last five years. I put the journals back in the drawers. I used to read them before I went to prison, so I already know what their pages contain.

Her computer is dead. I plug the charging cord into the laptop, then press the power button. The machine whirs to life. Concerned Mother taps her foot.

Instead of wasting time waiting, I tear the comforter, then the flat sheet, then the fitted sheet from the bed. All I find is the blankie I sewed for Rose Gold when she was a baby. I'm surprised she still sleeps with it. I toss the shredded blanket aside.

Grunting, I heave the mattress off the box spring, sure I'll find something between them. Nothing. I get down on my stomach with a flashlight and check under the bed. There's a stack of dusty *Cosmopolitan* and *National Geographic* magazines, the same publications Alex used to read. While I flip through each magazine's pages, I imagine Rose Gold sitting here, alone and friendless, trying to copy the life of her cool older friend, Alex—buying the same groceries, using the same makeup, reading the same magazines. Pathetic.

Nothing falls out of any of them. Nothing odd is written on any of their pages. I turn back to the laptop. It's password-protected.

I try different combinations of Rose Gold's and Adam's names, their birthdays, even my own name, though I know the last one is unlikely. After the sixth failed attempt, the computer locks me out. I pound my fist on the desk. Concerned Mother is past desperate by this point. I wipe my forehead. My hand comes away damp.

Sitting in my daughter's desk chair, I peer around her bedroom—

a mess now, thanks to me, but nothing unusual or suspicious. No secrets to uncover.

Why has this door been locked all these weeks?

I check my watch—nine a.m. Gadget World should be open now.

I redial the number from last night and wait. The phone rings. On the third ring, someone picks up.

"Gadget World, Zach speaking. How can I help you?" says a chipper young voice.

"Hi, Zach. Is Rose Gold there?" I ask.

"She's not, but we just opened, so she could be running a few minutes late." Zach sounds like he doesn't have a care in the world, the little prick.

I debate how best to word my next question without sounding any alarm bells.

"Did she come in yesterday?" I say as breezily as possible.

"I'm not sure. I didn't work yesterday. Hang on. I'll transfer you to my manager's office."

Zach puts me on hold. The phone rings twice.

A miserable voice fakes enthusiasm. "Scott Coolidge, Gadget World manager, speaking. How can I help you?"

"Hi, I'm calling about Rose Gold Watts," I say.

"What about her?" Scott says after a beat.

I hesitate. "This is her mother, Patty."

Scott doesn't say anything.

"I was wondering if she came into work yesterday?" I close my eyes, trying to sound natural.

"No, she didn't," Scott says, annoyed. Bingo.

I make a clucking noise that could mean anything.

"Didn't even bother to call and tell me," Scott grumbled. "I called her phone three times. No answer."

"I'm sure she's sorry about that, Scott," I say. "I'm having trouble getting ahold of her too."

"So she's not coming in today either?" Scott says, not at all concerned about Rose Gold's well-being. "Listen, she knows I run a tight ship around here. You give one of them some slack, and the rest think you're a pushover. That's strike one for her."

"That seems fair. I know she respects your authority," I say, trying to wrap up the call. "I'll tell her to contact you as soon as I hear from her. Bye now."

I end the call before Scott can give me another lecture on responsibility, and dial Rose Gold's number again. Appearances are everything. She doesn't pick up. I put my phone on the desk.

A loud wail breaks my focus. Adam. I forgot he's been in the other room all this time. Oh, well, he can cry it out. Self-soothing is an important lesson to learn early—some of us do it our entire lives.

Hands on my hips, I wander around the room, trying to concentrate, to figure out what I've missed. After a minute, Adam's wails escalate into shrieks, stopping me short. Those are more than the cries of a hungry or tired baby or one who just wants to be held. I've heard it enough times. I'd recognize the sound anywhere.

I rush toward the bassinet. Adam is on his stomach, flailing his arms and legs.

Beneath his head is a puddle of green vomit. He stares up at me with a tear-streaked face.

Just like Rose Gold used to.

22

Rose Gold

November 2016

My mother leaned in and lowered her tone, though the nearest inmate was clear across the visitors center and sobbing to an elderly woman.

"I have a new cellmate," Mom said. I was trying to stay positive, but I didn't like the way her eyes lit up when she said it. Before I could respond, she continued. "Her name is Alicia. She can't be more than twenty. Guess why she's in."

"Why?" I asked. My first trip to the visitors center was two weeks ago. We'd gotten off to an okay start, but I wanted more from this second visit. I needed her to explain why she did what she did, to take responsibility for the ways she'd hurt me. In a year she'd be getting out of prison.

"Guess," Mom insisted.

"Burglary?"

"Nope."

"Drugs?"

"Nope."

"Too many DUIs or something?"

"You're never going to guess," Mom said with glee.

I sat back, thinking. I didn't care about Mom's cellmate, but decided to play along so we could get to the important stuff.

Mom leaned forward. "During her senior year of high school, she gave birth to a baby boy. When he was about two weeks old, she took him to the zoo—and left him. In a bush by the gorilla enclosure."

I looked up, startled. "Did the gorillas hurt him?"

Mom shook her head. "One of the zoo's staff members found the baby the next morning. He was hollering his head off, but he wasn't hurt. They traced the baby to Alicia after a few days."

"Then what happened to him?" I said.

Mom shrugged. "CPS or some such took him. Alicia was arrested."

"Why didn't she want the baby?" I asked.

"I haven't gotten that out of her yet. She's pretty tight-lipped. But a baby is a lot for a young girl to take on." Mom kept glancing over at the sobbing inmate, trying to suss out the drama. The woman was middle-aged, built like a linebacker. Her jowls flapped when she shook her head.

"Wouldn't the staff have found him when they were closing the park down for the night?" I tried to imagine being the employee who had found Alicia's son. I'd never held a baby.

Mom rolled her eyes. "What is this, Twenty Questions? I don't know, Rose Gold." She tilted her head back and stared down her nose at me. "We've been cellies for a week. Last night she went to the emergency room after cutting herself."

I covered my mouth with my hand. "That's awful."

Mom nodded. "I found her bleeding out on our cell floor." She sounded almost cheerful, like she used to when she'd gotten a deal on deli salami. When she saw my horrified expression, she put up a hand.

"Don't worry about me. I'm a trained medical professional, remember? I got her where she needed to go. Saved her life."

And with such humility too.

"They'll patch her up and send her right back to me. There's no 'talking through our feelings' at this place. I'll have to fix her myself. I think I can make a real difference in Alicia's life," Mom droned on. "The other women have made her life a living hell. They tend to look down on child abandonment."

This was my chance. "Yeah? How do they feel about child abusers?"

"I haven't conducted a formal poll," she said, not missing a beat, "but they're probably not big fans."

The sobbing inmate had quieted down, no thanks to the stony woman across from her. The inmate stood and turned to leave. When she saw my mother, her jaw stiffened and her head lifted.

Mom wiggled her fingers and half-smiled, half-sneered. "Stevens," she said, nodding a greeting.

The inmate ignored my mother and marched past her, slamming the door to the visitors center behind her. Mom chuckled to herself.

I was curious about my mother's relationship with this woman, but had to stay on topic before she eluded me again. "Do you know why you're here?" I asked.

Mom returned her attention to me. "Of course I do, sugar plum," she said.

We both waited for the other person to say something. When it became clear she had no intention of elaborating, I cleared my throat. "I want to hear you say it."

Her eyebrows furrowed, questioning.

I tried again, gaze focused on the table between us. "I want to hear you say—out loud—what you were convicted of." A trickle of sweat ran down my chest.

Mom stretched her arms out wide, forming a T. Like Jesus on his crucifix, she might have said.

"Aggravated child abuse."

Goose bumps popped up on my arms. I couldn't believe she'd come out and said it. My mother was finally taking responsibility for all the ways she had hurt me. Was she ready to admit she'd ruined my childhood? Maybe this would be the turning point in our relationship. Maybe I didn't have to shun her for the rest of my life.

When I glanced up, Mom stopped humming a cheery tune I hadn't heard her start. She sniffed. "But you and I both know that's a load of horse hockey."

No, I thought. *No, no, no.* I hadn't realized how much I wanted things to work out between us until this moment.

Mom gripped my hands in hers. "You know how much I love you, baby. I would never, ever hurt you."

I pulled my hands, red and throbbing, from her grip. I might explode into a million tiny pieces. Lava would boil from my ears and eyes. "So you're saying you're innocent?" I asked, teeth starting to clench.

Mom snickered and waved me off. "I never said I was a perfect mother," she said, "but I did my best."

"Don't do that."

"Have I told you about—"

"That thing where you give the vague answer," I said, speaking over her like she'd done to me countless times. "Draw a line in the sand. Are you saying you did or didn't poison me as a kid?"

My heart jerked in my chest. I was sure it was either going to sink through my stomach or project up my throat and out of my mouth. Mom watched me wipe my hands on my jeans. She sat there, observing me for a while, an amused expression on her face.

She tittered. "This is why I limited your TV time growing up.

When you watch too much drama, it melts your brain. You start thinking real life is like a movie."

"Yes or no?" Any semblance of pleasantness had left my voice.

Her smile faded. She gave me a withering stare. "No, of course not," she said. "Now, knock it off. You're way out of line. Don't forget who raised you, you ungrateful brat."

I shrank back. She hadn't changed at all. I should have known. Every single person to pass through my life disappointed me.

"It's not my fault you have no friends and a dead-end job," she ranted, face reddening. She was seething now. "If you're awkward and ugly, you have no one to blame but yourself. I gave you every opportunity. I gave up my career and my independence, plus any pretense whatsoever of a romantic relationship. I gave you everything, all of me—can you get that through your thick skull? And you thank me for my sacrifice by turning on me the first chance you get? By marching straight to the witness stand? You believed that wench Alex and her bigmouth mother over me? It's *your* fault I'm in here, not mine."

Keep going, I begged her. *Burn the whole thing down.*

"How dare you storm in here, after four years of silence, demanding apologies," my mother yelled. "You should be the one apologizing to me. I can't imagine what in high heaven I did to deserve a daughter like you. When I was a kid, I got beaten far worse for far less. You thank your lucky stars I don't believe in the belt."

"Quiet down, inmate," the guard in the corner of the room boomed.

His voice reminded me where we were. I loosened my grip on the arms of the chair. She couldn't hurt me here. I didn't need to be afraid.

Mom sat back, losing steam the way she always did. In the past, I would have scrambled to figure out a way to make up for whatever I'd done to her, to be the perfect daughter I was sure I could be. But I didn't have to make nice anymore. I was no longer my mother's possession. I was free to go.

I gathered my things, jaw set. I took out my sunglasses case from my purse. She would continue to grow old in her cell while I enjoyed this sunny day. I pushed back my seat.

"I'm sorry," my mother blurted. "I shouldn't have said the thing about the belt. That was too far. You know I would never lay a hand on you."

I sat there, chair pushed back from the table, too angry to formulate a response.

My mother gestured for me to scoot closer. "Come on, come on now. I brought this photo to show you of another inmate's dog." She pulled it from her pocket. "Broccoli—that's the dog's name—lives with the inmate's husband in California. He just won the World's Ugliest Dog Contest. Come see." I didn't budge, arms crossed, so my mother stood. "Here, I'll come to you."

She hovered over me, jabbing the photo in my face, prattling about the hilarities of this hideous dog—back to sweet, funny Mom. I didn't hear a word. For the first time in a while, I was thinking clearly.

In less than a year she'd be out. She'd start this Jekyll-and-Hyde cycle all over again. The warmth and jokes, followed by the inevitable mood swing, which then morphed into abuse, and then back to being the village sweetheart. A onetime screaming match or slap across the face was not enough to address this level of evil.

She needed a scar. Something permanent.

I glanced at the clock on the wall: six minutes until the guard announced the visit was over. I could do anything for six minutes. So I pretended to listen to her stories. I grinned and laughed and gasped in all the right places. I played the doting daughter right up until the guard signaled to me that time was up. To beat my mother at her own game, pretending was key. She once told me, after sweet-talking her way out of a speeding ticket, that it was easier to manipulate someone if they didn't perceive you as a threat.

I pushed back in my chair, walked around to her side of the table, and gave her a big hug.

"No hard feelings?" she asked, searching my face for hints.

I beamed and shook my head. I walked toward the exit, calling back to her with the enthusiasm of a thousand cheerleaders. "See you next week!"

In the parking lot at Walsh's, I sat in the van, fuming. I took my hands off the steering wheel and watched with awe as they trembled; I had never shaken with rage before. Most of the time, my emotions tumbled out in the form of tears or fear.

I couldn't imagine crying ever again. I'd aged forty years between walking into the visitors center and leaving it. Duped, again. And again. And again.

I wasn't ready to face my neighbors inside the grocery store yet—I needed to calm down first. Deep breath in, deep breath out. I took my phone out of my purse.

I scrolled through the social media app where I had the most friends: thirty-five. Christmas was a few weeks away, so everyone's status updates were about the holiday-themed activities they were up to. Here were the Johnsons, ice-skating at Riverfield Park. There was Kat Mitchum, posting photos of the puppy her parents had given her: an early Christmas present. I paused at Sophie Gillespie's name; she, Dad, and the rest of the Gillespies were standing next to a tall pine at a Christmas tree farm. Dad was flashing a thumbs-up and a cheesy grin. He was as happy as I'd ever seen him. Clearly not losing sleep over losing me.

Sighing, I got out of the car and traipsed into the grocery store. I needed a bunch of frozen dinners—I didn't have it in me to cook this week. Then I'd be on my way home to hang out with Planty.

I steered my cart down the frozen foods aisle, loading up with Salisbury steaks. Someone called my name. "Rose Gold? Doll, is that you?"

I knew before I turned that it was Mrs. Stone. I groaned internally. The last thing I needed right now was her peppy bullshit.

I contorted my face into a grin and turned to face her. "Hi, Mrs. Stone."

She hugged me, then surveyed my cart. "Are you getting enough to eat? You never eat your vegetables."

Shut the fuck up, I wanted to screech. Why did every person I know feel the need to tell me how to live my life? Where were all these adults when I was being poisoned in my own house for eighteen years? None of them had known better then; why on earth would they think they did now?

"Produce is up next," I lied, although now I would have to pick up some vegetables in case I ran into her again at checkout. All I wanted was to go home, microwave some popcorn, and watch *Amadeus*, the next Oscar winner on my list. Was that so much to ask?

"Oh, good. You know, a vitamin deficiency can lead to hair loss. And you've always been so sensitive about your hair—"

"Tell me about your day," I said, relaxing my jaw. "Anything newsworthy?"

"Oh, not really," she said. Mrs. Stone was the office administrator at Deadwick Elementary, so I didn't doubt she was telling the truth. "Actually, you know Karen? Ms. Peabody?" she added. Karen Peabody was my old neighbor and school principal before I started homeschooling.

When I nodded, Mrs. Stone continued. "Her parents are thinking about selling their house on Apple Street. Gerald's cancer is back.

Things don't look good, bless his heart. Mabel doesn't think she can manage the house anymore. Such a shame."

I had no idea why Mrs. Stone thought this story was interesting to the average person. Lucky for me, it was.

"Two-oh-one Apple Street?" I asked, in what I hoped was a neutral tone.

"That's right," Mrs. Stone said. She paused a moment. "I think that was your mom's childhood house, come to think of it."

I nodded, mind whirling.

She gave me a haughty smile and patted my arm. "You must sleep well at night knowing she's finally where she belongs." She had no idea I'd started visiting my mother in prison. As I'd learned recently, there were a lot of other things busybody Mrs. Stone didn't know about her former best friend.

I said good night and whistled on my way to the produce section. Maybe I'd buy a few mangoes or something, really live it up.

Two weeks ago Mom had told me—zipped-lips Rose Gold, her sweet little confidant—exactly what had gone on at 201 Apple Street. She said she'd never told anyone the horrific details before. Patty Watts had told me her secrets because she trusted me and me alone. Or maybe she didn't trust me. Maybe she just never thought I'd use her weaknesses against her.

Maybe she had underestimated me.

23

Patty

I pull Adam from his bassinet, cradling him in one arm and feeling his forehead with the back of my hand. He isn't burning up—no fever. I rock him back and forth a few times, but he keeps on wailing. The stench of vomit reaches my nostrils. I can't leave it pooled there in his bassinet.

I place my grandson in his crib in Rose Gold's bedroom.

"Just for a few minutes, sweetheart," I call over his shrieks.

Running to the kitchen, I grab a roll of paper towels and antibacterial spray. Adam's cries haven't subsided, but they're harder to hear now. I could walk out the side door and pace the yard for a while until he quiets down. Of course I won't. Overbearing? Maybe. But I have never been neglectful.

I square my shoulders and walk back to my bedroom, cleaning products plus trash bag in hand. I scoop the puke out of the crib and whistle the *Mary Poppins* song "A Spoonful of Sugar," struggling to drown out the baby's cries.

When the bassinet is clean, I return to Rose Gold's room, lean over the crib, and watch Adam. He's still crying, but losing steam.

I pick him up. "We're a team now," I tell him. "You have to be good for Grandma."

Adam's lower lip trembles, breaking my heart a little. His cries sound pitiful.

"What's wrong, sweet pea? Are you hungry?"

I carry him to the kitchen and pull a bottle from the refrigerator. A couple days ago, she was still here, pumping breast milk and feeding her child. Now she's left me alone.

When I bring the bottle to Adam's lips, he sucks hungrily, which means—oh, thank baby Jesus—he stops crying. I slump into a chair and try to feed him the bottle slowly, delighting in every second of quiet. That old maxim is true: children are better seen and not heard.

With the baby calmed down, I can think again. I need to make a plan, figure out where my daughter is.

When the bottle is empty, I return Adam to his clean bassinet in my room. He whimpers a little, but nothing that can be heard through a closed door. I leave the door open a crack when I leave.

I have been searching the living room for clues for no more than four minutes when he starts bawling again. I bite my lip. This is the last thing I need in the middle of a crisis. I head down the hallway to check on him.

He's vomited again, more this time. I rack my brain for answers: the flu? Reflux? A stomach bug? I sniff his diaper and wince, carrying him to the changing table in Rose Gold's room. He has diarrhea because of course he does. I put a new diaper on him before he makes a mess in two rooms.

His howling is giving me a headache. I put him in his crib and set to work cleaning the bassinet for the second time this morning. I've almost finished scrubbing when I hear the sound of spit up. I run over to the crib to catch him throwing up in there too.

"Panicking won't solve anything," I say aloud. The tremor in my voice is unmistakable. My heart is thumping in my chest. I should be used to this—I dealt with a sick child for years and years. But it's been a while, and I am out of practice.

I clean off Adam's face, then rush to the bathroom. Yanking open drawers and pulling on cabinet doors, I toss bottle after bottle on the floor next to me. There has to be some Pedialyte here somewhere. Is that even the recommended treatment for vomiting children anymore? I don't know. I haven't been a medical professional in a long time. Adam's cries get louder.

I have ripped the bathroom apart, hunting for a relevant treatment, but I can't find one. Rose Gold has very few bottles of children's medicine; she is wholly unprepared for a sick baby.

I dash across the hall, back to Adam's side. His cries have morphed from short bursts to a steady wail. I lift him from the crib. "Please be okay, little one," I beg, trying to soothe him. He vomits all over my shirt.

"What's wrong with you?" I cry, trying to rip my shirt off with one arm while holding Adam in the other. He's going to get dehydrated if he keeps puking like this.

I should call his doctor, to be safe. That way, someone else will know what's going on. Someone else can help me find a solution to this problem. And if it turns out to be a twelve-hour bug, then fine. There's nothing wrong with calling to be safe.

I pick up my phone from the nightstand and press the address book icon before realizing I don't know the name of Adam's pediatrician. Maybe Rose Gold wrote it down in her physical address book. I ransack the kitchen junk drawer, pull out the address book, and flip through every page. When I get to "Z" and still haven't found an entry with a "Dr." title, I want to join Adam in his crying.

"What about Mommy's desk?" I say to the baby. I carry him back to Rose Gold's bedroom. I've already turned every drawer inside out, seeking clues about her disappearance, but I wasn't looking for doctor's information then. Maybe I missed something.

I search the desk's cubbies again, more frantically this time, not bothering to put everything back where I found it. Nothing in the file folders. Nothing on the side shelves. Nothing in the pencil drawer. She must keep the pediatrician's contact information on her phone. I yell in frustration.

An hour later, Adam is still crying and throwing up. I'm no closer to having a plan. I've reached my breaking point, wanting nothing more than to collapse on the floor and throw a tantrum. *I don't know what to do,* I keep thinking. *Someone tell me what to do.*

I get a flash of inspiration: I'll give him another bottle. He quieted down for ten or so minutes when I gave him one earlier. Ten minutes is all I need—a little block of time to think straight and choose a course of action. And I don't want him getting dehydrated. A little milk will be good for him. For what must be the fiftieth time today, I dart from the bedroom to the kitchen.

Adam latches onto the rubber nipple. His screams subside. I nearly crumple to my knees in thanks. I watch Adam's tear-streaked face while he drinks. I need help. Then I have a thought.

I can—nay, should—take him to the hospital.

A tingle shivers down my spine. I imagine the doctors and nurses crowding around us, hurrying to attend to my sick baby, asking me questions, hanging on my every word.

What else is a worried grandmother to do? I have no way of contacting Adam's pediatrician. He has been vomiting for five hours. This is, by definition, an emergency.

I let Adam drink the rest of the bottle, then put him on Rose Gold's bed. Scurrying around the house, I pack the diaper bag with bottles of milk, wipes, and so on. I rush to my closet to put on a clean shirt. I run outside, open the garage door, and start the van so the interior will be warm by the time I bring Adam out.

Turning on my heel, I march back into the house again. When I open the side door, the first thing I notice is the quiet. Inside is as silent as outside.

My heart stops.

I realize I left Adam lying on Rose Gold's bed. He might have fallen off of it and hurt himself—or worse. I sprint past the kitchen and down the hallway, terrified. What if someone . . . No, I can't let myself go there. I was only gone for a second.

"Be okay, be okay," I chant to myself.

I cross the threshold to Rose Gold's bedroom. Adam's cries slap me like a glass of ice water. I'm flooded with relief to find the baby flailing around on his mother's bed. For a moment, I don't even mind that he's thrown up in here too. He is here. He is safe.

I vow never to let him out of my sight again.

My relief is short-lived. Is it possible his cries have gotten louder? I know in my gut something is wrong. Adam needs medical attention.

"Okay, bub, let's go," I say. I pick up Adam. I put his diaper bag over my shoulder and take one last glimpse at Rose Gold's destroyed room. This is not how I hoped to leave the house. If she comes back, she'll know I've ransacked her belongings. But by then I will also have restored her son to good health. I'm calling it even.

I buckle Adam into his car seat and remember again where we're going. I wonder what the doctor will be like—convivial with a perfect bedside manner or more formal and facts focused. I bet the nurses will pat me on the back, whispering I did the right thing. The other people in the waiting room will coo over Adam, say he looks like me, touch his forehead, and offer their own solutions. This is what I love about the medical community: everyone wants to help.

I back the van down the driveway, feeling a small twinge of fear. Some of Rose Gold's old doctors and nurses probably still work at the hospital. Worse, there's a chance Tom will be there. Then again he always worked night shifts. Besides, what choice do I have? Even if people there hold grudges against me, they still have to care for my grandson. We all took the same oath: *First do no harm.*

Maybe Adam has severe food allergies that need to be diagnosed and treated. That would make sense, after all. His mother has a long history of gastrointestinal issues.

I press on the gas pedal. Perhaps little Adam needs a feeding tube too.

24

Rose Gold

December 2016

I examined the three TV dinners on the folding table in front of me: Salisbury steak, lasagna, and a stuffed green pepper. I decided to start with the lasagna and pulled it closer to me. I couldn't be bothered to cook for myself anymore—what was the point of making elaborate meals if I was just going to eat them alone in front of the TV? I refilled my cup with more Sutter Home White Zinfandel.

I scarfed down the food and flipped through show after show on Netflix. The new live-action *Beauty and the Beast* film had just come out—Mom's favorite Disney movie. I stabbed at the remote, pausing on a documentary about weasels, but they reminded me of her too. I kept scrolling. After I'd been through every option, I turned off the TV and finished my dinners in silence.

For two weeks, a constant cry had run through my head: *Liar! Liar! Liar! Liar! Liar!*

It was like a car alarm with no deactivation button, and I couldn't turn it off. I'd cracked a plate last night thinking about it.

After clearing away the plastic cartons, I flopped onto the recliner, drumming my fingers on the armrest. I'd already watched *The Little Mermaid* four times this week. I spotted Planty in the corner. By the time I found a pair of scissors, I realized I'd already trimmed her dead leaves yesterday. I stuck my finger in the soil: already watered.

I wandered the house. Opening the fridge, I stared at the alphabetically organized condiments. This was the way she'd stored them, I remembered. I swiped at the bottles, messing up the neat rows until I had three shelves of chaos. My elbow caught on a jar and sent it flying to the ground, glass breaking and dill pickles flying everywhere.

I squeezed my hands into fists and screamed.

Screaming felt good. I'd been doing a lot of it. Normally I screamed into pillows so my neighbors wouldn't hear and call the police.

I left the pickles on the floor and stomped to my bedroom. The first thing I spotted was the pillow on my bed. I picked it up and pulled one end as hard as I could, arms shaking from the effort or rage. The satisfying rip of the cotton made me shiver. The stuffing tumbled out, landing in piles at my feet. I was standing on a cloud.

A knock at the front door broke my trance. I blinked, then tossed what was left of the pillow back on my bed and ran to the door.

When was the last time someone besides me had been in this apartment? I'd had an Amazon package delivered six months ago. . . .

I swung open the door. Mrs. Stone stood in the hallway. How had she gotten into the building? I thought about closing my door in her face. Then again, a little human interaction with someone not affiliated with Gadget World would be all right. I might need her down the road.

"Hi, dear," she said, scanning me up and down, like I might have a bomb strapped to my chest. I wondered what she saw. I hadn't looked in a mirror today or showered. Why bother on my day off?

"To what do I owe this pleasure?" I asked, pasting a smile on my face.

"You haven't been over in a while. I thought I'd visit. Can I come in?" Mrs. Stone gestured inside my apartment.

I opened the door wider and let her enter, taking her coat and draping it over a chair. She walked past me, eyes sweeping the living room. I didn't know what she was searching for. This woman deserved a plaque for annoying people in record time—she couldn't have been here more than thirty seconds.

"How's work been?" she asked, moving onto the kitchen. She stopped short at the refrigerator. "What's this?"

I remembered the pickles on the floor. "I was just cleaning those up," I said, bending down to pick up the soggy vegetables. "Had a little accident."

Mrs. Stone brought her hands to her face, a gross overreaction. "Oh, honey, are you all right?"

If I never heard that question again, it would be too soon. I was beginning to think there were worse things than loneliness—like unwanted company.

I tossed the pickles and dragged the trash can over to the fridge. Kneeling on the floor, I picked up the shards of glass.

"Oh, honey, don't use your bare hands. You're going to cut yourself. Be careful."

I closed my eyes, fingering one of the shards, thinking of not very nice things the glass could do to some very important veins in Mrs. Stone's neck. I picked up piece after piece of glass and tossed them into the trash, ignoring her warning. I glanced at her when I spoke.

"Everything okay, Mrs. Stone?"

She hemmed and hawed a bit. Then: "I heard you've been visiting your mother in prison. That you lifted the restraining order."

Jesus Christ, would it kill her to mind her own fucking business?

I tossed the last big piece of glass in the bin, then began wiping up the pickle juice with a towel. I glanced at Mrs. Stone, but didn't say anything.

"So it's true, then?" she asked, playing with a button on her fuchsia cardigan.

I walked to the hallway closet, yanked out the broom and dustpan, then returned to the kitchen. "Yes, it's true." I swept the smaller shards of glass into a little pile. Mrs. Stone watched, then hurried to grab the dustpan and held it next to the pile. I swept the debris onto it, and she dumped the remnants into the trash can. Taking the dustpan from her, I returned it and the broom to the hall closet. Mrs. Stone followed me into the living room. I sat in my recliner. She remained standing and kept fidgeting.

"Maybe it's none of my business," she said, clearing her throat, "but why?"

Damn right it's none of your business.

I made my eyes big and innocent. "Well, she is my mother, after all."

Mrs. Stone made a face, as if I'd suggested she eat the jar of pickles, glass shards and all. "After what she did to you, you don't owe her a second of your time."

She and I had avoided the topic of my mother in the past. I guessed neither of us cared to revisit how Mom had conned us, how stupid we were for falling for her lies all those years. At least I was a kid. Mrs. Stone must have felt like a real idiot, being tricked as a grown woman. I saw now how furious she was—I'd never seen her nostrils flare before.

"She's been in prison for more than four years," I said, knotting my hands in my lap. "Don't you think she deserves a second chance?"

Mrs. Stone's lips tightened to a thin line. "No. I don't think you should have anything to do with that woman."

Now was probably not the time to tell her I'd met with Gerald and

Mabel Peabody. They had agreed to sell me their house way below the asking price. Mabel said it was the least they could do after my "trying" childhood. She had been friendly with my grandmother and said she'd always suspected my mother was something of a "bad seed."

Buying the house meant giving up on my beautiful white teeth. I didn't take the decision lightly. For as long as I could remember, every time I was happy, every time the corners of my mouth inched upward, my only thought had been: stop. Smiling was a bad thing. I'd been *this close* to kicking those thoughts to the curb. For years I had dreamed of what joy without self-consciousness would feel like. What could be more worthwhile than my confidence, my happiness?

How about a satisfaction so deep, every inch of your skin tingles? How about a different kind of happiness—the kind people who have never been mistreated would call perverse?

When my mother got out of prison, I knew she would want—no, expect—me to take her in. I'd gladly spend my hard-earned cash to screw with her while she lived under my roof, in her childhood home. There would be time to fix my teeth later. The opportunity in front of me required action now. This time I was the one in control.

Mrs. Stone kept blathering. "She's dangerous, Rose Gold. She already hurt you once. I wouldn't be surprised if she tried again."

The idea of my mother hurting me now, as a twenty-two-year-old, amused me. "I'm not a kid anymore, Mrs. Stone," I teased kindly. "I think I can handle a mind game or two."

"I'm not just talking about mind games," Mrs. Stone insisted. "She brainwashed us, you most of all. What's to stop her from doing it again? What if she poisons your food when you're not paying attention?"

The idea was preposterous. Or was it?

"You believe she'd do that?" I asked.

She didn't hesitate. "I'd be more surprised if she didn't. If she comes back to Deadwick when she gets out, we'll all be watching her like hawks."

All this time, I'd been thinking too small. Pulling juvenile pranks around the house might have scared my mother, but they wouldn't teach her a lesson. Buying the old house was the first of multiple steps.

Mrs. Stone interrupted my train of thought. "Honey, promise me you won't let her back into your life."

"I can't promise you that," I said, arranging my features in what I hoped was an earnest expression. "I want to start over with her."

Mrs. Stone opened her mouth to argue, but I stood up and put my arm around her shoulders.

"I'll tell you what: if she starts up her mind games again or lays so much as a finger on me, you'll be the first person I call." I stared her dead in the eyes so she knew I was telling the truth, because I was. "I promise."

Mrs. Stone sighed, unhappy with this deal. "I don't know what you hope to gain from this. She's not a good person, dear."

I smiled. "She's my mom, Mary," I said sweetly, noting the surprise on her face when I used her first name. "The bond between a mother and a daughter is sacred. You know better than anyone that no matter how awful they are, we still find it in our hearts to love them."

Mrs. Stone—Mary—looked confused, as though she was trying to puzzle out whether I'd just insulted her pride and joy. "Speaking of daughters," she said, "Alex says the two of you aren't friends anymore."

Alex and I hadn't spoken in almost two years, and she had just now told her mother. Unbelievable.

I nodded sadly.

"When did this happen? I had no idea."

Of course you didn't. Because your daughter is a two-faced bitch who tells you nothing.

I tilted my chin to the floor. "I hate to say anything bad about her, but she wasn't very nice to me. I caught her talking behind my back to her college friends."

Mrs. Stone looked mortified. "Alex told me you were the one to blame. But if what you're saying is true, then I'm sorry. I didn't raise her to behave that way."

No, you raised her to walk all over you and everyone else she knows.

I picked up her coat and handed it to her. "I'm so sorry to have to cut our visit short, Mary, but I'm meeting a friend from work for drinks," I said, ushering her toward my front door. "But thank you so much for stopping by. It means a lot."

I scooted her across the threshold. She tried to keep the conversation going. "Is this a new friend? What's their name?"

"Arnie," I said, the first name that came to mind, almost laughing at the thought of him and me spending time together outside of work.

"Is Arnie a special friend?" she said, smiling.

For Christ's sake.

"Just a regular friend." I smiled back and waved. "Bye now."

Mrs. Stone turned and walked down the hallway. "Bye, dear," she called.

I closed the door and walked to the other side of the apartment, waiting for her rotund body to appear in the parking lot. A minute later, there she was, standing on the sidewalk, peering into the dark. Wary of the nonexistent crime in Deadwick, no doubt. I left the window to finish tidying the apartment.

Five minutes later, I walked by the window again. Mrs. Stone was still in the parking lot, sitting in her car. She'd started the engine and had her lights on, so she wasn't trying to be sneaky. But what was she waiting for? Was she checking up on me?

"Shit," I groaned. I was going to have to get in my van and go somewhere she wouldn't know I'd lied. Once you were caught in a lie, no one ever trusted you again.

I pulled on a jacket and grabbed my purse. Jogging to the van like I was in a hurry, I pretended not to see Mrs. Stone's car two rows over. The parking lot was full. Most of my neighbors would be plunked in front of their TVs at nine o'clock on a Wednesday night, myself included.

I drove five minutes to the town dive bar, checking my rearview mirror. I didn't think Mrs. Stone was following me, but just in case, I went inside.

The bar was quiet, except for two old guys sitting in a corner booth with a lot of empties on their table. One of them noticed me walk in. I sat at the bar, on the opposite side of the room from them.

The bartender approached—a scruffy guy around my age—and asked what he could get me. I ordered a vodka and cranberry. He placed the drink in front of me. I'd been watching the front door of the bar for five minutes. Mrs. Stone wasn't coming. I breathed a sigh of relief.

I took a sip of my drink and thought through my new options.

It would take some dedication to make them all believe I was back in her clutches. I'd have to play the role well, although I had sixteen years of experience being Patty Watts's victim, so that shouldn't be difficult. I'd have to be convincing. Nothing short of total commitment would suffice if I were going to send my mother back from where she came.

The corners of my mouth turned up.

"What's a babe like you doing all alone in a bar?"

The bartender had reapproached, hands on hips, eyes glinting. I had never been called a babe before.

"What's it look like?" I said, holding up my empty glass.

"Another?" he asked, cocking an eyebrow.

"That's your job, isn't it?" I put an elbow on the bar, rested my chin on my knuckles.

The bartender grinned. He picked up a bottle of cheap vodka. "I like them sassy."

I didn't say anything. I watched him add cranberry juice to the vodka in my glass.

He opened the ice bin. "Out of ice. I'll be right back." He moved toward the back room with my drink in his hand.

"Hey," I called. He turned around. I gestured for him to come back. "That's okay. I don't like ice in my drink."

A flicker of disappointment crossed his face, but he brought it back and set it down in front of me. He stuck a fresh straw in the glass before sliding it across the bar.

I put my lips to the straw and sucked. The cool liquid eased down my throat. We locked eyes.

He winked. "I wish I was that straw right about now."

I lifted my head from the drink and sat back in my chair. "Do you?" I asked, tilting my head to the side.

I grinned, putting every rotten tooth in my mouth on full display. The bartender recoiled, then mumbled something about needing to restock the ice. I watched him scurry away to the back room.

Once he was gone, I hopped off my barstool. I tipped my drink over the bar. Red liquid began to drizzle out.

"This is for trying to slip something into my drink," I muttered.

I walked the length of the bar and back, dripping the liquid from my glass the entire way. As someone not part of society until semirecently, I could by now confirm it wasn't all it was cracked up to be. Other people were exhausting.

I returned to my barstool, leaned over the bar into the half-full ice bin, and pulled out a piece, cracking the ice between my teeth. Then I scanned the rows of liquor against the wall for the most expensive-looking bottle, and hurled my glass as hard as I could at it. My glass shattered, and the bottle fell to the side, knocking other bottles off the shelves. I jumped at the noise, feeling more psychotic than badass.

Looking around the bar, sure that someone would arrest me, I noticed for the first time a cute guy with sandy blond hair sitting in the corner. He watched me with a lopsided smile and winked.

I smiled back. "Oops," I mouthed.

The bartender would be back any second—I had to get out of there. I picked up my purse and walked out the door, forcing myself not to turn around to see if the cute guy would follow.

I had work to do.

25

Patty

I burst through the hospital doors with Adam in my arms. The half dozen people in the waiting area turn when we walk in—Adam's wails are hard to ignore. I scan the room. A few upgrades have been made since Rose Gold was a child, but, for the most part, the lobby is unchanged. I hurry to the receptionist's desk.

"My baby needs to see a doctor," I cry when the young man doesn't turn away from whatever game I'm sure he's playing on his computer. He strikes me as someone who's been living in his mother's basement too long.

His eyes flick from the screen to the bawling baby in my arms. Sympathy crosses his face. Then he glances up at me, and skepticism replaces sympathy.

"This is your child?" he asks.

I scoff. "Not unless he's Benjamin Button. This is my grandson. He's been vomiting for more than six hours. I can't figure out what's wrong, in spite of all my training. See, I'm a certified nursing—"

The receptionist cuts me off. "Is he a registered patient here?"

"Yes, he was born in this hospital," I say.

"What's his name?"

"Adam Watts."

The receptionist types Adam's name into the database and waits.

"He never throws up like this. I'm worried he somehow swallowed something when I wasn't watching. Or maybe he has late-development pyloric stenosis. I read—"

The receptionist cuts me off again. "I don't see an Adam Watts in the system."

I lean over the counter, trying to see his screen. "Maybe you spelled it wrong. Watts is W-A-T-T-S."

The receptionist bristles, but I don't care.

"And Adam is A-D-A-M."

"I know how to spell Adam," he sniffs, "and that's how I spelled both names before." He types them again anyway and jabs the enter key.

After a few seconds, he (smugly) says, "No one under that name. You'll have to fill out a new patient form." He winces when Adam lets out a mind-numbing shriek.

I force myself to take a deep breath. "What about his mother, Rose Gold Watts?" I ask. "She has to be in your system."

The receptionist hands me a clipboard with a blank form. "That's not going to help you here, ma'am. Every patient needs their own medical file." He gestures for me to choose a chair and is relieved when I move the screaming baby away from him.

The rest of the people in the waiting room don't look excited as I approach with Adam. I give each of them a small "I'm sorry" smile; one elderly woman smiles back. I choose a seat next to her.

I begin filling out the form. I could have sworn Rose Gold told me she planned to give birth to Adam here. I remember saying how special it was that she was having Adam in the same hospital where I'd given birth to her. She hadn't seemed moved by the thought, but I'd chalked it up to pregnancy nerves. She must have had to change hospitals last minute, maybe to Westview twenty miles away.

When the form is complete, I bring it back to the surly receptionist. I have half a mind to tell him off, but if there's one thing I've learned about the medical community, it's that you want to keep them on your side or you'll never get anywhere. I hand him the clipboard and smile.

"Someone will be with you soon," he says.

I want to ask how soon, but know this will irritate him, so I don't. Instead I turn my attention to Adam. His face is bright red from crying. We head back to our seat. I pull a bottle from his diaper bag. When I put it to his mouth, he starts to suck and stops crying.

"Oh, thank God," a middle-aged man dressed in matching sweatpants and sweatshirt mutters. I shoot him a dirty look. People can be so cruel to children.

After thirty interminable minutes, a nurse calls Adam's name. I hop up from my chair and sling the diaper bag, plus my purse, over my shoulder. Adam has started to cry again, and I'm eager to get away from the others in the waiting room—their patience is wearing thin. Sweatpants Monster's eyes are in danger of rolling out of his head. I accidentally stomp on his toes as I pass.

I follow the nurse through a door and down a sterile white hallway. The patients' rooms line the left and right sides. I remember a childhood game of bingo I made up for Rose Gold—she got to fill in a square every time we visited a new room. She'd finished the board by the time she was seven.

We turn right at the end of the hallway, leading us down another long corridor. The nurse walks much faster than I do, although in my defense, I am carrying a fifteen-pound bowling ball, plus all his accessories. I glance down to check on Adam and run straight into someone.

"Patty?"

I recognize the voice before I look up: Tom. This will not go well.

Stepping back, I tilt my head toward my former friend, dressed in scrubs. "Hi, Tom."

"What are you doing here?" he asks with genuine confusion. He scans me for injuries, then sees Adam. His eyes narrow.

"Got to go, Tom. Chat later?" I try to sidestep him and run after the nurse. She's disappeared around another corner by now.

Tom steps with me, blocking my path. "Why are you here?" he asks again.

"My grandson is sick," I say impatiently.

Tom leans in toward Adam, his medical training kicking in. "Sick how?" he says.

I know this is going to sound suspicious. I'm going to look bad, but I don't see a way around him. I meet Tom's stare. "He won't stop vomiting."

Tom's eyes fill with fear, then with anger. He takes a step toward me, giving me just enough room to inch around him. He grabs my wrist, but I bat him away.

"I didn't do anything," I hiss. I pick up my pace and run after the nurse. Right before I turn the corner, I glance over my shoulder at Tom. He stands there, watching me go.

I nearly collide with the nurse. "I was wondering where you went," she says, leading me into room sixteen. Rose Gold used to call this the lucky room because sixteen was her favorite number.

The nurse introduces herself as Janet and closes the door behind us. She asks me routine questions about Adam's symptoms while checking his eyes, ears, and mouth. She pulls out her stethoscope to listen to his heart and lungs. She checks his skin and genitals for rashes. When she presses Adam's belly, he starts to cry again.

"I'm sorry, buddy," Janet says. She sounds like she means it. She plays with Adam's foot and tries to calm him. I sit back, exhausted, glad to be with someone else who knows how to care for children.

"Is Adam breastfeeding?" Janet asks.

I nod.

"And you're Adam's grandmother, correct?" Janet keeps trying to quiet Adam.

I nod.

"What are his mother's and father's names?" she asks, handing him back to me.

"Rose Gold Watts and Phil . . . I don't know the father's last name."

Janet stops typing.

"My daughter isn't in touch with him anymore," I say.

Adam's cries get louder, so Janet has to yell to be heard over him. "And where is Rose Gold today?"

To my relief, Adam vomits on me. Saved by the smell.

"See! This is what I'm talking about," I say, vindicated. "He's been doing this since nine o'clock this morning."

Janet jumps up from her chair and grabs a handful of paper towels. She helps me clean the baby and myself.

When all the soiled paper towels have been thrown away, Janet heads for the door. "Dr. Soukup will be right in." I beam. I love meeting new doctors.

Rocking the sobbing baby, I say, "We're going to get you some medicine, sweet pea. It'll make your tummy all better." Adam continues to cry, but his face is dry. He's dehydrated. I hug him tighter.

A while later, Dr. Soukup knocks and enters. She's a put-together woman with streaks of gray hair and a warm-but-no-nonsense bedside manner—my favorite breed of doctor. Maybe we'll become friends. I can meet her at the hospital on her lunch break, and she can show me the newest pharmaceuticals. Then I remember Adam and I won't be staying in Deadwick long. Too bad. I'll have to find a Dr. Soukup in our new town.

Reading from her computer screen, Dr. Soukup summarizes the symptoms I explained to Janet. I nod, eager to get to a treatment.

Dr. Soukup studies me over her stylish tortoiseshell glasses. "And where is Adam's mother?"

I can't very well say, *You know, I haven't seen or heard from her in thirty-two hours, so I'm not quite sure.* Wherever my daughter is, she deserves what she got.

"At a work conference," I say. "I'm watching Adam for the week."

Dr. Soukup shakes her head. "A work conference the week before Christmas? Companies these days have no heart."

I nod in agreement. "She works such long hours, it's like I've become his primary caretaker. I try to do the best I can. I mean, I'm a certified nursing assistant, so I like to think I know what I'm doing. But on days like today, I feel so inadequate."

Dr. Soukup pats me on the shoulder. "Not to worry, Patty. You're doing a terrific job."

The old familiar warmth starts in my chest and spreads across my body like an electric blanket. Her approval, her encouragement—I try to remember her words verbatim so I can store and use them in the months to come.

"I'd like to start with small doses of an oral electrolyte solution to rehydrate Adam," Dr. Soukup says. "See how there are no tears when he cries? That's a sign of dehydration."

"But, Doctor," I say, "based on how much he's vomiting and for how long, this is more serious than your average stomach bug, wouldn't you say? What about all the diarrhea?"

"It's only been eight hours," Dr. Soukup says. "Generally we don't start to worry unless it's been more than twelve. Do you have Pedialyte at home? You should wait to give it to him thirty to sixty minutes after he vomits."

I came all this way for some stinking Pedialyte? I don't think so.

"I think it might be pyloric stenosis," I say, fretting.

Dr. Soukup looks surprised. "Is he vomiting after feeding?"

"Yes," I say. "He's vomiting all the time." Which would include after feeding.

Dr. Soukup presses Adam's stomach. "Usually with pyloric stenosis, we feel an olive-shaped lump in the abdomen—the enlarged pyloric muscle. I'm not feeling that here."

Dr. Soukup is about to leave, but I need her to stay. I don't want this visit to be over yet. I want a prescription, a real treatment—not some over-the-counter strawberry liquid that college ne'er-do-wells drink when they're hungover. But my brain isn't moving fast enough; my encyclopedic knowledge of medical conditions is dusty, out of practice. I can't think of another illness.

"Let me grab a bottle of Pedialyte. We'll give Adam a first dose here, okay? I'll be right back." Dr. Soukup is out the door before I can protest. A kind but efficient treatment of patients—she's a professional, all right..

While she's gone, I think through my options. I could tell her he swallowed a piece of a small toy. She would ask why I hadn't mentioned this to begin with, but I could feign shame, say I didn't want her to think I was a bad grandmother. If the toy piece was big enough, she might be worried about letting him pass it on his own. She might suggest surgery.

I'm hit with déjà vu: rushing Rose Gold to the hospital, our endless waiting—for the doctor, for the treatment, for her to get better. Even the way Adam is vomiting reminds me of Rose Gold.

With my daughter missing, an extended hospital stay isn't a good idea. Complicating the situation is the opposite of what we need. I want Adam to stop throwing up so I can focus on next steps. Maybe I should give him the Pedialyte and hope for the best.

I check my watch. What's taking so long? Did the doctor forget where the hospital's drugs are kept? I open the door and poke my head into the hallway. I turn to my left and right: nothing. I take a few steps outside and peer around the corner.

At the end of the corridor stand Dr. Soukup and Tom. He's gesticulating like a lunatic. They're too far away for me to hear what he's saying, but it can't be good. Why does this yahoo have to butt into my business every chance he gets? No one asked you to play the hero, Tom Behan.

He turns his head and spots me. Before I can duck back around the corner, Dr. Soukup turns and sees me too. They both stare. I go back to room sixteen. Dread has replaced the warmth brought on by Dr. Soukup's praise. But I can't leave now.

A minute or two later, Dr. Soukup returns with a bottle of Pedialyte in hand. I search for evidence she's turned against me: a lack of eye contact, crossed arms, a clipped tone when she speaks. But she carries on in the same courteous manner as before.

"You know, Patty, I think you might be right," she says, unscrewing the bottle's cap and pouring a tiny amount of liquid onto a spoon. "Given how violent Adam's vomiting is, I think we should keep him here a bit longer. To be safe." She gives Adam the rehydration solution.

An involuntary shiver of anticipation runs through me at the idea of an extended hospital stay. Some folks like camping or going to the beach. Me? I've always liked a nice, long hospital visit. But not today. Not now. I'm too terrified to even think of enjoying myself.

"How long?" I ask. Tom is trying to trap me here.

"At least a few hours. Maybe overnight," Dr. Soukup says, watching Adam. "We want to run a few tests. Rule out anything more serious." She gazes at me over those elegant glasses. "That won't be a problem, will it?"

"Of course not," I say, swallowing hard.

I can't decide if the throbbing in my chest is elation or panic.

26

Rose Gold

March 2017

I waved to Robert the security guard as I left Gadget World and headed for the parking lot. It was a warm day for early March. Soon it would be spring, my favorite season. In spring, everyone appreciated the things they took for granted in summer. It was a time for fresh starts, new plans. I'd done a lot of thinking since Mary Stone's visit three months ago.

I climbed into the van and reversed out of my parking spot, forcing myself to ignore the four white cars in a row across from me. I'd wasted too much time on my stupid omens and superstitions. It was time to get serious: Mommy dearest was getting out in eight months. I would be ready for her.

By the time she and I were living under the same roof again, I would be skeletal. It would be too cold to walk around in a tank top in November, so I'd decided to take up running to give me an excuse to jog around the neighborhood in little clothing. With any luck, I might even faint on one of my runs and cause a scene. I could already picture

Tom Behan or Mary Stone helping me back home, ringing the bell and glaring when my mother opened the door. They'd picture her at the stove, rubbing her hands together and cackling with glee while she tilted drop after drop of the sickly-sweet liquid into my bowl of stew.

Their outrage would be just the beginning.

I didn't need to seriously start restricting calories for several months. I was already thin, so losing the extra weight wouldn't take long. But I wanted to make sure I was up to the task when the time came. I had come to love food like it was a person. In some ways, food was better—reliable and nourishing and it never talked back.

I was *not* looking forward to giving up burgers and blueberry pancakes and mac and cheese. Nor was I excited to act like I didn't know my way around the kitchen. I could make a pretty mean frittata by that point. Still, sacrifices had to be made in the service of a greater good.

To prepare I'd instituted a training program of sorts. I'd spend two hours making a beautiful roast chicken, then pour nail polish remover over it so I couldn't eat it. One night I put a bag of Skittles on the tray table in front of me and tested how long I could go without opening it. (My record was forty-two minutes.) Last month I baked a gorgeous Funfetti cake, took one bite, then forced myself to throw it away. After that, I knew I was ready.

Were these drastic measures necessary? Not strictly, but don't underestimate the importance of boredom.

When I reached the parking lot of my one-bedroom apartment, I remembered I didn't live there anymore. I swore. An elderly man gave me a dirty look. I gave it right back.

Ten minutes later, I paused at the stop sign at the intersection of Evergreen and Apple. To the right, a beat-up old treadmill stood at the end of Mr. Opal's driveway. If he was throwing it away, I might as well ask if I could have it. Tomorrow I'd go over there after work to find out.

I turned the van left on Apple and drove until the street dead-ended.

Number 201 Apple Street: home sweet home. I waited for the garage door to open, then pulled the van in and parked.

Two weeks prior I had moved into my mother's childhood home. Mabel Peabody had been hoping to wait to move out until the end of the year, but Gerald's cancer worsened faster than either of them expected. He bit the dust two months ago. I went to the funeral—to mourn, but also to remind Mabel I was ready to move in. She was so overcome with grief, she couldn't wait to leave. "Too many reminders of happy memories here," she said.

What a hard fucking life you've led, I didn't say.

I unlocked the door to my house. *My* house—I still got giddy saying it. It was old and creepy and falling apart in places, but it would do for now. I didn't have enough furniture to fill the two spare bedrooms, but one of them would be filled with a warm body soon enough.

I kicked off my shoes and flipped through the mail. Bills, delivery flyers, and one thick envelope. I ripped it open—it had taken me months to find this online. When I was a kid, you could buy it at pharmacies and in grocery stores, but now you had to crawl to dark corners of the Internet to get ahold of it. Reaching my hand inside the envelope, I felt for the cool, round glass and pulled it out: a small brown bottle with a white cap. Printed on the label in blue letters was "Ipecac Syrup."

"This is it, Planty," I said to the fern in the corner.

I stared at the bottle—no bigger than my hand, yet it had wreaked so much damage on my body. As a kid, I had only seen it once, at the back of Mom's sock drawer. She must have changed hiding places, keeping the bottles away from "nosy noses," as she referred to me. I closed my fingers around it, feeling powerful and sick at the same time.

I didn't revel in the prospect of poisoning myself, but it was the one concrete way to prove my mother was back to her old tricks. I wasn't sure a jury would believe an adult could be starved against her will, but she could sure as hell be unknowingly poisoned. Only an idiot would fall for the same trick twice, but I'd have to be that idiot, I guessed.

On the bright side, I wouldn't be the only one getting sick. It was my turn to play God.

I tucked the small brown bottle into a sock in my bedroom dresser. On my way back to the living room, I paused in the doorway of my mother's soon-to-be bedroom. I'd planned a nice surprise for her in here before her arrival. I didn't want Mom stuck staring at four boring old walls—she deserved a flourish.

Sometimes I was convinced I felt my grandfather's dark presence in this house. How, I wondered, had my mother hidden from his wrath? Had she gone for the obvious spots at first: her bedroom closet, under the bed, behind the shower curtain? And then as she got older, had she become craftier? Hidden in the car inside the garage, up a tree, in the giant freezer in the basement?

"What do you think?" I asked Planty as I moved through the living room. "I'd guess the Wattses didn't spend much time in the basement after dear old Uncle David died."

In the kitchen I checked the calendar on my refrigerator, cursing when I found "RESTRICTION TRAINING" written on today's date. I'd been hoping to order a pizza tonight. But a plan was a plan, and I hadn't tested myself in several weeks. I brought my dinner—saltine crackers, Bush's baked beans straight from the can, and one perfectly microwaved chicken nugget—to a tray table in the living room so I could eat in my recliner. I didn't see the point of eating meals at the kitchen table anymore, not when I'd have to stare at the empty chair across from me.

I turned on the TV and let *The Godfather* play in the background. I'd already seen the movie a few times; Don Corleone's voice soothed me. How far I had come—when I was a kid, Mom would only let me watch Disney movies and *Blue's Clues*. The thought of watching Steve get the mail one more time made me want to choke myself with his green sweater.

I allowed myself five saltines and two spoonfuls of beans before moving the aluminum can and sleeve of crackers away so I wouldn't be tempted to eat anymore. I picked up my phone and scrolled through a handful of social media apps. I discovered Mrs. Stone had created a Facebook account and rolled my eyes.

"Another way for her to insert herself into other people's business," I said to Planty. I clicked my tongue and kept scrolling. Everyone's lives were so boring, so diminished. All they did was change jobs and boyfriends and apartments.

I stopped scrolling when a name caught my eye.

"Well, look who it is," I crowed to Planty.

Sophie Gillespie of the insufferable Gillespie clan. I hadn't spoken to any of those imbeciles in a year and a half. They hadn't tried to reach out to me, so why should I bother getting in touch with them? I refused to let myself dwell on how much I missed Anna. This was their loss, not mine.

I examined Sophie's post: a family photo Kim had posted first. Sophie had reshared it.

All five of them stood in a field wearing matching outfits: white pants and blue shirts. They were laughing and glowing, happy as could be. They gazed at their matriarchal hag in the middle of the group. Kim was holding a blue balloon.

Printed on the balloon was a cartoon stork carrying a baby. Underneath the stork was shouty text: "IT'S A BOY!"

"No," I said.

My eyes flicked to Kim's photo caption: "Billy and I are so excited to welcome the newest member of the Gillespie family in September."

"No," I said again, taking in the dopey grin on Dad's face.

I kept reading. "We have wanted a fourth child for years and years. Our prayers have been answered."

"YOU. HAVE. A. FOURTH. CHILD!" I shrieked. I whipped my phone across the room. It hit the wall and crashed to the floor. I did not care. A violent sob jerked in my chest, stirring the long-dormant grief of all I had lost. But I would not let these people make me cry again. I refused to sit here and bawl until my stomach hurt. Anger was so much easier.

I kicked the legs out from under the tray table. Beans and crackers went flying. I punched my fist into the back of the recliner until a knuckle cracked. I screamed for so long and so loud my ears rang for several seconds after I stopped. I bit down as hard as I could on my fist until the pain of my teeth sinking into flesh made me scream again. When I pulled my hand away, it was bleeding.

I paced the living room, pulling at my hair in agitation. These assholes traipsed around the country acting like they were wholesome and wonderful, but nobody knew the way they tossed aside people they didn't give a shit about. Nobody knew how awful they were.

I stopped moving for a minute and studied my shaking hands. I was holding several strands of blond hair—when had I ripped it out?

They had—have—a fourth child. They rejected me.

None of them deserved this baby, especially Dad and Kim. They couldn't be allowed to keep doing whatever they wanted, getting the best of everything in life while the rest of us suffered. Someone had to punish them, to show them the pain they were inflicting on other people. To show them how it felt to have your family taken away against your will.

I sat, stewing long after the sun had set and all my neighbors' lights had turned off. I could see nothing but my father's dopey smile in that photo. I vowed not to leave my chair until I'd thought of a way to wipe that grin off his face.

Around two a.m., as I sat on the floor picking crusty beans and crushed crackers off the carpet, I realized that, once again, I'd been thinking too small. I was not a natural strategist, but if you gave me enough time, I could come up with an idea. And now I had a good one.

"A really good one," I said, turning to Planty. I saw Planty had been hurled at the wall, her pot broken into a million small pieces, dirt scattered across the carpet. I shrugged—I'd clean her up later. Sometimes you accidentally hurt the ones you loved.

Grinning, I scooped a few beans off the floor and held them between my thumb and forefinger before slipping them in my mouth. This once, I'd break my own rule and eat a little extra. We were celebrating, after all.

I was so happy and proud of myself, I could have burst into song. A classic nursery rhyme popped into my head—a perfect choice, very maternal of me. I sang along and picked up more beans.

And down will come baby, cradle and all.

27

Patty

One of the overhead fluorescent lightbulbs flickers on and off, interrupting the quiet with irritating buzzing noises. I stop pacing to give the ceiling a dirty look. I should tell one of the nurses to get a repairman in here.

I check on Adam, who has fallen asleep on the cot. I've aged twenty years in a day and a half. With real longing, I think of the twin bed waiting for me on Apple Street. If I wanted to, I could even sleep in the queen bed, now that Rose Gold is gone.

Adam and I have been in this hospital for hours without anyone coming to see us. These four walls have become a holding cell. I usually love the smell of hospitals; there's something so comforting about their sterile, clean odors—a constant reminder that help is around the corner. Now the smell is making me gag a little, suffocating me.

Maybe I should sneak Adam out of here and treat him myself.

I start to gather the contents of the diaper bag when a knock sounds at the door. I drop the bag and step back, as if it's a crime to take care of a baby.

I turn toward the door, expecting Dr. Soukup or Janet the nurse. I can handle anyone but Tom.

What I do not expect is two police officers in uniform. I can handle anyone but Tom or the police.

The first officer is tall and thin like an exclamation point. The glint in her eye suggests she's partial to corporal punishment. She steps into the room, the other officer trailing behind her.

"I'm Sergeant Tomalewicz with the Deadwick Police. Are you Patricia Watts?"

"Patty," I say. My father called me Patricia. "Is this about Adam?" I ask. "He really is sick."

"We'll get to the baby in a minute," Tomalewicz says. She points to her lackey. He barely looks old enough to drive. "This is Officer Potts."

Officer Potts waves at me, as if we're meeting at a beach party. Tomalewicz frowns, then turns back to me.

"Where's Rose Gold, Patricia?" she asks, piercing me with dark eyes. She reminds me of a vulture.

"Patty," I correct her again. "And I don't know." My hands are starting to shake, so I cross my arms against my body.

"When's the last time you saw her?"

"I dropped her off at work yesterday morning. She said she would jog home at the end of her shift. She did that sometimes. But then she never showed." My hands have somehow escaped their hold and are wringing themselves at my waist. I tuck them into my back pockets, then take them out again, worried the stance is too flippant. I need to look innocent.

Tomalewicz continues. "Why didn't you call the police or report her missing?"

Careful now, Patty.

"It hasn't been much longer than twenty-four hours," I say. "I thought she might be blowing off steam somewhere."

"Is that like Rose Gold, to 'blow off steam'?" Tomalewicz asks, using air quotes.

No, I think. "Yes," I say. "Sometimes." I realize I don't sound very concerned about my daughter's whereabouts, so I add, "Being a new mom is hard. I wanted to give Rose Gold a little space."

"I see," Tomalewicz says. I don't like her tone. "I have an officer at Gadget World talking to the store manager. He says Rose Gold never showed up to work yesterday—or today. He says the last time anyone saw her was five p.m. on Saturday. That was fifty-two hours ago, if math isn't your strong suit."

I need a drink of water. My throat feels like I've swallowed four pounds of sand. I gulp. "I don't know what you want from me. I don't know where she is."

Tomalewicz appears unconcerned. She saunters to a chair across from the hospital bed and lowers herself into it, her long grasshopper legs bent at sharp angles. I sit on the bed, relieved to have support, some way to hide my trembling legs.

"Dr. Soukup says you told her Rose Gold was at a work conference." Tomalewicz watches me, waiting for my response, but I can't think of one, so I stay quiet. "I'll take your silence as a yes. Why did you tell her that if you just told me you don't know where Rose Gold is?"

I clear my throat. "I needed to deal with one problem at a time. Adam was—is—so sick. I couldn't take care of him and find my daughter."

"That's what the police are for," Tomalewicz cuts in, eyes narrowed. "Officer Potts here is going to take a look through your things."

I nod my permission, though she didn't ask for it. To illustrate how cooperative I am, that I have nothing to hide, I hand over my purse and the diaper bag.

Potts begins with the diaper bag. The bag weighs at least ten pounds and has dozens of little compartments, zippered pockets, and snap pouches. Potts begins removing each item one at a time and placing them in a pile on the side table—diapers, wipes, pacifier, portable changing mat, diaper rash cream, hand sanitizer, backup onesie, pacifier clip, hat, burp cloth. From the side pockets, he pulls two bottles of milk and examines them before placing them on the floor, separate from the rest of the stuff.

He keeps digging farther into the bag, pulling out tissues and Rose Gold's hair ties, all the junk that gets us through the day. My heart jackhammers in my chest.

By now, Potts is elbows deep into the diaper bag, unzipping small side pockets we never use. From one he pulls a small rectangle—an iPhone. I had no idea it was in there.

I think I might throw up.

"Is this yours?" Potts asks me. This is the first time he's spoken. His voice is much deeper than I would have guessed. He touches a button on the phone, but the screen remains black—it's dead. Potts rummages through his own bag and pulls out a charger. He searches the wall for an outlet, then plugs in the phone. Satisfied, he glances up at me, waiting for the device to power up.

I could lie. I could say it's mine. I could say I don't know whose it is. But I bet there's an easy way to tell whom the phone belongs to, and I don't know enough about technology to outsmart the police on this one. Potts looks like he was born with an iPhone in hand.

"It's Rose Gold's," I mutter. Both officers' eyebrows rocket skyward in surprise. Tomalewicz's lips are starting to curl up at the corners.

"I've been calling her and leaving frantic messages for days," I protest. "Check the call log."

"Days? I thought you said it's been twenty-four hours," Tomalewicz says.

"Hours, then," I say. "Maybe it just feels like days. I'm so worried," I say, which is now true. "I'm so worried about both of them."

By now the iPhone is back up and running. Potts starts scrolling, tapping, hunting. I can't see the screen, so I don't know what he's searching for.

"The thing is, Patricia," Tomalewicz says, "we got a call today from a concerned resident. Someone who received an alarming letter from Rose Gold."

Who? I think, then glance up, hoping I haven't said it aloud.

Tomalewicz crosses her legs, resting her right ankle on her left knee. "Rose Gold sounded very frightened by you in the letter. It sounds to us like you were back to abusing her."

That accusation again. This town will never let it go.

Potts puts down Rose Gold's phone and picks up the diaper bag, continuing his search anew. He hunts through every compartment, runs his hands along every inch of liner. He makes no comment, doesn't even glance our way. Tomalewicz keeps talking.

"She said you *made* her take the baby."

"What?" My eyes flit from Potts back to Tomalewicz.

"You made her pretend the baby was hers and threatened to hurt her if she didn't. You told her it was time for revenge, that no one ditched Patty or Rose Gold Watts and got away with it. Rose Gold said she went along with your plan at first. But then she got worried you were starting to hurt Luke the way you hurt her. She said when she confronted you—told you this had to end—you threatened to hurt both of them before that ever happened."

My head spins. "Luke?"

Tomalewicz's jaw tightens. She stares at Adam. "Luke Gillespie."

At the sound of that name, a rush of nausea hits me. I see stars. The room starts to darken.

I gaze at the baby sleeping on the cot and ask, "Are you saying this baby isn't my grandson?"

"Rose Gold's story checks out," Tomalewicz says. "We called the Fairfield police. Billy Gillespie—Rose Gold's father and your ex-lover—reported a child missing two and a half months ago. They've been searching for him round the clock in Indiana."

Potts pulls a Swiss Army knife from his pocket and cuts a small hole in the diaper bag's lining. He pulls out a small brown bottle with a white cap. "Found it," he says with triumph.

Tomalewicz and Potts turn to me, watching. They want me to say something, I realize. They think that bottle of ipecac syrup is mine.

But it isn't mine. I drove mine to the next town over this morning and smashed it to pieces behind a Subway. Then I swept up the pieces and threw them in a dumpster. I couldn't take any chances if I was bringing Adam to the hospital.

"Why would I bring a baby I poisoned to the hospital?" I ask.

Tomalewicz shrugs. "Excellent question. You used to do it all the time."

I ignore her comment. "Why would I bring the poison with me?"

Tomalewicz fixes me with a withering stare.

"If I had something to hide, why wouldn't I go to a different hospital where no one knows me?"

Tomalewicz turns to Potts, gesturing at the bottles full of Rose Gold's breast milk. "Let's pack these up and get them tested."

At her command, Potts repacks the diaper bag. He drifts out of the room with the bottles and Rose Gold's iPhone. I watch him go in disbelief.

"I haven't spoken to Billy Gillespie in twenty-five years," I protest. "I didn't even know Rose Gold knew his real name. I didn't know about any of this."

Tomalewicz uncrosses her legs and leans forward, elbows on

knees, chin in hand. "Yes, we know all about your long record of claiming innocence. You're never guilty of anything," she says. "It's always everyone else's fault. Funny, the justice system didn't agree."

I have a decision to make, but not a lot of time to make it. My instinct is—always has been—to deny, deny, deny. But I realize the gravity of the charges I could be facing: kidnapping, aggravated child abuse a second time, and I don't know what else. I'm backed into a corner. I take a deep breath.

The words tumble out. "Okay, I admit I sometimes mistreated Rose Gold when she was a child," I say.

I expect a flood of relief in finally saying the words out loud. I've been holding this in for so long, pretending I'm innocent, acting like I didn't know any better. But all I feel is empty, defeated, like a loser. No one would ever smile at me or pat me on the back again, tell me I was good enough, even *great* once in a while. Superhuman mother is the one role I know how to play. Without it, I am nobody.

I swallow hard. "But I have never, ever abused Adam—I mean, Luke. I had no idea he was kidnapped."

The door to the room swings open. Mary Stone barges in, irate. "I knew you were guilty!" she shrieks. "We all did. We knew you hurt Rose Gold then, and now you've done it again. What did you do with her, you monster?"

Tomalewicz jumps to her feet, alarmed by the intrusion. She puts a hand on Mary's arm. "Mrs. Stone, I told you to wait in the lobby," she says calmly. "Now I'm going to have to ask you to leave."

Mary rips her arm from Tomalewicz's grip and keeps raving, jabbing a finger at me. "You poisoned them both and then killed Rose Gold. You wanted her out of the way so you could ruin that poor baby's life the same way you ruined hers. She told me all about you in her letter. And when she started standing up to you, you destroyed her."

Mary bursts into tears.

Tomalewicz speaks into her radio, "Welch and Mitchell to room sixteen."

"I didn't see Rose Gold for a month after the baby was born," Mary cried. "She told me she had to go to a hospital in Springfield because of pregnancy complications. Where is she?"

Mary's rants have woken Adam. He starts to cry too.

"The baby," she shouts, reaching for him with red-rimmed eyes and snot running down her face. Tomalewicz plants herself in front of Adam, blocking both of us from him.

"That poor, poor baby," Mary wails, folding herself in half with sobs.

Two more officers enter the room. Their eyes go straight to Mary. One of them turns to Tomalewicz for confirmation. She gives a short nod. The officer holds Mary by the arm, helping her stand upright.

"Let's go, ma'am," he says, pushing her toward the door. I can still hear her shrieks once the door has closed.

Tomalewicz addresses the other officer. "Get Dr. Soukup or a nurse for the baby."

The officer nods and leaves. Thirty seconds later, Janet—our original nurse—rushes through the door.

Tomalewicz nods at Janet. "We suspect the baby has been poisoned with ipecac syrup. I'm not sure what testing or treatments should be done—"

Janet interrupts, smooth and confident. "We'll take care of him."

She strides to the cot. When she tucks Adam—Luke—into her arms, my stomach heaves. She whispers to him as she heads for the door, trying to calm his tired cries. Shifting him to one arm, she opens the door. Before she takes my baby away from me forever, she gives me an evil look, one full of hatred and disgust. Then she is gone, and so is Adam—I mean Luke.

The room is silent.

I am numb.

Tomalewicz and I don't wait long before the two officers reenter. I spot the handcuffs right away. I put my hands behind my back while the officers cuff me.

"I'm innocent," I protest. "I'm telling you the truth!"

Tomalewicz begins reading me my rights, but I don't listen. The accused don't have any rights. Innocent until proven guilty? What a load of horse hockey.

Tomalewicz keeps talking. "These officers will escort you to the station. I'd love to take you myself, but I have an important call to make to the Fairfield Police Department. I think we're about to make an entire town very happy."

But Rose Gold visited me while pregnant. She pumped all that milk. She thought her father was dead, that his name was Grant. I never used my bottle of ipecac. None of this makes any sense.

"You need to find my daughter," I say. "She has the answers you want."

Tomalewicz pierces me again with those vulture eyes. "Trust me, we'll find her."

She nods at the other officers and leaves.

The officers escort me out of the patient's room and into the hallway. I keep my eyes glued to the tile floor, hoping Tom is either on a lunch break or fell through the earth's crust and is boiling somewhere in its inner core. We shuffle toward the exit. I see the stares but am too shocked to be humiliated.

Adam's name is Luke. My grandson is Billy's son. I don't have a grandson.

The police car has already been pulled up to the front doors of the hospital. One of the officers guides me into the backseat while the other gets behind the wheel. Their faces are a blur. Their words are a blur. This car is a blur. All of it, this whole town, is one big whirly blur. I try to reason my way out of this, try to string a coherent thought together. I have only one.

The little bitch set me up.

28

Rose Gold

Of course I set her up.

You've wanted to do the same. You have lain in bed at night thinking of all the exquisite ways you could punish the person who wronged you. You know the one—even now, their face hovers in your mind. *If only,* you think, not daring to finish the thought.

The difference between you and me is follow-through. I made it happen.

When Ursula was about to destroy Ariel, Prince Eric didn't make a peace offering. He didn't divvy up sides of the ocean, settle for living amicably with a sea witch. He drove a ship's mast straight into her gut and killed her. I'm my own Prince Eric. I saved myself.

A week has passed since my mother was arrested again. It still tickles me pink to say that, although maybe I'm sunburned. Every day here has been blue skies and seventy degrees.

I wait in line at the bakery to pay for my sweet bread. The shop's walls are covered with colorful murals of local historical landmarks. The customers chat and gesticulate, ignoring me. I keep returning to this shop, mostly because the cashier here is nice to me. When it's my turn, I hand him my money. He smiles, and for a second, I feel less alone.

I leave the bakery and stop to gawk again at the beautiful brick church across the street. For the third morning in a row, I admire its bell tower, topped with a wrought iron crown hoisted by angels. I soon become aware of how exposed I am, standing here slack-jawed. I keep moving, taking a bite of the sweet bread while I walk the bustling streets.

A few minutes later, I reach the side street where I parked my car, a beat-up white sedan by a well-known automaker I'd like to keep anonymous. Google says it's the most popular car on the roads here. I blend right in. I could be anyone. I don't want to be found.

And boy, are the cops searching for me. I bet Vinny King from *Chit Chat* would get down on his knees to interview me now.

I unlock my car door and climb into the driver's seat, smoothing the bangs of my wig in the visor mirror. Short jet-black hair wasn't my first choice, but the color disguises me well. I bring another piece of sweet bread to my mouth. A rank smell invades my nostrils: body odor. I sniff my armpits—I stink. I'll need to shower soon or at least take a dip in the ocean. It's a few streets away.

I've traveled farther in the past seven days than in my entire life put together. This is all part of the new me. I wanted a fresh start, which meant I needed a clean break.

———————

On that Monday morning last week, I got ready for work, like any other day. My mother dropped me off at Gadget World around eight fifty, like any other day. But unlike every other day, I turned around and walked back home instead of going into work. I hid in the unlocked abandoned house across the street for a few hours, until Mom left to take Luke to the park. Once she was gone, I was a busy little bee.

I had to clean out my closet, add ipecac syrup to the milk, then bury my phone and the small brown bottle in the diaper bag. After dropping a letter in the mail, I was on my merry way.

I had planned to mail the letter to the cops in Fairfield, but I realized putting Mom's destiny in Mary Stone's hands would really piss her off.

Bonus point.

Fourteen hours later, I made a pit stop at a PO box in Denver to pick up my new identity documents, courtesy of my former boyfriend. I wasn't worried about him turning on me when my name hit the papers; forging passports gets you up to ten years behind bars.

Then I headed south.

I walk around to the backseat of the car and fold my blanket (an old beach towel) and pillow (my purple hoodie). The floor is littered with fast-food wrappers and dirty underwear. Maybe I'll wash my clothes while I shower.

I start the car, not sure where to go. I don't know my way around this city. I'm not used to cobblestone roads, to telephone wires everywhere, to being surrounded by mountains. I've never seen so many palm trees—I had never seen a palm tree in real life before this week! I want to go everywhere, but I'm scared of taking a wrong turn. I have to keep reminding myself there are no wrong turns, that I don't have a destination in mind.

I've been thinking about getting a job cleaning rooms or working the reception desk at a resort here. I could speak English with the guests—it'd be nice to have a conversation, even with a stranger. I haven't spoken to anyone in seven days. I don't want to leave this place, but I have a constant nagging feeling that I should go.

Is it easier to stay lost in a big city or a small town? The biggest big city is eleven hours east. The presence of millions and millions of people on the streets would keep my face from standing out. Then again, there are probably way more cops around. If I pick a small, dusty town instead, I bet I won't see many police officers. But I'll stick out like a sore thumb. I drum my fingers against the steering wheel, not making eye contact with any passersby. Any of them could be hunting me.

I'd thought once I'd pulled this off, I'd be scot-free. I didn't realize the strategizing would have to continue for who knows how long. Backing the car out of the parking spot, I decide to head for the highway. I can always come back. For now I don't stay anywhere long.

It seems like all anyone cares about is the baby. Luke is fine. He's been reunited with Dad and Kim. I made sure to only put a few drops of ipecac in each bottle. The effects won't be any longer lasting than a bad stomach bug. I wouldn't kill my own brother. I'm not crazy.

Taking him wasn't even that hard. I pored over Sophie's social media accounts come September. Then one day, boom, there he was, out in the world. All the Gillespies shared photos of him in the hospital; he was healthy, Mom was healthy, blah blah blah. I waited a few weeks, then drove to Indiana on my day off and parked the van at the bus station. After walking a mile or so to the Gillespies' house, I waited for Dad to take the kids to school and himself to work, and then I listened.

So much can be achieved by listening.

I watched Kim head upstairs with Luke, then snuck into the house through the back door and hid in the tiny seasonal closet Dad said no one ever goes in. Once I heard the shower running, I slipped into the guest room—what should've been my room. It had been turned back into a nursery. Those stupid ducklings still lined the walls, like they had when I visited. And there he was, one month old, sound asleep in his crib. I picked him up carefully so as not to disturb any sweet dreams he might be having of puppies or fire trucks. He nestled his little body into mine, and every fiber of my being ached with love. "I'm your big sister," I whispered. "I promise to keep you safe."

Sure, I could have framed my mother with a baby from any maternity ward or park. But this baby killed two birds with one stone. Both of my parents deserved to pay for their cruelty.

I didn't have it easy during those months. After I brought Luke home, I nearly drove myself crazy with fear that I'd slipped up and the Gillespies would catch me. True, two years had passed since Dad had thrown me out of his life, and I'd given him no reason to suspect I harbored ill will toward his family. Never once did I contact any of them, and I did nothing but stammer pathetic apologies that day on the soccer field. Still, I worried I'd left a shoe print in the house or some other piece of evidence that could be traced to me.

When Dad called me on the night I picked Mom up from prison, I nearly passed out in panic. I needn't have. He was calling everyone in his phone book, asking them to keep their eyes and ears open for news of his missing child. He awkwardly blundered his way through our phone call, and that was when I knew he had no idea. I sank to the floor with relief and said the right things at the right times. I even offered to drive up and help him look for the baby. Of course he immediately said no—even in his time of need, he wanted to keep me far away from his family. The next morning, when Mom asked if Adam's father had been the caller, I nodded. I wasn't lying.

Do you know how hard it is to fake being a new mother? The pregnancy suit—you can buy anything on Amazon these days—was a cakewalk by comparison. I had to keep an enormous supply of formula locked up in my room; I even poured it through a breast pump three times a day so the pump would look used. I didn't start adding the ipecac until the very end. Other than that small deviation, I was a model mother. Luke got off easy, compared to me.

I miss that little nugget so much. He was my best friend, the one person in my life who never left me. In some ways, I knew how my mother felt. Giving him up was the hardest thing I've ever had to do.

I knew I would only be forgiven for my role in the kidnapping if I died for the baby. The police are looking for me, but I doubt they expect to find me alive. If they do, the public will crucify me. They'll judge me and call me evil. But I needed a child for the abuse to look authentic. A grown woman being poisoned by her mother is a fool. But a helpless infant? Nothing enrages the masses—or juries—like hurt children. I would know. Good luck worming your way out of this one, Mommy.

———

I drive for a couple hours, marveling at how green this place is, even from the highway. The mountains are a constant presence, always looming large in some direction. They are infinitely prettier than cornfields. I turn on the radio. Eurythmics' "Sweet Dreams" is playing. My mother loves this song.

I wonder where she is right now. I turn off the radio.

Eventually I notice I'm low on gas and get off the highway. I need a pick-me-up. While stopped at a light, I grab my burner phone and rewatch the clip of Mary Stone talking to the press. I fast-forward to the forty-second mark and press play. There she is, standing at a podium, shouting into a bouquet of microphones with tears streaming down her face. Her flair for drama makes her the perfect unwitting accomplice.

"I heard Patty Watts say, with my own two ears," Mary cries, "that she poisoned and starved Rose Gold."

I press pause and sit back in my seat. I watch this video at least a dozen times a day. The light turns green. I step on the gas.

You brought this on yourself.

All my mother had to do was take responsibility for ruining my life, to tell the truth for once in her miserable existence. She blew her chance. And underestimated me every step of the way. Mom thought I couldn't—wouldn't dare—put one over on her. She refused to let go of the image of the little Rose Gold she'd raised: weak, spineless, and dependent on Mommy. She assumed her dolt of a daughter was no match for a brain like her. Don't make me laugh.

Oh, she's trying to make up for it now—telling every reporter who will listen that she's been framed, that I set her up and am in hiding somewhere.

But nobody wants to hear the truth from a liar.

I pull into a run-down gas station and park my car next to a pump. When the tank is full, I head inside and pay the clerk in cash. Then I walk to the back of the store and lock myself in the bathroom. I take off my wig and wet my face in the sink, trying not to get any water in my mouth.

When my face stops dripping, I splash some water on my armpits. I turn my clothes inside out so no one can see any stains, and stand there for a minute, fanning myself.

My eyes drift to the mirror and settle on my hair, finally long like

I've always dreamed of, the ends resting on my chest. I toss it over my shoulder and realize whom I look like. A few years ago, I wanted nothing more than to be her carbon copy—to become Alex Stone. But I don't want to be that person anymore. I'm not a woman who loses her shit over some missing hair. I'm much, much stronger than Alex.

I leave the gas station and park at a small general store. It only takes a few minutes to find what I need.

With my new purchase in hand, I head back to the gas station bathroom. If the attendant recognizes me or is surprised to see me again, he doesn't show it. With the door locked, I pull the clippers from the bag and set to work.

Long strands of dark blond hair fall to the floor.

I work my way around my head. The buzz of the clippers brings me back to the small bathroom in the town house. I'm six years old again, sitting cross-legged in a tutu on the counter while Mom shaves my head, reminding me my hair will fall out in clumps if we don't keep it short. She promises me I'll look better this way.

For the first time, I've made the decision.

I shave and shave and shave until it's gone—all of it. My feet have disappeared under my hair. Bye-bye, Alex.

Running my hands over my downy head, I grin. My face is filling out now that I'm eating again. My eyes are less sunken. Two rows of rotten teeth gleam back at me from the mirror. I haven't tried to cover them in months. I can't remember now why they bothered me in the first place. They're not so bad. They may look brittle, but they're sturdy enough to feed me, to keep my secrets, to contain my rage.

Most people don't like holding on to anger. They feel it crushing and consuming them, so they let it go. They try to forget the ways they've been wronged.

But some of us cannot forget and will never forgive. We keep our axes sharp, ready to grind. We hold pleas for mercy between our teeth like jawbreakers.

They say a grudge is a heavy thing to carry.

Good thing we're extra strong.

Acknowledgments

Thank you—

To my dazzling agent, Maddy Milburn, who plucked this manuscript from her query pile and took a chance on me. Working with you is the best decision I have ever made for my career. I will never stop thanking you. To the rest of the MMLA team—Anna Hogarty, Georgia McVeigh, Giles Milburn, Chloe Seager, Georgina Simmonds, Liane-Louise Smith, Hayley Steed, and Alice Sutherland-Hawes— thank you for helping me keep my head on straight. You are all total stars.

To my brilliant editors, Amanda Bergeron in the US and Maxine Hitchcock in the UK. Your insights and ideas have strengthened both this book, and me as a writer, in countless ways. Thank you for making me sound smarter than I am and for sharing (or at least tolerating) my love of spreadsheets. Every single day, I am so happy my books and I have found homes with the two of you.

To the Berkley team: Loren Jaggers and Danielle Kier, the best publicists in town; Bridget O'Toole, the newsletter ninja; and Jin Yu, master of all things marketing. I wish we lived in the same city so we could get together all the time. Emily Osborne and Anthony Ramondo, your cover design is perfection. Thank you too to the rest of the Berkley team: Craig Burke, Stacy Edwards, Grace House, Jean-Marie Hudson, Claire Zion, and everyone else at Penguin Random House in the US.

To the Michael Joseph team: Emma Henderson, Rebecca Hilsdon, and Hazel Orme, the superb editorial squad; Ellie Hughes and Gaby Young, my magnificent publicists; Vicky Photiou, Jen Porter, and Elizabeth Smith, the marketing dream team; and the unbelievably talented designers Lee Motley and Lauren Wakefield. A million thanks to everyone else at MJ, including: Louise Blakemore, Anna Curvis, Christina Ellicott, James Keyte, Catherine Le Lievre, and the broader team at Penguin Random House UK.

To Mako Yoshikawa, my first reader, my thesis chair, and my mentor. You believed in this book back when only three chapters of it existed. Your feedback shaped Rose Gold's voice, you taught me the importance of causation in fiction, and perhaps most importantly, you urged me to keep going. This book owes its existence to you.

To Rick Reiken, my thesis reader and former professor, who went above and beyond what was required for workshop, gave me brilliant craft advice, and helped me navigate the publishing industry. Were it not for you, I might still be languishing with that (awful) first draft. Thank you for gently helping me realize I had to start again.

To Steve Yarbrough, who was my first-ever workshop professor and kept encouraging me even though my stories in his class were . . . rough. Week after week, I soaked up as much of your wisdom as I possibly could. I hope at least a little bit of it comes through in these pages.

To Emerson College, who supported this novel as my MFA thesis project. Thank you to the faculty for making me a better writer; to the college for your generous program fellowship, which afforded me a single-minded focus on writing; and to my classmates, especially Beth Herlihy, who read early drafts of this story and cheered me on.

To the following people and texts for helping me understand the medical history and psychological impact of MSBP: Julie Gregory's *Sickened: The Memoir of a Munchausen by Proxy Childhood*; Michelle Dean's Buzzfeed article covering the story of Dee Dee and Gypsy

Blanchard; and Marc Feldman's *Playing Sick?: Untangling the Web of Munchausen Syndrome, Munchausen by Proxy, Malingering, and Factitious Disorder.* Any errors are my own.

To Dr. Jim McKee, DDS, for your time and expertise on all things teeth-related.

To Ashley Chase, Ray Ciabattoni, Sarah Coffing, Guy Conway, Maddy Cross, Lauren Hefling, Annie and Todd Hibner, Christy Holzer, Jen and Tristan Kaye, Dave and Sara McCradden, Ali O'Hara, Dave Pfeiffer, Kelsey Pytlik, Shiv Reddy, Tara Reddy, and Savs Tan, for your unwavering love and support on this book and in everything I do.

To Allison Jasinski, for all those long chats on the blue couches at our Geneva Terrace apartment. You ignited my interest in psychology and obsession with society's outliers. Thank you for always believing in me.

To the Wichrowskis: Sheila, Taylor, and Paul, for being some of my earliest readers and the first book club to discuss my novel! These last few years, I've asked for your opinions so many times—on my query, the back jacket copy, the cover design, the list is endless—and you were always ready with the smartest comments. Your excitement during this process has meant the world to me. I am beyond lucky to be part of your family.

To my grandparents, Pat and Jim Soukup. Thank you for always loving me and for fostering my fondness of reading. For thirty-plus years, every time I've gone to your house, one or both of you has had a book in hand. I am so proud to be your granddaughter.

To the Malichs: Jackie, Matt, and Cadence, for your tireless encouragement. Jackie, thank you for being one of my first readers. Thank you for the hours we spent discussing twists—the good, the bad, and the predictable. Thank you for answering hundreds of uncomfortable questions about pregnancy, being a new mom, and every other facet of motherhood. You continue to blow me away with your strength and love. And thank you, Cadence, for gracing us with your presence—you are the sweetest baby I've ever known. It is one of life's great honors to call you my niece. Please do not read this book for a very, very long time.

To Vicki Wrobel, for helping me get my Colorado geography right; for weighing in on all the things, big and small; for making me laugh and having my back, always. Thank you too for believing you saw a Toys "R" Us in Mom's belly—you will officially never live that story down. I am so lucky to have you for a sister.

To Mom and Dad. You knew long before I did that I would write books someday, so it's only fair I state it for the record: you were right. From *The Girl Who Got Lost in the Zoo* to *Accelerated Reading* to *Adventures of Misty Creek* and beyond, no one has bolstered my love of reading and writing more than you two. Your constant support made writing this book easier, but your parenting made creating Patty's character harder—because I have no idea what it's like to have parents who are anything but loving, selfless, and one hundred percent behind me. Dad, thank you for being the only person who thought writing a book and training for a marathon at the same time was a good idea! Your drive pushes me to work harder and get better. You told me a million times when I was a kid that it didn't cost any more to dream bigger. I guess you finally got through. Mom, I would be hopeless without you. You've printed, FedExed, and hunted jewel-toned tops— no task was ever too big of an ask (and there have been a lot of asks). Thank you for never batting an eyelash at the dozens of weird questions I asked during book research. I feel your love an ocean away. I love you both so, so much.

To Moose. People sometimes ask if I feel isolated working by myself all day, but I haven't been lonely since the day we brought you home. That said, I wouldn't hate it if you stopped farting under my desk.

To Matt. For being my partner. For moving to Boston so I could go to grad school. For supporting us while I got my MFA. For thinking this novel was a good idea. For arguably the best joke in the book. For Drip Feed (the only time you will see it in writing). For celebrating the highs and weathering the lows. For being the first person I want to tell everything, even after all these years. On our first date way back in 2011, I confessed I had this crazy dream of writing a book someday. Your eyes lit up, and you leaned in, wanting to know more. You have been leaning in every day since.

Readers guide for *Darling Rose Gold*

Questions for Discussion

1) Who is the victim? Who is the perpetrator? What does it mean to be a victim in the context of this story?

2) Who did you most empathize with throughout the book? Did your sympathies change chapter to chapter? If so, how?

3) Patty's actions are attributed to Munchausen syndrome by proxy, a mental health disorder. Should she have gone to prison if her behavior was caused by an illness beyond her control?

4) Do Patty and Rose Gold love each other? How did your view of their relationship change throughout the book?

5) Toward the end of the book, Rose Gold says, "Nobody wants to hear the truth from a liar." Did you trust either of the narrators? At what points, if any, was that trust shaken?

6) What did you think of Rose Gold's final decision not to fix her teeth? To shave her head? How do societal beauty standards affect Rose Gold throughout the book?

7) How much of our personalities are shaped by nature vs. nurture? Do you think Rose Gold and Patty would have committed their crimes had their childhoods been different?

8) "Some of us cannot forget and will never forgive." Do you think Rose Gold will ever be free of her mother's influence? Were Rose Gold's actions justifiable? What do you imagine her future will hold?

9) What role did the residents of Deadwick play in the story? What characters had the biggest impact on Patty and/or Rose Gold? Why do you think Patty was able to keep her actions hidden for so long?

10) Does Patty know she's lying or has she convinced herself she's telling the truth? What makes you think so?

Photo by Simon Way

Stephanie Wrobel grew up in Chicago but has been living in the UK for the last three years with her husband and dog, Moose Barkwinkle. She has an MFA from Emerson College and has had short fiction published in *Bellevue Literary Review*. Before turning to fiction, she worked as a creative copywriter at various advertising agencies.